BANTAM BOOKS BY LOUIS L'AMOUR

NOVELS

Bendigo Shafter
Borden Chantry
Brionne
The Broken Gun
The Burning Hills
The Californios
Callaghen
Catlow
Chancy
The Cherokee Trail
Comstock Lode
Conagher
Crossfire Trail
Dark Canyon
Down the Long Hills
The Empty Land
Fair Blows the Wind
Fallon
The Ferguson Rifle
The First Fast Draw
Flint
Guns of the Timberlands
Hanging Woman Creek
The Haunted Mesa
Heller with a Gun
The High Graders
High Lonesome
Hondo
How the West Was Won
The Iron Marshal
The Key-Lock Man
Kid Rodelo
Kilkenny
Killoe
Kilrone

Kiowa Trail
Last of the Breed
Last Stand at Papago Wells
The Lonesome Gods
The Man Called Noon
The Man from Skibbereen
The Man from the Broken Hills
Matagorda
Milo Talon
The Mountain Valley War
North to the Rails
Over on the Dry Side
Passin' Through
The Proving Trail
The Quick and the Dead
Radigan
Reilly's Luck
The Rider of Lost Creek
Rivers West
The Shadow Riders
Shalako
Showdown at Yellow Butte
Silver Canyon
Sitka
Son of a Wanted Man
Taggart
The Tall Stranger
To Tame a Land
Tucker
Under the Sweetwater Rim
Utah Blaine
The Walking Drum
Westward the Tide
Where the Long Grass Blows

SHORT STORY COLLECTIONS

Beyond the Great Snow Mountains

Bowdrie

Bowdrie's Law

Buckskin Run

The Collected Short Stories of Louis
L'Amour (vols. 1–7)

Dutchman's Flat

End of the Drive

From the Listening Hills

The Hills of Homicide

Law of the Desert Born

Long Ride Home

Lonigan

May There Be a Road

Monument Rock

Night Over the Solomons

Off the Mangrove Coast

The Outlaws of Mesquite

The Rider of the Ruby Hills

Riding for the Brand

The Strong Shall Live

The Trail to Crazy Man

Valley of the Sun

War Party

West from Singapore

West of Dodge

With These Hands

Yondering

SACKETT TITLES

Sackett's Land

To the Far Blue Mountains

The Warrior's Path

Jubal Sackett

Ride the River

The Daybreakers

Sackett

Lando

Mojave Crossing

Mustang Man

The Lonely Men

Galloway

Treasure Mountain

Lonely on the Mountain

Ride the Dark Trail

The Sackett Brand

The Sky-Liners

THE HOPALONG CASSIDY NOVELS

The Riders of High Rock

The Rustlers of West Fork

The Trail to Seven Pines

Trouble Shooter

NONFICTION

POETRY

LOST TREASURES

LOUIS L'AMOUR'S
Lost Treasures:
Volume 1

LOUIS L'AMOUR'S
Lost Treasures:
Volume 1

Unfinished Manuscripts, Mysterious Stories, and Lost Notes

from One of the World's Most Popular Novelists

Louis L'Amour
with
Beau L'Amour

BANTAM BOOKS

New York

Published in the United States by Bantam Books, an imprint of Random House, a division of Penguin Random House LLC, New York.

BANTAM BOOKS and the HOUSE colophon are registered trademarks of Penguin Random House LLC.

LIBRARY OF CONGRESS CATALOGING-IN-PUBLICATION DATA

Names: L'Amour, Louis, 1908–1988, author. | L'Amour, Beau, writer of introduction.
Title: Lost treasures, unfinished manuscripts, mysterious stories, and lost notes from one of the world's most popular novelists / Louis L'Amour ; [introduction by Beau L'Amour].
Description: First edition. | New York : Bantam Books, 2017. | Includes bibliographical references and index.
Identifiers: LCCN 2016021929 (print) | LCCN 2016041495 (ebook) | ISBN 9780399177545 (alk. paper) | ISBN 9780399177552 (ebook)
Subjects: | GSAFD: Western stories. | Adventure stories. | Detective and mystery stories. | Historical fiction.
Classification: LCC PS3523.A446 A6 2017 (print) | LCC PS3523.A446 (ebook) | DDC 813/.54—dc23
LC record available at https://lccn.loc.gov/2016021929

Printed in the United States of America on acid-free paper

randomhousebooks.com

2 4 6 8 9 7 5 3 1

First Edition

Book design by Caroline Cunningham

To my father, Louis L'Amour,

whose world was so much wider than the West he loved.

WHAT IS LOUIS L'AMOUR'S LOST TREASURES?

Louis L'Amour's Lost Treasures is a project created to release some of the author's more unconventional manuscripts from the family archives.

Currently included in the project are *Louis L'Amour's Lost Treasures: Volume 1* and *Volume 2*, which will be published in the fall of 2017 and 2019 respectively. These books contain both finished and unfinished short stories, unfinished novels, literary and motion-picture treatments, notes, and outlines. They are a wide selection of the many works Louis was not able to publish during his lifetime.

In 2018 we will release *No Traveller Returns*, L'Amour's never-before-seen first novel, which was written between 1938 and 1942. In the future, there may be a selection of even more L'Amour titles.

Additionally, many notes and alternate drafts to Louis's well-known and previously published novels and short stories will now be included as "bonus feature" postscripts within the books that they relate to. For example, the Lost Treasures postscript to *Last of the Breed* will contain early notes on the story, the short story that was discovered to be a missing piece of the novel, the history of the novel's inspiration and creation, and information about unproduced motion-picture and comic book versions.

An even more complete description of the Lost Treasures project, along with a number of examples of what is in the books, can be found at louislamourslosttreasures.com. The website also contains a good deal of exclusive material, such as even more pieces of unknown stories, personal photos, scans of original documents, and notes.

All of the works that contain Lost Treasures project materials will display the Louis L'Amour's Lost Treasures banner and logo.

LOUIS L'AMOUR'S LOST TREASURES

CONTENTS

INTRODUCTION

By Beau L'Amour

This book may drive you crazy.

What it contains is mysterious and fascinating, frustrating and, more often than not, tragically incomplete. It is a look behind the curtain into a world of what might have been. It is a look under the hood at how the machinery of a writing career that lasted over half a century functioned. It is also a look at the struggle to express an idea, and how difficult it can be to bend the unruly process of creativity to one's will. This is the story of the debris, the chaff, the waste heat that a writer produces. The stuff that never makes it to the editor's desk. The stack of pages never graced by a final "The End."

It is humbling to think that, with a career that produced ninety-one novels and nearly four hundred short stories, articles, screenplays, and poems, Louis L'Amour also left behind hundreds of unfinished works. It is comforting to know that, regardless of how prolific he was, he was human, that he had failures, weird ideas, and dreams he couldn't quite fulfill. It is amazing to realize that his imagination stretched well beyond the tremendous variety of work that he eventually published, from Westerns and crime stories, high adventure and historical romance, to stories he planned in science fiction, horror, and what can only be called the genre of mystical or spiritual adventure.

You may not find a hidden literary masterpiece between these covers, but you will get a sense of the entirety of a prolific writer's journey, an idea of the scope of all a truly creative person can struggle to wrap his or her mind around.

Within these pages I have included some of the most interesting material from what is a considerable archive. Many examples are stories that Dad discussed with us around the dinner table; others were completely unknown to me and inspired a good deal of research. I am reluctant, however, to do too much explaining, reluctant to organize this book too carefully. Exploring these manuscripts for the first time gave me a wonderful feeling of surprise and discovery. It is an experience that I do not wish to deny to others.

But I will try to create some context. . . .

It is still dark. Early morning. A late 1960s winter and the previous night's rain is still dripping from the eaves.

The neighborhood is just off the Sunset Strip in a neglected sliver of Los Angeles County sloping down from the Hollywood Hills. It is a community of nightclubs, gas stations, and small offices where, up narrow flights of stairs, the agents of rarely employed actors ply their trade.

West Hollywood is the dark sibling of Beverly Hills, which lies right next door. Beatnik poets and hungover movie stars frequent the coffee shop on the corner. The Doors, Led Zeppelin, and Buffalo Springfield play at clubs like the Whisky a Go Go, the Roxy, and Gazzarri's, and crowds clash with police when the neighbors complain about the noise and traffic. The edges of parking lots and the overgrown hillsides, even the sidewalks themselves, are dotted with hippies, camping (for lack of a better word) any place they can find a spot where no one will hassle them. They have come to this part of LA following a dream, or the music, or just one another. The place is a motley riot of counterculture, creativity, and confusion.

The sound of typewriter keys clacking greets me as I wake. I come downstairs dressed for school. The hallway that leads to the kitchen ends in three doors. Ahead, a bathroom; to the left, my father's office, a small room choked with books and papers in a small house choked with books and papers. The light is on above his desk, but his chair is empty. To the right is the kitchen, the coffee percolating and my mother delivering eggs and broiled bacon, condensed strips with the fat cooked off (my favorite), to the breakfast table.

In a few minutes my sister will join us. My mother doesn't have to dress her anymore; she's old enough to manage by herself. Then, Dad will put down the newspaper, take up a book, and read to us while we eat. It's a morning routine that will not end until I start driving myself to school nearly ten years later. The books he read were things he was interested in, Thor Heyerdahl's The Kon-Tiki Expedition, Adventures in the Apache Country, *or something from his youth, like* Tarzan and the Jewels of Opar. *We were surrounded by stories in every manner imaginable.*

By the time Mom was backing our aging and road-weary Cadillac out of the garage, Dad was back at his desk, typewriter rumbling, keys whacking out an irregular pattern. He'd still be there when I came home from school, after dinner, and sometimes, long past my bedtime.

I would wake up to that sound the next morning and the next and the next. . . .

This is how I remember my dad at work.

Louis's schedule, to be specific, was to always be the first one in the house out of bed. He took great pride in this, no matter what the circumstances. He wrote before breakfast and then immediately afterward. He worked until lunch, which, unless he had a business meeting, didn't last long. In the afternoon he would break to exercise, lifting weights in the backyard, whirling a jump rope, or shadowboxing. Before we got home from school he was back at it, and after dinner would often work until the late news came on the TV. He wrote seven days a week. He never took a vacation that wasn't a research trip . . . and sometimes, when we did travel, he would pack a tiny portable typewriter that had been "liberated" in Germany, and would write then, too.

I'm not sure when he took on this type of schedule, but I think it started in Oklahoma in the late 1930s. There was a certain point when he got serious; you can see it in his work. At first he wrote poetry and stories that were both personal and dark. Louis Lamoore (the way he was spelling his name when the Lamoore family arrived in Choctaw) was a bit of a pretender, an "artiste." He was a young man who, though he had talent, traded a great deal on his personality and good looks. In many ways he seemed to be writing more to augment his social life than to found a career.

Then something happened. Perhaps it was a sudden sense of vulnerability, of the years passing, of the realization that, though he had roamed the world, he was over thirty, living with his parents, and there were few things he could actually *do* that would earn him any money. Maybe it was the advice of a mentor or a warning from his father or elder brother. Maybe it was some small success that made him recognize that his future could be realized, rather than simply dreamt about. Whatever it was, it left him a changed and highly motivated man.

The point of view of his writing shifted. In the early period, the characters were stand-ins for himself, the stories drawn from his life or those he had known. In *some* ways these stories were actually better written, and certainly more polished, than some that came later . . . but to succeed professionally, he was going to have to learn to communicate in a manner that was more universal than personal. He would need to entertain the masses rather than members of writers' groups and readers of minor literary magazines.

It was just before this moment, through accident or the hand of destiny, that Louis also met an angel. In *Education of a Wandering Man* he said:

> At one time, trying desperately to write some-
> thing that would sell, I rented a typewriter. For
> several months I paid the rent. Then came a time when
> I could not, so I wrote him a note and explained. I
> never heard from him again. No bill, nothing. That
> typewriter meant more to me than anything. . . .

Being able to write every day opened the creative pathways and kept them open. Becoming good at it wasn't quick or easy, but eventually Dad had practiced so much that creativity became somewhat automatic. He set himself detailed goals and worked hard to achieve them, crossing projects off of typewritten lists with a proud, red grease pencil. By the late 1940s his goal was to sell a short story a week.

Not to *finish* a story a week. Sell.

Even though he'd had a fair amount of success by then, publishers would not take everything he wrote, so he had to complete quite a few more than fifty-two stories a year in attempts to make his quota. The work didn't pay much. Even that volume of writing did little more than pay the rent. Speed was essential.

I have no memory of how we were trained, my sister and I, but we knew how to approach my father if he was working and we wanted his attention. We would enter his office, picking our way through the piles of books and papers. We would stand to one side of him, just within his peripheral vision, and silently wait while he worked. Sometimes he would lift his fingers from the keys and say, "Just a minute." Then he would go on and complete a thought or get himself to a place in the story that would remind him what he had been intending to say next. Then he was yours . . .

. . . for about ten minutes. Before long, you could see the story or some innate discipline calling him back. We never had to worry about interrupting him because, while he was happy to be briefly distracted, he guarded his work time very carefully, and it never occurred to us that he might behave in a different way. "You run along now, I have to get back to work." He would lean forward then, hunting and pecking at the keyboard, back in the story and perfectly in tune with where he had left off. It seemed as if he always knew exactly where he was going and no interruption could confuse him or even make him pause for very long.

The descriptions of Louis L'Amour's writing process were legendary. According to publicists and popular myth, he did not outline and did not rewrite. He embodied every young writer's fantasy of what the process would be like. He cranked a page into the typewriter, started typing, and with absolute confidence, didn't look back until he reached the end of the story. All action, no agonizing.

Everything he wrote was good enough to immediately sell, or so the story went. The words simply flowed out of him. He did not get writer's block. He was not temperamental.

These may have been exaggerations, but they were not utter falsehoods or public-relations hype. He bragged he could sit with his typewriter on his knees and write a novel in the middle of Sunset Boulevard . . . and when a German magazine asked to shoot some pictures of him doing so, he did it, producing half of his day's output during the photo shoot. He was already so well-known for that particular boast that a motorist leaned out the window of his car and yelled, "You've *got* to be Louis L'Amour!"

Mom and Dad in their apartment in West Hollywood.

Before I was born, Louis made the transition from writing short stories to writing novels. The length of the stories changed, the publishers changed, the way the material was distributed changed, but Dad's work habits did not. His income grew, but he also had a family to support. We had a very comfortable middle-class lifestyle as long as he could write three or four books a year. If he sold a movie, then maybe my mother could redecorate a room, or we'd buy a new car. Financial considerations aside, Dad still took great pride in having a lot of story ideas and in the speed with which he could produce a page or a chapter or a novel.

Progress was his byword. Louis claimed he could "simply" put himself and his characters in a situation and the story would take off, virtually telling itself. He loved beginnings . . . loved them to the point that he occasionally shortchanged the ending of a story because he was so excited about starting the next one. He was powerfully optimistic, focused on productivity, the future, whatever was next. His frame of mind was such a potent force that, occasionally, Dad would announce stories that he had only just thought of as if they were finished. . . . In the reality he made for himself, there was little difference between thinking of something and completing it.

His presence was big and happy and generous. He made what he did look easy and, for the most part, it was. A great deal of the magic behind his sales was that he wrote so effortlessly that the material read the same way. . . . The energy that *any* writer puts into their work is the energy a reader will take out of it. And rare among writers, Louis loved the writing process.

Smoggy summertime. The early 1970s. A major transition in our lives. The L'Amour family—my father, mother, sister, dog, bird, and myself—are leaving West Hollywood for a new home in another part of town.

After many years of hard and constant work, Dad's fortunes have changed. The new street is quiet and elegant, not far from the campus of UCLA, the opposite of the bohemian funkiness of our old neighborhood. Louis is ensconced in the new house, typewriter set up on a carpenter's bench in a room just off the entrance hall. The boxes containing the books and papers he needs most are stacked around him. It will be a couple of years before the new house is fully furnished, before my dad's new office is built. Right now the move and the stress of buying a bigger home is enough for all of us.

My mother and I trek back and forth across town. Packing Dad's papers and books is not something she is willing to trust to the movers. She's got a borrowed station wagon and a twelve-year-old kid, me, to help her haul a considerable amount of stuff. Dad stays home and works.

It's not three or four trips we have to make, it's dozens. *There are nearly eight thousand books, most of them hardback. I have always wondered what the new owners of the West Hollywood house thought; every wall was covered in shelves. We had nearly been forced out of the house by the sheer volume of Dad's books and papers.*

The job takes weeks, moving from the echoing, dusty rooms of our old home to the new one, which, though larger, is rapidly filling with piles and boxes. To be sure, most of the boxes are full of books, but many contain papers, notebooks, and random stacks of manuscripts. It's hard to believe Dad actually fit all this stuff in our old place.

For a few years after the move that "stuff" remained stacked in the living room of our new house, and I occasionally saw my dad sorting through it, searching for one thing or another. Later, after his new office was built, most of those materials migrated down there, and the new room was big enough for him to add exponentially to their number. I can't say that the rest of us thought much about what this mass of papers contained. "Dad's work," or "Dad's mess"—that was as far as we went with it. It was only after his death, over fifteen years later, that we discovered many unexpected things. . . .

In the 1970s and '80s, after paying his dues for forty years, Louis L'Amour was the rock star of the paperback-book business. No title he put his name on had ever gone out of print, and his books were translated into more than twenty languages. When he appeared to do

a signing, lines stretched around the block. The movie business has given a name to that kind of success: blockbuster.

Critics and commentators were either swept away by his infectious writing style or they struggled desperately to explain away his popularity. If audiences had found his work to be no more than disposable, momentary entertainment, dismissing it would have been easy—but those readers kept coming back, not only buying every new book, but rereading the old ones until they fell apart and were purchased again. By 1980, Bantam Books estimated he had sold one hundred million copies. By the time he passed away in 1988, that number was topping two hundred million.

His success, though long in coming, was also limiting. Since the end of World War II, Louis had made his name writing Westerns. He loved the West, and he loved being successful and making so many people happy with the entertainment he provided . . . but he also felt trapped. Trapped in the Western genre. Trapped by his own success.

The Walking Drum, Louis's epic twelfth-century adventure novel, was published late in his career. However, it was written in 1960, a time when no publisher wanted anything but a Western from Louis L'Amour. It was not his only attempt to break away into new territory during that era. All of them failed, at least in the short term, though the blow of not being able to expand his horizons was softened considerably by the increasing success of what he eventually began to call his "frontier" stories.

By the time the mid-1970s rolled around, Louis was a lot smarter about his approach to working in other genres . . . and he had become a good deal more successful, which made publishers feel less need for caution. Incrementally approaching the issue of change, he published *The Californios* in 1974, a Western to be sure, but one that included some strange and otherworldly elements. He followed that with *Sackett's Land,* utilizing the characters of his popular Sackett family to open the door to novels set in the sixteenth and seventeenth centuries, long before the classic "Western" period. By the 1980s, his publisher was happy to experiment with tales like *Last of the Breed,* a contemporary thriller about an American military pilot escaping from the Soviet Union, and *Haunted Mesa,* a science fiction novel that adapted elements of Native American lore. Like *The Walking Drum*, both of these stories were conceived twenty or even thirty years earlier. By the time of his death, Dad was finally able to sell stories in a wider array of genres than just the Western.

Certainly, what held Louis back, when it came to the more adventurous and interesting material that he dreamed of writing, wasn't just the conservative nature of publishers or his core audience—his own limitations played a part, too. To complete many of the ambitious projects he envisioned, a great deal of planning and revision would no doubt have been necessary.

As you will see in this book, and contrary to popular myth, Louis *did* outline to a certain extent, and he *did* rewrite, or at least *restart*, stories that hadn't taken off in that magic way that would carry him all the way through to the end. But writing was not as intellectual an experience for him as it may be for many writers; over the years it had become instinctual and reactive. To complete some of these projects, which in their personal nature and distance from the Western genre were more like his earliest work, Louis might have needed to relearn the planning and revision skills he had developed at the start of his career.

For Louis, the key to almost every story was the beginning. He was both renowned for and proud of how he started stories. Using action or mystery or a particular turn of phrase, he would propel the audience into a situation in a way that made them lean forward, eyes leaping ahead to the next sentence. Getting *himself* to react to that moment was a trick he used to unlock the story. If the narrative "took," then he went with it, forging ahead until he had followed his characters through to the end. After a certain point he rarely looked back, and the story wrote itself in an unstoppable stream of the *unconscious*.

One day I was speeding along at the typewriter, and my daughter--who was a child at the time--asked me, "Daddy, why are you writing so fast?" And I replied, "Because I want to see how the story turns out!"

Working all day, every day, for decades on end had pretty much programmed him to write this way; having a story in the back of his mind for months or years before he put it down on paper allowed him to work out many of the details unconsciously. Once he started work, he really had little idea what was going to come out, and that kept his approach and the reader's experience consistently fresh.

Although he was occasionally accused of writing in a formulaic manner, by the 1950s Louis found it difficult if not impossible to accept *any* influence imposed from the outside. Whatever his formula was, it was based on some internal and little-understood aesthetic. This made working under the direction of publishers and movie executives nearly impossible. A number of the stories that you will read within these covers were victims of those limitations. At times of financial stress, or in moments when he dreamed of doing something different, Louis would hammer out a treatment (a "treatment" is much like the description of a story, rather than the story itself) and then try to get a publisher or movie studio to pay him up front for executing the final, finished story.

However, if he was lucky enough to receive that advance, he would soon become frustrated by corporate executives' attempts to get him to conform to their "creative" expectations or their schedules. It is true that very few writers of any sort like writing treatments, and even fewer do them well. In Louis's case it was so antithetical to the way he liked to work that on a number of occasions I remember him returning the money, regardless of how much we needed it, and going back to the methods he came by naturally. Writing a treatment was nearly always a recipe for disaster; if Louis was lucky enough to work out the story all the way through to the end, he was not very interested in doing so again when the time came to write the finished version. He knew what was going to happen. He was ready to move on to something else.

The day after my father died, I walked down into his office. It was shuttered and dark; for the previous four months, Dad had rarely left the second floor of the house. The room was more than four times the size of the space he had worked in in our old house in West Hollywood. The walls were lined with double bookshelves, twelve feet tall, the outer set mounted on huge hinges to allow it to swing out of the way, like a giant pair of doors, in order to access more books behind them. Few of these could be opened, however. The floor, his desk, and a sofa at the far end of the room were all stacked two to three feet high with papers and books and odds and ends of various sorts, left over from the different aspects of Dad's life.

In the preceding decades, the mess, like an occasionally rising tide, had moved up the hallway and into my mother's dining room. It happened a couple of times a year. We have never been able to prove that the expansion of that great mass of Dad's papers was connected to the phases of the moon or to solar weather, but sooner or later Mom would put her foot down and tell him to clean it up. His work space always looked like a disaster area, but she kept the rest of the house squared away in a manner that would have made the navy envious. If she had taken on the job of cleaning up his office after his death, it would have been both horribly emotional and completely exhausting on top of the crushing weight of settling his estate and renegotiating our publishing contracts. I knew this particular job was going to be up to me.

It was literally tons and tons of material, thousands and thousands of pages, and the sorting and copying had to be done with extreme care. Even-

The new office. Louis L'Amour surrounded by his work.
(Nancy Ellison © 1985)

tually, after two or three years, all that was left was our dining room table, piled high with random unidentified manuscript pages, some with numbers, some without. None were titled. The challenge was to match them to existing stories by recognizing the name of a character, or finding the continuation of a sentence at the top of a page or the beginning of a sentence at the bottom of another, in this way we pieced together unfinished and unknown manuscripts, all going into their own individual folders, the pile of which grew larger and larger. By this time a number of friends and family had joined in the effort, and it was like a giant game of literary Concentration.

It had never been easy to keep track of what Louis was working on. He kept lists of everything: what he had sold, what he planned on accomplishing in the next six months, what physical exercises he did and how many repetitions, his weight, what books he had read and the ones he planned on reading. He made several journal entries a week. And he made hundreds of pages of notes on unlined paper with a felt-tipped pen. He outlined speeches and articles and even jotted down jokes and poetry. The number of pages he generated was substantial even before adding the things he considered to be his actual work. A great many of the projects in this book had been hidden from us by the avalanche of paper he was constantly producing.

Somehow, even with all that *and* the novels that actually got published every year, he managed to write quite a few treatments and start scores of stories we had never heard of. In addition, we found partial manuscripts where Dad had made several different attempts to start many of his now well-known works, and piles of notes relating to that same successfully published material.

In some cases, he tried to start over and over. Often he would produce nearly identical drafts, each attempt allowing him to forge a few pages—or sometimes just a few words—further. Other times he would explore whether a completely different beginning, or different characters, would get a story to take off. On occasion he even considered changing a story concept from a novel to a TV series or even a play in order to see if he could make an idea work. Dad never *seemed* to agonize over anything, yet as I explored the materials he left behind, I realized that his writing was a much more laborious process than I had ever imagined. Possibly it was a more laborious process than he would even admit to himself! Working through these mysterious fragments of stories made us all realize how much we had taken for granted.

However, as this book will show, some of his most interesting material came to a halt after a few pages or a few chapters. In some ways, this is the archive of his most ambitious work . . . and, of course, that is *why* it was difficult to write. In my opinion, what Louis was unable to complete is often more revealing than what he *did* complete.

Because of the unfinished nature of some of these manuscripts, I am sure that reading this book will be a frustrating experience. For many readers, I suspect two particular questions will come up over and over. I will answer them as best I can right now. . . .

The first: "Yes. That is *really* where that story ended." Sometimes materials in this book will end in the middle of a sentence or thought. Louis either knew what he was going to write next and so didn't need to hint at what it would be, or he *didn't* know what he was going to write next and he ripped the page out of the typewriter and moved on to something else.

The second: "No. With a possible few exceptions, we are *not* going to have anyone finish these manuscripts or otherwise change them from what you see here." We are *intentionally* leaving this as the final form for many of Louis L'Amour's unfinished materials.

I believe deeply that, at its best, fiction is a partnership or collaboration between the author and the audience. Even with a finished work, a good writer hints, suggests, and directs, but then allows the reader to complete the scene, or the character, or the plot, or the meaning of the story. Imagination is the gift that you bring to the work and there is plenty here for you to imagine. In the end, however, *Louis L'Amour's Lost Treasures* is not so much about what these treatments and fragments of stories might have been, but what they tell us about their creator.

I find myself to be content with the unknown, and recognize

that what you see (or don't see) here were the mysteries that Louis confronted too, the uncharted waters of unrealized imagination, the ideas that lurked, misty and half-formed, in the terra incognita of his mind.

Ladies and Gentlemen, Here There Be Dragons. . . .

LOUIS L'AMOUR'S
Lost Treasures:
Volume 1

JEREMY LOCCARD

The First Four Chapters of a Western Horror Novel

CHAPTER I

At the top of the rise Duro Weaver pulled in his team
to let them catch their wind . . . He pointed with his
whip. "She lies right yonder, young feller, and I envy
you none at all."

The valley was several miles wide at that point, and
the tiny huddle of buildings seemed lost in the vast expanse. On their left the valley narrowed into the pass,
and beyond the pass lay the Mojave Desert, stretching
into infinite distance.

"Twenty Mile Station they call it," Weaver said, "and
it's a good twenty mile from the last stage stop. In any
direction but along the trail it's more'n a hundred mile
to anywhere else at all."

The mountains loomed dark and ominous in the late
evening shadows. "Them mountains," commented Weaver, "are
better left alone. There's deer in them, and bear, too.
Almighty big ones . . . grizzlies. But that there ain't
the reason. The Injuns tell queer stories . . . mighty
queer. You just fight shy of them."

Jeremy Loccard shrugged his heavy shoulders. "I've spent most of my life at sea, and we're used to strange stories."

"Mebbe," Weaver spat. He was skeptical of tales from other worlds. He preferred his own. "Mebbe so. But don't you get to thinkin' the West is all Injuns and fellers huntin' gold. This here's a strange, wild country, with queer tales aplenty.

"You ever hear tell of the Frog People? Injuns got their tales about them, and they're said to live yonder in the mountains. Or the Little People? If you figure all the ha'nts is in old castles you got another think a-comin'.

"You just walk them mountains alone. Or down in the desert yonder, an' you'll _feel_ them. You'll feel _watched_. Yes, sir. You surely will. You won't see nothin' but you'll know they're there.

"Somewhere around here there's a canyon full of writin' on the rocks . . . only this here is dif'rent writin'. I mean real dif'rent. No Injun will even _look_ at it.

"A few years back some fellers I knew went off into that desert. Everybody was findin' gold an' these fellers decide to have a try at it theirselves. They'd heard tell of that canyon and decided there must be gold there, so they set out huntin'.

"Those who claimed to know said it was deep an' narrow and couldn't be seen until you stood right on the rim. Mebbe some folks couldn't see it at all.

"One night they figured they was close, so they went into camp. Come daylight they'd scout around. Johnny Haskins . . . an' I knowed him well . . . he was huntin' firewood when he come on a trail. The others said it could wait until daylight, but it still lacked a mite of bein' dark an' Johnny was impatient. He taken off into the desert.

"Mornin' come an' no Johnny. They come on his tracks,

but the trail petered out in the desert yonder. Johnny
was gone.

"They told the story their ownselves. I never did see
Johnny after, but I heard tell of him.

"He come back, all right. On the mornin' of the
fourth day they woke up to see Johnny settin' by the
fire. They seen him plain, although his back was to them.
They knowed it was Johnny, all right, because he had a
funny white scar right back of his ear.

"They spoke to him and he turned around. Now this
here is their story, not mine, but they do say Johnny
turned into an old, old man. Three days had passed for
them, a lifetime for Johnny.

"He wouldn't tell them nothing, but he was almighty
anxious to get shut of the desert, and believe me, once
he got back he never went into the desert again. Wouldn't
go for love or money.

"Of a night they say he wandered in his dreams, and
they'd hear him cry out . . . scared-like. Sometimes he'd
whimper like he was in mortal fear.

"Sometimes in his sleep he raved about great build-
in's . . . castles, like. On'y thing we could get clear
was that he'd been a prisoner somewhere, held a long time
until he broke loose and got away into the desert. He
found that ol' trail again. He took off down that trail
runnin' until he ran smack into somethin'. He fell, an'
when he got up he seen the fire and come on in. Three
days for them, sixty years for him. You figure it out."

Weaver spoke to his team and the horses leaned into
the harness, starting the stage once more. "There's canyons about here where no man ever walked, and there's
valleys you can find sometimes that are greener than any
desert should be, but no Injun lives there, where you'd
expect them to be . . . won't go near 'em."

He paused, spat, and then said, more quietly, "Was I
you I'd not git off the stage. That there Twenty Mile

Station . . . there's been two men vanish from there. Just disappeared complete.

"An' don't you get to thinkin' all the spooky things happen of a night. There's things happen by day. . . .

"Why, there's a deep canyon back yonder, cuts off into the mountains. Up that canyon maybe ten, twelve mile there's a place. You cross the creek to go into it . . . narrow, winding canyon between low hills but with mountains all around . . . digger pine an' blue oak . . . and some of them ghost trees . . . you know, they're kind of white an' misty-lookin' after their leaves shed. Buckeyes, some call them.

"There's a little basin back up that canyon. There's a couple of springs there, too. I heard some mighty strange stories about that place. Ties in with the canyon I spoke of."

Loccard listened with only half his attention. Twenty-six years old and for two years chief mate on the four-mast bark Annandale, he had heard such tales many times before.

He had once sailed on a vessel unlisted in any port he'd ever come across, and found her a good ship. Good enough, at least. Piracy had more than one method, and with the passing of Blackbeard and Kidd other ways had been attempted. A quick change of name and a coat of paint with some alteration in the rig . . . who was to say what happened after she left port?

Nor was he in any position to choose his berth now, any more than when he sailed on the mystery ship.

He had come up from the seaport town of Wilmington, recently established on the California coast, to look for an old friend in Los Angeles. He was hunting no trouble, a fact that helped him none at all when trouble came. He emerged from the hospital to find his ship had left without him. What money he had carried with him was gone for the doctor and what care he needed while recovering.

No ships were hiring off the West Coast . . . a seaman, perhaps, but no mates. After a few weeks of trying
he accepted the job no one wanted, to handle the stage
station at Twenty Mile.

Shadows were deep in the canyons when the stage
rolled up to the station. Loccard looked at the buildings
with interest, crouching dark and forlorn beside the
stage trail.

Duro Weaver tied the lines to the whipstock and
climbed back over the tarp-covered luggage. From the back
he handed down the sea-chest, a battered carpetbag, and
two heavy canvas bags belonging to the company.

"There's grub in the bags. I hope you can cook." Duro
straightened up, putting a hand to the small of his back.
Jolting over rough, rock-strewn roads was hard on a man's
kidneys. "There's a well yonder. Water's good when used
reg'lar. Boss will get you some horses up here soon's he
can find a man to drive 'em."

"Thanks. I'll do all right."

Weaver looked doubtful. From the boot he took Loccard's rifle. It was brand, spanking new. "You're likely
to need this. Keep it by you."

A worn holster and gun-belt followed. The butt of the
gun carried five notches.

Weaver glanced sharply at Loccard. "Five? I never
cottoned to carvin' notches, but five's quite a few."

"They aren't mine. They belong to the man I took it
off of."

Weaver looked at Loccard again. Loccard was at least
three inches shorter than his own six feet, and Weaver
guessed his weight at one-sixty. "You took that gun off a
man who'd killed five men?"

"It seemed like a good idea at the time. He was
shootin' it at me."

Weaver exchanged a glance with Cottonmouth Porter, who had been riding inside the stage. Porter shrugged. The only other man riding passenger besides Cottonmouth was a slender man in a black broadcloth suit. Loccard picked up his sea-chest, shouldered it, then took up his carpetbag and took them to the stage station.

"I saw it," the stranger commented, biting the end from his thin cigar. "It was in Los Angeles."

"How could anybody miss at that range? It's unbelievable."

"It was Steve Darnell. Loccard was hit, all right, but he just kept coming. He took Darnell's gun away from him and slapped him silly with it. You never saw such a beating in your life. Then Loccard took his gun, stripped off his gun-belt, and walked to the nearest doctor. He spent the next three weeks in bed."

Weaver climbed back to his seat as Loccard walked back to pick up the rest of his gear. "Mr. Loccard, if I were you I'd be sure I had water enough and fuel enough before dark."

He held the lines as if reluctant to leave Loccard alone. "No travelers come this way except by stage, and the stages only come by daylight. So, don't open up for anyone . . . or any<u>thing</u>."

His whip cracked like a pistol shot, the horses dug in, and the stage vanished in the pursuing dust. Loccard watched it until it was only a dot in the distance. He glanced then at the mountains, at the looming blackness of them. They revealed nothing, offered nothing, and might conceal much.

The corral, across the road from the stage station, was empty. Until the horses arrived there was no way out of here but to walk, and he had no intention of walking. Or of leaving, for that matter. He had come to do a job and do a job he would . . . at least until he had money

enough to take him to San Francisco and keep him there
until he could get a ship.

There were three buildings and the corrals. The station itself was of good size, with a peaked roof a story
and a half tall and no porch. The side facing the trail
had a door and three small windows.

The barn for the housing of the horses was as stur-
dily built as the station itself. There was a lean-to
back of the corrals for the temporary housing of additional stock. Behind the corral was a low hill.

Loccard went to the door. It was fastened shut from
the outside with a hasp held in place by a whittled
stick. Removing the stick, he let the door swing open. It
creaked on rusty hinges and inside the air felt heavy,
the dead air of a room long closed. For a moment he hesitated on the threshold, for there was something clammy
and unclean about the smell.

With a shrug, he entered. Glass from a shattered bottle littered the floor and the pieces of a broken chair
had been brushed to one side. At the end of the room was
a bar, a long table with two benches, and one intact
chair. On the back-bar were several bottles and a few unwashed glasses. The cash-drawer was empty. Nearby was a
scale for weighing gold-dust.

The fireplace was large, occupied by two half-burned
logs.

In back was a kitchen, which housed a range, a
boiler, and a good stack of cut wood. The pots and pans
were clean and polished. Wonder of wonders, there were a
couple of flatirons.

On the left of the door where he had entered was a
room with an unmade bed, a bed with a wooden frame and
leather straps for springs. An old coat and a slicker
hung on pegs, and alongside them a gun-belt and holster.
There was a pistol still in the holster.

All else was dust and cobwebs.

He glanced again at the gun-belt, frowning. Odd that a man should leave without his gun.

Returning to the kitchen, he put on water for coffee, brought in his gear, and closed the door. Hesitating a moment, he turned back smiling at himself, and dropped the bar in place.

Yet he had one more thing to do. He lifted the bar again and taking the former station keeper's clothing outside, he set fire to it. No telling how many lives were lost.

With the water on, he puttered about, cleaning up, putting things to rights. He discovered an ax, razor-sharp, and a cross-cut saw. There were several wedges for splitting logs as well as a pick, shovel, and gold-pan.

Suddenly curious, he checked the pistol. It had been fired not long since . . . three times. Never liking the presence of unloaded guns, accidents always seeming to happen with guns suspected of being empty, he slipped cartridges into the empty chambers and returned the gun to its holster.

Outside it was now quite dark. The stars seemed very close because the mountain air was clear. Stepping outside, he walked to the middle of the road, looking both ways. All was dark and still. Suddenly there was a swoosh in the air above him; involuntarily, he ducked. An owl . . . and a big one.

Not since childhood had he lived in the mountains, and the mountains he had known were far different from these, for even the trees and flowers of the eastern mountains were different. Since that time he had been at sea, the shallow seas of the Malay archipelago as well as along the China coast and Japan.

Returning to the station, he rebarred the door, poured a cup of coffee, and sat down at the table. The gun-belt and pistol he had taken from Steve Darnell lay on the table. It was a fine weapon, nicely balanced and easy to the hand. That had been trouble he had not wanted, but Darnell was evidently a known man and considered a dangerous one. Seeing in Jeremy Loccard a stranger and obviously not a western man, he had thought to have some amusement. Darnell had a few drinks under his belt, and in such circumstances, apparently he often became quarrelsome.

Loccard had not been wearing a gun, as he had much of his life, for the islands and the waters where he'd sailed were infested with pirates, and had been from as far back as records existed.

Two men had vanished from this place . . . how?

Of course, there were men who could not accept solitude. A few days of silence and loneliness were all they could stand and they must get away, no matter how. That could have been it.

Uneasily, he glanced at the black squares of the windows. Anybody or anything could be out there . . . or at least that's what Duro Weaver had suggested.

What did he mean by anything?

He went from window to window, checking. Cobwebbed and dirty as they were it was unlikely anything within could be seen from without, beyond the light itself. For the first time he was struck by the smallness of the panes and the strength of the windows themselves.

A skilled workman, he realized these were not the original doors or windows. The doors were of double thickness and strongly hinged, mounted obviously by someone who wanted stronger, thicker doors.

Why?

He tried to recall what Duro Weaver had said about the Indians of the vicinity. Pah-utes, and further east the Mojaves. There were other tribes who lived close about whose names he had forgotten, and a tribe called the Tehachapis who lived in the mountains of the same name. They were rarely seen, but seemed friendly.

He added fuel to the fire and poured a fresh cup of coffee. Then he opened his sea-chest and got out a pair of black dungarees, a black and white checked shirt, and fresh socks and underwear. He was taking out the shirt when something fell to the floor.

It was an amulet, a good-luck charm given him by an old priest of some obscure religion of which he knew nothing. Actually, he heard later, it was a coin of Krananda, believed by many to be the oldest coinage of India. On it were several symbols: a Tree of Life, a swastika, and others. He had worn it from the day it was given him but had taken it from his neck while undergoing treatment for his wounds.

Not one to place faith in luck, either good or bad, he treasured the charm as a memento, not only of the priest and his daughter whom Loccard had helped out of a bad corner, but as a memento of the girl herself.

She had been a dainty, lovely thing with whom he had no means of communication beyond a few clumsy signs. All he had been able to discover was that they had come from some far land, both as a pilgrimage and in flight from some unnamed danger.

Yet, superstitious or not, he had emerged reasonably unscathed from a half-dozen brawls and two dozen hand-to-hand fights with pirates as well as the fight with Darnell, all while wearing the charm.

"What the hell," he muttered, and slipped the charm over his head. "It never did me any harm."

Hours later he was awakened by a faint sound. His fingers closed around the butt of the pistol. Then he lay still . . . listening.

He heard it again. Something outside the station, something silent, stealthy, creeping. Gently he eased himself from under the blankets and swung his feet to the floor.

Very carefully someone was lifting the latch, then pushing against the door. The door itself was heavy, the bar a formidable piece of timber. Nothing happened beyond that first creak. After one push the man or creature desisted.

Pistol in hand, Loccard edged to the window and peered out. He could, of course, see nothing. Vaguely through the unclean window he could see distant stars and the outline of the barn roof against the sky, and nothing more.

Yet something or somebody was out there, something that moved very quietly, something that did not wish to be seen, something with intelligence enough not to waste strength on a barred door.

CHAPTER II

Loccard waited, straining his ears for the slightest sound; moving silently, he went to each of the other doors and windows, but he could see nothing.

He was a tough, hardened young man, and as mate on a windjammer he was accustomed to responsibility, and to facing whatever trouble came. On such a ship it was always the chief mate who checked things out first, then reported to the captain, who usually made the decisions.

Now he was mate and master both, and he considered the situation. He was tempted to go outside and face whatever was there, but if he was wrong about someone trying the latch, and it happened to be a grizzly, he would be in serious trouble. Moreover, at this time he had nothing to protect outside, so there was insufficient reason for taking the risk.

Moving in the dark, he went to the kitchen. The glow from the coals was faint, so he added fuel, then put on the coffeepot.

Taking up his watch, he brought it to the grate, where he could check the numerals. It was two-fifteen.

Restless and curious, he went from window to window, listening. When the coffee was hot he filled a cup and sat down.

Something had pushed hard against the door, but finding it firm, pushed no more. That argued for an intelligence beyond that of an animal. Yet the push against the door had given him an impression of great weight, and what could have such weight but a grizzly?

With the coming of daylight he finished the last of the coffee over a few strips of bacon and sourdough bread. As he ate his eyes studied the doors and the windows.

Whoever had strengthened them had been a cunning workman. He had built strong against whatever might come. . . . Had he known something? Felt some premonition, perhaps? Had he built the windows higher in the walls and the doors to their new strength before or after he began to fear what might be outside?

Before, quite possibly, or he might not have remained to build them.

Obviously they had strength enough, for they were unbroken. Despite that, the man was gone.

It was unlikely Indians had taken him, for they would have looted or burned the station.

Nevertheless, the man was gone, and another, also.

Which one had done the building? He who had first disappeared? Or the man who followed him?

That they had been taken while outside seemed apparent, which meant that when outside he must be wary at all times.

When he had finished eating he took up the new rifle, loaded it, and went outside, drawing the door to behind him.

There were no tracks on the hard-packed clay around the station. He walked to the barn and found twelve stalls, six on either side. There was a small tack room containing some worn harness, a fairly good saddle, and a rawhide lariat of the type used by the vaqueros of California. There was also a pitchfork and a scythe.

He refilled the water-barrel near the well, carried several buckets of water to the trough in the corral, and while doing so saw the tracks of a deer. There was another track, also, but it was oddly smudged and could not be identified. Yet it was a fresh track.

Mindful of what he had been told, he carried fresh water into the house, filling two buckets and the boiler. As he moved about he kept the rifle in his left hand, and his eyes strayed from time to time to the surrounding hills. The hills close by were bald, covered only by some close-setting growth that he did not recognize. On the more distant slopes were trees and occasional outcroppings of boulders, worn by wind and blown sand.

Far overhead a bird soared. Twice he looked at it, brow puckered. It was a large . . . a very large bird. Perhaps it was a condor, for it was said condors inhabited some of the mountain valleys they had passed coming hence from Los Angeles.

Finally, he returned to the station, got a broom, and swept out; then, rigging a crude mop, he took water and swabbed the floor as he would a ship's deck.

He was a man to whom cleanliness was a habit, developed over long confinement to close quarters at sea and the necessity of setting an example for those who served

on the ships with him. He decided what he must do was rig
a holystone so he could clean the floors properly.

Loccard walked to the door to wring out his mop, and
was standing there when his nostrils caught a strange,
fetid odor, an odd scent that made the hair prickle on
the back of his neck.

For a moment he looked about. A skunk? It could be,
of course. The smell was not unlike that of a skunk, yet
different somehow. He was turning to go back inside when
his eyes caught several long hairs trapped under slivers
on the outer surface of the door. They were coarse hairs,
a kind of a dirty whitish yellow in shade, and unlike
anything he had ever seen.

There were three of them, and carefully, he took them
from the door and went inside. Why he did so he did not
know, but he placed them in a folded paper for future ex-
amination.

Certainly, he had never seen such hairs. A silvertip
grizzly? No . . . these were different.

When Weaver came next with the stage he would ask
him, as being long in this country, he might recognize
them. The hairs had been more than two thirds the way up
the door, and standing on the flagstone doorstep they
would have been at eye level for him, or even a mite
higher. He shook his head, irritated by the puzzle.

A grizzly standing on his hind legs could have left
them. Probably hairs from the white part of his chest, he
thought.

Cleaning up the place took most of the day. He stored
his food, gathered extra wood, and made ready for the
night. The horses would be coming any day, and he found
himself looking forward to their arrival. They meant more
work for him, but they would also be company.

He glanced toward the flanks of the mountains, thick
with a stand of timber. Suddenly, he thought of his telescope and went within.

When he had been unable to return to his ship they
had put his gear ashore, and the telescope had been
stored in his sea-chest.

Getting the glass from his gear, he returned to the
door, where he spent some time examining the mountains.
They were rougher than they at first seemed; he saw among
the trees more of the outcroppings of boulders, and what
could be cliffs.

As darkness came on, he found himself growing uneasy.
He retreated within the station, rebuilt his fire, and
settled down for an evening of reading. As a boy he had
no access to books, and had worked most of the time from
daylight until dark, finally going to bed so tired he was
at once asleep. Not until he went to sea had he any experience of reading for pleasure.

He had but one book, a copy of a novel by Bulwer-
Lytton given to him when he lay recovering from his
wound. It was <u>Rienzi, the Last of the Roman Tribunes</u>. He
settled down to reading, taking time out only to replen-
ish the fire. Several times he went to the door or windows but heard nothing, saw nothing. At last, his eyes
growing tired, he turned in.

At daylight he took his rifle and scouted the area.
He found no tracks, no sign that anything had come near
the station. Relieved, he went back inside, taking care,
however, to bar the door.

He had fried bacon and put out some bread and dried
apples which he had soaked well during the night, and was
preparing to sit down when he heard a sound of hoofbeats,
then a shout.

He went to the door, took down the bar, and glanced
out. Seeing a herd of horses and two men driving them, he
put his rifle down beside the door and stepped outside.

The older man rounded up a bay with three white

stockings that seemed inclined to stray while Loccard walked across the road and took down the gate-bars.

When he saw the last of the sixteen horses through the gate, he looked around at the riders. "Coffee's on. Come on in. You had breakfast?"

"We done et," the younger man said. He was scarcely more than a boy, but tall and strong. "We camped up the road a piece."

"You could have come on in last night," Loccard suggested.

"Never git me to come up here of a night," the older man said grimly. "This here's no place to be once dark comes."

"He stopped away back yonder," the younger one said. "I'd have come on in."

"Ain't got no sense. Not a durned bit. Not after what happened to them others."

"What did happen?" Loccard asked, following them through the door.

"Disappeared, that's what. Vanished. One day they was here, next day gone. I come up here bringin' grub an' such. They was gone."

"Well, not both t' onct. Each in his own time. Jed Slocum . . . he was a good man. Sharp man, too. He wasn't feared of no ha'nts, but little good it did him."

"What do you think happened?" Loccard asked.

"Who knows? Somethin' got 'em. Jed, he lived it out for nigh three months. Got thinner an' more peaked by the day. Looked like a dead man last I seen of him, but he wouldn't say nothin' about it."

"He said something to me," the boy said.

The older man stared at him. "You?"

"He ast me if I ever seen a yaller bear." The younger man sat down on a bench and stretched his long legs. "I said I never. There was no such thing. Brown bears, black bears, an' them polar bears. They're white. But no yaller bears."

Jeremy Loccard shrugged. "Who knows what's in those mountains? There could be bears of a kind no man has ever seen."

"Or other things," the older man spat, and Loccard winced. He had just swept and mopped that floor.

He helped himself to bacon from the frying-pan. "You ever really _look_ at this here country? She's good country. Grass, timber, water if you know where to look, but there's no Injuns . . . or mighty few. Now I say that's odd . . . mighty odd. I come west along the Humboldt River. Godforsaken country, but there's Injuns there, so why not here? I say they either was run off or somethin' took 'em."

Loccard got the pot from the stove and filled cups for them. "Those horses out there," he asked, "any of them riding stock?"

The younger man shrugged. "That grulla mustang has been ridden a good bit. Fact is, that's why we brought him along. If any stock gits away you can round 'em up ridin' him.

"There's two or three others been rid some, too, but mostly they're drivin' stock." The older man glanced at Loccard. "Heard your name. Jimmy, ain't it?"

"Jeremy . . . Jeremy Loccard."

"Jed Slocum, he was a nice ol' feller. Good man. I never did cotton to that Zimmerman, though. He looked mean . . . kind of sullen, like."

"He was the man here before Slocum?"

"Uh-huh. He was here three, maybe four months. Always had his nose in a book, big ol' books, like of which I never did see . . . kind of worried pictures in them."

"Worried?"

"Uh-huh. There was devils and such."

"Weird?"

"That's it. Worried. He seen me lookin' at a book left open on the table and he got mad as hell. He come over here and slammed it shut, said something about me bein' nosy. Anybody else an' I'd have took it up, but not him. He was a mean . . . mighty mean."

"He'd of killed you, Tom."

"Mebbe. An' mebbe I don't kill so easy." Tom glanced at Loccard, indicating the gun he wore. "You any good with that?"

"Good enough."

The older man chuckled. "All y'have to be!" he said. "That's all you have to be!"

A thought occurred to Loccard. "That Zimmerman, now? Somebody come an' get his gear?"

Tom looked over at his companion. "You get it, Beak?"

"Must still be around. I know Duro never brought it down . . . all them books, too. It would have taken some liftin' to get them aboard. Heaviest boxes I ever did see, an' I helped him off-load them."

"Them?"

"There was three . . . not so big but almighty heavy."

"Hid 'em, prob'ly. He was that kind. Wanted nobody nosin' around. He said as much, more'n onct. He had some notion . . . I dunno what . . . but some kinda notion about this place . . . these mountains. Maybe the desert.

"Asked all kinda questions. What was the Injuns like? Was they on' Paiutes? I ever see any other kind? Ever hear tell of any stories the Injuns tell?

"Hell, like I tol' him, these Injuns don't tell no stories. They don't even talk much. Anyway, what would they have to talk about? Nothin' but ignorant savages, runnin' around with no drawers on."

Loccard nodded. "Maybe so, but I've sailed on some far waters, and I've seen things. . . . It doesn't pay to take too much for granted with any people, no matter how primitive they seem."

"Bah! The sooner they're all gone, the better. I seen aplenty of them, here and there. Good for nothin'."

Loccard did not reply. To protest would do no good. The man had his mind made up and what he had decided pleased him, and left room for no further consideration of the subject. A neat pigeonhole was often a substitute for thought and a means of isolating ideas that might otherwise become disturbing.

"That Zimmerman, now. He was a canny one. Mean, but canny. I think he had something, some burr under his saddle. He didn't come here just for no job. He was looking for something, something he figured was worth plenty."

"How could that be?" Loccard suggested mildly. "In a country where there was nothing but savages?"

The contradiction irritated the older man. "Mayn't always have been Injuns here. Who knows who was here before? I tell you, I seen things . . . well, they was things no Injun ever done."

"What sort of things?" Jeremy asked.

"Mummies, an' such. Seen 'em in caves."

"Probably just the dry air," Loccard suggested.

"Mebbe. Mebbe so. I was just tellin' you what I seen. I seen aplenty, I have. That Zimmerman, though. He was no tin horn. He was a mighty big, mean man but he was knowledgeable. I never figured nothin' would happen to him."

The older man squinted at Loccard. "We got us a bet, down to Los Angeles. We got us a bet on you. I'm sayin' you don't last out the month. Somethin' will git you, or you'll run."

Loccard had disliked the man before; he liked him even less now. "Who'd you bet with?" he asked.

"Weaver. He says you'll stick it. I say you won't. I say something's goin' t' git you."

"I hope it was a good-sized bet," Loccard suggested. "Something worthwhile?"

"Bet him a month's wages, mine against his'n." He grinned, showing broken teeth. "He makes three times what I do, so I got me a good bet."

"No bet is good if you lose," Loccard said. "And I am going to make sure you do."

The older man shot him an angry look, then went outside. The boy lingered. "Mister," he said. "What he said about that Zimmerman was true. Those books now . . . There was some kinda strange signs inside. One book had some o' these funny signs where one end points one way, and the other end the other way."

"A swastika?" Loccard sketched the design in the air. "That's it."

Loccard stood in the door and watched them ride away. He glanced toward the horses, who seemed at home in the corral, but he went out and added several buckets of water to the trough, his eyes restless over the mountainside and down the trail toward the desert.

Zimmerman had brought three heavy boxes and none had been taken away, so either they were here or they'd been taken by someone. He hesitated but did not add, something.

Slocum had lost weight, had been under strain, had asked the boy about yellow bears. Had he seen such a bear? Or was it something else? Some other kind of creature?

The articles found in the living quarters of the station had obviously been those of the last occupant, who was Jed Slocum, so where were those of Zimmerman, who had preceded him?

Walking to the corral, he glanced over the horses. Before going off to sea he had known a little about

horses, and these were good stock. He located the grulla
and offered him a handful of rich green grass, pulled
from near the well. The grulla took it gratefully and
held still while Loccard rubbed his neck and talked to
him, but shied away when no more grass was forthcoming.

Yet it was the beginning of a rapport between them,
and Jeremy hoped the grulla understood who he was: the
man in charge, the man who fed him, the man who would be
riding him.

Nothing had been said as to when the next stage would
come through, but he assumed it would be today. He had
turned back toward the house when from the corner of his
eye he caught a flicker of movement near the corner of
the barn.

He turned sharply, glancing that way, cursing himself
for not having the rifle. His pistol, however, was in his
holster, easy to his hand.

For a moment there was nothing, and then he saw them.

An Indian man appeared suddenly, ghostlike, at the
corner of the barn. Loccard blinked, and a woman was
standing beside the Indian. Then one by one, a slim, wiry
boy, a girl of perhaps eight or nine, and one still
younger, of perhaps but four.

They stood, silent, staring, their eyes upon him as
though he himself were a ghost.

CHAPTER III

"Hello there," he spoke quietly, not wanting to alarm
them, for they seemed poised to run. "Come on in!" He
swung his arm at them in a gathering gesture. He knew
nothing of sign language but hoped they would understand.

They did not move, just watching him. He smiled at

them, and then went about the corral, checking it for
strength. On the far side he came to an abrupt halt.
There in the earth was a smudged track, a huge track, not
unlike that of a bear, yet different, somehow.

He glanced at the Indians. The man had come a little
closer, so he motioned them on again, then pointed to the
track in the earth. This time the Indian came on, whether
from curiosity or because he was getting over his fear,
Loccard did not know.

When the Indian was only a few feet off, Loccard indicated the track, then stepped back a little, spreading
his hands and shrugging, as if to say he did not know
what it was.

The Indian took one glance, then stepped back so
quickly he almost fell. He backed away quickly. "Bad!
Bad!" he spoke hoarsely, obviously frightened.

"Bear?"

"No bear! Bad! Ver' bad!"

"No bear? Then what is it?"

"Bad!" The Indian backed away. His fear was obvious.
"More big! Ver' bad!"

Loccard gave it up, for the time being at least.
"Eat?" he suggested.

The Indians had been about to walk away; now they
hesitated. The man wanted to go, the woman was protesting.
Her gestures indicated she was speaking of the children.

"Come!" Loccard said. "There is meat."

Reluctantly, they followed him, avoiding the area
near the track. Loccard was puzzled, for their fear was
obvious and he had never known Indians to fear any animal. To respect them, to be wary of them, but not to
fear. He had known no Indians so far west, yet he had
known other primitive peoples, and fear of wild animals
was rare among them.

There might be fear, however, if the animal was possessed of an evil spirit, or believed to be so.

He thought of that. There was something here, and he must know more. He must know more to satisfy his growing curiosity, and he must know more simply to survive.

He led the Indians back to the station and sat them down on the bench at the door. Then he went inside, put together some bread and meat, and brought it out to them. He did not know these Indians, and they might only be scouts for an attacking party lying somewhere nearby, awaiting a signal. Others had vanished from this place, and no man knew how. He doubted that Indians were involved, but who could be sure? He would take nothing for granted.

He brought out meat and bread for himself, then squatted on his heels where he could see the road, and ate with them, asking no questions, saying nothing at first.

Finally when he did it was in his halting Spanish. He spoke of a good day, asked if they'd traveled far.

"Not far," the Indian replied in English.

"You are alone?"

The Indian indicated the woman and children. "They are with me. We look."

"For a place to live?"

The Indian shook his head. He seemed to be searching for a word, then gave up and said it in Spanish. "Amigos."

"Friends? Here?" Then he said quietly, "I will be your friend."

The woman glanced at him slyly, almost hopefully, but she said nothing. The children watched him with large dark eyes.

"I have just come," Loccard said. "I like it here."

"You go," the Indian said quietly. "It is not good place for man."

"I serve the stage. The stage goes through. I help."

"You go."

Loccard was silent. He went inside and got cups from the shelf and filled them with coffee.

"You know this place?" He gestured around, taking it all in. "You have been here before?"

"I am Kawaiisu. This my land. One time I live"--he pointed toward a place to the northeast--"there."

He sipped his coffee. Obviously he had once known more English, but now was feeling his way with a language long unused. At least, that was what Loccard thought. Having partially learned many tongues himself, he knew how quickly a language only slightly known can disappear. That was the trouble of being a seafaring man. One rarely stayed long enough in one place to learn a language well. He knew a smattering of marketplace, waterfront language from fifty ports.

Suddenly the Indian said, "One time many mans here. All gone, maybe." He looked at Loccard. "You see?"

"No . . . not yet. I have not been here long," he said. "You are the first Indian I have seen. But," he added, "I was not expecting to see any yet. Maybe they have not made up their minds about me yet. Maybe they look at me to decide what to do next."

"_They_ look, too. Soon they take you."

" 'They'? Who are '_they_'? And where would they take me? And why?"

The Indian shrugged. He wiped his hands on his legs. "Is no good here. Many mans here . . . where now? Gone . . ."

He finished his coffee and Loccard refilled the cup, adding sugar. The Indian sipped his coffee. "All around . . . bad places here. Ghost places. You no stay. You go . . . _now_."

"I must stay."

They sat silent. The children finished their eating and their mother likewise. They sat silently beside Loccard while the minutes passed into a half hour, then an

hour. Finally, Loccard got up. "You stay . . . rest. We
talk."

The Indian stirred a little, but made no reply. The
man seemed lonely, hungry for more than food. Or was that
something Loccard was simply reading into him? It was
hard to tell with an Indian, for all peoples do not mani-
fest interest or joy or dismay in the same manner.

Shortly before noon he harnessed six horses and led
them out of the corral and tied them to the corral bars
to await the stage.

"That animal?" he said, after a while. "The one that
made the track, he is bigger than a bear?"

The Indian held up two fingers. "Big like two bears.
Maybe three. Long hair . . . yellow. No bullet kill him.
No arrow."

"He lives in the mountains?"

"No live here . . . other place."

Loccard went back inside and began making fresh coffee. The stage would be coming along soon and the passengers would want some refreshment. He built up the fire
and when he looked outside, the Indians were gone.

Loccard walked onto the road and looked up and down.
The family, if that's what they were, had vanished.
Well . . . He shrugged and went back inside. In such a
short time they could not have gone far, and they might
return.

He heard the stage before he saw it, heard Duro Weaver's halloo and then saw it coming in the distance. He
went out to the roadside and was standing there when the
stage came wheeling up and stopped. He caught the horses
by their bridles, steadied them a bit, and then he began
unhooking the traces as the passengers got stiffly down.
There were three men and two women.

One of the women was scarcely more than a girl, and
she looked frightened. The older woman was tall, slender,
and very beautiful in a cold, somewhat haughty way. The

men moved toward the stage station, and the younger woman
made as if to follow, but was stopped by a sharp word. The
other woman stood in the road and looked carefully about.

When the team was taken to the corral and the fresh
team harnessed, Loccard walked back to the station with
Duro.

"You all right?" The stage driver spoke softly.

"Sure. Everything's fine."

"Didn't know whether to expect you or not," Weaver
said, "the way thing's been happenin' up here."

"I'll make it," Loccard spoke with more assurance
than he felt.

They went inside and he took up the coffeepot and
filled cups. He glanced at the girl, smiling when their
eyes met. She seemed startled and shot a quick glance at
her companion, who seemed not to have noticed.

She was pretty, Loccard decided, almighty pretty. She
was frightened, too, but why he could not guess. All
three men were well dressed, and seemed to have no connection with each other or the women.

The older man, who might have been one of those who
invested in mining ventures, or began them, waved a hand
at the country around. "It must be lonely here. Do you
have many visitors?"

"I like wild country," Loccard said, "but visitors?
Only some Indians."

"Indians?" It was the older woman who spoke. "I
thought . . . I mean, I believed there were no Indians
here. It is not true, then?"

"There was a family," Loccard said. "They came by
just before you did. It is said there are Indians in the
higher mountains. Some call them the Kawaiisu, some the
Tehachapis."

"This is excellent coffee," a man whom Loccard took
to be a gambler commented. "Better than I expected from
the tender of a stage station."

The third man, who wore a black suit, spoke up. "You have not looked at him, my friend. I detect a certain air, a certain style. It is the style of command."

"An Army officer?" The gambler studied Loccard with interest. "I believe not."

"Will you have some more coffee?" Loccard suggested.

Duro Weaver, who sat at the end of the table, knew how Loccard felt. "Better drink up," he said. "We've little time and I want to be out of the pass before dark."

The older woman glanced at him, but her expression did not change. She was, Loccard thought, a remarkably beautiful woman who for some reason was trying not to appear so. . . . Was it simply that she did not wish to draw attention to herself? Her eyes were large, her bone structure delicate yet strong.

The mining man, if such he was, glanced at Weaver. "Any special reason to be out of the mountains before dark? Like the lady here, I didn't think there were Indians in this part of the country."

"Could be outlaws," the gambler suggested. "There's one named Vasquez--"

"I didn't think that was what he meant," the man in the black suit commented. "I think our good driver had something else in mind."

Nobody spoke for a minute, and Jeremy Loccard went to the door. The sun was sinking behind the mountains. It would soon be dark here, although light upon the desert, only a few miles away. He glanced toward the corral. The grulla had its head up, nostrils flared, looking north toward the darkest mountains.

He glanced down the pass toward the desert. A weird yellow light showed there. "Weaver?" he spoke in a casual tone. "Got a minute?"

The stage driver got up and walked to the door, wiping the back of his hand across his handlebar mustache.

Loccard indicated the yellow look over the desert. "Is
that what I think it is?"

"Sandstorm," Weaver said, "a bad one. You're sheltered here, don't get much of it."

"The wind is picking up, though."

Weaver went outside and walked along the road a little, looking down the pass. He walked back. "You got
comp'ny, son. No way to get a team to face that. Sometimes the sand'll take the hide right off a man."

Loccard shrugged. "Means you'll have to spend the
night at Twenty Mile," he commented dryly.

Duro Weaver swore softly, bitterly. "I'll tell 'em,"
he said, "then we better put up the team." He paused
again. "Put 'em in the barn."

They walked back to the station together, and as they
stepped in, the older woman started to rise. "Is it not
time?" she asked. "It seems to me we have stopped overlong."

"We'll be here longer," Weaver said. He took out his
pipe and began to fill it. "There's a sandstorm blowin'
out on the flat, blowin' like the mill-tails of Hell!"

Loccard was looking at the older woman. Her features
had suddenly seemed to harden and for a moment he saw
something in her face that seemed wholly evil, something
so--

She turned toward him, and her expression changed
swiftly. She smiled, beautifully. Her teeth were very
even, very white. "We will be all right here, won't we? I
mean, we don't have to be afraid of those Indians, do
we?"

"Of course not." He gestured about. "This place is
very strong. . . . Nothing could get in, unless we let it
in. And we are well armed."

She looked at him, and he thought her eyes were
faintly amused, even taunting. "Are your rifles the answer to every<u>thing</u>?"

"Sometimes they have to suffice," Loccard replied quietly, "although I've had no trouble here."

He followed Weaver outside and they led the horses to the stable and stripped off the harness, hanging it on pegs inside the stable. They forked hay into the mangers, and then went outside. Loccard caught the grulla then and took him into the stable, too.

Weaver hesitated in the road. "Loccard, tell me honest. You seen anything out here?"

"No," he said. "I've <u>seen</u> nothing." He paused. The wind caught dried leaves and scattered them down the road, moving a little ripple of sand along with them. The wind would get into the pass soon, and they'd be feeling it. And that was the trouble . . . they would not be able to hear.

"I've seen nothing, Duro, but there was something."

Weaver took his pipe from his mouth, looking at him.

"Something almighty big, something bigger than the biggest grizzly you ever heard of, something that pushed against the door, something that might have weighed a ton or more."

Weaver swore, slowly, emphatically, solemnly.

"I found a smudged track . . . long claws, and I found some yellow hairs. Long hairs, maybe seven or eight inches, mighty coarse. Smelled awful."

He listened to the wind, saw the trees bend with it. A tumbleweed went rolling by on the road.

"The Indians saw the track. They were scared. I fed 'em, tried to get them to stick around. They disappeared."

"Don't do no good to feed Injuns," Weaver said. "Underfoot all the time."

"I wanted to know what they know. They said I'd better go . . . something would <u>get</u> me, like it got the others, and the Indians."

"Indians, too?"

"That was my impression. There used to be Indians
here. Now there are none. Maybe they just went away, but
that Indian didn't think so, he didn't think so at all.
He was scared."

"What d' you think it was?"

Loccard shrugged. "Look, I've been in fifty countries, talked to a hundred kinds of people. The white man
thinks he knows it all because right now he's running
ahead of the pack. I came to one conclusion, knocking
around in foreign parts, and that was that there was just
a whole lot I didn't know.

"Maybe there's animals we've never seen, maybe there
are things we've never seen. I had a dog whistle once
that I couldn't hear, but my dog could hear it.

"I picked up cargo along the coast of Sumba a couple
of times. It's an island in the East Indies east of Java,
but off the mainline of those islands. We picked up san-
dalwood there, bird's nests--the Chinese make soup from
them--skins, shells, and sometimes horses. There's a lot
of wild horses on the island.

"I went back inland to see the high plains where the
horses ran. They were there, all right, but here and
there I saw stone walls surrounded by thickets of brush
through which no path seemed to go.

"These were said to be villages long deserted, although they were not unlike some of the villages in other
parts of the island. The people avoided them. Or perhaps
they only wanted me to avoid them. In a thicket near one
of those villages I saw a piece of what looked like rocks
fitted together into some sort of a floor or platform.
There were low trees around, a few boulders. I started to
go near but they advised against it.

"Few minutes later I looked back and there was a man
standing there beside that flat rock. He was looking at
me. Or I thought he was. He hadn't been there a few minutes before."

The wind was blowing harder. Duro Weaver started across the road, then stopped again. "Those tracks you seen? Those claw marks? You ever see anything like them before?"

Loccard looked at him, leaning closer so Weaver could hear over the rush of wind down the pass. "One time. We were loading tar down at those brea pits out there west of Los Angeles. There were a lot of bones in that tar; made trouble for us, as they were always in the way. I came on a forearm or foreleg of some creature with claws like that. Whatever it was, it was mighty big, and it must have had tremendous crushing power in those forelegs."

"I never seen no such animal," Weaver protested.

Loccard gestured. "You ever been back in those mountains?"

"No."

"Well, neither have I."

CHAPTER IV

They went inside, closing the door on the wind, which was now blowing a gale. The fire on the hearth was warm, there was a smell of coffee in the air, and the men were gathered about the table, talking.

At the fireplace the two women sat . . . not talking.

The master of a ship, as Jeremy Loccard had occasionally been, or the chief mate, which he had been since he was nineteen, learned to be reticent, sharing his thoughts but rarely. Such a man learned to judge the shades of feeling among a crew, the way the ship creaked in different seas and winds, the way the lines handled and the look of the sails. There was so much in the handling of ships and men that could be found in no book.

Loccard knew that Duro Weaver was a brave, confident man. In any situation he would be where he needed to be and he would be doing what was necessary.

He closed the door and put the bar in place. They had fuel enough, for the nights were cold at this time of year, and they had food enough. The sandstorm might blow itself out overnight, but if it followed the way of storms at sea they might be in for two or three days of it.

The man in the black suit looked around at Loccard. "Any bears in these mountains?"

"Lots of them," Weaver spoke up. "When we built the barn, yonder, we killed a grizzly had to weigh eight or nine hundred pounds."

"Are they really dangerous?"

"Mister"--Duro Weaver got out his pipe--"any wild animal is potentially dangerous. I seen a man badly mauled by a buck deer. Up Frisco way I saw a woman half-killed by a cub bear she thought was mighty cute. She just had to ruffle his fur, she said.

"Wild animals are wild, you got to remember that; also, they're like folks, and they have their moods. Bears more than most. Bears are notional. A body has to be wary where a bear's concerned."

"You've hunted this country?"

"No." Weaver stuffed his pipe with tobacco. "I never hunted about here and I don't know of anybody who has . . . 'less it was Zimmerman."

Suddenly Loccard realized Weaver had sharpened their attention. Even the women at the fire were listening.

"Zimmerman?" The man in the black suit was too casual. "Who was he?"

"Station man here . . . a while back."

"What became of him?"

Weaver had not wanted to answer that question but had seen it coming. "Disappeared," he replied coolly. "He was

here one day, and the next day he was gone. Maybe," he
added, "he come onto one o' them cute bears."

"Disappeared? Did anybody look for him?"

Weaver stooped to the fireplace and took up a burning
twig to light his pipe. "Look? Where? Mister, there's a
sight of country out yonder. Take a mighty big army with
lots of time to comb it.

"Nobody," he added, "knows what's out there. Maybe
nothing. Maybe things no man has ever seen. Maybe things
no man wants to see.

"I've heard tell of a canyon back yonder to the
northwest . . . maybe twelve, fifteen mile from here.
Maybe not so far. Injuns used to go there. Left holes in
the rock where they used to grind acorns. There's two
good springs in that canyon, grass, wood for the burning,
shelter from the wind . . . but no Injuns. Not no more."

"Why?"

"Your guess is as good as mine. They follow the creek
up the main canyon, but you'll never catch an Injun going
up the south side of the creek. Least, that's what I been
told."

"Superstition," the mining man suggested.

"That there," Weaver said, "is an easy word. It's a
word used to sidestep many an explanation, or a belief or
idea a man don't understand."

"Or don't want to take time to study," Loccard added.

Weaver nodded toward the outside. "You ever been out
in those mountains alone? Who's to say what's there?
Maybe what the Injuns believe in is only there because
they believe in it. Maybe in places like this there's
things left over, things that ceased to be a long time
back . . . except in places like this."

"You're talking nonsense," the mining engineer commented. "I only believe in things a man can measure and
weigh. Whatever else there is doesn't matter."

Loccard added fuel to the fire. He crouched beside

it, staring into the coals. On such a night, in such a wind, they would hear nothing outside. Maybe it was just as well. He thought of the horses. If there was trouble there he must go out.

The older woman came to him. "I am Andrea Ritter. I must speak with someone who is familiar with all this." Her gesture took in the country around.

"I just arrived," Loccard said. "Duro there, he knows as much as anybody and that's little enough."

Loccard paused a moment, and then in a lower voice he said, "What's your interest, ma'am? If I knew, maybe I could help."

She hesitated, seemed about to speak, then shook her head. "I cannot. It is too much, too, too much!"

Duro walked over, a cup of coffee in his hand. "Heard what you asked, ma'am," he said, "but there's nobody knows much. Some figure there just isn't nothing to know. It's empty country. The first white man along here so far's anybody knows was a Captain Pedro Fages, exploring for the Spanish folks. Jed Smith come through, but we don't know exactly where. Been a few white men back in yonder huntin' gold, an' that's about it.

"So far's anybody knows the Spanish never paid it much mind. Even the Injuns mostly pulled out an' left."

"Why? Why would they do a thing like that?"

Duro sipped his coffee. He had no answer to that and attempted none. He glanced at Loccard and raised an eyebrow. Neither could understand why a woman such as this was so interested in what was to all obvious view a barren and empty land.

Loccard's eyes went to the girl. She was very pretty, but the scared look was there, too, and she seemed scared of Andrea Ritter as much as anything. Or was he imagining things?

He went back to the kitchen and began putting to-

gether a meal. There were supplies enough, and he saw no
sense in stinting.

The girl followed him into the kitchen. "May I help?"
she asked. "I can cook."

"Sure." He held out a hand. "I'm Jeremy Loccard."

"I am Jennifer Kernaby. . . . Call me Jen."

"I'll do that." He waved a hand about. "We don't have
much. For now we'll just make up some cazuela . . . one
name for stewed jerked beef. You can chop up some onions
for me, if you're of a mind to."

They worked in silence for a few minutes, and he
asked, "Goin' far?"

She did not look at him. "Not far. At least, I don't
think so. Maybe we'll go back to Los Angeles soon. Andrea
wanted to come here."

"Here? This place?"

"I . . . I don't know. She wanted to come here, and
she wanted me along. Maybe she's going on up to San Francisco. We talked about it. I think . . . maybe she's
looking for land."

Loccard glanced at her. "Ma'am . . . Jen . . . this
is no place to look for land. There's land aplenty nigh
to the sea, better land than this, I'd say, and it's
closer to market. This here is wild country, and it will
be for a good time to come."

Suddenly she was close to him. "Mr. Loccard . . .
Jeremy? I'm afraid of her."

Instantly she stepped away from him. There was a
sound of boot heels clicking, and Andrea Ritter was in
the door. "Oh? There you are! I wondered what had become
of you."

"I am helping Mr. Loccard," she said primly. "There
seemed such a lot to do."

"I am sure he can manage." Andrea's tone was grim.
"Come! You'll be all smelling of onions."

She rinsed her hands in the basin, and dried them carefully while Andrea waited, then turned and left the room without a backward glance.

"Make's no sense," he commented, to himself. "Why would she be with someone who scared her? And why would a woman like that be hunting land up here?"

He finished fixing their supper and served it. The mining engineer, whose name proved to be Delphin Rickard, came to the kitchen to help Loccard carry the food to the table. He suspected Rickard came more from a desire to look around than from any desire to help. "That man in the black suit? Do you know him?"

"I never saw any of you before," Loccard said, "and it is unlikely I will see any of you again. I'll make some money here, then be gone."

"Probably a wise choice," he agreed. "This Zimmerman now? Did you know him?"

"No. I don't believe even the man who followed him knew him. Mr. Weaver, your driver . . . he knew him to talk to."

"You've never been out in the mountains?" He took up a platter of sliced beef. "Hunting, or the like of that?"

"I haven't been here long enough."

"Odd that Zimmerman would come here," he mused, looking about. "It's unreasonable."

"You should know enough by now that there's no way of judging people. Just when you think you've got them figured, they'll cross you up. But why Zimmerman? What made him so different?"

"Zimmerman? Ah? There was a strange one! I did not know him, you understand, only of him. He was a scholar. An authority on the occult, a delver into mysteries."

"You must have him mixed up. This Zimmerman was a mean man by all I hear, a big, strong, and mighty difficult man."

"Of course. He was all of that. I had friends who

knew him, or knew of him. He went his own way, shared
what he knew with nobody. But why should he come here? To
such a place as this? What was he looking for? What did
he expect to find?"

"Maybe," Loccard said dryly, "he just needed the job,
as I did."

"Zimmerman? I doubt it. The man always had access to
money. I mean he would seem to be on his uppers, then he
would show up with money. And money was a prime requisite
with Zimmerman. He liked to live. Champagne and fine
wines, the best food, the best women. I think the man
loved nothing but his appetites."

Rickard took his platter and went into the next room
and Loccard followed with biscuits, cheese, and a pot of
stewed fruit.

The puzzle of Zimmerman allied itself to the puzzle
of Rickard himself. Why was he here? Where had he come
from? What was his connection with Zimmerman?

Yet, he might have given Loccard a clue. Zimmerman
could always come up with money, and that implied a
source. Was he a wealthy man? Had he wealthy friends or
relatives? Or was there some other source for his
wealth?

A delver into mysteries, Rickard said. Well, he found
his mystery here, surely, and disappeared. Or had he?
Suppose he was somewhere about?

Well, suppose he was, thought Loccard. That meant
nothing to him. Zimmerman had left his job, gone off on
his own. Or been killed.

Killed? By what?

The word brought Loccard up short. Why not by "whom"?
Was he already imagining something else? Was he filling
his world with creatures of the imagination? Was he not
creating a mystery where there might be none?

Once the food was served Loccard sat down with the
passengers. The talk about the table seemed so much idle

chatter, and only Jen and Duro were silent. That was unusual for Duro, for he was a man who liked people and who
talked well, and his long years on the frontier had given
him a wealth of stories. Now he merely listened, and if
anything, he seemed puzzled.

The fire blazed cheerfully on the hearth and the
coal-oil lamps, backed with reflectors, gave added light
to the room. Outside the wind howled and sand rattled
against the windows.

The coffee smelled good, and slowly Loccard began to
relax. He glanced once toward the door of his room. His
rifle stood just inside the door.

As though reading his thought, the man in the black
suit asked, "Do you always wear a pistol?"

"This country," Duro replied for him, "a man better.
No tellin' what a body'd run into on the road."

Andrea Ritter smiled. "I am sure there's noth--" Her
voice broke sharply off, for they all heard it: an eerie
cry, heard faintly but clearly enough during a momentary
lull in the wind.

It was no human cry, nor like any animal. . . . A
bird maybe, but what bird? What strange sound in the
night? Andrea's eyes went wide; her lips parted as if to
scream, but no sound came. All were transfixed, all but
the man in the black suit.

"There it is," he said coolly enough, "all that was
needed. It's out there."

They looked at him, staring, nor did any one of them
speak. The cry came again . . . closer.

"It is coming then," the man in the black suit said.
"It's coming."

COMMENTS: Dad found the Southern California wilderness to be a spooky place. He touched on it in *The Lonesome Gods* and used that strangeness to a much greater extent in *The Californios.* I agree with him. We used to talk about the feelings we'd get back in the hills and the hot, chaparral-choked arroyos. It is a haunted landscape, even more so than a Colorado or Utah canyon full of cliff dwellings. I have no idea why that should be the case, but we shared the feeling nonetheless.

The location of this story seems to be very near to Tehachapi Pass in the area along Highway 58 between Bakersfield and Mojave. The idea of seeing a sandstorm come up from the desert makes complete sense; these days the area is near a giant wind farm. I'm confident in saying this story was written in the early 1970s because Louis mentions a narrow canyon where buckeye trees grow and the Kawaiisu Indians left *pa-haz*, or grinding holes, in the rocks—a description of a piece of property we owned not too far from the pass.

My mother and sister sitting in that narrow canyon at
the base of the rocks with the grinding holes.

By the time he gets to Chapter 4, it seems Louis had reached a decisive moment in the writing process. The arrival of the odd group of stage passengers suggests that the mystery of the disappearing station agents, and even the existence of some sort of monster, is just the tip of the interdimensional iceberg. The place where Louis stopped writing is probably the place where he was going to have to commit to what the book was going to be about. Dad usually worked this sort of thing out unconsciously, but whether it was a conscious or unconscious process, it is obvious to me that he wasn't quite ready to take the next step. No doubt several of the passengers are in on whatever is happening and it would seem that Jeremy Loccard's amulet will also play a role.

It is amusing to see a moment of Chick Bowdrie–style forensics when Loccard places the smelly hairs in a folded piece of paper. (Bowdrie was a Texas Ranger character Louis wrote about early in his career.) The monster may be a giant sloth, though even as big as they were, I'm not sure they'd be all that aggressive. Perhaps it was a short-faced bear, an extinct carnivore of colossal size . . . which would definitely have been something to fear. The bones of both have been found in the La Brea Tar Pits in Los Angeles.

As I mentioned, Dad was working with ideas here that were very similar to ones he experimented with in his novels *The Californios* and *The Haunted Mesa*: strange animals that come from somewhere else, another reality of some sort, and people who know about this other place and, regardless of the danger, wish to exploit it in some way. In his notes on this story Dad mentions checking into Harold Courlander's *The Fourth World of the Hopis* and Frank Waters' *Book of the Hopi*. Both were also inspirations for *Haunted Mesa*. Additionally, Louis considered rereading some of the work of Talbot Mundy, a writer who influenced Dad's more occult-oriented adventure fiction, and Charles Fort, an early collector of unexplained phenomena.

In some ways it seems as if Louis was about to expand on, or even write a sort of sequel to, *The Californios* with this story. His notes mention "a lost city in the desert and the people who lived there." Juan, the old Indian in *The Californios* who can travel between worlds, told the tale of such an Atlantis-like city. Louis jotted down the following bit of dialogue for one of the characters to impart:

```
    "People throw things out of kilter. The Old Ones
knew. Young folks lost a lot of knowledge. There was
a wall in that town, and on the Wall were inscrip-
tions. This wall could be read by the Old Ones, but
when the storm came they were suffocated in the dust,
all but a few who had gone through the Portals. When
they came back all was gone, their folks, temples,
houses everything gone. They live on the Other Side
now and just return for pilgrimages, but they don't
want folks in the way. . . . This here is on the
route, the temple is in the mountains yonder, and the
Portals are there. There were other Openings. . . ."
```

This idea of portals to other worlds is a significant element in *The Californios* and *Haunted Mesa*. In both there is another plane of existence that invites exploration and offers a sense of possibility that our world has been running low on recently. Louis grew up in a time when the ends of the earth had yet to be completely explored, but by the time he wrote these chapters, the likelihood of discovering *King Kong*'s Skull Island or *Lost Horizon*'s Shangri-La had been reduced to nearly zero. A parallel universe was the next step for a writer of the frontier.

Dad also jotted down one final note, possibly of what was intended to be the last scene in this story:

```
    A vanishing stagecoach? A Lurch of the stage, a
jolt, a cloud of dust, then a trail the driver has
never seen before. A shining city in the distance.
Stage picks up Loccard, he warns them to turn around
and drive fast, before the Opening closes. They
escape--"Still, that city now. I'd like to have seen
it."
```

TRAIL OF TEARS

The First Seven Chapters of a Historical Novel

CHAPTER 1

She stood poised and naked upon a point of rock,
caught in a beam of light that fell through clouds rifted
by some far wind.

For an instant she stood upon her ledge beyond the
trees, and upon the high trail where he rode his horse,
Miles Tolan drew up sharply, astonished by the sudden
glimpse of beauty . . . and then he reached for his glass.

Yet even as the glass found her figure she sprang out
into the still air, arms flung wide, and vanished from
sight beyond the trees.

The minutes marched, but he did not ride on. Far from
any settlement, riding through a mountain wilderness,
what he had just seen was clearly impossible. Yet he had
seen her. How far away had she been? Was it four hundred
yards or a bit less? The clear mountain air made the distance deceptive.

The sky was overcast with lowering gray clouds, and
the shaft of sunlight where the girl had stood was the
last, anywhere. Now it, too, was gone. A few scattered

drops fell, and he went to his saddlebags for his
slicker. Huge drops spattered and rattled on the leaves
of the forest, and from afar he heard the coming of the
cold battalions of rain.

Lieutenant Miles Tolan rode through wild country upon
dim trails known only to wild game and the Cherokees
themselves. He had chosen this route to Atlanta in making
his change of station, for he loved the wild and lonely
mountains and now it was late summer with the nights carrying a promise of early autumn. It had been three days
since he had seen anyone at all, and to see such a girl
in such a place . . . It was preposterous.

Slowly, he walked his horse forward. In the last ten
miles he could remember no trail that turned off in her
direction, but he searched for one as he rode. The trail
he followed was a narrow passage between two walls of
towering forest, and under the trees there was a thick
tangle of undergrowth and brush. Then, when he had traveled more than a mile, he dipped down from the rise into
a wide green meadow where a mountain stream tumbled over
rocks and beside it ran the thread of a rarely used path.
Despite the impending storm, he turned the black horse in
that direction and rode swiftly along.

Almost at once the trail left the meadow and went up
into the trees. With mounting excitement he knew he was
riding toward the rock on which he had seen the girl.

The trail seemed unused, yet suddenly he emerged from
the brush into a small parklike space, and here at the
base of a huge rock was a pool. Deep, clear, shadowed by
surrounding trees, it was a place of eerie enchantment,
but it was empty.

Arrested by the strange stillness, he sat his horse
in absolute silence, listening. There was another swift
patter of rain upon the leaves, and somewhere beyond the
pool and cloaked by the trees he could hear a trickle of
running water. Turning his horse, he rode around the

pool's edge to the towering mass of rock. The ledge from which the girl dived was at least fifteen feet above the water, but due to a rise in elevation, it was all of a hundred feet above the trail where he had been riding when he had glimpsed her.

On the far side, near a small stretch of sandy shore, he found natural steps and a path leading upward. In the sand at the base of a rock was a small, smudged print like that of a moccasin.

Dismounting, he climbed the rock and looked all about him. The land was deserted, empty, still.

Turning slowly, he surveyed the entire scene, and for the first time saw another trail leading westward. It must have been this path the girl had taken. Reluctantly he turned to go, then wedged between the rocks he saw a book.

Apparently the book had fallen there and been forgotten, perhaps by the girl who had only just left the ledge, for the book showed no mildew or dampness. Careful not to damage the covers, he extracted it from the crack. It was an almost new copy of Thomas Moore's Lalla Rookh. There was no name on the flyleaf.

Glancing around for some sheltered place where the book might be left, he found none. After a moment's hesitation he thrust it into his pocket.

The rain came across the forest with a rush of strength that belied the preliminary showers, and Miles Tolan scrambled down from the rocks and into the saddle. Reluctantly, he rode back to the trail he had been following. There would be adventure enough waiting for him in Atlanta; what he wanted now was an inn where he might get a hot meal and a bed.

Six feet and two inches tall, Miles Tolan was a lean and powerful one hundred and ninety pounds with a dark,

Hamlet-like face and green eyes, and he was riding toward
an assignment he did not want and had not requested.

It was beautiful land, this country of the Cherokees.
He did not blame them for wanting to stay, yet the government had decreed they must move, and move they would.
It was the last job he would have asked for, and was definitely not an assignment he had expected after his service in the field, but an Army officer did not question
his orders, he merely obeyed.

The rain fell steadily. His thoughts returned to the
diver. . . . What would a woman, especially one familiar
with the writings of Thomas Moore, be doing in such a
place? From all indications there was no plantation or
house within miles, and yet there she had been.

The smashing sound of a shot cut across the day like
the crack of a teamster's whip, and then, just ahead of
him, Tolan heard a high-pitched scream.

Leaping the gelding into a run, Tolan raced down the
trail to swing around a bend into a small clearing. Beyond the clearing and facing him was a long, low house
built of logs.

A girl was running toward him, a child half-blind
with fear. Only a few steps behind and rapidly overtaking
her was a lean, rawboned man whose features were filled
with a savage exultation that revolted Tolan. Even as his
horse pounded toward them, the man overtook the girl and
threw her to the ground, grasping her dress at the shoulder to rip it away.

The black covered the ground in a breath and Tolan's
hand dropped to the scruff of the man's neck and seized
him by the collar. The horse had not slowed and the man
was jerked from the girl, and Tolan dragged him a dozen
feet before he let go.

Beyond the shed Tolan heard the report of another
shot and a crackle of flames.

The man got shakily to his feet, fell, then got up

more slowly. "What right you got, buttin' in here?" he yelled. His lean jaws were covered with a coarse stubble of mixed-gray beard and he was almost frothing in his fury. "She's nothin' but a damn Cherokee! The state says they got no rights, so what's to stop a man?"

"I am. I'm stopping you."

His eyes ugly with malice, the tall man rubbed hard palms on his coarse jeans. "Are you now? I reckon Hallett will have something to say about that."

Tolan reined his horse around. "Walk ahead of me." He indicated an opening between the shed and a corral. "Walk out there into the open."

He turned to speak to the girl, but she had chosen the moment to disappear into the trees. Girl? A child rather; she could have been no more than fourteen.

There was a pile of loot in the clearing, and nearby an old Indian woman sat on the ground staring dumbly at the flames that consumed her home, her face seamed with age and grief. A man was stretched upon the ground, a patch of blood covering most of his back. Standing nearby superintending the rounding up of horses and cattle was a big man in high boots, carrying a blacksnake whip.

"Mr. Hallett"--the man Tolan had interrupted in his attempted rape was, Tolan noticed, both respectful and fearful of Hallett--"this here sojer says we got to leave them Cher'kee gals alone."

The big man turned sharply around, his face hard-set, ready to command. He had a strong-boned face with the skin drawn taut over the bones. His eyes were intensely black, his mustache was black, and it was obvious he was a man accustomed to command. Yet as he saw Tolan's uniform and recognized his rank, his manner changed. "How are you, Lieutenant? I am sorry you came up when you did, but we have to let the men have their fun. This is disagreeable duty."

"Since when did looting and rape become a duty?"

Hallett's features stiffened. "Obviously, Lieutenant, you are a stranger to Georgia. It is our business to root these people out, and that's what we'll do. I will be obliged if you would not interfere."

Tolan's expression did not change. "I have interfered." He sat straight in the saddle. "I am sure you can do what must be done without murder and rape. Now call off your men and get out of here."

For an instant Tolan believed Hallett intended to strike him with the whip. All the planes of Hallett's face seemed to flatten out and the skin around his eyes tightened. "I take no orders from you," he said, "nor from nobody else but my boss and the state of Georgia."

"You will take these orders." Tolan's tone was crisp. "I have been directed to report here by General Winfield Scott, and my orders are to see the Cherokees are moved with every care to their comfort and security. My orders do not condone rape."

Hallett hesitated. It was obvious to Tolan, and the fact surprised him, that the big man cared not a whit for Tolan's orders; but Hallett apparently was not sure exactly how far he might go in such a case. Miles Tolan, who had estimated many a man's potential before this, knew now that Hallett was not only a dangerous man but a capable, intelligent one as well.

"Very well, Lieutenant," Hallett said finally, "we will move along, as you suggest. This is a matter that can wait, and we can always return when we see fit. We will simply have to see that you are put right by your superiors."

"I have my orders."

"Ah? From General Scott, I believe you said? General Scott is not in Georgia, sir, and your orders here will be very different. You are to report to Colonel Loren White, I presume?"

"I am."

"You will learn, Lieutenant, that Colonel White is in command here, and your future orders will be from him. And one of those will be to refrain from molesting or interfering with citizens in pursuit of their business."

Miles Tolan was suddenly angry. He did not relish being told off by a civilian, nor did he like the implication that rape and murder would be tolerated by the American Army. "Be that as it may," he repeated coolly, "you will now get your men together and move along. The Indians will be brought in by the Army, and all in good time."

Hallett's smile was equally cold. "And if I choose to ignore that order, Lieutenant? What then?"

"I should be obliged to enforce it, sir."

Hallett made a great show of looking around and behind Tolan. "You are alone, I see. Doesn't it strike you that enforcing such an order might be difficult?"

"I should require no assistance, nor should I request it."

"You're very sure of yourself, Lieutenant. Too sure for an officer in a bright new uniform. One day I may decide to find out what is behind those shining buttons . . . if anything."

"I shall look forward to the moment, Mr. Hallett. And just so you will not be deceived by this bright new uniform, I might say it replaces a number of them worn out in service during and since the Black Hawk War."

He sat his horse as if on parade, watching Hallett get his men together. They came grudgingly, and one of them started to drive the small herd of gathered stock.

"Leave them," Tolan ordered.

When the drover hesitated, Hallett spoke to him in a low voice. Reluctantly, they mounted their horses. The man whom Tolan had interrupted had a rifle across his saddle. "Got a notion to bury me a sojer," he said.

Tolan was looking at Hallett, although every man in the group was under his gaze. "Mr. Hallett, if that man moves that rifle muzzle I am going to kill you."

Hallett's shock was evident. Tolan's holster flap was unbuttoned and the pistol butt was near his hand. Hallett's eyes lifted from the gun to Tolan's eyes and he knew that Tolan would do just as he warned.

Hallett's rage was evident. "Turn around and get out of here, you fool!"

Watching them ride reluctantly from the clearing, Miles Tolan was profoundly irritated with himself. Why had he made such a point of letting Hallett know that he was no desk soldier? Explanation to such a man was a weakness. Still, it might have averted a fight. When the riders had disappeared from sight, Tolan looked slowly around.

He was alone but for the aged woman and the dead man. For he was dead; no man could lose so much blood and live. Dismounting, Miles Tolan crossed to the dead man and turned him over. It was the face of a middle-aged man, careworn and tired, yet a face possessing that innate dignity he had seen in many an Indian before this. The dead man's clothing was clean; his hair had been neatly combed.

His pockets had been turned out and everything of value stolen.

Tolan drove the small herd of stock into the corral and put up the bars. During all this time the old woman had neither moved nor spoken, and the girl he had rescued seemed nowhere about.

The house was burning and nothing could be done about that. Tolan walked toward it, disturbed by something here that he could not quite fathom. The swept yard, the carefully constructed buildings . . . This was evidently the farm of an Indian of some consequence. Too many Indians he had known previously, those who had taken to the

white man's ways, had often been lazy, drunken, or indifferent.

Not so the warriors he had met in battle. Tall,
splendidly built men, many of them, and they could fight
like so many cougars.

Sudden hoofbeats sounded on the trail down which he
had lately come, and from the trees rode a small caval-
cade of Indians. Several of them were young men, stripped
to the waist and in buckskin leggings, but the two men
who rode at the head of the group were dressed as prosperous planters might dress. The oldest of them, a short,
powerfully built man obviously their leader, wore a black
hat, and although his clothing showed wear, it was also
neatly brushed. The young man beside him wore a cabin-
spun shirt, open to the belt. He had a ragged scar across
his cheek.

This man glanced from the dead man to the old woman,
and then to Miles Tolan. "Does the white man's army now
make war upon old women? What would he do if he faced
warriors?"

"I have faced warriors," Tolan replied brusquely. "I
have faced the fighting men of the Sac and Fox, Sioux,
and Kiowa. What warriors have you faced?"

"My people are at peace." The young man spoke haugh-
tily, but Tolan realized he had touched a sensitive spot.

"It is of no importance whom we have faced," Tolan
replied quickly. "We are not at war here, and what has
been done was not of my doing. I am sorry for it."

"He speaks true." The girl he had saved from being
raped slipped from behind the saddle of one of the riders.

She had repaired the tear in her dress, and now she
came up to the older man and spoke rapidly in what Tolan
believed to be Cherokee. When she had completed what was
obviously an explanation the older Cherokee said, "We
thank you, Lieutenant, for what you have done, but we

must warn you also. The man Hallett is a dangerous enemy, and he will not quickly forget. We have come to know him well."

"Won't the law protect you?"

"The law!" The young Cherokee's fury exploded into words. "There is a law for the white man, but there is no law for the Indian! The law here is a club to beat us down and rob us of all we possess!"

"It has been arranged for you to migrate," Tolan suggested mildly. "If you are dissatisfied, why don't you go?"

"A man does not willingly leave his home, Lieutenant," the older man said. "This is the land of our fathers, and of their fathers before them. The dust of Cherokee bodies has helped to build high the mountains, his blood flows in the sap of the trees, and his stories have grown into these rocks. This is our home."

"It is a good land in the West."

"So we have heard. But the Cherokee have lived here since the memory of our oldest men. These hills have been our hunting ground, and these valleys have known our crops.

"Now we are asked to go . . . to live among alien spirits and the ghosts of strange peoples. We are asked to abandon the graves of our fathers, the fields we cut from the forest, the homes we built with our hands. I ask you: How can we?"

He gestured toward a huge oak beside the clearing. "Beneath that oak my grandfather died fighting the Creeks, and my mother is buried beside him. Here I played as a child, and by this stream I killed my first deer.

"The Cherokee, White Man, is born of these hills. He was not a homeless people. Here he was born, here he has lived, and here, God willing, he shall die."

Miles Tolan was profoundly moved. What reply had he to such a statement?

"You have been kind," the old man added, "and because of us you have made an enemy. Moreover, the man who employs him will become your enemy as he is ours."

"Who is this man?"

"His name is Rounce . . . Wilson Rounce."

Miles Tolan was shocked. "Rounce? Did you say . . . Rounce?"

"The name is familiar to you?"

They stared at him as he absorbed the information . . . and remembering Will Rounce he felt, for the first time, something of apprehension.

"We were children together," Tolan replied. "Yes . . . yes, I know him."

CHAPTER 2

"He is the worst of our enemies."

"I shall speak to him."

"Tell him," the old man said proudly, "that it is I, Tsali, who call him enemy. If he will come among us I will repeat it, and stand before him when I do so."

Miles Tolan sat very still, watching them go to the old woman and help her from the ground, but he was remembering Wilson Rounce.

Seventeen years had gone by since they had parted. Had they ever been friends? Had Will, beneath his friendly exterior, ever been anything but an enemy? As boys they had hunted and fished together, and they had fought side by side against other boys. Everyone else had considered them friends. Everyone, Miles remembered, but old Elias Rounce, Will's grandfather. But then, nobody ever outwitted old Elias. Not even Will.

And now Will Rounce was here. . . . What could have

happened to Rounceville, the town old Elias had founded,
and which should have been Will's?

Why would any sane man leave those broad planted and
forested acres? Why would someone give up ownership of
the mills, plants, and factories that Elias Rounce had
broken from the wilderness? With such an inheritance a
man of Will's intelligence and training could have built
a great financial empire.

The sense of apprehension returned to him. Will
Rounce was the only man who had ever beaten him . . . and
he was the only one who had ever beaten Will.

Suddenly, he thought of the girl who had dived into
the pool. He swung the black horse over to the old Indian. "Tsali, back up the road I thought I saw a woman
dive into a pool. It was west of the road."

Tsali's face was expressionless. "I know of no one in
that area."

Tolan had a feeling the Indian was lying. "Is there a
pool up there? Or a lake of some kind?"

"I know of none."

"Thank you." Miles Tolan turned his horse into the
trail and cantered away. Now he knew he had been lied
to . . . and if Tsali would lie about the pool he might
also lie about the girl. But why should he lie? What was
the secret there?

Tolan shrugged. It was unlikely that he would ever
know, and even more unlikely that he would ever come into
these mountains again. His way led westward, guiding the
Cherokee to the new lands beyond the Mississippi, and
there would be no time for searching the mountains. Anyway, he reflected philosophically, she was probably unat-
tractive, married, or both.

It was very still. The clouds hung dark and low and
secretive sounds stirred in the forest. The trail widened

now, and occasionally smaller trails turned off into the
green, mist-shrouded hills. Here and there great crags
jutted from the forest, thrusting their serrated edges
against the sky. It was a lovely land. There were running
streams and small meadows, parklike stretches of forest
and occasionally now fenced fields where corn grew.

His thoughts reverted to the woman on the rock. It
was an unexpected place for anyone to be at such a time.
The Cherokee Removal was far advanced and many had already taken the westward route. With their going the land
was, as he had just witnessed, filling with renegades
ready to profit by what the Indians had been forced to
leave behind.

Miles Tolan had no feeling one way or the other about
the Removal. In a vague sort of way he had been aware of
the discussion for some time, and aware of the violent
animosities that had arisen from it. He knew that Clay,
Calhoun, and Webster had all spoken against it, but that
Jackson himself was for it, all the more surprising because he had heard many of his brother officers speak of
the excellent service rendered by the Cherokees in the
Creek War . . . and they had been led by Jackson during
that war.

Knowing nothing of the arguments pro or con, Tolan
recalled only that Davy Crockett had made excellent
speeches in the halls of Congress for the Cherokees. For
an Indian fighter this was unexpected, but Davy had the
reputation of being a fair man, and he had fought both
against and beside the Cherokees. He had, in fact, sacri-
ficed his political future by taking a course in opposition to that of the Jackson party with which he was
affiliated.

Politics was not a soldier's business. Miles Tolan
had been given a task to perform and he would carry it
out to the best of his ability and leave the arguments to
the civilians.

Of one thing he was certain. Indians could not hope
to survive by their old way of life. They represented a
hunting and food-gathering society in conflict with an
agricultural and industrial society, and when two such
diverse cultures opposed each other the less productive
was sure to fall by the way. Right and wrong might be de-
bated, but the outcome was certain.

Yet the farms he had lately seen, including the one
where the trouble had taken place, had been well-tilled
farms, with compact buildings and an atmosphere of productivity and well-being about them. If these farms were
examples of Cherokee industry, then the picture had to be
far from one-sided. But of course they must be the exceptions. They had to be.

The presence here of Will Rounce was a disturbing
fact. Since the day when Elias Rounce had called Miles
Tolan into his office and told him he must leave Rounceville, he had known a sort of freedom such as he had only
dreamed of before. Only the fact that he owed a debt to
the old man, who had taken him in and educated him, had
kept him in Rounceville so long. What the others saw as
ignominious dismissal he saw only as a door being opened.

Before him the trail dipped into a wide, shallow valley and in the bottom of the valley lay the post road.
Further along he could see a stage station. Slow smoke
rose from the chimney and a private carriage had only
just drawn up at the entrance.

Two women, one young, one elderly, were getting down
from the carriage. As the younger turned to wait for her
companion, their eyes met.

They were wide, lovely eyes, either blue or gray, and
nothing in his training as an officer hinted that he
should be laggard. "How do you do?" He swept off his hat
and bowed. "I am Lieutenant Miles Tolan."

"And I," she replied sweetly, "am not interested."
With that she was through the door and into the station.

From behind him he heard an unpleasant laugh. "You sure didn't make no hit, Sojer! An' just as well, too. Will Rounce wouldn't stand for nobody sparkin' around his woman . . . even if she ain't nothin' but a 'nother Cherokee!"

It was Hallett's man, the one who had attempted the rape. He was loafing near the corner of the building, and now he grinned broadly in appreciation of Tolan's discomfiture.

Ignoring him, Tolan turned his horse over to the Negro stable boy.

Will Rounce's woman.

Was it to be Will Rounce wherever he turned? How would it be between them after seventeen years? What had Will become? And if it came to a struggle between them, who now would win when old Elias was no longer in the background? Slapping his hat against his thigh, Miles knocked dust from it and from his clothing. Then he opened the door and stepped within.

The long room served the functions of office, waiting room, dining room, and saloon. Its floors were of hand-hewn plank, the furniture of rough homemade construction, including four tables with four chairs at each. When Miles entered the room the girl and her companion were already seated. Only one other table was occupied . . . by a group of card players, and there were several rough-looking men at the bar.

As he seated himself at a table not far from the girl and the elderly woman who was her companion, a young man, clad as befitted a gentleman of fashion, entered from the rear door and joined them. Rounce's man had called her a Cherokee, which was obviously a mistake. He had also called her Rounce's woman. . . . Was that another mistake?

He thought she glanced toward him, but when he looked

toward her she was busily in conversation with her
friends. She was, he decided, even more attractive than
he had at first believed. Almost, in fact, uncomfortably
beautiful.

There are women, he reflected, so beautiful that men
are awed by them, and many a man who might otherwise be
interested is inclined to stand off, doubting that such a
girl would be interested. He grinned at his hands, reflecting that no such inhibition had ever held him back.

A man had come from behind the bar wiping his big
hands on his apron. From the deference in his manner,
Tolan decided he both knew and respected the newcomers.

"Sam," the young man was saying, "we'd like some of
that home-cured ham of yours. Whatever else you have . . .
we'll trust your judgment."

"Leave it to me, Mr. McCrae."

Sam crossed to Tolan's table and hit the boards a
swipe with his cloth. "I'll have the same as the people
at the next table," Tolan said. "They seem to know your
food."

"You'd do better not to wear that uniform here-
abouts," Sam advised, low-voiced. "There's some around as
don't care for it."

"It's our country's uniform," Miles replied quietly.
"I wear it with pride."

Sam's face changed. "Comes to that," he said, "I've
worn it myself. Only there's some, the Cherokees and
their friends, who don't care much for it."

"From what I've heard," Miles replied, "it is less
the Army that makes the trouble, and more some of your
Georgia politicians."

Sam glanced toward the men at the bar. "That's right
enough. And those are some of their friends. What they're
doing is a rotten shame."

Sam left for the kitchen and Miles Tolan carefully

avoided looking at the men at the bar. They were drinking, and as they drank they grew progressively more
noisy, and such men were inclined to become quarrelsome.

Moreover, Hallett's man had come into the room and
from the glances cast his way, Miles was sure he had been
telling them the events of the morning. From words over-
heard Miles learned the man's name was Adam Couch.

When the food arrived Miles realized for the first
time how really hungry he was. The long ride in the mountain air had been invigorating, but strenuous, too, and
the ham had proved all that McCrae had implied. He ate
hungrily, aware that the loud voices from the crowd at
the bar had dropped to a conspiratorial mumble. From what
he could hear the women at the next table were growing
increasingly apprehensive. McCrae was stubborn, and refused to be hurried.

Suddenly a pockmarked man with a tough swagger de-
tached himself from the group and strode to the table
where the women sat. Leaning over, he put his big palms
flat on the table. "You got the on'y woman here, fella,"
he said, grinning at McCrae, "I think we ought to give
you some comp'ny."

"The lady you refer to is my sister."

"Is she now?" Grinning insolently, the man pulled up
a chair and sat down. He was, Miles observed, just drunk
enough to be both mean and dangerous.

McCrae got to his feet. "Shall we go? It is quite
late."

The man in the chair grinned up at him. "You can go
anytime you like," he said, "but she stays."

One of the men from the bar was strolling casually
across the room, his intent to get behind McCrae. Another
man moved to the table where Miles Tolan sat.

Miles continued to eat, alert to every shift of position. The man behind McCrae could seize him if he offered
any opposition, and the third man was obviously supposed

to keep Miles from interfering, but Miles had already
planned to shove a chair into that man before he could
move, and a pistol would cover the others. Such affairs
were far from new to him, and though he savored the coming action he was worried for the sake of the women. His
dislike for the men at the bar was surpassed only by his
dislike for Adam Couch.

"We will go," McCrae said quietly. "I advise you not
to interfere."

"You'll have the law on us, I suppose?" The man at
the table grinned insolently. "There ain't no law for Injuns, so we can do what we want. You've no comeback, not
none a-tall." Outside there was the sound of hooves and
harness.

Miles put down his cup and thought of an alternative
that was equally pleasing and less physical. From his
waistband he took a pistol and placed it on the table,
and as he did so the man watching him spoke quickly. "The
sojer's got a pistol, Stanky."

Stanky's head turned sharply around, glancing from
the pistol on the table to Miles Tolan quietly sipping
his coffee. His cup was rather obviously held in his left
hand. He had said nothing. Only the cold steel of the
pistol lay there, more eloquent than words.

"Your carriage has just drawn up, Mr. McCrae," Miles
said then, "and you have some distance to go, I believe."

McCrae's poise did him credit. "Of course . . . Will
you join us?"

"No." Miles Tolan looked over at Stanky as he spoke.
"I am sure these gentlemen would like to arrange some entertainment for me here, and I would dislike to miss it."

"We would enjoy having you for our guest," McCrae insisted politely, "and our accommodations, begging Sam's
pardon, are somewhat more satisfactory than his. It would
be a privilege to have you, sir."

Miles Tolan got to his feet and picked up the pistol.

"In that case, I shall accept. I am sure these gentlemen will understand and postpone whatever plans they had until a later time."

Stanky's face was set in ugly lines. His drunkenness seemed to have disappeared. "I think," he said coolly, "I think I'll make you use that pistol."

CHAPTER 3

"I would not advise it."

The voice came from the doorway, and Miles was irritated with himself for hearing no sound from the opening door. "I would not advise it, Stanky. Mr. Tolan was always a most excellent shot . . . one of the best I have ever seen."

Miles Tolan did not turn his eyes from the man he was watching, but said quietly, "It has been a long time, Will."

Stanky backed off hurriedly. "We didn't mean nothing, Mr. Rounce. We was just havin' some fun."

"Get out."

Will Rounce did not lift his voice, but there was something in its tone that could not be missed. "Get out . . . and if you ever speak to Miss McCrae again, or trouble her in any way at all, I'll kill you."

Thrusting the pistol back into his waistband, Miles turned to meet Will's outstretched hand. "Miles! Man, but it is good to see you!"

Rounce turned. "Laura, I want you to meet Miles Tolan. We were boys together."

Her acknowledgment was brief. "Will! Why did you not tell us you were coming? We had no idea!"

"It was a surprise, Laura. I was on my way to visit

and hoped to surprise you, and now it is you who surprised me."

Miles Tolan knew Rounce was lying. He had no idea why he was lying, but this advantage he always possessed over Will. He had always known even though old Elias, for all his shrewdness and judgment of people, seemed never to be aware of it. Miles, with better judgment than he had normally shown, knew, but had never let on that he knew.

Will had been a handsome boy, and he had grown into an even more handsome man. He possessed a noble head, finely carved features, and was even bigger than Miles, at least an inch taller and probably thirty pounds heavier. He had a shock of golden hair above a fine brow, and blue-white eyes, piercing and shrewd. He looked like a younger and much more handsome Andrew Jackson.

Standing to one side, Miles watched Will talking to Laura and her brother. Laura's eyes glowed with excitement, and if she were not already Will's woman, Miles reflected, she well could be, for she was obviously infatuated.

As always, Will dominated the room. All eyes were on him, and all hung on his words. With a curious sense of relief, Miles Tolan realized that he did not. Was it because he remembered Will from old? Or was it something else--something new and different? In any event, he felt that there was something shallow and false about the entire scene. For seventeen years Miles Tolan had dealt with the harshest kind of reality, and in those years he had known many men, but he was realizing that he had never liked Will. They had been thrown together by circumstances and others believed them inseparable friends, but such had never been the case. Under the apparent friendship they had always been rivals, but that rivalry had, on Miles' part, always been tempered by the debt he owed to Will's grandfather.

"Come!" Will caught Miles' arm. "We will go on to Brignole."

Outside, once he had helped Laura into her carriage, Will swung astride a fine-looking sorrel and cast an admiring glance at Tolan's black, which the stable boy led out.

"Still a taste for horses, I see." He met Miles' eyes with a smile. "It's good to see you," he said sincerely. "We should never have lost track of each other. Believe me, I've needed a man I could trust, and often wondered what had become of you."

The McCraes' carriage clattered off and Will gestured widely. "This is a growing country, Miles. Look what's happened in Texas, and then look at what is happening here. Within the next few months the last of the Cherokees will be out of Georgia. Believe me, Miles, I am very close to the men behind this, and when that land is redivided I expect the best of it. You should give up your commission and join me."

"I'd have to think about that." Miles remembered that Will Rounce had always been full of plans, large plans. There was no denying his intelligence, and Miles knew the training they had both been given was such as to place them in an advantageous position in any bargaining that would be done. Too many times in the past men had underrated Will Rounce. To outward appearances he was a stalwart and handsome man who looked the soul of honor; only long familiarity allowed one to realize the devious cunning that lay beneath the surface.

Yet the offer was tempting. Will was a man who might go far, particularly as he was devoid of the scruples that might hold others back or make a more honorable man somewhat cautious.

"You'll report to Lorin, I suppose. We're very close, he and I, and you'll do very well if you listen to me and work with me." He was silent for a few minutes. "For the time it would be better for you to stay in the Army. I can use a man like you."

Miles Tolan shifted his seat impatiently. It irked

him that Rounce should so readily assume that he was not
doing well, and that he would so readily fall in with
whatever schemes Rounce had in mind. He was about to say
as much, but restrained himself. Nothing was to be gained
by starting trouble.

Rounce lowered his voice. "There's gold here, Miles.
Have you heard of that? Gold . . . and better than that,
there is fertile soil. Once the Indians are out of here
we'll have a chance to get rich fast. Much of the land is
already cleared and planted to crop.

"Reap the crops and sell, cut the marketable timber
and sell, take the cream off the gold mines and
sell . . . then move west. This is a big country, Miles,
and all of it open to development."

"If you go west you'll be coming up against the Cherokees again. They may be tired of moving."

Will Rounce chuckled. "They're Indians, Miles. They
had this country to themselves for thousands of years and
did nothing with it except hunt, fish, and plant corn.
We're building a country, Miles, a big country. Nobody
can stand in the way of that."

Miles switched the conversation. "This place to which
we're going tonight . . . what's it like?"

"Brignole? It's the country home of the McCraes, and
a lovely place, a very lovely place. I would hate to see
it fall into the wrong hands."

"There was some reference to the McCraes being Indian. That's nonsense, of course."

"It was not. . . . You must realize, these are by no
means the wild Indians of which you've heard. They have
gone the white man's way, or tried to. They've something
like their own legislature, their own newspaper, and even
their own courts.

"Some of these Indians are planters and businessmen,
Miles, and not a few of them are very well-off. Some,
like the McCraes, are truly wealthy."

"But if they are moved west, what happens to that
wealth?"

Will Rounce smiled into the dark. "That, my friend,
is something to which we must give our attention. It
would be a pity, a great pity, to have all that fall into
the wrong hands."

Brignole stood upon a tree-clad knoll well back from
the high road, and was a long manor house of two stories
with wings running back from either end. Across the front
was a broad veranda and six columns. The house was
painted white, and made a lovely sight surrounded by the
huge old trees and fine expanse of lawn and garden that
surrounded it. A drive surfaced with gravel swung in an
easy half-circle from the high road to the door and back
again to the road. The house possessed all the quiet dignity and elegance Miles had come to associate with the
Virginia homes where he had often been a guest.

The slaves who met the carriage were tastefully
dressed in dark livery and conducted themselves with
pride and deference.

Inside, the house was tastefully and beautifully done
in a style much less cluttered than was usual, and the
room which he was shown had wide windows that opened upon
a hillside. It was dark, but he could appreciate what the
view must be. When he had bathed and changed into fresh
linen and a carefully brushed uniform, he descended the
stairs and found his way to the library.

A man of slightly more than medium height got up from
his chair to greet him. He had black eyes and a faintly
olive skin topped by pure white hair. "Lieutenant Tolan?
I am John McCrae. Welcome to our home, sir. Please consider it your own."

"Thank you, sir."

"And may I present John Ross?"

Miles Tolan turned with quick interest. John Ross, a
chief of the Cherokees, was a man of medium height,
rather squarely built with a shock of graying hair and
keen blue eyes. He was, as Miles had heard long before,
only one-eighth Cherokee, yet having grown up among them
he considered himself one of them. Both his father, Daniel Ross, and his maternal grandfather, John McDonald,
had come among the Cherokees as traders.

"How do you do, Lieutenant? Yours is a familiar
name."

"Mine, sir?"

"A friend of mine served with you during the Black
Hawk War. He had much to say of your gallantry . . . and
your marksmanship."

"He was exaggerating, sir, I'm sure." Miles hesitated. "Are you among the Cherokees who are migrating,
sir?"

Ross chuckled. "I doubt it, Captain. I doubt it very
much. Tell me: You rode down through the mountains, did
you not? What did you think of them?"

"What is there to say? They are beautiful, sir, beautiful beyond belief."

"Then you can understand why we do not wish to leave.
This is our home. . . . We have grown up here, lived
here, and we wish to die here."

"That was what Tsali told me."

Ross glanced at him sharply. "You have met Tsali?"

Miles accepted a glass of sherry and sketched briefly
the circumstances. "It is a pity," he said at last, "that
violence could happen, but I have no doubt it was a rare
occurrence."

"We wish it were. . . . Unfortunately, Georgia passed
a law denying the right of any Cherokee to institute a
suit against a white citizen, or to appear as a witness
against him. The rougher element have taken this as giving them the right to rape, plunder, and murder."

Laura McCrae came into the room, and John Ross turned
to her at once. "My dear," he said, "I've never seen you
look more lovely than tonight."

She smiled at him, then her eyes swept the room,
searching for Will Rounce, no doubt. Miles felt a little
twinge of irritation, and was amused at himself for the
feeling. Yet there was no question that Laura McCrae was
a girl of singular beauty. Her black hair was parted on
the side and combed back, several carefully composed
ringlets dangling in front of her ears. The long hair was
built into loops on the crown of her head, and her eyes,
he noticed, were gray . . . gray and very beautiful.

The gown she wore was one that left her lovely shoulders bare, and the tight bodice tapered down to a small
waist and a loose gown that flowed to the tips of her
toes. With surprise, Miles realized it was the first gown
he had seen in America that followed the new Paris fashion where the ankles were no longer visible. The material
was of tulle over satin, and of a soft green that empha-
sized the color of her skin.

Miles felt uncomfortable, and hated himself for the
feeling. It was not as if he were a stranger to good society, for he had traveled some in those seventeen years
since he had last seen Will Rounce, but he was not accustomed to being ignored by pretty women, or any women at
all, and he was vain enough to be irritated by it.

He turned to the bookshelves, drawn by curiosity as
well as a genuine love for books. He could never leave
them alone, and until he had scanned the books in a house
he was never completely at ease.

Whatever else John McCrae might be--and from all the
evidence he was a very successful planter--he was also a
man who knew and appreciated good books. For these were
not only well chosen, but all showed evidence of use. Out
of curiosity he looked to see what poetry there was, but

found only the Greeks. Of the contemporary poets such as
Byron, Keats, Shelley, and Moore, he found no sign.

Could the girl who dove from the rock have been Laura
McCrae?

The thought came unexpectedly. It was odd, Miles decided, that the idea had not occurred to him before. She
had come from that direction, the timing was about
right. . . . He turned to look at her. . . . No . . .
there was something, some scarcely definable difference.

She turned at that minute and their eyes met. Excus-
ing herself from her father and Ross, she crossed the
room to him.

"That was a strange expression, Lieutenant. Do you
usually look at girls that way?"

"No . . . probably not about you." He looked down at
the book in his hands, a copy of the odes of Horace. "Do
you read poetry, Miss McCrae?"

She glanced down. "Horace? No, that is Father's."

"I mean . . . do you read the contemporary poets?
Thomas Moore, for instance? In particular, have you read
Lalla Rookh?"

She was startled; he recognized that at once. When
she lifted her eyes to his they were innocent and her expression was bland. "No . . . I can't say that I have
read anything of his. Of course, I've heard of him. Why
do you ask?"

"It is a beautiful poem. It is natural to think of
beauty when one speaks to you."

"You are gallant, Lieutenant." She looked directly
into his eyes. "I appreciate the compliment, of course,
but that was not at all why you asked. You had a reason,
Lieutenant, and I am curious."

"And if you talk to Miles any longer, I shall be
quite jealous."

Will Rounce had come up to them, and he was smiling.

At the same time Miles noticed that there was irritation
present, too, and he liked the feeling that Will could be
irritated. He was always so sure of himself, so perfectly
possessed.

"We were talking about poetry," Miles commented.
He recalled very clearly how disdainful Rounce had been
toward anything related to the arts.

"Oh . . . then I came just in time to rescue you,
Laura," Will said. "Miles reads too much. I was hoping he
had gotten out of the habit over the years. Perhaps he is
incurable."

"No, really," she protested, "we were talking about
Lalla Rookh."

Will Rounce turned slowly and looked searchingly into
Miles' eyes. It was an utterly cold, probing stare.

Miles felt a queer, leaping excitement. For some reason the title had some special meaning for Will, and
whatever the meaning was, Will was not pleased that Miles
might know of it.

"Why that poem?" Will inquired abruptly.

"It is one of Moore's." Miles brushed the comment
away as if no longer interested. "We were talking of
Moore and Byron."

"I am not interested in poetry," Will replied
abruptly. "Poetry is for women."

"Many of us in the Army," Miles replied quietly,
"found poetry very interesting. It is easy to recall, and
sometimes on the long marches one can remember it with
real pleasure. You might be interested to know, Will,
that every war brings on a new interest in poetry . . .
and it is the soldiers who are interested."

During the meal that followed Miles found it difficult to believe that the people among whom he sat were
mostly of Cherokee extraction, and that at least two of

them were full-bloods. Yet they had been in contact with
Europeans for upward of three hundred years, some say
from the time of de Soto and his conquistadors. After the
Spanish had come Frenchmen, and then the Scots, Irish,
and English traders.

Will Rounce was in great form. Always an easy,
graceful conversationalist, he was at his best tonight,
turning from topic to topic with ease. Strange, that
with his admitted attitude toward the Cherokees he should
be here. Miles' thoughts returned to Will's queer reaction to the title of the poem. Obviously it meant something more to him than just the title of a book . . .
but what?

Laura's laughter drew his attention and he found all
eyes on him. "Will was telling us about the time you were
thrown from the black horse."

"Did he tell you," Miles replied dryly, "that it was
because he'd put a burr under the saddle blanket?"

"Will!" Laura protested. "Did you do that?"

Rounce looked up, laughing. "Probably . . . Miles was
growing too sure of himself, and I thought the fall would
do him good."

As he spoke the last words he looked down the table,
but his expression was cold, almost threatening.

So here it was again, Miles thought: They sometimes
worked together but they always fought . . . and who
would win this time?

CHAPTER 4

Yes, that was the way of it. Will had put the burr
beneath his saddle to give him a fall. What Miles neglected to tell his dinner companions was that it was a

contest with a gold guinea as the prize, offered by Elias Rounce.

Trust Will to pull a stunt like that with a prize at stake. It was a good thing to remember, Miles told himself, and helpful to have recalled it just now. He would remain with the Army and let Will make his money with whatever scheme he had planned.

There were other stories Will Rounce could have told, like the time the four Dutch boys had set upon them. It was four to two, but unequal at that, for the two had been trained at fighting, well taught in boxing, wrestling, and the quarterstaff by that man of many wisdoms, Phineas Cronkite.

The first thing Phineas had taught them was that most such fights are won by the first blow, so to strike first and strike hard . . . and strike hard they did, and from then on it was two and two, and a fair fight except that the remaining two Dutch boys had seen what had happened to the first two. Victory had been complete.

There had been a subsequent occasion when two rough-looking men had set upon them in Philadelphia. Neither boy was yet sixteen, and the two men had followed them up a dark street and demanded their money.

Miles struck first. He was quick with his fists and the two men were expecting no trouble, and Miles' blow had been an underhanded blow to the belly, and in the darkness the man had not seen it coming. As he doubled over with pain, his face made a perfect target for Miles' jerked-up knee, and as he fell, Miles hit him again. It took Will Rounce little longer to finish off his man.

It was a time when little was known of boxing and wrestling beyond the usual frontier sort of back-heel and hip-lock, a strong back type of gripping and throwing with relatively no science to it. Phineas Cronkite was a master at Cornish-style wrestling and while in England he had picked up a fancy bit of fist work, which he taught

them. No doubt about it, the school directed by Elias
Rounce had been an odd one, but efficient.

It was seventeen years since then, and Will a man of
importance now, far more than any mere lieutenant of cav-
alry who owned a few blocks of land out west, land of so
little value that a neighbor traded off three square
miles of it for a pair of red-top boots.

Yet it was good to be here, dining in the candlelight
on the fine old silver and crystal, with the soft movements
of Negro servants and a distant sound of music to lend
background to their talk. It was a long way from the campfires of the Comanche or the Sac and Fox, and farther still
from the fo'c'sle of a windjammer beating up to Vigo Bay.

Seventeen years . . . What a lot could happen to a
man in that time! And what a lot had happened to him. He
was a different man now than he had been when he left
Rounceville to go out into the world by himself.

Later, alone in the library, Laura found him. He was
looking over the books again, a glass of Madeira in his
hand.

"Do you find time to read, Lieutenant?"

"There is always time. Those who say they do not have
time for books simply do not want to read badly enough.
Often they have been my only companions, and their advantage is that they say the same words to everyone."

"And people do not?"

"They tell you what you wish to hear . . . or what
they believe you wish to hear."

"And what about Will?"

"It is for you to make your own judgment on that
score."

"You don't like him?"

"I did not say that, nor did I mean to imply it. How
can one judge a man one has not seen in seventeen years?"

"You are quibbling."

"Perhaps."

"But you were his best friend!"

He considered that. "Yes . . . yes, I believe I was."

"Then how can you talk so against your best friend?"

Miles returned the book to its place on the shelf.

"Miss McCrae, they were your words, not mine. I have said that I believed I was his best friend. It does not necessarily follow that he was also my best friend."

She studied him curiously, and without, he suspected, much liking for him. "You make me very curious, Lieutenant. Will has told me of the education you two received, and unless I am mistaken you two were together for twelve years. He said you came to them when you were five."

"Yes."

"Who were your people?"

He hesitated, then he said, "I do not know."

She tilted her head to the side a little. "Do you know, Lieutenant, Will told me the same thing, and I believe he told me the truth, but I do not believe you have told the truth. I believe there is something you knew that you never told them, not Will, nor your Phineas nor Elias Rounce."

He smiled, listening to the drum of horses' hooves upon the road outside.

"What would it matter?" he asked.

"I don't know." She was puzzled. "But I _am_ curious."

Several people came into the library and Miles walked toward the door. He was in time to see a horseman arrive, the same he had heard approaching.

The rider was a uniformed soldier who swung alongside the veranda, dismounted, and tendered him a letter. "You are Lieutenant Tolan, sir? The Colonel's orders, sir. You are to go to him at once!"

"You mean I must leave tonight?"

"Tonight, sir. The Colonel was most explicit."

Miles ripped open the envelope.

Report to me at once. This station.

I will accept neither delay nor excuses.

Miles spoke to a waiting slave. "Have my horse saddled and brought around."

He went hurriedly to his room and gathered his few
possessions together. He was hurrying down the steps when
he met McCrae. Laura was right behind him.

"Here! What's this? You're not leaving?"

"Sorry, sir. Orders from Colonel White."

John McCrae was serious. "I hope you are in no trouble. Colonel Lorin White has the reputation of being a
very difficult man."

Laura walked with him to the door. She looked up at
him, her expression showing her curious indecision. "I
can't make up my mind about you," she said.

"Is it necessary?"

"I don't know. Somehow I feel that it is. I want to
thank you for helping us tonight. I am afraid there would
have been trouble. James . . . my brother . . . is not
very coolheaded at times."

"It was nothing."

"I was rude to you, too. I could at least have been
polite."

He chuckled. "It was nothing."

It was very late and he was bone-tired. He walked to
the horse, who looked at him reproachfully. "Nothing for
it, old fellow," he whispered. "Believe me, I'd rather
you rested."

There was a step on the porch behind him and he
looked around to see Will Rounce standing there, and he
was smiling.

"You see, Miles? This comes of interfering with my

men. You will find it much simpler to keep out of things
that do not concern you."

Anger choked him. For an instant he felt like striking Rounce, and then he asked calmly, "So this is your
doing?"

Will grinned at him, a taunting, challenging grin.
"If you want to work for me, Miles, I could use a man of
your training. It is hard to find good men . . . who know
how to take orders."

"Go to hell, will you?"

He stepped into the saddle and reined the black horse
around. As the horse leaped into a run, Will's sardonic
voice came to him.

"Good-bye, Miles," Will said.

And then it began to rain again, a soft, drizzling,
soaking rain.

Laura McCrae awakened to the sound of rain, and for a
long time she lay still, listening to the drops pattering
on the roof and looking out her window at the far-off
hills, veiled now with streamers of moon-touched cloud.

The old house was silent, for it was very early. The
old stones and timbers slumbered with their memories of a
hundred years of McCraes who had lived and worked, loved
and dreamed within its walls. It was impossible they
should be forced to move, to leave their home, the soil
they had tilled, the forests they had used and protected,
the land that meant so much to them all. Wide awake now,
she looked up at the ceiling. All her memories of childhood and girlhood were here; the few years she had been
away had been filled with longing for Brignole. . . . To
her it had always been home, and she had never thought
seriously of leaving it.

Angus McCrae had been the first to come here . . . a
lone man with a rifle, ax, knife, and blankets. He had

brought with him a few odds and ends of trade goods, having landed from a ship that lay briefly off the coast and
that had put him ashore at his own request.

He had been a strong man, Angus McCrae, but a kind
man. A fighting Highlander, he had feared neither man nor
devil, and had the gift of making friends, and from the
first he had found a place among the Cherokees. He studied their customs, found much in them to admire, and remained among them, taking the daughter of a Cherokee
chief to wife. That had been in 1680. For several years
he had been hunter, trapper, and trader.

That same year he had come upon the site of Brignole
and laid the foundation stones with his own hands, completing the first room that first season, and using it
for a one-room cabin. Yet he had never thought of it as
one room, only as the beginning of a mansion. He built of
granite and he built solidly, as a man would descended
from a long line of working masons.

Three sons had been born of that union, the first
killed fighting the Spanish from Florida, the second to
die in war with the Creeks. The third son had gone north
for a wife, selling his furs in Virginia and finding a
Devonshire girl there, who took readily to Cherokee ways.
And that same year they had added a fourth and fifth room
to the house on the hill, and William McCrae had gone
north again to Virginia, this time to drive back a bull,
three cows, a ram, and seven sheep to Brignole.

It was William who added to the lands Angus had
bought from the Cherokees, and who began the fur trading
business. Old Angus had already begun farming, planting
wheat, barley, and rye, as well as Indian corn. William
set up a smithy, and brought hand looms into the area. On
that ground the family had lived for one hundred and
fifty-eight years, and now they were being forced from
their lands, driven out because they were Cherokee.

They bore the name with pride. How much Cherokee

blood did they have? Nobody knew exactly; there was no
generation or branch of the family that had not seen in-
termarriage. Regardless, they considered themselves Cherokees and were so considered by others.

The Cherokees were a proud people, and a great nation
among the Indians of eastern America, related although
not allied to the Iroquois, a strong people, vital, energetic, and filled with love of the land in which they
lived.

They had learned early that the way to survive was to
study the white man's way. They had fenced their fields,
tilled them carefully, and learned the crafts and the
small arts. But they were still Cherokee, and now they
lived upon land the white men wanted.

Intelligent and keenly perceptive, the Cherokee had
among them men who not only understood their old ways,
but who grasped the effect changing times were to have.
The result was that by 1830 great herds of cattle grazed
the Cherokee hills, and their fields produced corn, tobacco, wheat, oats, indigo, and potatoes. Their cotton
was exported to New Orleans on their own boats, apple and
peach orchards were common, and butter and cheese of
their own manufacture was upon their tables.

A printing press and a newspaper were established. A
metalsmith named Sequoyah had devised an alphabet, one so
well designed that within a short time several thousand
Cherokees had learned to read their own language. A library and a museum were built, and the schools increased
in number each year.

Yet each success angered many of the white citizens of
Georgia and each success became an additional tool for the
politicians. Throughout the state there were many who found
much to admire in Cherokee progress, and who had done what
they could to prevent encroachments on Cherokee lands. Unhappily, these men of goodwill were in the minority.

Laura McCrae got up and slipped into her robe, then

went to the window. It was light now, and the sun would
soon be over the trees that crested the hills in the
east. Yet she never saw the sun first in the east, but
from the west, for the western hills were higher and the
first rays always brought to them a crown of pale light
that strengthened and grew rose and red with growing dawn.

How could she leave this? How could she trek west
riding in a wagon or walking behind one? It was unthinkable! But no, it would not happen. Will would not let it
happen. He loved Brignole as she did, and he would do
what he could to keep it for them, and to see that the
McCraes did not have to go.

Was she selfish to think of herself and her own family now? What of the others? She had heard her father and
John Ross discussing the arrival of Tsali at the raided
farm on the previous day, and they had worried for fear
something would happen, some incident that would give the
Georgia militia an excuse to move into the Cherokee Nation in force. Tsali was a recalcitrant, a hard old man
who loved his hills and would fight to the death for
them. Those who hoped for a reprieve feared what he might
do as much as they admired his convictions.

Her thoughts returned to Miles Tolan. There was something disturbing about him, and he kept coming between
her and her thoughts of Will. Somehow it was hard to feel
the old excitement for Will since she had seen Miles. Yet
there was no reason for it. He was nothing to her and she
was not interested in him.

She was, she told herself, very sure of this. She was
not interested in Miles Tolan.

He was a striking man . . . not so handsome as Will
Rounce, but a fine-looking figure in his uniform, with
such splendid shoulders. . . . Yes, she admitted it reluctantly, he was exciting.

She could imagine the girls in Atlanta. What a fuss
they would make over him!

For some reason the thought made her impatient. After all, he was a friend of Will's, and she would not like to see them make a fool of him. Remembering the dark, clean lines of his face, the quiet amusement of his eyes, she was suddenly not so sure the girls of Atlanta would make a fool of Miles . . . or that any girls would, or could.

And then she remembered the book. He had mentioned Lalla Rookh . . . but it must have been a coincidence. Surely, there could be no connection.

She must talk to Will . . . but could he tell her? Would he tell her anything at all? He had never talked to her about it, had always brushed off all her questions. Yet something was going on that she did not understand.

Books by Thomas Moore were just not very common in Georgia at the time. He was a modern poet, and only slightly more acceptable than Lord Byron. But then Lord Byron was quite shocking and no nice girl read his poetry . . . at least, not in public or where it could be seen.

It was impossible that Miles could know her, and his mention of Lalla Rookh must have been an accident, although Laura knew that Will had gotten her a copy of the book just before she disappeared.

The rain fell steadily. It was a pity Miles Tolan had to leave in the middle of a storm . . . it was a long ride to Atlanta.

It would be a longer ride to the lands on the Arkansas, and so many of her people had already taken it, marching through forest and swamp, dying of fever, falling by the way, pillaged and robbed by those who pursued them with their hatred. Already thousands had gone . . . and there was bitterness among the Cherokee for those who had not proved loyal, or those who yielded.

Should she go? Should she herself take that march, take it despite all Will might do?

She knew there were Cherokees who thought they

should--that if they were forced to go, all should go.
Others were already talking of taking to the remote
hills, fighting it out there and dying rather than leave.
She had no taste for that life either.

Yet Chief Ross still hoped there would be a chance,
despite the growing pressures and the orders from Washington. He would return there soon in a last attempt to
get Van Buren to allow them to remain. But even if he
succeeded, there would be trouble if they stayed, for already many of the Georgians had come into the Cherokee
Nation, had burned homes, looted crops, even driven off
cattle the Cherokees had hoped to take west. Others had
been robbed on the road west, robbed in Alabama and in
Tennessee by bands that had followed the march from Georgia.

Let them go. She would stay. Will would arrange that.
They would keep Brignole; after all, they had a Scottish
name and a well-known ancestor. They could stay on. She
would marry Will, and in a few years this would all be
forgotten.

She bathed, dressed quickly, and went down the
stairs. Her father had just seated himself at breakfast,
and he looked up with a smile. She was suddenly aware
those smiles were all too rare these days.

"Laura! You're up early."

"I could not sleep."

He nodded. "Few of us can, these days."

"What does Uncle John think?"

"He's going to try again. He never gives up, that
man. I don't know what we could have done without him. He
has given most of his life to the Cherokee Nation, and
few people appreciate it."

She paused. "Father . . . what do you think of Will?"

He chuckled. "What does it matter? When a man has a
headstrong daughter and she decides what man she wants,
what can a mere father do?"

"Do you like him?"

John McCrae hesitated. Will Rounce had been a guest in their home many times. The fact that they were so far unmolested was due entirely to the fact that Will stood between them and potential depredations. He was a strong and capable man with excellent connections. He was very close to the military command, and even closer to the governor. That he had influence in Washington was undoubted. Chief Ross frankly admitted that doors closed to him had opened as a result of Will's influence . . . not that it had done Ross much good. But then, nothing much did, nowadays.

"Yes," he said after a minute, "I like him."

Even as he said it, he had a disturbing thought that maybe he did not like Will Rounce. . . . But if he did not, why should he dislike him? Certainly Will had been a good friend, and he was an affable, agreeable companion.

"He's a very able man," he added. "I think Will Rounce will go far. I should not be surprised to see him a United States senator one of these days."

"Not if he befriends the Cherokee much longer." Laura realized suddenly that she had never considered it in that light. "We may be the cause of him making enemies."

McCrae smiled. "Not us. I know we consider ourselves Cherokee, but I doubt many others do. Not in Washington, anyway."

James came down the steps and joined them at breakfast. He was still excited over the events of the evening before. "He was so calm," he told his father. "I never saw a man like him. He was calm, yet he seemed perfectly sure of himself, as though it were something that had happened many times before and he knew just how it would go."

"He's a soldier. John tells me he made a fine name for himself in the Black Hawk War, and that he's been into the far west."

"Fighting Indians," Laura said.

Her father looked up. "Yes, Indians," he said. "If we go west we may have to fight them ourselves."

They were silent. The thought of going west hung heavily above them all. So many had been forced to go, and now the threat faced them every morning when they awakened; yet despite the number who had already gone, the idea that they, too, might go was unreal to them. Angus had been the first McCrae to cross the ocean to the New World, and this had been the only McCrae home since the day he had first come upon the knoll where the house stood.

True, members of the McCrae family had gone out to other parts of the Cherokee Nation and established places of their own, but to them all, Brignole was home. It had been named for the ship Angus McCrae's father had long sailed in trade to the West Indies.

McCrae looked up. "James . . . I wish you would not go to Atlanta this week. You may be needed here."

"You think there might be trouble?"

"I hope not. But stay here."

Laura went to the door again, and stood looking down the road. Will was still asleep in the guest's quarters, and she wanted to talk to him. She was becoming frightened, more frightened than she had ever been, and it was because her father was worried. Only Will could protect them; he had constantly assured them there was nothing to be concerned about.

Only a few weeks before, her father had suggested they might still sell out for a good price, but Will had laughed at the thought, and they had wanted to be reassured. Sell Brignole? It was unthinkable . . . but suppose they lost everything?

It was then, and for no reason, that she remembered what Miles Tolan had said. That he might have been Will's best friend, but Will was not his best friend.

What had he meant? She felt the remark was somehow

disparaging of Will, and was nettled by it. Yet as she
turned back inside the house the remark stayed with her,
irritating and troublesome . . . like a burr under the
saddle.

CHAPTER 5

Colonel Lorin White stood with his feet solidly apart,
his fists resting on his wide hips. His round, fat face
was set in hard lines. "Lieutenant Tolan"--his voice was
high, but its tone showed his peevish anger--"you are not
a Moravian missionary, but an officer of the Army of the
United States sent here for escort duty! Your orders give
you no right to interfere with private citizens going
about their legitimate business!"

"General Scott's orders were--"

"He placed you under _my_ orders! I will tolerate no
interference with civilians! You are to escort a group of
Indians that I shall designate, and nothing more!"

"Am I to understand rape and murder are licensed by
this command?"

White's face stiffened; he took a step away from the
window and his voice lowered. "Lieutenant, I will not tolerate impudence from you. I have given you your orders.
You are to take what men you need and ride through the
backcountry and make a thorough search for all Indians
that may be hiding out. These Indians are to be brought in
to the camps and to be held until they can be taken west.

"You will observe there is nothing in those orders
that will allow you to interfere with civilians in any
way. You are especially to refrain from interfering with
Mr. Hallett."

"Or Wilson Rounce?"

Colonel White came around his desk. "I did not mention that name. Nor is it to be mentioned."

Miles relaxed a little. "But Mr. Rounce is an old
friend. I might say, a very old friend."

White stared at him doubtfully. "I did not understand
that you knew him."

"I know him very well." Pleased that White was no
longer so sure of himself, Tolan gathered his gloves
and turned to go. "I know him well enough to know that
those associated with him usually find themselves in
trouble . . . but Will Rounce gets off scot-free."

"That is none of your business," White said firmly.
"You will follow your orders."

Miles Tolan walked outside and stopped on the steps
of the building. Inwardly, he was furious. Obviously,
White was playing it cozy with the local politicians, and
certainly Will had wasted no time in demonstrating his
influence.

Well . . . they were right, of course. It was none of
his business. A law had been passed and a treaty signed,
and it was not his position to ask questions, but only to
obey. Yet Will Rounce's position here intrigued him, and
whatever else might happen Miles knew very well that he
was not through with Will. There was that in Will that
would never leave well enough alone.

It had begun long ago, in Pennsylvania. Miles Tolan
had been five years old when he fell under the supervi-
sion of Elias Rounce of Rounceville, and despite his
mixed feelings for Will, Miles could never feel anything
but affection and respect for that stern, just, and ec-
centric man who for twelve years had been guardian, fos-
ter father, and mentor to him.

He had never been addressed by any name other than
"Mister Elias." He ruled his household as he ruled his
varied businesses, with a firm hand. Never in his presence did anyone laugh or speak loudly, nor did anyone who

worked for him ever idle at a task. Not only would such a
man have been dismissed at once, but he would have found
it difficult to find work of any other kind in the community. Despite this, Elias Rounce was a man not only
feared, but admired by many and respected by all.

His family were reported to have been fisherfolk, although it was rumored there had been shipbuilders among
them too. He rarely spoke of himself, and Miles could recall only three occasions when he had made any reference
to his past.

It was Mister Elias's firm belief that education was
for the purpose of building character. He did not believe
in the way schools were traditionally managed; he main-
tained his own school for his grandchildren and for the
children of a few of his immediate associates. Their
teacher was a man imported for the purpose by Mister
Elias.

Phineas Cronkite was tall, almost as tall as Mister
Elias, who himself stood six feet and four inches in his
size-fourteen boots. Whereas Mister Elias was a solid man
of broad chest and shoulders, Phineas Cronkite was lean,
hollow-cheeked, and sparse of hair. His skull was long
rather than broad like Mister Elias's, and what little
hair he did possess was thin and pale. His nose was long
and busy as a ferret's while his thin lips were tightly
compressed, as though he feared to say something extraor-
dinary.

Phineas Cronkite, who was the only teacher Miles
could remember, possessed an amazing fund of knowledge on
a peculiar variety of subjects, but Miles had never been
able to discover where or how he had come by such knowledge or the skills he had at hand.

When he instructed his few students he did so in a
dry monotone that yet held some strange quality of fasci-
nation, for Miles could never recall finding him either

dull or uninteresting. Somehow, the moment he began to
speak one's attention was captured, and from that instant
no one in class ever thought of anything else.

His instruction would have been considered radically
unorthodox in any other school, but Miles did not believe
that Phineas saw it in that light at all, or even gave
any serious thought to the opinions of others.

Miles would never forget those classes. There were
six students, ranging in age from ten to fifteen during
the years Miles remembered them best. Phineas would look
past them with his yellow eyes and begin to talk, and
from that moment their attention was captured. Yet looking back, Miles could never remember Phineas showing excitement, pleasure, or sadness.

No matter what he taught, his manner remained the
same. He instructed them in cheating at cards with the
same dry, empty-faced manner in which he taught the
Psalms, and he taught them how to kill a man with a knife
in exactly the manner in which he instructed them in
Thucydides. If he was able to distinguish one pupil from
another, Miles could recall no indication of it.

Mister Elias was a successful man. It was impossible
that he could have been anything else, being the sort of
man he was. Miles never knew all the details of Mister
Elias's business, but Rounceville was Mister Elias, and
vice versa. He owned and operated the tannery, blacksmith
shop, carriage shop, and a gunsmithy. He operated a pro-
vision store, and employed cobblers, tailors, and dress-
makers. Rounceville was an economy complete in itself.

Yet all this was but a small part of his business,
for Mister Elias bought things. It was said of him that
Elias Rounce would buy anything, and it was also noted
that he sold everything he bought, and invariably at a
substantial profit. If no profit was immediately available, he waited. As a result there were warehouses of

amazing odds and ends, through which Miles and the others
had rummaged and searched for things to excite their interest or with which to play.

Mister Elias's orders were that each child was to be
out of bed at four a.m. and after a cold bath to breakfast at four-thirty. They were to be employed by five
o'clock. Each Saturday morning the boys were called to
the desk by Phineas and each was given a rifle and six
loads of powder and ball. By sundown they were expected
to report to him with at least five rabbits, squirrels,
or game birds.

On this day the boys were not allowed to carry a
lunch, so if they ate at all, it must be from food found
in the forest or fields. These rules were laid down by
Mister Elias and given to Phineas Cronkite for our instruction, and remarkable as it might seem, Miles could
not recall that after the first few months any of them
ever went hungry.

Once each month Mister Elias would receive each of
the students alone in his study, and at that time questioned them on topics connected with their work, study,
or hunting. Each of them might be called upon to speak
extemporaneously upon a topic selected by him from their
field of activities. These meetings with Mister Elias
began when they were ten and proceeded, with rare inter-
ruptions, until they were freed from their education.

Never during the twelve years at Rounceville could
Miles recall any evidence of favoritism, despite the fact
that two of the students were his own grandsons and one a
granddaughter. Mister Elias had been strict with them
all, yet perceptive of their individual traits, attri-
butes, and talents. Later, Miles realized Mister Elias
knew more of their faults than he had suspected, and that
he was prepared to deal with them.

When Miles was sixteen Mister Elias came to the room

where Phineas held class and placed on the desk before
Phineas a volume of Blackstone. "Miles Tolan will read
this," he said, "and he will report to me after examina-
tion by you. Every man should know the rudiments of law."

At intervals, following Miles' fourteenth birthday he
was given a horse, a small wagon, and a load, usually not
large, of trade goods. With this he was expected to go
out and trade, and he was expected to show a profit; if
such a profit did appear it was put into Miles' account in
Mister Elias's bank. It was the same for each of the boys.

At the trading he had been moderately successful, but
never so successful as Will, who had concluded some
rather fabulous deals.

All that had ended rather suddenly when Miles was
seventeen.

On the morning that Mister Elias sent for him, Miles
had been surprised, because during the year that had just
passed these visits had grown increasingly less frequent.
Mister Elias was seated behind his huge desk, and he had
surprised Miles still more by suggesting he be seated.
Mister Elias not only kept most standing at attention
during their recitations and examinations, but he would
tolerate nothing slovenly nor lacking in respect in his
charges' conduct.

He had been occupied with some figures when Miles entered, and seated in the high-backed chair, Miles watched
him. How old he was Miles had never known, but at the
time he must have been nearing seventy, although still a
powerful man, physically active and showing no more evidence of the passing years than a huge old oak tree. His
square-cut beard was streaked with gray, but so it had
been when Miles first saw him, and his face seemed un-
changed.

Mister Elias looked up suddenly. "Miles, you are no
relation of mine."

Of this Miles was aware, but he sat awaiting what might follow, and his curiosity was keen.

"When I die I shall leave you nothing, nor do I believe you have expected it, so the time has come for you to act for yourself.

"I have never felt that advice was important. Men of my years are far too ready with their advice, and it is rarely worth the bother. All too rarely they have thought out the advice they offer, and the further you go in life the more you will realize that few people think. They follow lines of least resistance or take advantage of opportunities that occur. If you think, Miles, the world can be yours."

He paused. "I now have something to say to you that I know you will not repeat. I have observed you carefully, and have found many qualities in you to admire, and one of them is that you invariably keep your own counsel. I like this, and I know there are many things you might have discussed of which you have said nothing.

"I want you to leave here, Miles, and I want you to go far away. I ask you to do this because one of the things I have observed is the unhealthy rivalry that has developed between you and Will.

"No." Mister Elias lifted a hand. "Do not explain or protest. I know the rivalry is mostly on Will's side. Will is a boy who has to win--he cannot take second place, and will not. You are aware of this, and in a number of cases you have deliberately allowed him to win because, I believe, you feel you owe a debt to me."

Miles started to object.

"Please! I have thought this out, and I know the character of each of you. You have no reluctance to let Will win because winning is important to you only when the issue is itself important. Regardless of that, Will has lately taken a new course. For some reason, through some insecurity I cannot fathom, competing with you and

winning has become more important to him than anything
else in the world.

"During these past few years he has lied, cheated,
and stolen. His 'successful' trading was not successful,
Miles. He was selling his goods and then stealing because
of his need to be absolutely sure he bested you.

"I want you to go away, Miles. Go far from here, and
stay away from Will if you can possibly do so. Will has
great ability, but you have qualities he will never have.
You have character and you have persistence. If you remain in the same area, sooner or later a time will come
when an issue or a woman would become so important to you
that you would not allow him to win. I fear then that he
would try to kill you. He would try; whether he could
succeed or not I have no idea . . . but whatever the result, it would be disastrous.

"I am not a foolish old man, Miles. There is something lacking in my grandson, some moral sense that I
have been unable to provide. I have watched you both
grow, and I could wish, Miles, that you were my grandson.
I would admit that to no one else. I am proud of you, and
wherever you go, I know you will survive and you will
achieve whatever it is you wish to achieve."

"That will be due to you, sir."

"In part, perhaps. The education I have given here is
different. Many believe it is severe, but life is not
mild. Many believe I have concentrated too much on some
aspects, but I do not think so. Here we try to build
character first--self-respect, independence of spirit,
self-reliance--and to offer the equipment for survival
and for citizenship."

Mister Elias got to his feet. "No one has been told
of your going and I would prefer you to tell no one. You
will ride Ambrose, my Irish stallion; he is now yours.
Your clothing has been packed, you have a bill of sale
for the stallion, and your money is here. You will find

on your saddle a new rifle and a brace of pistols. You are to go as if on a business dealing for me. You are not to come back."

Miles remembered how he had gotten to his feet. He looked across the table at Mister Elias with a lump in his throat. "Thank you, sir. Thank you for everything. You have been more than a father to me, and I shall try to follow your advice."

Elias held out his hand, and Miles suddenly realized that it was the first time they had ever touched. Then the boy turned toward the door.

"Miles?" Something in Elias's voice had turned cold. "I send you away in hopes that by being apart each of you may grow naturally, and my grandson will live out his days. But I would do you no favor to leave you unwarned. If ever you and Will meet again, do not think of what I have done for you, but simply protect yourself. You are my son also, in my feelings if not in blood."

And now what Mister Elias had feared had come to pass. They were together again . . . and the Army had ordered him here, and the Army would not permit him to leave.

Already battle had been joined, mildly so far, but joined nonetheless.

There was only one thing to do. Avoid Will. Avoid Hallett, avoid Adam Couch, avoid anyone or anything that led to him or was close to him.

Avoid Laura.

CHAPTER 6

During the days that followed there was little time for thinking of Will Rounce, nor of Laura McCrae. Oddly

though, it was the girl in the forest to whom his
thoughts reverted again and again; the mystery of her
presence there and her sudden disappearance haunted him.

Not less did he wonder about the peculiar reactions
of both Will and Laura to his mention of Moore's Lalla
Rookh. Certainly, there was nothing in the contents of
the book that could create such an effect. It was simply
a rather charming and romantic love poem with some interesting overtones.

However, it was Mister Elias's admonition that remained most in his mind, and he took care to avoid any
further meeting with Will Rounce. For the moment Miles'
duties were more than sufficient to keep him busy, and it
would not be long before he would again be going west,
and this time with a party of Cherokees. Once west he
would contrive that he not come east again, one way or
another.

How could a man dedicated to pushing the Cherokees
from their land still remain a friend to the McCraes? Especially when that man was an avowed enemy of Tsali's?

More and more he found himself puzzled by Will's
presence here at all. What had become of Rounceville?
Mister Elias must certainly have divided among his three
grandchildren a sizable fortune, if all had survived
until his death. Will would have been a fool to leave a
going business in a community where he could assume the
mantle of his grandfather's prestige and be immediately a
personage of some importance, in every sense.

What had happened?

As the weeks passed, bitterness increased among the
Cherokees who remained in the mountains at the corner of
Georgia, North Carolina, and Tennessee. The Treaty of New
Echota, signed by fewer than five hundred of a tribe of
more than sixteen thousand, required the Cherokees to

surrender their lands in Georgia and move to Indian country beyond the Mississippi.

The Cherokee Nation was to be given five million dollars, an equal amount of land in the new Indian Territory, an educational fund of half a million dollars, and
compensation for abandoned property in the East. But
there was open talk of bribery, and the known fact that
many of the Cherokees present at the treaty signing had
been made drunk and were in no condition to know what
they were signing. The situation was made even more com-
plex by the passions involved, passions that led to several of those in favor of the treaty having been
assassinated and what amounted to a Cherokee government
in exile being established over the state line in Tennessee.

Reports of a gold discovery in the Cherokee country
increased the cupidity of those politicians who were ex-
erting pressure on Washington and Atlanta, but the
rougher element were not inclined to wait upon the Removal. Rushing in, they tore down Cherokee fences, ruined
their crops, and defiled the pure waters of their
streams. Ignoring both the tribal government and the fed-
eral treaties, the state of Georgia passed laws extending
her jurisdiction over the Cherokee country, and even went
so far as to forbid any Cherokee to hold office in the
tribe, or any white man to live in Cherokee territory
without swearing allegiance to the state of Georgia. The
Georgia Legislature, eager to preserve the gold for the
white man, even made it illegal for any Cherokee to dig
for gold on his own land.

Rarely, Miles Tolan thought, had the legislative
right been so abused. It was at a time when throughout
the United States there was strong sympathy for the
Greeks in their war for Independence, yet only a few went
so far as to speak out for the Cherokees in their own
land.

Detachments of soldiers were sent out to scour the
fields and the mountains with rifle and bayonet, to
search every cabin hidden away in the coves of the hills
or the deeper valleys, and to seize and bring in Cherokees wherever found. From dawn to dusk they were in the
field, rounding up the Indians and escorting them to
stockades, where they were concentrated prior to their
movement westward. It was cruel work, and few in the Army
liked it.

Resistance was rare. The Cherokees had been worn out
by the long struggle to keep their hills and by the continual inroads of white men seeking gold, stealing stock,
or merely searching out land they wished to claim. More
than once the people had scarcely been moved from their
cabins before looters had them in flames.

In all of this, Miles Tolan was a part. He had been
given a job to do and he did it, acting with speed, effi-
ciency, and with whatever kindness was possible. With
care, he managed to avoid the parties of looters, or
bands he suspected might be directed by Will Rounce.

In the fifth week he again met Laura McCrae.

They recognized each other at the same instant, and
she rode up to him at once. "Have you seen Will?" He
thought there was a note of anxiety in her tone. "He has
not been to Brignole."

He hesitated, and despite himself he was worried,
worried for this quiet, attractive girl who seemed to
have placed her faith in Will Rounce. "No," he said finally, "I haven't seen him . . . but then I have been
very busy."

"My father is worried. We have received orders to va-
cate."

Miles glanced down at the reins in his hands. "It is
the law," he said. "All Cherokees must move."

"We won't be forced to." He thought there was a
shadow of doubt in her voice. "Will assured us we had no
reason to worry."

"I think he was wrong." He heard himself speak the
words almost without volition. "I don't believe it is a
good policy but I do believe you will be forced to move.
No word has been given to me to provide for any exceptions . . . and there are other factors to be considered."

"Will is very close to the governor," she replied,
"and to Colonel White. He told us just to stay where we
were, that everything would be all right."

"He has given you false hope."

She was not convinced. "I do not know what you think
is wrong, but I assure you, you are mistaken. Will is a
fine man, a very fine man. My father admires him very
much, and so does James."

"And John Ross?"

"No," she admitted, "I do not believe they like each
other."

"And Tsali?"

"Tsali?" She was surprised. "Why, Tsali is nobody.
Just an old mountain farmer."

"But a Cherokee," Miles interposed, "Tsali told me to
tell Will that he was his enemy. And the men whom I
stopped from looting that farm were under Will's orders."

"I do not believe that. Oh," she added quickly, "he
may claim some of the land now that people are forced to
leave, the same as many others. But he would not allow
such things as you saw there. I know he wouldn't."

Miles did not like the way the conversation was tend-
ing, and gathered his reins. "My only advice to you is to
place your trust in no one concerned with this movement.
Listen to Ross if you will. He is trying to do something."

"That is strange talk from a soldier," Laura said,

"advising me to place no faith in anyone concerned with
the movement."

"A soldier does what he is told, but that does not
mean he does not have his own opinions. I only know that
what has to be done, will be done, so far as I can arrange it, without hardship to those involved." He spoke
stiffly, feeling an antagonism from her he could not
quite understand. Unless she was resenting his attitude
toward Will Rounce. "I believe no one is in any position
now to promise anything, and I have no faith in Will's
promises."

"You hate him, don't you?"

"No," he said honestly, "I do not hate him. I really
do not even dislike him. I simply do not trust him, and
my lack of trust is based on past experience."

"I think you hate him more than you suspect because
he was always better than you in everything you two did."

Miles laughed. "Did Will tell you that? Well, sometimes I know he was better than I. He could jump farther
and higher than I could, but he could not run or walk as
far. He was always a little better in shooting at tar-
gets, but I usually came in with the most game. I just
think Will was born lacking some other quality the majority of us have."

There was no warmth in her eyes. "I do not like you,
Lieutenant Tolan. I believe you have no right to talk of
Will that way. Someday he may thrash you for it."

Miles chuckled. "He may, at that." Then he added more
gently, "But it will take some doing."

Both were prepared to ride on, yet neither moved. The
sun dappled the trail with leaf shadow, and somewhere off
under the trees they could hear birds scratching and rustling among the leaves.

"Miss McCrae," he asked suddenly, "did Will ever tell
you what happened to Rounceville?"

"No. So far as I can recall he's never mentioned it.

When you appeared he did tell me something of your early
life there."

"It should have been his. I believe Mister Elias had
planned it so, and he was a man who thought things
through. Often I've wondered what happened to Phineas
Cronkite, our teacher."

"Will never discusses it." Her curiosity was aroused.
"What was it like?"

"Mister Elias . . . he was Will's grandfather . . .
was a man of original mind. I never did hear how he
started it all, except that the first time he came
through the valley where he built Rounceville he was a
wagon-peddler. He traded with the Indians, fought them on
occasion, then bought cattle, horses, and hogs. When the
country began to settle up he was the main source of supply, and he invested in shoemaking, tanning, and a blacksmith shop. It developed for thirty years until he owned
an entire community, and had put by a good bit of money."

"Will told me you left when you were seventeen."

"By invitation. I mean, Mister Elias educated me,
cared for me, and at seventeen I was old enough to fend
for myself."

"What did you do then?" Laura asked curiously.

"Saw some country . . . went down the river to New
Orleans . . . joined up with the Missouri Fur Company."

"You were a trapper?"

"Trapper, hunter, trader. I came back to St. Louis
and then made a trip over the Santa Fe Trail to the Spanish settlements there. I did pretty well."

Laura watched his eyes curiously. "You're a strange
man, Lieutenant. I don't quite know what to think of you."

"We're all much alike." He made a move to start
again, and said, "You could tell me something, however. . . ."

"What?"

"Who is the Beloved Woman?"

CHAPTER 7

Laura had evaded his question--that was Miles' first thought upon opening his eyes. He lay very still with his hands clasped behind his head, knowing it was time to get up, yet wanting to think.

It was Sunday morning, he was without orders, and for this one brief day he was once again his own man.

For more than a week he had been hearing references to the Beloved Woman, and his curiosity had been excited. She was without a doubt a personage of some importance, but to questions asked of the Cherokees he received only evasive replies, replies that had whetted his interest. In general he had found the Cherokees a courteous people, and usually willing to explain any of their own customs that aroused interest.

Among the Georgians themselves he found few who knew anything about the Cherokees, and most of them doubted they were interesting. Here and there he found a degree of sympathy for their plight, but these people felt that decisions had been based upon much that had gone on before their time--and seemed less aware of the role played by a few self-seekers and politicians who wanted the vote. There was also a hard core of people who saw the Cherokees prospering and believed it was something in the land they owned rather than their own energy that brought them such prosperity. These shiftless ones wished to drive the Cherokees from the land so that they might have it.

There was also, deep-seated within all peoples, the desire to seek out anything different from themselves and destroy it. That desire was not exhibiting itself for the first time, nor would it be for the last. It was blind, unreasoning hatred of all that was different.

Miles sat up in bed, then swung his feet to the
floor, staring irritably across the room. He wanted a
transfer. He wanted to get out of this situation, to get
away from what was happening here. Uncle Elias had done
much to shape his thinking, and had fostered within him,
among other things, an appreciation for industrious people; and now, everywhere his eyes turned, he saw clear
evidence of the sort of work he understood best.

No craftsman, whether blacksmith, weaver, carpenter,
or leather-worker, had been allowed to live among the
Cherokees unless he had taken Cherokee youths as appren-
tices. No missionary was allowed in the territory of the
Cherokees unless he also conducted a school. All he could
learn of this people indicated a keen appreciation of the
necessity for change and the best way to go about it.
True, some had taken to drink, and there were laggards
among them, but they were few. Fewer, Miles reluctantly
admitted, than among his own people.

As he shaved, bathed, and dressed, Miles grew annoyed
with himself for pondering a problem beyond his control.
What could he, Lieutenant Miles Tolan, do? He had authority, but limited authority only. He was subject to orders
from his government, from any superior officer, and, it
seemed, from Will Rounce. At least, that is, if they came
via Colonel White.

Already, Miles knew he had overstepped his orders to
a degree. Wherever possible he was careful to inflict no
additional hardship upon the Cherokees who were to be
moved. Fortunately, the rank and file of the Army were
men from the frontier or farms, and they understood what
had been done here and how much work it entailed. As a
result they had little but sympathy for the Indian.

Only yesterday a man had struck an old Cherokee with
a whip, and Miles had coolly walked his horse between
them as the Indian got to his feet. The man had attempted

to walk around Miles' horse, but seemingly without a
glance at him, Miles kept his horse between them. And the
Cherokee, seeing his chance, walked away.

Angrily, the white man demanded, "What's the matter?
You sidin' with these Injuns?"

"What?" Miles Tolan asked as if noticing the man for
the first time. "You were speaking to me?"

Disconcerted, the man protested, "I was givin' that
Injun what he had comin' when you come between us."

"I did?" Miles had looked astonished. "Why, I didn't
even see you!" Confidentially, Miles leaned toward him.
"They give us a lot to do, these days. Riding all the
time, rounding up these Indians. I must have fallen
asleep in the saddle."

He rode on, Sergeant Turpenning following. Turpenning
had said nothing, for he was a man who held his ideas inside his head, and rarely ventured opinions unless asked
a direct question. Sergeant Turpenning was forty-two
years old, with thirty of those years spent on the frontier and most of them in the Army. He was a man who knew
his place, but he also had his own ideas about the Indians, for he had fought them.

COMMENTS: Although I remember some work being done on this
novel in the early 1970s, I believe the majority of the material you
have just read was created between 1958 and 1960. *Trail of Tears* was
considered a potential move toward more "serious" work, both the
first time (the late 1950s) Louis tried to break out of writing Westerns, and during his more calculated, and more successful, attempt in
the 1970s.

Dad often joked that if a novel was written about the nineteenth century and set west of the Mississippi, it was labeled a Western and deemed inconsequential by the critics, yet if it was set east of the Mississippi, it might be thought of as a historical novel, and be taken more seriously.

Not only is *Trail of Tears* set firmly in the historical novel territory of the East, but its time period is earlier than most consider appropriate for a traditional Western. Better yet, it deals with themes and moments in history that both Easterners and Westerners would consider highly significant culturally and historically.

Prior to its completion, Louis wrote a proposal in order to sell this book. It was offered to both a publisher and a movie studio, though, ultimately, he did not conclude either deal. Hardcover publishers were a quandary for Louis. They got books reviewed. They got respect. They earned you a bit of extra money if your book sold well, because they cost more . . . but they also took part of your paperback earnings (for having promoted the book, and for brokering the deal), they weren't really available at a price appropriate for the common man (something Louis cared about deeply), and they wanted a piece of the movie rights. With the exception of critical recognition, for a popular writer like Louis L'Amour there weren't many advantages in those days to publishing in hardcover.

Once Louis knew he could earn a good living selling directly to the paperback publishers, the only reason to try for a hardcover sale was prestige—but prestige was an important goal for Louis in the early 1970s. He knew he could knock the ball out of the park in the paperback arena, but he wanted to win over the critics, too.

While none of the proposal drafts took the story through to its completion, they do reveal a few additional details.

The inclusion of the intriguing, sylphlike Woman on the Rock, the girl who turns out to be the Beloved Woman of the Cherokee, was made late in the process. I can remember Dad talking about having discovered the concept of the Beloved Woman while he was doing research for one of his later attempts. He was excited by the opportunity it posed for the creation of a fascinating character. At times she seemed almost a Native American Joan of Arc, and would have been an interesting addition to a tragic story of this scope.

For the longest time, Westerns and science fiction were the two genres where anything but the most superficial love interest was a taboo. Not so the historical novel, which often showed a tendency to cross over into romance territory. In his proposals, Louis made sure publishers knew he would be playing by the rules of historical novels:

> There is a strong love story, and in certain phases of the story, a good bit of sex, tastefully handled but definitely present. Aside from the action, the love story will be, I believe, one of the most entertainingly developed of recent years. With proper promotion I believe this book will have a great sale, of which we can all be proud.

Louis intended to play on the hypocrisy that surrounded the Cherokee Removal, showing that the prejudice of the white men did not need a target as obvious as the Western genre's typical Indians.

> . . . these Indians were, in many cases, educated, well-informed men and women who lived in the same sort of houses as white men and who wore the same sort of clothing as the white man from preference. Their differences from white society were few; they were not a group of "outsiders." Many were at least as well educated as the average white man of his time, and several had qualities of genius.

Not only was he exploring the fact that many Cherokee did not look or act differently from their white neighbors (many were even Christian), but some of his characters among the Cherokee elite were meant to be pathetically tone-deaf to the catastrophe that was bearing down on them. To add irony upon irony, there are some indications that he also intended to add major characters who were the black slaves of those same Cherokee elites, slaves who traveled and died on the Trail of Tears.

Although, for Louis, being an entertainer came first and a historian a more distant second, he did quote some of his sources for research on this book, and mentioned a few of what I'm guessing are actual episodes that he intended to use in the narrative:

> Material for this book has been culled from the
> Library of Congress, War Department records, the Peabody Library in Baltimore, the Enoch Pratt Library in
> the same city; from family records of descendants of
> Indians who made the march, and many other sources.
> Some of the episodes likely to be included in the
> novel are the following:
> The massacre of Tsali and his family;
> The burial of Chief Whitepath;
> Gen. Scott's thwarting of the Georgia militia's
> efforts to publicly horsewhip sixteen Cherokees;
> The separation of the Indian, Epenetus, from his
> son while helping a missionary administer sacraments;
> The lashing of a Cherokee for striking a soldier
> who had goaded the Indian's wife;
> The attempt of the Cherokees to put to death members of the treaty party who betrayed them;
> The sinking of the overloaded ferry in mid-
> Mississippi and the drowning of hundreds on it.

A quote included in some of Louis's notes sums up the attitude of many of the military men involved (throughout the frontier period the US Army, while being the blunt tool of government policy, was, in my slight experience, often vastly more sympathetic to Native Americans than the private citizens who were their neighbors):

> General Wool, in command in the area, asked to be
> relieved rather than carry out the distasteful mission. In the majority of cases the Army was sympathetic, and before the end of the march, almost to a

man they were helping the Indians. General Wool is
quoted as saying, "The whole scene since I have been
in this country has been nothing but a heart rending
one. . . . I could not do them a greater kindness
than to remove every Indian beyond the reach of the
white men who, like vultures, are waiting to pounce
upon their prey and strip them of everything they
have or expect from the government of the United
States."

The final pieces of the narrative that lurk in the fragmentary
proposal drafts are set out here:

Meanwhile, Miles is rounding up Cherokees and
bringing them to the stockades to be held pending
movement to the west. He is disturbed to find them
totally unlike the Indians he had known. They are a
prosperous and successful people farming their own
land, running their own mills, in almost no way different from their white neighbors. It is a fact that
causes him to ask questions of himself and others. It
is a fact that causes him to reconsider his attitude,
which has been positive yet patronizing, toward the
Indians he once fought in the far west.

. . . Laura is confident they will not have to
go, for Will has constantly assured them not to
worry. Through beauty, wealth, and education, she is
able to straddle the divide between worlds and is unaware of the depth of the prejudice she faces. She
dismisses Miles' warnings as jealousy because Miles
doubts the honesty of Will's intentions. On one side
Will is seemingly friendly to the Cherokees, on the
other he is working with those who are looting them.

. . . Miles meets the girl he has seen diving
into the pool. She will tell him nothing of herself,
but they arrange several meetings in the deep woods.
She is hiding from someone. He becomes aware that
that someone is Will Rounce, and the powers that he
represents. She is, he later discovers, the Beloved
Woman, a personage of real influence in the tribe, an
influence even greater than that of many chieftains,
and to whom they all must listen with respect, a
leader they might rally around in time of war or
trouble.

During one of their meetings Miles hears a faint
sound and learns they have been watched. Following
the watcher to prevent him from telling what he has
seen, he comes suddenly on the body of the man. He
has been killed. Later, he sees one of the sons of
Tsali leaving the area. He is a Cherokee Miles has
met before.

Miles himself is subjected to searching inquiry,
for it is realized that he has won friends among the
Cherokee. It is believed the Beloved Woman knows the
location of a vast deposit of gold, for the gold discoveries on the Cherokee lands so far have been limited and the interlopers are unwilling to believe
there is no more.

Miles meets Hallett again, and this time in a
fight. Hallett attempts to strike him with a whip.
Miles gives Hallett a severe beating and is arrested.

Orders are issued for the McCraes to go west.
Shocked, Laura tries to reach Will, but she cannot.
They are driven from their home, and escaping, she
returns to find Will and some of his friends holding
court in her home, and for the first time she realizes that this was what he had always intended, that

he had pretended friendship to have first chance at
one of the best places in the Cherokee Nation.

The above would suggest that Will's short-term goal is to keep the
McCraes from selling their land so that he can grab it without having
to buy it ... but who his mysterious connections are and what the
long game is remains a mystery, as does what happened to Will's inheritance from Uncle Elias.

Louis was interested in the many utopian, often experimentally
socialist communities that sprung up on the American frontier, like
the Shakers and New Harmony. I know he had many more intriguing
details up his sleeve about the community of Rounceville and the
characters of Elias Rounce and Phineas Cronkite.

Here's a short breakdown that was done somewhere along the way.
It's the only indication we have of the shape of the entire plot. It's
important to realize that Louis rarely referred to outlines like this
once he started writing, so he might have gone on to do something
completely different. The "FIRST," "SECOND," "THIRD," and
"FOURTH" he is writing about are acts or the major sections of the
story.

FIRST:

Story opens, protagonists meet, problem is un-
folded. Hero's character is revealed, also that of
heavy and girl. Situation is revealed, conflict begins.

SECOND:

Conflict increases, characters revealed still
more, problem develops, and the whole condition and
state of affairs is revealed and made clear. Hero begins coping with problem, meets with failure. His
love for girl is revealed to him suddenly.

THIRD:

Removal begins: a long, bitter, brutal trek. Take much time with this, and with individual characters who have been developed in early sections, now meet with trouble, death, bereavement. Hero is recalled to Atlanta; refuses to abide by orders; attempt at assassination. Plans are revealed whereby heavies will cut off a small band of Indians and rob them. Heavy reveals his true attitude toward girl: He despises her as an Indian.

FOURTH:

Removal continues. After terrible trials, hero returns to girl finding much death, pity, and fatigue along the way, and afraid she will be dead or lost. He comes to her, but is pursued by hatred of heavy until final fight in the swamps or on the river's edge or on the plains of Oklahoma.

Begin writing tomorrow and do 1,000 words of the beginning. Do them over. Begin with action, poetry, power. Create a character worth reading about.

I love that last bit. Louis was always writing himself these sorts of affirmations. They are another facet of his lifelong motivation to keep moving, think positively, and improve himself. Below is the most interesting set of notes on this story, because they are written in first person, as if he, Louis, was the actual narrator. I don't know of another case of him doing this, even for a story that was ultimately written in first person.

OUTLINE: TRAIL OF TEARS

1. I arrive in Georgia, and meet girl and [illegible]; I meet old friend; develop acquaintance

with girl, find doubts of friend. Become friends
with some Cherokees. Told off by [illegible] in
Atlanta.

2. Trouble develops, affair with girl, acquaintance
develops with friend's girl. My girlfriend's father also involved. Old friend plots against me.
Break becomes definite. Fight at Cherokee town.

3. The Removal Begins: Harassed, betrayed, the first
fight, herds driven off, murder.

A different, handwritten version of the first-person notes.

Finally, there is this cryptic passage from some of the *Trail of Tears* materials:

```
1st section: in love but don't know it.
2nd in love but won't say it.
3rd in love but can't do anything about it.
4th can say, can do, no future
```

I'm not sure why this book wasn't eventually completed; possibly it was because of changing priorities in Louis's career. The struggle to break into the hardcover business may have become less important as his success replaced the need to be well reviewed. He also became more focused on planning his "three family" (Sackett, Chantry, Talon) series and recognized that sooner or later, because of changes in the book business, he was going to be able to publish in hardback without changing genres. While Louis very much wanted to write other kinds of material, he also wanted to win widespread acceptance for his Westerns, and as much as he liked a challenge, he preferred to succeed without having to accommodate others. It was a tension that ran like a subtle stream throughout his later life.

A WOMAN WORTH HAVING

A Treatment for an Adventure Story

COMMENTS: A "treatment" like the following document is the description of a story rather than the story itself. It is used as a sales tool when an author is attempting to present an idea for which he wishes to be paid, by a publisher or a movie studio, to write. In Louis's case, treatments were almost never intended to be an exact description of the finished work; they were much more like a very early rough draft where he experimented with the potential of different structures and ideas.

"A woman worth having must be fought for or stolen."

--Arab proverb

Hot and dusty were the crowded streets of Mosul on that afternoon in 1845, but the tall, erect young En-

glishman who made his way through the crowd was aware of
something more than the dust, smells, and flies of the
Near East. He was aware of a subtle undercurrent of revolt, of seething unrest. And Henry Layard was fully
aware of the reason for that feeling, for during his
short stay in the country he had seen much and heard more
of the sadistic cruelty of the local governor, Mohammed
Pasha.

Layard was a handsome young man, skilled in the arts
of diplomacy, which was his profession, and knowing in
all the languages and many of the dialects of the Near
East. Yet he was a man ridden by a driving urge to find
the fabled cities of Nineveh, to uncover the ruins he
knew existed in the valleys of the Tigris and the Euphra-
tes. Nor was this his first trip to Mesopotamia, for he
had been here before and had scouted the country carefully while hunting. Near the rivers he had found several
huge mounds that seemed geologically out of place, and he
had come to believe they were actually heaps of sand and
debris blown up and over the ruins of the ancient cities
mentioned in the Old Testament.

He was walking now to a meeting with Sir Stratford
Canning, British ambassador to the government of Turkey,
who was visiting in Mosul from his headquarters in Istanbul.

As he pushed through the crowd, his mind was fraught
with anxiety. He needed money to finance his project, and
he feared he would neither get it nor receive permission
to remain in the country until conditions became calmer
than they now were. The slightest wrong move could explode into revolt, and only fear of the bloody vengeance
of Mohammed Pasha was keeping the people quiet.

Ahead of him he saw a sedan chair carried by slaves
and preceded by two stalwart desert tribesmen. It was an
unusual sight, for sedan chairs were rarely seen and al-

most never in charge of Bedouins; it betokened a person
of some importance.

As he drew abreast of the sedan chair there was a
sudden outburst in a dark alleyway and a rush of men. In
an instant the marketplace had exploded into a fighting,
screaming, brawling mob. One of the bearers was knocked
to the pavement and the chair fell, turning half over and
spilling a very startled, and beautifully robed young
woman into the street.

The Bedouins who were her protectors had been separated from her by the fighting, and in an instant, Layard
sprang to her side and stood over her, fighting off the
brawling Arabs. Quickly as it had begun, the fighting
washed past them, and Layard helped the shaken girl to
her feet.

"Are you hurt?" He spoke as he helped her up, and he
found himself looking into a face covered by a heavy veil
but revealing a pair of large and amazingly lovely dark
eyes. For an instant she was in his arms, then she
stepped back and, to his surprise, thanked him in English!

Before he could ask a question the Bedouins had
reached her side and she had moved toward her chair,
which had been righted and was awaiting her. She looked
back once and thanked him again, but startled out of his
lethargy by the prospect of losing a girl he wanted very
much to know, he started after her, asking who she was
and where she lived.

The girl got into the chair without seeming to hear
and then was borne away, leaving him standing in the
street. This was not, he remembered unhappily, Paris,
London, or Naples. It was a Moslem city where the women
did not talk to men other than those of their immediate
family and rarely met foreigners or even set eyes on
them.

Disappointed, but excited by her touch and the memory of her eyes, he hurried on to keep his appointment with Sir Stratford.

Henry Layard is an Englishman of French parentage, a brilliant scholar, gifted in his command of languages, and a skilled hunter of big game. Yet his greatest interest is in antiquities. For a long time many people had believed the great cities of the ancient east, Babylon and Nineveh, to be mere fantasies of the imagination, like the Arabian Nights. Herodotus, who wrote many of the legends, had also written of other things too fantastic to be believed, and most of the scholars of the time either doubted the cities had ever existed or doubted their size and importance. When other students had been concerned with boating or cricket, young Layard had been studying Arabic, perfecting himself for just this task. With his dark, strongly boned features and his tall, lean build, Layard could, and in fact had, passed for an Arab himself.

Sir Stratford Canning was a tall, white-haired man of great dignity, and Layard was his personal friend and protégé. Far more than Layard realized, Sir Stratford shared his enthusiasm, but he doubted the time was favorable for such an endeavor as Layard had in mind. He knew this was reputed to be the home of the oldest civilizations on earth, older even than Egypt. The idea that fantastic cities, filled with the treasures of centuries, might lie beneath the sands had been rumored since the discoveries of Botta, but these wild theories were not discussed by sober men of science. Still, Sir Stratford knew Layard's enthusiasms and what to expect of this conference, though he had not made up his mind as to his reply.

He was torn between what he considered sane and sober reasoning, his duty to his young friend, and his friend's interests, as well as his own. Diplomat he might be, but beneath it, as with many of the greatest diplomats, there was a romantic strain, and had he been a few years younger . . .

Layard talked of the mounds, of the broken bits of marble mingled with the sands, of the fragments of pottery. He drew upon the stories of Daniel, of the Tower of Babel, of the conquests of Alexander.

"Fables!" Sir Stratford objected. "It is all too indefinite! If the cities had ever existed they would still be occupied!"

"Some things remain." Layard was positive. He had crossed the area, and he told of what he had seen and heard: the legends of cities buried in the sands; a great image of white stone, winged and mighty.

Finally, Sir Stratford agrees to finance him to a limited degree, deliberately making the amount a mere sixty pounds in hopes Layard would give up. Layard accepts eagerly and Sir Stratford admits himself defeated. Then Layard tells him of his exciting meeting in the bazaar.

The ambassador laughs. "I'm surprised she didn't agree to meet you. That must have been old Hakim's daughter, and from all I hear there's not a conventional bone in her body."

Layard learns the girl was probably Alissa, the only child of Hakim, of the Hadida tribe, from the wild deserts of southern Arabia, the land reputed to have been the home of the Queen of Sheba. Old Hakim was sheik of one of the most powerful desert tribes in Arabia, the master of ten thousand horsemen. Without a son, Hakim had reared his daughter with an amount of freedom considered disgraceful by other Moslems. She had ridden to battle with him as a child, had hunted with him, and she went about Arabia and the Near East, guarded by a handful of tribesmen and the knowledge of her father's power.

Layard leaves Sir Stratford with a parting warning from the older man that he must at all costs avoid the attention of Mohammed Pasha. If the governor learned of Layard's presence he would most certainly forbid any digging and might imprison him on some pretext. Stratford further warns him of the troubled state of political affairs.

All this Layard knows only too well. He has not mingled with the camel drivers and merchants for nothing. He knows the gossip, and knows that the Pasha has spies everywhere.

Mohammed Pasha was a short, squat man, possessed of a macabre sense of humor and a sadistic streak that made him relish the utmost in cruelty. If he suspects a man might begin plotting against him, that man could at any time be condemned to torture and death. Pockmarked, with an ear missing, and with queer, jerky movements and a hoarse, bellowing voice, the Pasha is as repulsive in person as his policies are to the populace.

Not satisfied with burdening his people with taxes to an extent almost unimaginable, even in the Near East, Mohammed Pasha had his own spies incite his people to riot or rebellion so these could be put down with cruelty and bloodshed. This retinue of spies, forming a network all over the country, allowed almost any conversation to be reported to him at once.

Layard knew this, so when he went again to the Tigris he went as a hunter of wild boar, a casual British sportsman, armed with several heavy rifles and a pig

spear. And so he returns to the area of his interest, and
makes an inspection of the mound where he has chosen to
dig.

Here he finds himself blocked, not by Mohammed Pasha,
but by Sheik Awad, the half-brigand, half-friendly sheik
who controls the area. Awad flatly refuses to allow digging. Layard is stalemated, and suddenly a new factor en-
ters the situation. A lavish caravan appears, tents are
spread, the black tents of the desert Bedouins, the tents
of the daughter of Hakim!

Unknown to him, Alissa has him spied upon by one of
his own men, and she has followed him here. He tries to
see her, and is refused admittance, yet when he sees Awad
again, the way is suddenly opened for him, and he is permitted to hire laborers. Alissa has interceded for him
without his knowledge.

Although he has seen her but twice (she passes near
him riding a magnificent stallion) he is half in love
with her. He wishes to meet her, but she refuses. Discon-
solate, he seeks the advice of the slave girls at the
well, but they will not talk to him. Yet on the following
night there is another girl among them, and as she turns
away with her jar of water she gives him a long, slow
look. He follows and talks to her, she flirts with him,
teases him, but assures him that if she, the slave of a
powerful princess, is not supposed to talk to him, how
can he expect to see Alissa the daughter of Hakim?

She taunts him with being an infidel, an eater of pig
meat, and they meet again, and then again. She taunts him
with being fickle. Who is it he is in love with? The
daughter of the Hadida? Or the slave girl?

Layard is himself in a state of utter confusion. He
will not admit he is in love with the slave girl, but he
finds himself making excuses to see her. Meanwhile, the
digging goes on.

A wall is uncovered and on it are amazing reliefs,

and some pottery is found: a small jar covered with gold leaf, some broken tablets. All are dusted and preserved with the greatest of care.

Meanwhile, the spies of Mohammed Pasha have reported the digging by the strange Englishman. The Pasha believes he is searching for treasure. He sends soldiers, and Layard is ordered to stop. Yet the Pasha knows now that the young man is the friend of the ambassador, and that he will have other friends in Istanbul. To protect himself he tells Layard that he is digging in a Moslem cemetery, that he is desecrating graves.

While Layard sleeps the soldiers carry stones and place them about to make it appear that the words of the Pasha are true: that this is, indeed, a graveyard.

Again, hopeful of assistance, Layard goes to see the daughter of Hakim, but again Alissa refuses to meet with him. So he leaves and goes to Mosul, determined to face the Pasha and demand an explanation, and also to get, if it is at all possible, permission to continue his digging.

At Mosul he finds the city wildly excited. A rumor is out that the Pasha is dying, that he left the palace in his carriage and was stricken suddenly, then rushed back to the palace, and now word is out that he is either dying or dead. Soon the wails of the mourners are heard, and a friend of Layard's rushes to him, overjoyed at the news. Layard is suspicious and holds back.

A huge crowd has gathered outside the palace and they are dancing and laughing, shouting for joy at the death of the tyrant. Suddenly, the Pasha appears on a balcony. He begins to roar with laughter as his soldiers rise suddenly and fire into the mob. Men fall, screaming and dying, and then other soldiers rush forward and those men still alive are made prisoners, their property to be confiscated, themselves to be tortured and killed.

Revolted at the bloody spectacle, Layard nevertheless

persists in his purpose. He goes to the palace, and the
Pasha, in a vast good humor, admits him. The Pasha is
suddenly sly. This man may have powerful friends--he suggests that if Layard is searching for gold, that he can
tell him and that something can be arranged.

The Pasha is by turns tyrannical and obsequious.
Layard suggests he will have nothing to do but return to
Istanbul and report to his friends there that the Pasha
will not allow him to continue. Disturbed, the Pasha finally allows him to return and continue digging. Se-
cretly, he plans to let Layard find the gold he believes
he is searching for, and then to murder him.

On his return Alissa arranges a meeting for him with
a Turkish official from the Ottoman capital who is traveling incognito. Layard explains the situation, and takes
the Turk through the ruins he has uncovered. An educated,
cultured man, the Turk is entranced, and Layard gives him
several presents, a vase and some polished tile, to take
back to the sultan in Istanbul.

Attempting to thank Alissa, Layard is cut coldly off.
Her act was mere courtesy, such as would be extended to
any honest man. She understands what he is about, and
wants to help; that does not mean that she can permit any
friendly overtures from an infidel.

Furthermore, she advises him, she understands he is
carrying on an affair with one of her slave girls, that
he is arranging clandestine meetings. Just what are his
intentions toward this girl? Does he not know that he is
upsetting her? Disturbing her heart?

She tricks him and teases him, asks him if he believes any slave girl is as beautiful as she? He hesi-
tates, flounders, then says he cannot say, he has never
seen her with her veil off. She seizes upon this: Then he
has seen the slave girl's face? She has removed her veil
for him? He defends the girl, says it was his fault, and
she leads him on, berates him, and finally sends him

away, angry and confused. She knows how he feels and is
vastly amused.

Then the stone carving of a huge Winged Bull is discovered with great excitement by the diggers. They rush
to him, and the spies, believing the treasure discovered,
and that only gold could induce such excitement, report
to the Pasha. Soldiers appear from nowhere and both he
and the girl (the slave girl, as she seems to be) are
made prisoners. They are to be tortured to reveal the
hiding place of the gold that the Pasha cannot find.

In the nick of time he escapes with the girl and they
get away into the desert. At a lonely oasis they hide,
and when they return, accompanied by Bedouins of her
tribe, they kill the Pasha's brutal soldiers and take the
Pasha prisoner.

Istanbul appoints a new Pasha who gives Layard permission to excavate as much as he wishes, and Layard visits the old Pasha in a filthy, leaking cell where the
onetime tyrant is now cringing and bemoaning his fate.

Layard is summoned then to the black tent of the
daughter of Hakim. She accuses him of infidelity again,
of pretending to be in love with her and all the while
carrying on with the slave girl. She forces him to admit
that he has found the girl lovely, that she is exciting.
She accuses him of loving two women--he says he can love
but one. She demands that he leave and see neither of
them again. He refuses and, angered, he seizes her. Her
veil comes loose and he sees the princess and the slave
are as one.

Furious, she sends him away.

That night the great Winged Bull, the statue that he
is sending back to the British Museum (where it can be
seen today), is at last taken from the hole. Upon a huge

wooden cart surrounded by workmen, the Winged Bull starts to move away.

And then a slave girl comes to him and, kneeling, hands him a note. It is from Alissa. The girl speaks in a low voice. "Alissa sends to her master a message of love."

"Love?" He is angry now. "Why, that--!"

The girl on her knee giggles, and he wheels around to stare at her. She stands erect and throws off the dark cloak, revealing herself as the daughter of Hakim--truly a woman worth having.

They stand together, watching the Winged Bull drawn away to the chanting of the workmen and the creaking of the great cart.

COMMENTS: Although modern, scientific archeology has both merit and morality in the real world, the swashbuckling adventurers/ grave robbers of the late nineteenth and early twentieth centuries have great appeal as the heroes of stories. Austen Henry Layard was a real person, a world traveler, archeologist, and diplomat who published nearly a dozen accounts of his discoveries and expeditions. Here is Louis's introduction to the character taken from some of the notes pertaining to this project:

Layard was a member of a French family that settled in England. He was born in Paris in 1817, lived in Italy for a short time with his father. Studied law. As a young man, an adventurer at heart, he traveled in the Near East, where he became impressed by the vast mounds which seemed geologically incongruous. He believed they covered ancient buried cities, known at that time only through the Old Testament and Herodotus. After long efforts he convinced Sir Stratford Canning and received limited financing, and at twenty-eight, in 1845, he began the excavations that were to write new chapters in world history.

Like those other archaeologists Lawrence of Arabia (later famed as soldier and author) and Belzoni (who was a strongman in a London music hall before going to Egypt), Layard was first and always an adventurer of romantic nature.

A highly abbreviated and romanticized version of Layard's adventures in the Near and Middle East, this treatment, I believe, dates back to the 1950s. The subject matter and style suggest it might have been intended as a potential sale to a motion-picture company, but since we have no contract to back up that suspicion, it is impossible to be sure. The following character breakdown offers a bit more detail about how some of the characters might be used:

CAST OF CHARACTERS

HENRY LAYARD. . . . . Englishman of French ancestry. Tall, handsome, energetic. Skilled linguist, amateur archaeologist destined to become one of the great names in the field. Obsessed with the idea of excavating the mounds along the Tigris, he refuses to be delayed by either the machinations of the local governor or the civil unrest prevailing. Sharp, intelligent, and courageous, he doesn't allow his interest in the dead past to interfere with his interest in the living female.

ALISSA. . . . . The daughter of Hakim, sheik of the powerful Hadida clan of southern Arabia. A girl with a mind of her own, who knows what she wants and how to get it but not

above having some fun in the process. A beautiful and
sexy wench with brains and education and more freedom
than Moslem women are usually allowed. The kind of a
girl to walk beside a man, not behind him.

MOHAMMED PASHA. . . . . The kind of a
man who would pull the legs off flies in private. One
ear and one eye missing, pockmarked face, short,
jerky, ugly, sly, cunning, tyrannical, and obsequious. His main interest is sadistic cruelty--and
money.

SHEIK AWAD. . . . . A coiled,
thieving brigand with a sense of humor, plenty of
courage, no conscience, but he catches some of Layard's enthusiasm for uncovering the buried city of
Nimrud. Willing to take orders from Alissa because he
knows where his bread is buttered and the Hadida clan
are notoriously lacking in sympathy for opposition to
the daughter of Hakim.

SIR STRATFORD CANNING. . . . Layard's friend and
superior. Dignified, and shrewd. Interested as Layard
is in the antiquities of the land between the rivers.

IDRISI PASHA. . . . . Turkish official who comes incognito to camp of Alissa. A man of
intelligence and enthusiasm, secretive yet the coun-
terpoint to the depravity of Mohammed Pasha.

ISMET & MAHMOUD. . . . . Gun-bearers
and assistants of Layard. Ismet a conniving boy, Mahmoud a giant in strength.

RAMIS. The
name Alissa assumes when she poses as the slave girl
of her own retinue. So she can see Layard more often.

While some of these characters are fictional and typical of Hollywood stereotypes of that era, Mohammed Keritli Oglu, Pasha of
Mosul, is actually reported to have been even more odious than the
way he is presented here. When traveling, he was known to tax vil-

lagers for the wear and tear their simple food caused his teeth and there are stories that he actually did, on occasion, allow his death to be reported, and then confiscated the property of all who celebrated his passing!

The Winged Bull was a colossal relief, carved on the sides of a block of stone, rather than an actual three-dimensional statue. It depicted a winged bull with a human head, and it was one of two protecting the palace of Ashurnasirpal II, an Assyrian king.

Whatever this treatment's intended market, it is unlikely that Louis considered it finished. As a careful read shows, its tense is somewhat unstable. He was used to writing fiction in past tense, but movie treatments are nearly always written in the present. A shorter version was also produced, possibly to coincide with the brief attention span of studio executives. Neither was edited well enough to have been ready for presentation.

True Louis L'Amour fans will note that the title *A Woman Worth Having* is also a title that Louis considered for one of the sequels to his novel *The Walking Drum*. This is a single case out of many where Louis switched titles from one project to another when the need arose.

JOHNNY BANTA

Several Beginnings to a Western Novel

LT

COMMENTS: Here are three attempts at starting a Western novel. As you read, you can track the changes Louis made as he figured out what he wanted the story to be, how he wanted to set up the characters, and the differences between them and the threats they would have to face. It's a nice, quick example of how a story would develop.

VERSION ONE

When we came up the valley of the Sweetwater the frost was white on the lowlands and upon the far slope of the mountain the aspens were clouded gold. At nineteen I was the youngest of the lot, although for seven years I had done a man's work, and proud of it.

Only there was a searching in me, for I had found nothing I wanted very much, nor any place I cared to stop, but the soft look on my face was only the softness of being young, and reflected little that was inside me.

When a boy is left alone at twelve he becomes a man or he becomes nothing at all.

Yet it was a hard land in which I had come to manhood, and the way I had found for myself was never easy. When a boy takes a man's place he is expected to be a man and not a boy, so it was stand up to a man's work and a man's responsibilities, and I did that, although it gave me difficult moments.

There were seven of us riding east, and until what seemed but a few days before we had been strangers. And now we were still strangers, but we rode together, shared our grub and our watchfulness and our awareness of danger.

East of us, a distance of hundreds of miles, was St. Louis, our destination, and we were seven armed and belted men, riding with our rifles ready, for we had passed the Pai-ute country and were heading into the land of the Sioux.

There was the Sailor Swede, Coyle the gambler, Harran who had been a trapper, and Seagrave, the only one of us who had done well in the gold fields.

Fleming had crossed the Plains seven times, he said, and Sheedy had kept a store in the gold country, and there was me, Johnny Banta, born in a west-bound wagon and now going to the States for the first time.

We rode with Fleming at point, the Sailor and Coyle on one flank, Harran and Seagrave on the other, and bringing up the rear were Sheedy and myself. In the middle of our group were our nine pack animals, three of them belonging to me.

We crossed the Divide short of noon, and when we crossed it was nothing like the Sierras, just a rise in an almost flat area . . . although it was high up, more than seven thousand feet where we crossed over. We found the Sweetwater and rode along it, riding loose in the

saddle and ready for trouble, for we had been lucky so
far and were worried by it.

We stopped for the night in a hollow among the low
hills near the Sweetwater and Fleming got down from his
saddle and turned his eyes on me. "You'll cook tonight,"
he said.

"I'll not," I told him straight. "Three times this
week I've cooked and no complaint. We're seven here, so
we share and share alike."

Coyle had begun a fire, and he looked up, mildly
amused but interested. I think he had been expecting
this.

"You talking back to me?" Fleming stared at me, but
I'd been stared at before.

"Telling you," I said, "and not only for today. It's
turn and turn about."

Fleming put down the pack he held in his hands and
looked at me. "I don't want to give you a whuppin', so do
as you're told."

"Anywhere we go," I said, "I'll make tracks as big as
you."

Coyle's pleasant voice intervened. "The boy's right.
From the beginning he's done his share, and more than his
share."

"You buttin' in?" Fleming was a man ready for trouble. He had an arrogant way about him that raised my
hackles, but he was unsure of Coyle, who might be a man
to leave alone.

"Trying to save your life," Coyle replied quietly,
and from the way Fleming took it I knew he figured it was
a threat from Coyle himself.

"I'll cook," Sheedy interrupted hastily. "I don't
mind."

Sheedy cooked, and I almost wished I had, it was that
bad, but I rustled wood for the fire before finding a

place to bed down with a natural hammock of earth to give
me shelter from the wind, and from bullets, if it came to
that. With my hunting knife I cut blocks of sod and
forted up a little.

"You expectin' a fight?" Harran asked me. "Ever'
night you build yourself a hole to hide in. How long you
gonna keep it up?"

"Until we're in St. Louis," I said, and meant it.

Coyle awakened me two hours before dawn to take over
the sentry duty, and I slid out of my blankets and rolled
them up for traveling.

"All quiet," Coyle told me, and then he went to his
blankets for a little sleep before daybreak.

It was almighty still . . . the sky was touched up
with stars, and along the Sweetwater the trees and brush
were a black snake winding among the low hills. This was
almost the hour when Indians liked to attack . . . in the
gray hour of first dawn.

Trouble was shaping for me among my own crowd, but it
was trouble I would have to handle my own way, and I was
set for it, believe me. None of this bunch knew anything
of me, and I was almighty sure they had let me join up
because I had horses and they needed pack animals.
Horses, those days, were bringing a fair price and hard
to come by even when a man had the money. And maybe because Fleming figured me for a camp flunky.

Fleming was a bullying man. He had wide shoulders
and was muscled like a wrestler, and he liked to throw
his weight around. Harran was of the same stripe, dark
and surly with an ingrown streak of meanness in him.
Sheedy . . . well, Sheedy was living in Fleming's shadow.
Figuring Fleming for the strong man, Sheedy latched onto
him for the trip.

Maybe I was young, but I was taking no pushing
around. If they wanted to drive this hoss they'd best get
set for trouble.

There was gray in the sky now. Individual trees were
standing out now, and the grass moved under the long
wind. My rifle lay easy in my hands and I kept my head
turning, trying to see everywhere at once. That rifle was
a Deane, Adams & Deane five-shot revolving-cylinder
rifle. An Englishman who was on his uppers in Frisco had
sold it to me, and I'd never seen a faster-shooting gun.

There was dew on the grass, and suddenly I saw a gray
streak in the grass . . . a difference, but it was there.
Reaching down, I picked up a stone and chucked it back
into the middle of camp and it hit near Fleming's foot.
He sat up and I lifted my rifle and pointed into the
grass where the streak stopped; somebody was crawling
there, and had brushed the dew from the grass as he
moved. There was no taking aim, I just squeezed off my
shot into the head of that wide streak.

There was a sharp movement there, and then the Sioux
came out of the gray morning, running low and running
fast. My second shot went wide, the Sioux was moving too
fast, but my third, held low down, dropped an Indian in
his tracks. On the other side of camp a rifle opened fire
and then still another from beside me. Sudden as it had
begun, the attack stopped.

Only the grass moved, rippling under the gray skies,
and leaves of the aspen whispered and chattered along the
hillside. Fleming crawled over to me. "How many did you
see?" he asked.

Reloading my Deane, Adams I laid out five extra paper
cartridges on a flat rock. If I got that many shots during the next rush I'd be mighty lucky.

"Maybe four," I said, "but if they're like Modocs
there might be fifty out there."

"You fought Modocs?" Fleming glanced at me.

"These here are Sioux," I said, "maybe they're different."

With my Bowie I dug out under my body and got deeper
into the ground. The others were doing the same, settling
down for

VERSION TWO

When we came up the valley of the Sweetwater the
frost was white on the lowlands and upon the far slope of
the mountains the aspens were clouded gold. At nineteen I
was the youngest of the lot, although for seven years
past I had done a man's work, and proud of it.

Only there was a searching in me, for I had found
nothing I wanted very much, nor any place I cared to
stop, but the softness of my face was only the softness
of being young, not of anything inside me, for when a boy
is left alone at twelve he becomes a man or he becomes
nothing at all.

Yet it was a hard land in which I'd come to manhood,
and the way I had found had never been easy, and with the
hardness this gave me there was a truculence, too, for I
had some of the urge to prove myself that is in every
boy.

There were but seven of us, and until a week or two
before we had been strangers. A week? It was more than
that, but on the trail there is a small sense of time,
and only distance by which to measure.

We were seven armed and belted men riding east from
the gold country with St. Louis a long way off. There was
the Sailor Swede and Coyle the gambler, there was Harran
who had been a trapper and Seagrave who had struck it
rich on the Feather River.

There was Fleming who had crossed the Plains seven
times, and Sheedy who had kept a store in the gold coun-

try, and there was me, Johnny Banta, born in a west-bound wagon, now going east for the first time.

We rode with Fleming at point, the Sailor and Coyle on one flank, Harran and Seagrave on the other and bringing up the rear were Sheedy and myself, and in the middle of us were the nine pack horses, three of the nine belonging to me.

We crossed the Divide short of noon and after that found the Sweetwater starting from the low hills and we rode along it, riding loose in the saddle and ready for trouble, for we'd been lucky this far and were worried by it. Too much good luck is a danger, for a man knows it must change. Back along the Humboldt we'd had a brush with the Pai-ute, but they had no stomach for what we gave them.

There was a hollow where a creek flowed down to the Sweetwater and there Fleming got down from his saddle. "We'll stop the night here," he said, and turned his eyes on me. I'd no liking for the man and knew what was coming before he opened his lips to speak. "You'll cook tonight," he said.

"I'll not," I told him straight. "Three times this week I've cooked and no complaint. We've seven here, so we share and share alike."

Coyle looked up from the fire where he was poking sticks into the new flame. He looked interested, and mildly amused.

"You talking back to me?" Fleming stared at me, but I'd been stared at before.

"Telling you," I said, "and not only for now. It's turn and turn about."

Fleming put down the pack he held in his hands and looked across the camp at me. "Now look, boy, I don't want to give you a whuppin', so do as you're told."

"Anywhere we go," I said, "I'll make tracks as big as you."

Coyle's pleasant voice intervened. "The boy's right. From the beginning he's done his share and more than his share."

"You buttin' in?" Fleming was ready for trouble but he was unsure of Coyle. He might be a man to leave alone; a gambler had to be tough to live.

"Trying to save your life," Coyle replied quietly, and from the way Fleming looked at him I knew Fleming was taking it for a warning and a threat.

"I'll cook," Sheedy interrupted hastily. "I don't mind."

Sheedy cooked, and I wished I had, it was that poor to eat, but I rustled wood for the fire and found a place to bed down with a natural hammock of earth to give me protection from the wind or bullets. With my hunting knife I cut sod and forted up a little.

"You expectin' a fight, kid?" Harran asked me. "Ever' night you build yourself a little hole to hide in. How long you gonna keep it up?"

"Until we're in St. Louis," I said, and meant it.

That night there was talk around the fire but little was said to me and none of it by Fleming. He had me marked for trouble, that much I knew, but it was no different than it had always been for me.

At daybreak I was out and around before any of them, and had killed a white-tailed deer, an easy shot at a hundred yards, and I was skinning him out when Coyle rode up. "Figured there might be trouble," he said. "I came running."

"Thanks." Rising from beside the deer, I gathered the hide around the best cuts. "Seemed a chance for some fresh meat, and as for trouble, I'm likely to find as much of that in camp as away from it."

"Fleming won't rest."

We rode back toward camp, riding side by each, and I said to Coyle, "He'll have you marked. . . . It will be trouble for you if you're seen with me."

"I'll accept that," he said, "and Seagrave will too, I think."

"Ah," I said, "now there's a thing. He's carrying plenty, I've an idea. Fleming has been watching him."

We rode on, but there was a difference now, for the unity that had been with us was gone; we were drawing apart. Coyle and Seagrave took flank together, and it might have seemed an accident, although Sailor Swede merely took the place alongside Harran and we rode east along the Sweetwater.

Our nooning was near a grassy bank, outcropped with ledges, and we built our fire close under the bank, of buffalo chips and a few scattered sticks.

We made coffee there and chewed on some jerky and gave ourselves talk about the trail behind and what lay ahead. This was Sioux country, and I'd heard a sight about the Sioux from my folks before they died, and from others in California. The Sioux were a lot of Indian . . . every one a fighting man from the high timber. At that, everything might have gone all right if Harran hadn't found that squaw.

She was young and she was walking. She was also a mighty pretty girl of maybe seventeen or a year younger. Hard to tell the age of an Indian.

She was carrying a small pack on her back and she came on us as we sat there eating, but the only one who saw her right then was me and I could see she was alone and scared, so I said nothing at all. Then Harran went down to the creek and the next thing we hear a fight.

All of us went down and Harran had caught him a squaw, and he was grinning. He looked around at Fleming and said, "Lookit here. Lookit what I found."

"Leave her alone," I said.

Harran looked at me like he hadn't heard me or couldn't understand, but Fleming knew, all right.

"Why, now," Fleming said, "finders is keepers. Ain't that right?" He looked around. "I reckon we found her, and we'll keep her, and if you want to leave her alone, Banta, you do just that. Fact of the matter is, we'll see that you do."

"Let her go," I said. "This is Sioux country. That's a Sioux squaw. You want to get us all killed?"

Nobody had said anything, although I had an idea that Coyle

VERSION THREE

When we came up the valley of the Sweetwater the frost was white on the lowlands and upon the far slope of the mountains the aspens were clouded gold. At nineteen I was the youngest of the lot, although for seven years I had done a man's work, and proud of it.

Only there was a searching in me, for I belonged no-where and had found nothing that I wanted very much, nor any place I cared to call home. It was a hard land in which I had come alone to manhood, and the way I found for myself was never easy. When a boy takes a man's place he is expected to be a man, and not a boy, so it was stand up to a man's work and a man's responsibilities, and that I did, although it caused me some bad times and some difficult hours.

There were seven of us riding east, seven who until a few days before had been strangers to one another. We were still strangers, although we rode together, shared our grub and our watchfulness, our awareness of danger.

East of us, hundreds of miles away, was St. Louis . . .
a distance not to be measured in miles but in hours of
danger, for the land we rode through was the land of the
Indian who wanted no such interlopers as we.

We were seven armed and belted men, riding with rifles across our saddles. There was the Sailor Swede,
Coyle the gambler, Harran, who had been a trapper, and
there was Seagrave, the only one of us who had done well
in the gold fields.

Fleming had crossed the Plains seven times, and
Sheedy had kept a store in the gold country, and of
course, and last of all, there was me, Johnny Banta, born
in a west-bound wagon and now going to the States for the
first time.

We rode armed for trouble, with Fleming at point, the
Sailor and Coyle upon one flank, Harran and Seagrave on
the other. Bringing up the rear were Sheedy and myself.
In our midst were our nine pack animals, three of them
belonging to me.

We crossed the Divide just short of noon, and it was
nothing akin to the Sierras, which is a fine, tall range,
but only a long roll in almost flat land . . . although
it was nigh to eight thousand feet, they said, where we
crossed over.

The Sweetwater was where we expected it would be and
for the night we camped in a hollow among sand hills.
Getting down from his saddle Fleming turned his eyes upon
me. "You'll cook tonight," he said.

"I'll not." I told him straight out. "Three times
this week I've cooked and no complaint, but we're seven
here, so we share and share alike. I'll be flunky to no
man."

Coyle had begun a fire, and there was a sparking interest and some amusement in his eyes when he looked up.
He was a pleasant man but a cynical one who derived a wry
pleasure from many a thing that would get most men's

nerves on edge. But this, I believe, he had been expecting.

"You talking back to me?" Fleming stared at me, but I'd been stared at before when I was more of a boy than I was now.

"Not talking back," I said, "but telling you. From this point on it will be turn and turn about."

Fleming put down the pack he had taken from the horse and looked at me. "If you don't want a whuppin', you do as you're told."

Now, I was not as big a man as Fleming by forty pounds, nor as tall by inches, but there is a time for all things, and one thing I'd learned was, not to be put upon.

"Anywhere we go," I said, "I'll make tracks as big as you."

"The boy's right." Coyle spoke casually, working his fire to build a bed of coals. "He's done his share and more."

"You buttin' in?" Fleming was a big man and one with an arrogant way about him that raised my hackles, but he was not too sure of Coyle, who might be a man to leave alone.

"Trying to save your life," Coyle told him, but Fleming took it as a threat from Coyle and not a warning.

"I'll cook," Sheedy spoke hastily. "I don't mind."

Sheedy cooked, and it was that bad I almost wished I'd not forced the situation, but I rustled wood for the fire before choosing a place to bed down beside a hammock of earth and grass that gave me some extra shelter from the wind, or might, if need be, stop a bullet. With my hunting knife I cut blocks of sod and forted up a mite, being of cautious nature and not my first time in Indian country.

"You scared?" Harran looked at me with a look in his eyes I cared little for. "Ever' night you build yourself a hole to hide in. How long you gonna keep it up?"

"Until St. Louis," I said, and meant it.

Trouble was shaping among my own crowd, for it was
Fleming considered himself our leader, knowing the Plains
as he did, and Fleming was a bullying man. Harran was
like him, and Sheedy a shadow for Fleming in all he did.
None of this lot knew anything of me, and I'd been thinking the only reason I was invited along was because they
had need of my horses, for horses at that time were hard
to come by.

It was curiosity taking me east, and maybe something
more, for it was in me to find a place for myself and as
yet I'd had none. There was nothing behind me but drifting and working, wherever a job could be had. A time or
two I'd tried panning gold, with no amount of luck, but
I'd saved a bit, bought myself some horses, and done some
packing for other owners of claims who worked deep in the
hills.

Coyle awakened me two hours before dawn to take over
the sentry duty, so I slid out of my blankets and rolled
them for traveling.

"All quiet," Coyle whispered, and crawled away toward
his blankets for a nap before daybreak.

It was almighty still . . . the sky touched up with
stars, and along the Sweetwater the trees and brush lying
like a winding black snake among the low hills. Soon it
would be growing light.

The night had a waiting in it, a sort of stillness
like something was set to happen. My rifle lay easy in my
hands. It was a Deane, Adams & Deane five-shot revolving-
cylinder rifle. I'd picked it up from an Englishman who
was on his uppers in Frisco, and I'd never want a better
gun.

Individual trees began to stand out from the dark,
and there was dew on the grass . . . then I saw a gray

streak there where it should not be. Picking up a small
pebble, I chucked it into the middle of camp, where it
hit near Fleming's foot. He sat up, looking at me, and I
lifted my rifle and sighted into the grass where that
streak in the grass ended. Somebody had been crawling,
brushing the dew from the grass where he crawled, so I
just squeezed off my shot into the end of that streak.

There was a movement down there, and then the Indians
came out of the grass, out of the gray morning, running
low and fast. My second shot was too quick and a miss,
but the third, held lower, dropped a Sioux in his tracks.
Beside me another rifle opened up and from the far side
of camp, another. And then no Indian could be seen, anywhere.

A faint dawn breeze stirred the grass; nothing else
moved. Reloading the Deane, Adams I laid out five extra
paper cartridges on a flat rock. If I got off half that
many shots during the next rush I'd be lucky . . . if
there was a rush.

Aspen leaves whispered. Fleming was beside me, and
Coyle off to my left. We waited through long minutes and
then Seagrave calmly slipped back into the hollow, just a
few yards behind us, and stirred up the fire and put on
the coffeepot. If a man was going to fight, he had to
eat. That was Seagrave's thinking and for my mind it was
right.

How many had we got? Studying the situation, it
looked like the two I'd nailed were the only ones, although the Swede thought he might have barked one. Their
surprise had failed and by now it was full light although
the sun wasn't over the eastern ridge.

Our situation was good. We had a fine field of fire
in every direction and some shelter for ourselves. In the
bottom of the hollow a man could stand almost upright
without being seen and we had both grub and water, so if
the fight continued we wouldn't run short for several

days. Our horses were in the hollow with us, as safe as
we were ourselves. So far, after that first attack we
had seen no Indians anywhere, but I didn't like the look
of it.

Harran wanted to go on.

"They've gone, so we'd best push on before they bring
help."

"If these were Modocs," I said, "they'd still be out
there. I don't figure Sioux are much different."

Waiting gets a man. It works on him, and nobody knows
that better than an Indian. He also knows that most white
men are the get-up-and-get-at-it type who have no patience. Therefore an Indian usually figures if he waits a
white man will move and give him a chance. That was what
Harran was all for doing, and Sheedy and the Swede were
right with him.

Not me. Not Johnny Banta. One time I nearly got my
fool head shot off like that, and nobody needs to show me
twice. In this sort of fighting, a man doesn't get many
mistakes. Mostly he gets a chance to make only one.

"You want to move," I said, "you go ahead. But you
leave my horses here."

"Suppose we decide to take them?" Harran was a mean
one, a most trying man.

"Why, anytime you get your mind made up," I said,
"you just try. Only there's two Indians out there with my
mark on them who offered a slight less target than you do
right now."

Harran, he didn't know what to make of me. He figured
me for a kid who wasn't dry behind the ears yet, but he
had seen me shoot, a time or two. He just wasn't sure.

"I believe Johnny is right," Seagrave said. "I believe there are still Indians out there."

So nobody went anywhere right then. The wind stirred
the grass out front and the sun came up and when the sun
was over the hill in our eyes, they came out of the grass

again, running swiftly, and shooting as they came. Fleming was quick; he shot fast and an Indian fell, and then
the rest of us were shooting and the attack stopped
again.

Harran had nothing to say about that, nor anybody,
all of them realizing how some would have been dead had
they tried to leave. It wasn't that I was smarter than
anybody, I had fought Indians before, was all, and maybe
I was more scared. Nobody wants to die at nineteen.

They pulled out then. The Sioux weren't a big party
and they decided there was easier hunting. They pulled
out, so a short time after, we left, riding away in the
same formation as before.

Only there was friction among us. Fleming didn't like
me, nor did Harran. Coyle had nothing to say; a watching
man like him couldn't be expected to take sides until the
last minute, if at all. Seagrave rode up to me and said
something that had been on my mind.

"Johnny, I think you're my friend, and I'm a man who
needs friends."

"Well, now."

"I mean it. I need friends, boy and you know why."

Fleming, Harran, Sheedy, and the Swede, they were
going back empty. Sheedy might have had a little put by,
but mighty little, and this was a lonesome country where
a man might die and no questions asked. Seagrave might be
just realizing that, but I'd had it in mind for some time
now, ever since I began to get windward of Harran.

He was a hungry man . . . hungry for all the things
he thought he deserved. A hungry man and one eaten by
envy and dislike is a dangerous man when opportunity offers, and here with us was Seagrave carrying gold home to
the States, and a lot of gold at that.

The Sailor Swede was a hard man. Big, powerful, and
sullen, he was a man with a violent temper and unless I
was mistaken, killing lay behind him. He was a fit one to

walk beside Harran, and Sheedy would follow the two of
them.

Fleming? The man did not like me, and he was a man
big with his own sense of importance, and little enough
reason for it. I did not know about Fleming, nor about
Coyle, for that matter. It was beginning to look as if it
might be Seagrave and me against the lot.

For I'd seen what he saw. Fleming staring into the
fire of a night, remembering that he was returning from
gold fields with nothing to show, and no answer to the
questions he would be getting except the admission of
failure. It comes hard for any man, but harder still for
one like Fleming. And there was Harran, hating and full
of envy, the Swede wanting gold for women and liquor, and
there was Sheedy, a coyote ready to snatch at the wolves'
leavings.

That I was one with Seagrave was a natural thing.
First, I was disliked, and secondly I owned some of the
horses, which were themselves worth a price. And they had
seen me friendly with Seagrave.

It was a far-off place, the California we had left
behind, where we had all been friendly enough, joining
together for the long trek across the Plains, and shaking
hands around, or eating together. Now that trouble had
come on us there were divisions obvious to us that had
not been so easily seen before.

We rode on, and after a time Seagrave dropped back
and offered to take the place of Sheedy, who gave up
willingly, not liking me, nor the dust we both had to
eat. So Seagrave rode beside me, and not another word was
said about what might come, only he talked of his family
in Vermont and what would come to them if anything happened to him.

There was nobody anywhere who gave a thought to me,
but I'd no wish to feed the buzzards or the coyotes out
on a grassy hillside somewhere, so we made it up between

us that one of us would always be awake and watchful. And that was the way it was right up until we came upon the woman.

Only she was no woman, only a girl. A scared girl of sixteen or so . . . there in the middle of nowhere.

Fleming was well out in front and when he saw her running along the grassy slope he drew up his horse, and we all bunched, a bad thing to do, and stared at that girl in the gray dress running like a frightened deer along the slope.

At first we thought she was chased by Indians, but there were no Indians in sight. We waited, wanting to rush into nothing but what we could handle.

"Must be a wagon train close by," Sheedy suggested.

"Off the trail," Fleming objected. "They hold farther south where there's fewer hills."

"Let's go," Coyle said. "That girl needs help."

———————————— LT ————————————

COMMENTS: This is how many of L'Amour novels got started. A number of tries, getting the tone or the particulars of the first scene or first few chapters set up. Sometimes the differences between the different versions were very minor, sometimes radically different. Then something would click and the narrative would take off . . . or it wouldn't. Quite a few of the story fragments in this book are pieced together from a number of parallel attempts such as these. Cutting and pasting them together I have tried to present a version that shows off the most complete vision or most interesting aspects of what Dad was trying to create.

These three attempts contain a favored plot of Louis's: a tough group of guys and a stash of money that isn't going to be big enough for the ones who steal it to share. What role the girl was going to play and why she was changed from Indian to white is anyone's guess.

Louis experimented many times with "the tough guys and a bunch of money" concept ... to the point where I've wondered if it was something he'd actually confronted in real life. The idea shows up in a couple of other places here in *Louis L'Amour's Lost Treasures*. In fact, we'll see it again and I'll discuss it a bit more thoroughly before we get to the end of this book.

JAVA DIX

The Beginning of a Crime Story

When I woke up that morning I was broke. Not even coffee money. Out on the street there was a slow rain falling and I walked along, wondering what to do. I was two days back in town from the Far East and I didn't know anybody.

Finally I stopped on a corner and was just standing there when this Buick convertible drove by. There was a girl in it with auburn hair. She was lovely . . . so lovely it made a guy catch his breath and start to hurt down inside. I watched the car until it turned the corner. Then, just as I was starting across the street, the convertible came up again and this girl stopped the car and looked at me.

She was young. Not more than twenty. Only the way she looked at me wasn't young . . . she looked me over.

"Want to make some quick money?"

"Sure," I said, and she opened the car door and I got in.

This babe I didn't figure. She was no tramp. Every
lino of hor broathod olass. Nor oould I figuro tho youth
of her along with that wise way in which she examined me.
The two things just didn't go together.

We drove on for a couple of minutes and neither of us
said anything. She had good legs, but I tried not to
think of that. This babe wasn't on the make and she
wasn't likely to go for a busted drifter.

"You," she said, not looking at me, "you haven't had
breakfast, have you?"

"No." I switched to tho far sido of tho soat whoro I
could look at her. "How'd you figure that?"

"It's nine o'clock," she said, "and you just came out
on the street. You walked past a diner and you walked
past a good restaurant. They wouldn't let you make coffee
in that hotel where you stayed. Then you stopped on the
corner looking around. You didn't know where you were
going. I'll bet you're broke."

"You're a smart kid."

"And you're a stranger in town."

"How'd you figure that one?"

"The way you look at the signs, the way you walked.
The way you hesitated on the street like you weren't sure
about the traffic."

"You do a lot of figuring. What's the gimmick? What
d'you want?"

"I want a man," she said quietly, "with nerve enough
to tackle hell with a bucket of water."

That about floored me. Somehow it didn't figure, not
this girl needing help, and not the way she asked for it.
She swung the car around a corner and pulled up at a
small restaurant. "They don't know me in here," she said,
"and it won't be busy now. We'll go to that booth almost
to the back. We can talk while you eat."

We got out of the car and went in. She was wearing a

green raincoat and she walked quickly, not minding the rain on her hair. We took a table and she watched me eat. And then over her coffee she started to talk. But not until after she had pumped me for plenty.

Me? I'm a big guy, not heavy. I weigh only one-seventy, but I'm six-two. I can do a lot of things, none of them usual and not many of them legitimate.

Name? They call me Java, and my last name is Dix. Merchant seaman, lumberjack, placer miner in New Guinea, and pearl poacher. I was with the OSS during the war and afterwards a freelance journalist. . . . That's the quick version. Fights? I've won and I've lost, but I won more than I lost and got off the floor a few times to win.

I can talk nine languages like I was born to them. I'm proud of that.

"I need a man," she said, "who has nerve and brains. I'm in trouble, real trouble."

"Somebody else is in trouble," I said, "not you."

She smiled a little, hesitated, then nodded. "Yes, you're right. It's my mother."

"If your mother is in trouble," I said, "then it would be your father you took after."

She smiled again, only this time it was not just a mechanical smile, it was warm and beautiful. "You're right," she said, "but my father is dead. If he were here I'd never have stopped you. I wouldn't have been looking for you."

"He must have been quite a guy."

"Dad was wonderful," she said quietly. "He was honest, and he had nerve. You would have liked him," she said, and suddenly she looked at me, a little surprised, "and he would have liked you."

"Fathers don't like seeing drifters with their daughters. Drifters without money."

"He would understand. He had been a drifter himself.

Only he was rich when he died. He made it in the oil fields. He was a big man," she said, "with red-gray hair, and--"

"Slasher Hannegan," I said, "he was Slasher Hannegan, of Spindletop, of Seminole, of Tampico and Balikpapan."

She stared at me, and tears came into her eyes. "You knew him? It . . . it's unbelievable!"

"Worked for him, kid. I worked for him in Tampico. I was a tool-dresser. I worked on a tower for him in Borneo. That was ten years ago. And I remember you now, all freckles and knees, living in a house on the bluff above the road that wound around from the port to the Dutch Club."

It was crazy, but there it was. She had picked up a tough-looking drifter off the street when she needed help, and I had worked for her old man. Only it wasn't so strange, in some ways. A lot of tough men had worked for her father during the wild days of the oil booms.

We were both quiet then, and after a while she said, "It's almost like he led me to you. I was desperate. I knew what he would have done, and knew I could not do it, so I started looking for the right sort of man. Yesterday I looked. I went to bar rooms, I rode along the docks, I looked everywhere . . . and then I saw you."

She opened her purse and took out five twenties. She handed them across the table. "That's a stake, Java. That's for nothing. That's what Dad would have given any man of his old crew if he was broke. You take it from Dad, and pay it back when you can."

Once the money was in my pocket she did not waste any more time.

"My mother drinks," she told me. "She drinks too much. She never drank when Dad was alive, and she never had reason to." She looked me right in the eye and said quietly, "My mother needs a man. When Dad was around, she was all right. She was happy. . . . Now she isn't happy anymore and she drinks. And sometimes when she is drinking she goes out."

This was tough for her. I could see how tough, only this kid was game. She must have been living with this for a long time, and it had not been easy.

"Usually she went out of town, but once it was the wrong man."

"Blackmail?"

"Yes . . . but not just a little blackmail. He wants it all . . . everything."

"You've talked to him?"

"Yes"--she looked up from her coffee--"he includes me."

Something in me started to get mad then. It was bad enough to take advantage of a woman's weakness, but to get this girl into it . . . "He's got evidence?"

"Yes."

"You said he wanted all of it? There's a lot?"

"There's eleven million, more or less," she said quietly. "But it isn't the money. It's mother, and it's Dave."

"Dave?"

"My brother. He's to be married soon, a girl from--a very prissy family."

I grinned. "I take it your brother doesn't take after your dad."

Little by little the story shaped itself. But there was something about it that did not quite fit. Her mother, I gathered, was just forty, a lush and lovely woman. She had been closemouthed, however, even when drinking, but somehow this one particular man had found out exactly who she was, and he had come to town, looked the situation over, and then moved in with his demands.

"She's already given him money?"

"Several times . . . about four thousand dollars."

She waited while the waitress filled our cups, then
she said, "He's not in it alone. There's somebody else."
    "What did you want me to do?"
    "Find out all who are involved. Get the evidence.
Prints, proof, everything."

COMMENTS· There is a nice reference to some of Louis's personal
travels hiding in this story. When he writes

        . . . a house on the bluff above the road that
    wound around from the port to the Dutch Club.

Louis is talking about Balikpapan, a town on the Borneo coast, now
part of Kalimantan, Indonesia. He visited there while working on a

Louis Lamoore in Balikpapan, Netherlands' East Indies.

tramp freighter in the 1920s. Seeing that it was part of the Netherlands' East Indies at the time, it was literally a club for the local Dutch
residents. Louis claimed that, on certain evenings, they ran movies
that, back in the States, would have been considered very out-of-date . . .
seeing that this was still in the period before sound, I have always
wondered exactly how old these films were!

INVESTMENT IN CHARACTER

A Treatment for a Western Story

Bill Ryan, carrying ten thousand dollars, is en route west to meet his future bride and her father. The money is to be paid for a partnership in a going business that promises well, and Bill is enthusiastic over his prospects. His girl's father has never approved of Bill, but has resigned himself to the inevitable--but Bill must produce the ten thousand to prove he is able to care for the girl and to provide a good living for her. The money is Bill's entire savings, combined with a small inheritance he has had since he was a child.

On the train he meets a kindly old gentleman who is both interested and sympathetic. He kids Bill about losing his freedom, and quotes frequently, among others the quote from Kipling,

"Pleasant the snaffle of courtship, improving
the manners and carriage.
But the colt who is wise will abstain from
the terrible thorn-bit of marriage."

At the hotel Bill finds his girl and her father will
not arrive until the following day and he is restless,
with time on his hands. His kindly old friend introduces
Bill to a tall, polished man who is "in the mining business" and the three have dinner together and Bill hears
much talk of "leads," "drifts," and "ore bodies" and is
impressed. The mining man picks up the check. Later, with
time hanging heavy on their hands, the mining man suggests a poker game to the old man. Both advise Bill to
stay out of it, but he decides to play a few hands. He
feels that his luck is in--that he can't lose.

And he wins, wins again--three straight pots. Then he
loses, wins again, loses, and wins twice more. Now well
ahead of the game, he is feeling good. He gets an excellent hand, and the betting runs high. Before he realizes
it he is out of his winnings and deep into the ten
thousand--and he loses. Then he wins and loses again.
Soon he is winning only small, occasional pots, but losing the big ones.

Disgusted, most of his money gone, he suggests they
call it off, and the others agree--though they all know
he still has well over two thousand dollars.

They leave the room and he sits there, then gets up
and paces around the room. Worried and restless. He drops
into the chair where the mining man had been seated,
starts to get up, but his fingertips brush something
pushed down between the side of the chair and the cush-
ion. He reaches back and draws out--an ace of spades!
Then the ace of hearts, and then the other two aces follow!

He has been cheated!

Then it all adds up: the old man on the train, his
own free talk about what he was going to do, his plans,
etc. The arrival in town, introduction, and the game. He
is enraged, but suddenly, he has a plan. Most of all, the
old man's continual quotations irritate him. He had be-

lieved them an amusing quirk; now that the man has been
revealed as a card shark, Bill's attitude is less toler-
ant.

At breakfast he meets the men, comments on the fact
that he is down to his last two thousand, and says he
might as well go for all or nothing.

Bill now knows their pattern. They will let him win a
couple of small pots, then get into a big one--and they
will see that he has what he thinks is a good hand--and
then they will take him. He doubts if they will delay
long.

As expected, he rakes in a couple of small pots. He
has carefully watched the mining man and noticed that his
hands have not been off the table. Bill Ryan is dealt two
queens and two kings. He discards the fifth card and
draws--another king!

A full house.

He acts--shows excitement--digs out another wad of
bills (actually, it is a Kansas City bankroll: newspaper
wrapped in a few bills), and gambling on their belief in
his gullibility, he ups the ante until everything he has
is in the pot, and all the money they have won from him.
He sees the gambler's hand drop from the table as if to
ease his position a little, and Bill Ryan calls--and
spreads his cards on the table: queen and four aces!

The mining man and his companion stare blankly at the
aces and Bill places a pistol on the table. "Brought it
along for rattlesnakes," he comments, and rakes in the
pot, stuffing the money into his pockets, and easing from
the room.

The two crooks sit staring at each other, then the
old man explodes with anger. "You had those aces!" he
shouts. "You had them in the chair!"

The mining man springs up, and the two lift the cush-
ion. A neat white typewritten card is in the position
where they had left the cards, on it the words:

"Lie to a liar, for lies are his coin; steal from
a thief, for that is easy; lay a trap for the trickster and catch him at the first attempt, but beware
of an honest man!"

COMMENTS: This feels like a treatment for a half-hour TV episode, but I have no idea if it was intended for any particular show. From the late forties until the sixties, there were dozens of "anthology series" on the air, shows where every episode was a different story with different characters. Some of these were exclusively Western and many others would accept Western genre materials. In the 1950s, other short stories and treatments of Louis's were purchased for shows like *Rebound, Fireside Theater, Ford Television Theatre, Climax!, Schlitz Playhouse,* and *Chevron Hall of Stars.* Selling quickly sketched out ideas like this one or repurposing old short stories was an additional way for Dad to scrape together some money. He also sold or created episode concepts for reoccurring character series like *Tales of Wells Fargo, Maverick, The Texan, Sugarfoot, City Detective,* and *Cowboy G-Men.*

Dad's relationship with Hollywood was as much a relationship with the TV industry as it was with feature films. *Cowboy G-Men* was produced as early as 1952, and he also wrote the pilot for 1956's *Hart of Honolulu,* which, if picked up, might have been TV's first "private detective in Hawaii" crime drama.

THE GOLDEN TAPESTRY

The Beginning of an Adventure Novel, and a Treatment

CHAPTER I

He lay upon his face in the wet sand, a tall old man
in shabby clothes, and looking down at the body, Ballantyne knew it had begun again, but this time he did not
know why.

It was an austere face, judging by the side of it he
could see, with a high-bridged nose and prominent cheekbones, a face worn and old, but strong with lines of
character and determination. Poor, he might have been,
but this man had been proud also.

Glancing swiftly to right and left, then along the
rim of the cliff above, and seeing no one, Ballantyne
lifted the edge of the worn coat and checked the pockets. . . . They were empty. The coat, no doubt purchased
secondhand years before, bore no label.

Gently, Ballantyne lifted the old man's hands, for
the hands of a man are revealing, and often tell more
than his face or the few odds and ends his pockets may
contain. These were strong hands, calloused but agile.

Ballantyne had seen those callouses before. These were the hands of a weaver, a weaver of rugs.

The dead man was unknown to Ballantyne, but the three stab wounds in the kidney indicated the hand of Mustafa Bem. In Samarkand, Damascus, and Kashgar, Ballantyne had seen similar wounds, and he needed no autopsy to know the blade had been long and thin, the blows hard-driven and slanted sharply upward.

Yet Bem took no action without orders. Somehow this old man had incurred the displeasure of Leon Decebilus, and soon so might Villette Mallory unless Ballantyne moved with extreme care.

Villette Mallory was alone, and unaware the man she had so recently met, Leon Decebilus, was one of the most ruthless criminals in the Near East. No matter the mask of refinement and culture he might have assumed, Decebilus was a ruthless and violent man, intolerant of interference and utterly without scruples.

Ballantyne stood up, and then walked quickly away from the body and mounted the cliff by a rarely used path. The last thing he wished was to become involved in an investigation by provincial authorities.

When his eyes cleared the edge of the cliff, Ballantyne paused and swept the area with a swift, practiced attention. Assured that he was unobserved, he went up quickly, and proceeded to stroll carelessly along the ancient path that skirted the cliff's edge.

The narrow beach where the body lay was on the shore of the Gulf of Izmit, known in classical times as the Gulf of Nicomedia, in Asiatic Turkey. Some fifty miles from Istanbul, the former capital of the once-great Byzantine empire, the Gulf was off the beaten track.

Whatever the reason for this man's death, it had to be big, for Leon Decebilus no longer involved himself in petty crimes--the thief, spy, panderer, blackmailer, and murderer had come into wealth and power.

Even the law moved warily where he was concerned, for
he was an international figure with friends in high
places, and he had been shrewd enough to implicate or involve them in his own dealings, involve them to such a
degree that their fortunes depended upon the success of
his.

The dead man obviously had been unaware of the risks
involved in dealing with Decebilus, a fatal disadvantage
in such affairs. That certainly could not be said of Ballantyne, but what of Villette Mallory? Did she recognize
the manner of man Decebilus was? Could she?

Ballantyne swore bitterly and impatiently, and he was
not an impatient or bitter man. He knew why he was getting involved, but he did not understand what was behind
the curious chain of events that had led him to this
place.

He was involved because of Villette. You are, he told
himself, a silly romantic fool. No, a guilty fool. And
guilt is never a good reason to dig yourself in deeper.

He was a man who lived by his wits, he told himself.
He liked this explanation better. Wherever Decebilus
showed his hand there was a profit to be made and where
there was a profit he could make it as easily as Decebilus. Well, almost.

Turning from the track along the cliffs, Ballantyne
walked through the short grass and up the slight slope to
the ruins. The area was known as Eski Hissar, Turkish for
"old castle," but the Byzantine tower for which it was
named was only one among the many ruins along the Gulf of
Izmit.

They were unimpressive ruins, without boldness or
beauty: a few crumbling walls, scattered stones, and
grass-covered mounds. The walls that remained were often
constructed of stones from still older walls; even the

most ancient ruins in sight had been built from the
stones of others.

On the crest of the hill not far away, tall cypresses
marked the tomb of Hannibal, and from that vantage point
one could look over the slope below and see an incredible
maze, design interwoven with design, the outlines of
walls invisible on the ground itself.

Seating himself among the ruins where he could observe without being observed, Ballantyne took the camera
strap from his shoulder and placed the camera beside him
on the grass.

A camera, he had discovered, automatically marked one
as a tourist, and tourists were apt to be regarded as
harmless, somewhat blundering and gullible creatures inclined to go almost anywhere. The camera was a visible
passport to almost anywhere but a military zone.

To Ballantyne all ruins were interesting, and from
time to time he emerged from such ruins with a stone tab-
let, an ancient vase, or even a fine stone head. Discreetly removed and even more discreetly disposed of,
such odds and ends had solved his financial difficulties
on more than one occasion. But today he was not scouting
such a midnight dig--there was larger game afoot. The
dead man had affirmed that suspicion.

Ballantyne settled back to wait. Warm and lazy under
the sun, the slope from where he waited was freshened by
a gentle breeze from off the Sea of Marmara and the Gulf.
If life had taught him nothing else, it had taught him
patience.

Yet when the gray car appeared, he felt a premonitory
chill. It left the village and came slowly along the goat
track, a track rarely used by carts, never by cars. The
Renault grumbled cautiously along the crumbling edge of
the cliff toward the ruins.

That they returned at all to where the body had been
left was evidence of their concern. The track they fol-

lowed led only from the nearby village to the pastures
beyond. Yet it might be possible, if one were a skillful
driver, to follow the track along the shore, over the
ridge, and then by a woodcutter's trail through the dark
patch of forest beyond. A dirt road somewhere over there
connected with the highway from Ankara to Istanbul. No
car had made the trip but in years past it had occasionally been done by carts.

He watched the gray car coming slowly along the
track; his own position concealed him and he had chosen
it for that reason. He was known to both Barbaro and Mustafa Bem.

Across the blue waters of the Gulf he could see
the thickly wooded shores that ended in the promontory
known as Boz Burun, and at the farthest point on the
southern horizon he could just make out the peak of the
Bithynian Mount Olympus. The closest town was the fishing
village Gebze, but, as with many places in this corner
of the world, history complicated the simplest of things.
Gebze had once been Libyssa, the spot where Hannibal had
spent his last years, hiding from the power of Rome. It
was there, in 183 B.C., he had taken poison to avoid capture.

Yet, he had fooled them at last, in one respect at
least, for the vast treasure he was known to have with
him disappeared when he died. Vanished also were the hollow bronze statues, gods sacred to Phoenicia and Carthage, which he had brought with him from Crete to
Nicomedia.

More than one adventurer, wandering soldier, goatherd
or peasant had entertained himself with the thought of
what he could do if he found that treasure, yet the story
was but one of many told along this coast. War and trouble lead men to conceal their riches, always with a plan
to return and recover them, but slavery, imprisonment, or
death have a way of intervening. How many such treasures

might lie buried within a hundred miles of Istanbul? Or even within the city itself?

The gray car had stopped some forty yards off, near the ragged boy who tended a flock of goats that grazed among the ruins. Mustafa Bem got out of the car, looking as lean and savage as ever, and called to the boy.

"Have you seen a blue Maserati? A blue car driven by a woman?"

The boy walked toward them, accompanied by his sheep-dog. "There may have been a car. I was far up the hill-side."

"Where does this road go?"

"It does not go. It is always here. For twelve years I have been coming here and the road is always as it is."

"Where does it end, boy?"

"The road has an end? Each road leads to another, yes? So all the roads of the world begin here at our feet."

Mustafa Bem grew impatient. "Do people come here? Strangers, I mean?"

The boy shrugged. "Why should they come? Here there are only the grass and my goats."

"The blue car . . . did it go on?"

"There are only pastures and forest beyond. I was with the goats. Perhaps the blue car went back when it discovered this was not a road for cars." Mustafa Bem returned to the Renault and talked to someone within.

The air was clear and their voices could be heard, but Ballantyne could no longer distinguish the words. He had not heard the woman's car or seen it, but neither would have been possible during the time he had spent on the beach. Had he missed his chance . . . ?

Mustafa Bem got into the Renault and drove on, but no great distance, for where the track ran past the base of the ruined tower the cliff's edge was of crumbling rock. Only a fool would try to go further unless on foot, and

for a minute or two the issue was in doubt and Ballantyne
watched them in amusement. At last they backed up, turned
around, and started back.

There was a route through the ruins, a route Ballantyne had himself located when he scouted the area on his
first visit. Ballantyne had the tactician's distaste for
a cul-de-sac. Was it not Plautus who said that not even a
mouse trusted himself to one hole only?

The goatherd seemed concerned only with his flock,
but Ballantyne was sure the boy also watched the car. He
was a thin boy of something around twelve years, with
large, expressive eyes and an olive skin. Yet he wore his
rags with a savoir faire that went beyond mere assurance.
Ballantyne had seen the boy on each of his previous visits and they had nodded to one another in passing but
they had not talked.

When the gray Renault disappeared in the direction of
Istanbul, the boy walked to where Ballantyne sat among
the ruins. Squatting upon his heels, the boy looked where
Ballantyne was looking.

"You see something?"

"I look at the sea . . . sometimes at the ruins."

"The sea?"

"I find it beautiful. The ruins, also."

The goatherd scarcely glanced at the time-blackened
stones. "The ruins are no good, even for goats. The roofs
have fallen in."

The boy glanced again at Ballantyne. "Why do you look
at the sea and not at the goats? I think the goats are
more beautiful than the sea. Look at them!"

To please the boy, Ballantyne turned to look at the
goats. Some two dozen of them browsed or reclined upon
the hillside. The boy seemed pleased that Ballantyne appeared to agree.

"They are not my goats," he explained, "but someday I
shall own goats. Perhaps as many as these. Then you shall

see beauty! They shall be as white clouds upon the green
sky of the hillside."

He glanced at the camera, leaning over it, curiously.
"You have a machine. What is it for?"

"To make pictures. I shall want some pictures of the
sea and of the ruins."

"Of the goats, too?"

To please him, Ballantyne agreed. "Yes, and of the
goats, too."

The reply seemed to satisfy the goatherd on that
score, but he still seemed restless and puzzled. Gravely,
they exchanged introductions. The boy's name was Rashid.
Ballantyne waited, aware of the boy's curiosity, and
aware that in some way he himself was undergoing examina-
tion.

There was something here the goatherd failed to com-
prehend. He broached the subject to Ballantyne as one
gentleman to another. "You make pictures of the sea, the
sky, and the ruins. Of the goats, too. Why do you do
this?"

"To catch their beauty, and to hold it. Then I can
look whenever I like."

"But why a picture? They are here! You can see them
without a picture."

"For you they are here, for you they will remain, but
I shall go away and it is good to have something with
which to remember. I shall look many times at the picture
and will see all this as I knew it today."

"You need a picture for this?" The boy was astonished. "I remember without a machine. I can remember the
goats, each one of them." He considered the problem, and
suddenly his expression brightened. "Ah, then! The machine is your memory! It is very strange to remember with
a machine."

Neither of them spoke for several minutes, each in
his own way marveling at the wonders of the world. "I

have heard men speak of this," the boy said, "that you have machines for everything. I should not like that."

Ballantyne watched the changing light on the sea and the shore. If the Maserati had come and gone it was not his plan to remain longer, but the conversation left him dissatisfied. He had an amusing feeling that he had, somehow, been bested.

He offered the boy a cigarette, which was accepted gravely.

"You have been here before," the boy said.

"Several times."

"Not many come to the ruins. Most who do merely look and go away." The boy lit his cigarette and puffed shrewdly, cupping it in his hand as do those who smoke much in the wind. "I think you come for a reason, and I do not think it is because of the machine or the pictures."

The kid was observant and he had something to say that he hadn't gotten around to yet. Ballantyne watched the white puffballs of cloud over the far, wooded shore.

"You have a woman?" the boy asked, finally.

"No."

"No woman? It is good for a man to have a woman."

"No doubt." It was a conclusion Ballantyne had no wish to debate. "And you? Do you have a woman?" He asked the question in all seriousness.

It was accepted in the same manner. "No, I am young for a woman and they can be much trouble."

The comment seemed to explain much. The boy smoked in silence and Ballantyne waited for him to speak.

"Do you have goats at home?"

"No," Ballantyne confessed, "I have no goats."

"A camel, perhaps?" Rashid was giving him every chance to prove himself a man of substance.

"No, I have no camel." Inspiration came to him. "Once I owned two horses."

Rashid pondered the matter. "It is good to have
horses, but a horse is like a woman. It is unproductive.
If you have a horse or a woman you must also have goats."

"I think you come here for a reason and I do not
think it is because of the machine." Rashid repeated himself. Ballantyne said nothing but the boy seemed to be
arriving at a decision. "There is a woman who comes to
this hillside," Rashid said. Then glancing at Ballantyne
as if to challenge his disbelief, he added, "A woman with
a rug."

When the quarry is sighted the hunter moves with caution. Ballantyne waited for several moments before he
asked, "She sits on a rug?"

"She looks at a rug. She sits on the grass, or sometimes on the stones. She is very beautiful," he added,
"and not old." Then reluctantly, "She is more beautiful
than the goats."

It was a compliment of the highest order. "That cannot be," Ballantyne said positively. "How could a woman
be more beautiful than goats?"

"It is difficult to believe," Rashid admitted.

A dead weaver . . . a woman with a rug. A pattern was
emerging.

"She comes often?"

"She is here now." Rashid got to his feet. "She has
much trouble, this woman, and she has no man."

"You protected her from the men in the gray car,"
Ballantyne suggested. "I know them, and they are evil
men."

Rashid looked at Ballantyne with interest. "You speak
Turkish then?"

"I am a man of many tongues." Ballantyne paused, and
then he took the plunge, knowing what icy depths lay before him. "I will help her if I can."

"Come, I will show you."

The woman was Villette Mallory.

The magazines called her "The Incomparable Villette," and whether it was modeling the latest design from Christian Dior or Jacques Fath or dropping a playful wink while presenting a cut-glass bottle of perfume, the term suited her.

On this day she wore a gray suit and a blouse of pale blue, and her hair, a dark auburn, was tied with a scarf of the same shade as the blouse. Her eyes were green and her cheekbones high, the bone structure of her face delicate yet strong.

This moment was what Ballantyne had come for. And, he feared, so had the old man on the beach.

"My friend Rashid has come to me with the story of a beautiful woman who sits among the ruins and looks at a rug. Being a romanticist, naturally, I came."

"A romanticist?"

"A romanticist when I think of women, Madame, a realist when I deal with them."

She measured him with cool eyes. He was a tall, athletic-looking man, something more than thirty. He was tailored well, if casually, but there was something indefinably down-at-heel about him, the sense that his fortunes had ebbed and flowed like the tides.

"Who are you?"

Rashid squatted upon his thin, bare heels and looked upon Ballantyne with dispassionate eyes, as if to say, "You know nothing of goats, let us see how you do with a woman."

"It is a question I have often asked of myself, Madame, but who can reply to such a question? Born of woman, I am a man . . . possessing no fortune and no family; it has been left to me to live by knowing, and if I have no wit, Madame, I have at least wits, and I live by them."

She wore no makeup today and was even more beautiful than he remembered, but it was not a cool classical beauty. There was some humor that showed in her eyes, but there was sadness too.

"One more thing I have, that is curiosity, and curiosity opens windows upon the world. And . . . I know something of rugs."

Something happened then, for her eyes were suddenly no longer green, but hazel, almost yellow, like the eyes of a leopard in the jungle.

"Do you know me, then?"

"Let us say that I have seen you several times before this. . . . Madame was in Honfleur, at the Auberge du Cheval Blanc. You were motoring along the coast and you had stopped for lunch. The food there is quite good."

"And there have been other times?"

"Twice in the Mouski marketplace in Cairo. The first time I sat at an adjoining table listening to your voice and enjoying your profile. The Marquis was quite annoyed."

"And the second?"

"I sold you an antique ring . . . a lovely green stone."

Her eyes were cold. "I remember the stone. It was fake."

"It was, Madame, and I regret it, but at the moment I had nothing else to sell. I would make it up to you if you would let me."

"I think you are a thief, if not worse."

"One lives as one can."

Ballantyne seated himself on the wall facing her. He was, she reflected, a graceful man for one so lean and tall. He handled himself like a fencer or a boxer.

"For example," he said, "by this time Madame has guessed that my being here is no accident. I came to meet you."

"That's absurd. How could you know I would be here? Or that having been here, I would come again?"

"It was a slight gamble, but there are few secrets in the East, Madame, and as I have said, I am a curious man.

"For example, your husband, the late Maharajah of Kasur, was an ardent sportsman. Suddenly, on the eve of an important polo match, he withdraws. His withdrawal was a serious blow to the chances of his team, and he was known as an honorable man. Nothing but a matter of life and death could cause such a last-minute withdrawal.

"Then came the news of his death in a plane crash while en route to Istanbul. Why the sudden flight? Why Istanbul?

"These questions sharpened my curiosity, and as I have said, there are no secrets in the East. I heard rumors, made discreet inquiries.

"Your late husband, like many others, had lost his estates when India and Pakistan were divided. He settled large sums of money on old family retainers . . . he was forced to modify his way of living . . . and still he owed many debts.

"Then a most curious thing. This Maharajah who had only a small income by his former standards recently assured his creditors that all would be paid . . . within a month."

"So?"

"So one could only assume that he expected, somehow, to come into a quite large sum of money from some hitherto undisclosed source. Then the unexplained flight to Istanbul, so I asked myself . . . was the money here?

"There was also a disturbing story. That in deciding to fly here the Maharajah knew that he caused his own death. The whisper was that had he not died in the plane crash he would have died in another way, and soon."

"Why would anyone wish to kill him?"

"That was what I asked myself. But behind many murders there is a matter of money. Somehow, in some way, he was coming into money and somebody else wanted it. It is as simple as that."

She was thoughtful, but finally she asked, "Do you have a name?"

"I am called Ballantyne."

"Merely Ballantyne? Nothing else?"

"If you must have more, I am Michael Surendranath Ballantyne. My mother was of a Rajput family of an ancient line. She named me for a great teacher, a scholar. I fear I have not lived up to her hopes."

"My husband was a Rajput."

"I know. . . . That is among the reasons I am here today, along with the ring." He paused. "Ballantyne is enough. Throughout Asia they know that name."

"I am impressed."

"You need not be. I am a dealer in chance, a liaison man, a go-between, an arranger of meetings. I said that I live by my wits, but it is equally true that I live by whom, and what, I know."

Her handbag, a large one, lay open on the rock before her, the open side within easy reach of her hand.

"For example, you have a gun in your bag. You will not need that for me, but keep it close. Today you lunched with Leon Decebilus."

"So?"

"He is a thief, and a master of thieves."

"I doubt if he would spy on me so obviously as you have done."

Ballantyne turned to the goatherd. "A gray car came along the track a short time ago. What did they wish to know?"

"They asked if I had seen a blue car with a woman driving it."

"You see? The men in that Renault were Mustafa Bem and Barbaro, and where they are, Decebilus is. They are his men."

Her eyes were cold. "I am sure you are mistaken. We have mutual friends. Mr. Decebilus is a financier, a respected man."

"If you said 'feared' rather than 'respected' I would accept that." He nodded toward the cliffs. "Walk down to the shore and you will find a tall old man in shabby clothes lying dead upon the sand. He was killed by Mustafa Bem. You are in greater danger than you realize."

She looked startled. "A dead man? Down there?"

"Do you know this old man?"

"With a scarred jaw?" She was thoughtful. "About sixty? In a worn black suit?

"He came to my hotel the day I arrived and wished to buy a rug from me. He said it was for sentimental reasons, that an ancestor of his was the weaver."

He looked at her seriously. "Madame? How many rugs have you sold in your lifetime?"

"Rugs? Why, none of course."

"You do not think it strange that immediately after you arrive in town a man comes to your hotel room and wishes to buy a rug from you?"

"Strange? Of course I thought it strange. But my husband--everyone wants something and many think he is still wealthy."

"You did not agree to sell the rug?"

"I refused. He started to argue so I closed the door in his face."

"But you did see him again?"

"He must have followed me. He was outside the Abdullah where we went for dinner."

"And you mentioned it to Decebilus?"

"I may have. In fact, I am sure that I did. After all, the man had followed me. Decebilus was amused."

"No doubt. But now the man is dead. You see no coincidence in all this?"

She was silent, and Ballantyne glanced at the ridge

and the cypresses at Hannibal's tomb. From the track
they were hidden, but an observer up there on the ridge,
especially if he had field glasses, could see anyone
here. In fact, he could see the three of them even without glasses . . . and no doubt the blue car was close by.

"Whatever it is," Ballantyne continued, "that your
husband knew, you may be sure Decebilus knows also, or
some of it. And you may also be sure that the knowledge
concerns money, for Decebilus is interested in little
else."

Villette looked away from him toward a wedge of blue
sea visible through a notch in the ruined wall. Her husband's sudden trip . . . without explanation . . . it was
so unlike him. And the rug? It was possible that Ballantyne was right, but what, then, of Leon?

She had known the name of Leon Decebilus for years,
it seemed. Friends returning from Monte Carlo, St. Tro-
pez, and Paris had mentioned his name as they mentioned
the names of Onassis, Pignatelli, or King Farouk.

When they met . . . quite by accident . . . they had
talked briefly. Then they had lunched together, and last
evening there had been dinner.

He was a brute. Instinctively, she knew that, but a
fascinating brute. He dressed with extreme care . . .
with too much care. His manners were perfect, too perfect
again . . . as they are apt to be when acquired late in
life and not from childhood. Yet there was also a bizarre
touch: the rings on his fingers, one huge one on his left
hand, two slightly smaller rings on his right.

He had been gracious. He had offered his car, even a
chauffeur, anything she might require. He offered his
sympathy for her loss; he had not known the Maharajah,
but had known of him.

Who had not heard of Dhyan Jai Rathore? She had known
of him for several years before they met. Their pictures
were often in the same magazines, he gambling in Monte

Carlo . . . attending the movie festival at Cannes . . .
fishing in the Bahamas. He was exotic, a Rajput, educated
at Cambridge, a man with a gift for friendships and for
sports. If "Jay," as his friends called him, was known
for something in particular, it was making the most demanding feats like climbing mountains, blazing across the
finish line at Le Mans, or leading a champion polo team
look easy and fun. After her first year in New York it
was almost fated they would meet.

Her success had been spectacular. A farm girl from
Oklahoma, she had started modeling for Neiman Marcus in
Dallas but quickly moved into the world of New York and
Paris fashion. She photographed well from any angle and
wore clothes with an easy grace. The ready wit for which
she had become famous was rather a gift for quick, deft
characterizations, a quality inherited from her father.
Though never an actress, her ability to banter and poke
fun at herself had made her a favorite on TV variety pro-
grams.

She had never been sure whether she really loved Jay.
From the first they had fitted into each other's lives
easily and naturally. They liked each other and liked
many of the same things, and he was at home anywhere. She
had been happy with him, he seemed to love her, and when
he had proposed she accepted.

Ballantyne interrupted her thoughts. "Your husband
gave you no clue to his secret? Could it have something
to do with the rug?"

"The rug that the man wanted to buy? It is a prayer
rug . . . but what could a rug mean? I think it was just
a talisman, a good-luck piece. I know it had been in
Jay's family for years."

"A prayer rug, a rare one, can be worth as much as a
valuable painting. And, believe me, I'd rather have one. I
could talk for a year on the subject of rugs. But . . ."

Ballantyne was thoughtful. All he had said of rugs

was true, yet somehow it did not make the kind of sense
he was seeking. If Decebilus wanted something it would be
worth millions, not thousands. Was it then the prayer rug
of some religious leader? Something of importance in the
Moslem world? He could think of no story of that sort,
but such a rug might exist.

"Do you have the rug with you?"

She paused, still suspicious. "Not today. Jay asked
me to keep it for him in Paris. When he wired me to meet
him in Istanbul, he asked me to bring the rug . . . not
under any circumstances to forget it."

Villette turned to him suddenly. "What do you expect
to get out of this, Ballantyne? You have admitted you
sold me a stone that was not genuine--why should I trust
you?"

"You need not trust me. Go to the police. Ask for
Hamid Yalcinkaya, only him. Tell him what has happened,
tell him of me, of the man on the beach, then get on the
first plane and fly back to the United States."

All Ballantyne could do was make his play. "Or you
can see this through," he said. "See it through with
me . . . or with Decebilus. You will choose one of us,
because he will give you no alternative and I will try to
take it from him . . . whatever it is. I, however, will
accept any deal you think is fair--a bargain, if you ask
me."

She arose suddenly. "I must go." She extended her
hand.

He took it, touching the fingers lightly with his
lips. "Do you know the Pandeli?" he asked. "In the old
town? Lunch with me there tomorrow . . . at twelve?"

She studied him coolly, then assented. "Very well,
Ballantyne. At twelve."

"And in the meantime . . . be careful."

She started away, then hesitated. "Do not forget that
I have a pistol."

"Your eyes, Madame, are the greater danger." He
bowed, smiling a little.

She laughed. "Ballantyne, I think you're a nineteen-
karat phony. You would lie in your teeth for money or a
woman."

"Madame . . . let me assure you. Your money is safe
with me. Until tomorrow, then?"

The blue Maserati had been hidden in an angle of the
wall. She pulled the car from its place of concealment
and, with a rasp of exhaust, started slowly back toward
the track.

Rashid moved up beside Ballantyne, and there was no
childishness in his face. "Treat her well. She is my
friend. If not"--he drew a dagger from among his rags--"I
shall have your heart."

The words were theatrical, the gesture boyish, borrowed no doubt from some story heard in the marketplace.
But some stories are not to be taken lightly, for they
form the instruction and discipline of a people, and the
goatherd, boy though he was, meant what he said.

"And do you take care," Ballantyne warned, "if you
are questioned, to know neither of us."

A man could walk almost as fast as a car could be
driven along the goat track, so he reached the village
only a few minutes behind the Maserati. His battered Land
Rover awaited him, hidden in a ruined camel shed.

The Maharajah . . . or Jay, as Villette called
him . . . was dead. And it appeared the only one who
might keep Decebilus from attaining what he wanted was
Villette herself.

Nor had she taken Ballantyne's warning seriously
enough. There are some who will believe nothing ill of
those they meet socially . . . and there are many who
will accept anyone who has the money to put up a good ap-

pearance and be introduced by the right people. Leon Decebilus appeared to be what he wished people to see him
as: the operator of a number of freighters and tankers,
of a small airline, and, through various associations,
several nightclubs and restaurants in Cairo, Alexandria,
Athens, and Aleppo.

That Villette knew and understood men, Ballantyne had
no doubt. A beautiful woman becomes habituated to using
her beauty, learns subconsciously, at least, that men are
not only willing but eager to serve her. Her smile, her
frown, her graciousness--all these can be used, almost
without thinking, on all ages and types of men. None of
this would have any effect on Decebilus.

Prostitution had long been one of the sources of his
income . . . the first stable source. Refugees were his
stock in trade and with the shifting of borders, wars and
civil wars, supply was never an issue. His orders shipped
women, like so many head of cattle, from Marseilles to
Genoa, Cairo to Tangier, Alexandria. He had no desire
that could not be satisfied merely for the promise, or
the threat, of a transfer from one better or worse
brothel to another. There was no experience he could not
have, or had not already had, for safe passage for a family or one more dose of heroin or hashish. Villette Mallory was a beautiful woman, but she would need to rely on
other qualities if she was to defeat Decebilus.

Ballantyne drove swiftly and with the knowledge of
many roads, and as he drove he worried over the problem
as a dog worries a bone. He had too little, all too little with which to work.

The sudden, unexplained flight of the Maharajah and
his subsequent crash. The arrival of Villette in Istanbul, and the quickly arranged meeting with Decebilus. The
man who came to Villette to buy a rug and was immediately

murdered. It all meant something, yet what it was he
could not guess.

To put a period to the matter, Mustafa Bem and Barbaro had followed Villette to the ruin, inquired about
her. Had they followed her to kill? Or merely to watch?

Until he knew more, Ballantyne would assume that Villette's rug was the joker in the deck. He had to get a
look at it, one way or another.

By the time the outskirts of Istanbul were reached,
Ballantyne was close behind the Maserati. Or rather, he
was close behind the car that followed the Maserati.

The battered Volkswagen had appeared from nowhere in
the vicinity of Kartal, falling in behind the blue car,
but clinging too close for a man experienced at his job.

Ballantyne had been watching for the Renault, not a
Volkswagen, and when he realized it was following Villette, he drew up during a crush of traffic and studied
the driver.

He was a stranger, yet hauntingly familiar. A narrow
face, badly pocked, with a pointed beard and a trimmed
mustache. The man's shirt collar was greasy, the uphol-
stering of the car torn and old. At the instant Ballantyne came abreast of him, the man's coat gaped somewhat,
revealing the butt of a heavy pistol.

Falling back to a discreet distance, Ballantyne
watched the Volkswagen trail Villette into the sweeping
drive that led up to the looming modernist rectangle of
the Istanbul Hilton.

The stranger locked the Volkswagen, then almost ran
to catch up as Villette went through the doors.

Parking alongside the car, Ballantyne took time for a
quick glance inside. An ancient cardboard valise, a few
old newspapers, and a paperbacked American novel. Whoever
the man was, he apparently could read English.

Walking swiftly toward the hotel, Ballantyne stopped just in time to keep from being run down by the gray Renault. Behind the wheel was Barbaro, beside him Mustafa Bem.

They drew up, and Mustafa Bem darted for the doors. Neither had paid any attention to Ballantyne.

CHAPTER II

Following Mustafa Bem inside, it became immediately obvious that although Bem knew the stranger, the stranger did not know him.

The driver of the Volkswagen turned to glance back toward the entrance at the moment Mustafa Bem stepped through, and although the latter turned sharply away, the Volkswagen driver paid him no attention. In turning away, Mustafa Bem came face-to-face with Ballantyne.

"So!" His eyes flared. "The wolves gather!"

Indicating the driver of the Volkswagen, Ballantyne replied, "Decebilus must be hard up to bother with such as that."

"He is no business of yours! Stay out of this!"

"Tell Dice that I'm in town, will you? He will be pleased, I am sure."

"He wishes nothing to do with you, Ballantyne, and consider yourself fortunate, for the next time he gives the word I shall kill you." And then he added, "And do not call him Dice. You know he doesn't like it."

Ballantyne strolled away and going to a booth, bought a newspaper. The dark-eyed girl who took his money scarcely moved her lips as she said, "Leon Decebilus is staying here."

Ballantyne's face revealed nothing, but he was star-

tled. For years Decebilus had stayed nowhere but at the
Parc Oteli, formerly the town's leading hostelry. Could
the sudden change mean that he wished to be near Villette?

"No," the girl whispered when he asked if Decebilus'
arrival was unexpected, "he reserved a suite just one
week ago today."

The same day the Maharajah of Kasur reserved his
rooms. "Thanks." He glanced at the paper. "Tell Johann I
wish to see him."

"He expected you. He is in the barbershop."

The fact that Decebilus had reserved his suite on the
same day as the Maharajah might be pure coincidence, but
Ballantyne did not believe it for a moment. It was another small link in the chain of evidence tying Decebilus
to the visit of the Maharajah and Villette.

Suddenly a man was beside him, a slender blond man
with a saturnine expression, neatly dressed in a dark
suit and a snap brim hat. The man paused to light a cigarette, but as he lifted the match it served to cover the
words he spoke from the corner of his mouth. "The Scylax
is lying in the port of Galata."

"Thanks, Johann."

"Arrived last night . . . in ballast."

The blond man walked away and Ballantyne stared at
his newspaper with unseeing eyes. The Scylax, named for
an ancient Greek navigator of the Indian Ocean, was a
freighter of Decebilus' Green Star Line. To bring the
freighter in ballast to Istanbul represented a contradiction for a shipping man as shrewd as Decebilus; it would
not pay to sail empty unless some very valuable cargo was
expected.

There were many pieces of the jigsaw, but fit them
together as he might, they refused to represent any in-
telligible picture. And here in the lobby of the Istanbul
Hilton were several of the pieces.

Obviously the man in the Volkswagen wanted to watch or speak to Villette Mallory . . . and just as obviously, Mustafa Bem was here to watch for her . . . or for the Volkswagen man.

Ballantyne had a theory that the way to defeat a careful enemy was to keep his plans from developing, and Leon Decebilus was a planner, a conniver. Shrewd, careful, and unemotional during the early stages of planning, Decebilus left little to chance. Yet if his plans became disturbed or frustrated, he was inclined to become enraged. And when aroused he gave way to fits of fury and brutality that could be shocking, a fact known to but few of those who now surrounded him. Ballantyne knew it, of old, and it was a gap in Decebilus' armor that could be exploited. It was a very dangerous gap, however.

Ballantyne had succeeded in outmaneuvering Decebilus on two previous occasions, each time by forcing him to move before he was ready. When such men move hastily they make mistakes, and the mistakes of others belong to the man prepared to seize what opportunity has offered.

Now Ballantyne made such a move. Crossing the room, he walked directly up to the driver of the Volkswagen, and as he did so, he saw Mustafa Bem turn sharply toward him, a hand half-lifted as though to prevent the meeting.

"My friend," Ballantyne said quietly, "you are in great danger. Unless you are very careful you will be killed as was"--suddenly Ballantyne knew he was right-- "as was your brother."

"Brother?" The Volkswagen man stared blankly at Ballantyne. "I have no brother."

"Perhaps your father, then? A tall old man in a black suit?"

The man grabbed his sleeve. "What are you saying? Where is he?" The voice echoed in the glass and marble lobby.

Heads turned. Mustafa Bem, his face pale with shock, had headed toward the exit. He had, however, to pass them in reaching it.

"He lies dead on the sands below Eski Hissar," Ballantyne said, speaking so only the Volkswagen man could hear, "of three knife thrusts in the back."

The man's face was yellow and sick. "You are lying!" he gasped hoarsely. "It cannot be true!"

"You may see for yourself."

"The woman! That foul--!"

"She had nothing to do with it. He was killed by a man sent by Decebilus."

"Decebilus!" Again people turned to look.

"It was he who gave the order," Ballantyne said. Then, turning, he pointed at Mustafa Bem, who had just edged past them, and said, "But there is the man who actually killed your father!"

Mustafa Bem sprang for the entrance and the Volkswagen man leaped after him.

There was a wild scramble at the door as people rushed to either get out of the way or to see what was happening. Ballantyne stepped back, watching.

Behind him a cool voice said, "You are a fool, Ballantyne, a pitiful fool."

Turning, Ballantyne looked into the eyes of the one man he really had reason to fear.

It was Leon Decebilus.

He was three inches over six feet with black hair and intensely black, piercing eyes. His cheekbones were high, the bone structure of his face massive. He wore a dark suit of excellent tailoring and material.

"You could stay out of this," Decebilus suggested, "and we could forget the past."

"You might forget it, Dice. I would not."

Ballantyne saw a dark flush of anger under the swarthy skin at Ballantyne's use of the old nickname.

"I never liked you, Ballantyne. You interfere with me and I shall have you killed."

"Again?"

"You were lucky before. I could have you taken away, then drowned or burned."

"Aboard the Scylax?"

Ballantyne saw the jump of fury in Decebilus' eyes, and for an instant he thought the man would strike him. Instead, Decebilus hissed, "Stay out of this!" and turned sharply away.

Ballantyne went out into the night, stopping under the portico, the roof of which was the architect's inter-pretation of a flying carpet. He shook a cigarette out of the pack in his shirt pocket.

Suddenly he saw the Volkswagen man coming back up the drive. He was perspiring freely and Ballantyne stopped him before he could reenter the hotel.

"I would stay out of there if I were you. They will have you arrested."

The man stared at him from great, anguished eyes. "You are my friend, I think. . . . Why?"

"You have given me no cause to be otherwise, and De-cebilus is my enemy. It is as simple as that." He paused, then added, "Look, you are in trouble. Your father died because of the rug."

The man showed no surprise at the mention of a rug, accepting the connection without comment. "You are sure he is dead?"

"Three stab wounds in the back. It is the method of Mustafa Bem."

"I shall kill them all," the man said gloomily. "My father was a good man." He looked up at Ballantyne. "He knew nothing of the rug until I told him. But for me he would still be alive."

"Do not blame yourself--we are all in God's hands."
After an instant and keeping his manner casual, Ballantyne said, "Tell me about it."

He held his breath, expecting anger, suspicion, or that the man would walk away from him, but the Volkswagen driver was preoccupied with his own grief. "It was a dream. An impossible dream." He turned large, sad eyes upon Ballantyne. "Ours is a poor family; it has always been a poor family.

"We are weavers, and weavers have their own tales, whispered among themselves, stories half-real, half-fantasy, stories of rugs and magic and legend. To tell a tale comes naturally to a weaver, you understand?"

"It was the story of a rug?"

"Yes, and a story of my family and a knot, a knot that only we know how to use."

"A knot? You mean a weaver's knot for a rug?"

The man started to speak, then stopped abruptly, seeming to realize what he was about to do. He turned sharply and stared at Ballantyne, his eyes hard with suspicion. "You are not my friend! You want the secret for yourself!"

"I can tell what you wish Madame to know. I can speak to her for you."

"No! I will tell nobody!"

"Decebilus knows."

"It is impossible! Only a weaver could know! Only a weaver from--!"

He broke off and strode away, his skinny legs covering the ground in long strides.

Ballantyne swore softly. He had been close, very close . . . to what he had no idea, but it might have supplied him with part of what he needed to know.

The sun had gone down beyond the Sea of Marmara, beyond the crumbled ruins of ancient Troy. He stood where he was, enjoying the cool air and the pleasant evening,

trying to imagine what the story might be. He thought of
the storytellers in the Old City, not far from where he
himself lived. Which would be most likely to know and
which the most likely to tell a foreigner if he did?

He must move with extreme caution, for every step he
took now was a danger. Leon Decebilus had never liked
him, but for the past few years he had actively hated
Ballantyne, hated him because of all the men Decebilus
had known, Ballantyne was the only one ever to have seen
him weak and frightened. Had it not been for Ballantyne,
Decebilus would now lie dead under the searing desert
sun.

"Ah, Mr. Ballantyne!"

Ballantyne turned to face Hamid Yalcinkaya. He was a
man of medium height, extremely well built, with fine
shoulders and a strongly made face. An officer of the police, he was also much more than that, for he acted as a
liaison man between the highest powers in the government
and the police. Whenever he took an interest in a case,
it was sure to have international or political overtones.

"Hello, Hamid. Late for you to be out, isn't it? I
mean, a growing boy and all that."

"I could go to sleep earlier, Ballantyne, if I was
sure of just what you were doing. Not that I enjoy being
suspicious of an old friend, but I know you too well."

Ballantyne hesitated. Hamid might have just the information he needed, but the man was shrewd and from anything Ballantyne might say he could construct some idea
of what was involved. Ballantyne had no wish to cause an
old friend trouble; nor did he wish to be troubled by
him.

At this stage he was not altogether sure whether he
was thinking of Villette first, or of himself. To protect
her from harm was a debt he owed: The few dollars he had
bilked from her in Egypt had literally saved his life . . .

but when it came to a treasure or a new source of profit, if such existed, he would have to do some thinking.

"Now how do I keep you from sleep? I am out here only for a bit of fresh air."

"You should have found the air at Eski Hissar invigorating enough."

Ballantyne straightened his tie. So they knew about that? A little frankness then . . . just a little.

"Well, she didn't say no."

"Did she say yes?"

"No."

Hamid chuckled. "The lady is very beautiful, and very expensive, no doubt. I mean no disrespect in saying that, only her friends spend freely, I believe."

"You mean Leon Decebilus?"

"Old friends, aren't you? You and Decebilus?"

"Neither of us would use the term."

"And yet, you carried him out of the Empty Quarter. Three days, I believe, on your back."

"I should have left him there."

"You should have been a Turk. A Turk would have left him right where he was."

Hamid glanced at the tip of his cigarette. "What was all that inside just now? That business with Mustafa Bem?"

"Keep the enemy worried, keep them afraid of what you know, of what you might do."

"It is a philosophy of which we Turks approve, though perhaps not in our best hotels. . . . But why Decebilus? And just at this moment? Is it only because of the beautiful lady from America? Or is there something more? Something of which I should know?" Hamid paused. "How, for example, does it connect with a certain plane crash in Iran and the death of the lady's husband?"

"What do you know about that?"

Hamid shrugged a shoulder. "It was no accident, if that is what you mean. Someone planted a bomb in the tail. Very accurately timed to explode over one of the wildest regions in the Elburz Mountains."

"And you tied it to Leon Decebilus?"

"If we could connect it to him he would be under arrest. To you, my friend, I shall admit this much, no more. There were indications."

"There was a shift of hotels, and a suite taken near that reserved by the Maharajah, is that what you mean?"

"More than that. Tell me, Ballantyne, did you know the Maharajah of Kasur?"

"Only by reputation."

"Would you say he was an impulsive man? A dreamer? I mean, was he impractical?"

"No . . . I saw films of him driving in the Le Mans race, and I've read of him playing golf and polo. A realist, I would say, a very cool, hardheaded man, but with imagination."

"I see."

Ballantyne was watching the place where his car was parked. Was that a moving shadow? Or a trick of the eyes?

"What is she like?"

"Intelligent. She's been courted around Paris and Cannes by a lot of playboys, but she's more levelheaded than you might suspect."

"She was a model?"

"I'm guessing she could go back to it. She has something a girl is born with if she has it at all. Women always look to see what she is wearing that gives her that look, but it's the lady, not the clothes. She traveled a good bit following her business as a model, but she invested a little money in Broadway shows and a couple of them did very well. Being a beautiful girl, she meets everybody sooner or later. That's about the size of it."

"Did she tell you all this?"

"We met only today. We were introduced by a goat-herd."

"Rashid?"

Hamid never missed a trick. Ballantyne's surprise must have shown in his face because Hamid smiled with obvious satisfaction. "Oh, yes! I know Rashid. In fact, he reported a murder. A weaver named Yacub . . . stabbed to death, out at Eski Hissar."

Like the Ottomans of old, Hamid must have informers everywhere. Ballantyne made his decision suddenly: When in doubt, be frank.

He explained in detail his visits to Eski Hissar, hoping to meet Villette, his discovery of the body, his recognition of the wounds. And then he repeated what Villette had told him, that the dead man had followed her to the Abdullah. He did not mention the rug.

"Have you any idea why?"

"You're joking. Men always follow Villette. Only . . . she mentioned his following her to Decebilus."

"You're not suggesting he was killed because of that?"

"I suggest nothing. I comment, that is all."

He glanced toward his car once more, but saw no movement there. "Can I drop you somewhere, Hamid?"

"I have my own car." Yet Hamid made no move to go; he lingered, as if about to say something, then at last when he dropped his cigarette to the pavement he said only, "He has not changed, Ballantyne. Decebilus is the same."

"They tell me his fingers reach even into the government, to the police."

"If they do, I should like to know it." Hamid glanced at Ballantyne. "They do not reach to me."

"If it was shown to me in black and white, I still would not believe it," Ballantyne said.

"Thank you. Thank you, my friend." Hamid turned and walked away. He looked hard, capable, and tough. Hamid

was a true Turk, and it would never do to underestimate
him.

Ballantyne started for his Land Rover. He was thinking of what might be done before morning, for whatever
was to be done must be done quickly. Decebilus was not
one to waste time.

The VW had been replaced by another, larger car. Ballantyne dug out his key, his eyes sweeping the other vehicles, searching for that movement he had seen. He heard
the whisper of clothing behind him . . . too late.

A knife-point pricked his back, and a car door opened
behind him, the car parked directly alongside his own.
The knife must have been put against his back through the
window of the car. If that was so, when the door opened
for the man to emerge the knife must be for a moment
withdrawn while he moved it around the window frame.

Ballantyne stood very still, trying to judge from
where the knife-blade was how tall the man might be. It
was not Mustafa Bem, but a shorter man.

"Don't move!" the voice growled, in English. The
pressure of the knife-point slackened and Ballantyne spun
swiftly, hands shoulder high, knocking the knife-hand
aside.

His attacker lunged out of the car but Ballantyne
jerked a knee into his groin and knocked him back into
the car seat. Then he slammed the door on the man's leg.

The man screamed.

People around the hotel stopped, staring toward the
parking lot. Ballantyne climbed into the Land Rover and
backed out, taking his time. He could hear his attacker
moaning and cursing, but he ignored it. Turning his car,
he drove unhurriedly away.

When Villette Mallory closed the door behind her, she
stood for long minutes with her back against it, her eyes

closed. No matter how desperately she fought the feeling, she was frightened.

The poise that was so distinctly a part of her was endangered by the frightening realization that she was broke . . . and in a foreign country where she had no friends.

She had always earned a good living, but she had lived too well and there had seemed no end to the money or the opportunities. Planning for the future, saving, had seemed something she could put off for a while. Despite her reputation as a glamor girl, despite how easy it had been to accept the attention and the pay, she had never been truly comfortable in that world. There was a darkness at its core, a corruption that made her uneasy.

When Jay had come along she was at a low ebb, emotionally. She had almost despaired of finding the sort of man she wanted, the sort toward whom she was naturally attracted.

Like many another girl who becomes a success in the world of fashion, motion pictures, or the theater, she had not realized how much it would limit her choice of men. Instead of meeting more men when she became famous, she met fewer . . . fewer she actually trusted, at least.

Too many were alcoholic playboys, veterans of a handful of unsuccessful marriages; still others were simply not interested in women at all, or were those who pretended an interest for protective coloration. Many men merely thought she was unapproachable, others assumed she was too approachable, but among them she found no men of character.

Not, at least, until she met Jay. His fortunes had been up and down so many times that he had no illusions left. Born into fabulous wealth in one of the poorest countries in the world, when India was torn asunder he had rebuilt what was left of his inheritance, enough to allow him a comfortable living. More than money, it was

his dominance on the polo field and in the Team Lotus
cars at Le Mans and Monaco that had kept him in the public eye. He had a love of life and a great trust in himself and the hand of fate.

When his investments in Cuba had been lost to the
revolution, he found himself on the verge of going broke
again. Villette was concerned--she had passed up another
contract when they married. She made arrangements to fly
to Paris to see what work was available.

But Jay had laughed. "There's nothing to worry
about," he had said. "I've still got the rug."

"The rug?"

"It's a long story. And it will be quite the adventure for us."

Later he had commented on it again. "There's millions
in it, but it will take some doing."

He was excited by whatever plan he was making, but
then he was off with the team and their ponies to
India . . . and while there something had gone terribly
wrong.

Now Jay was gone, and if she was to believe Ballantyne, he had been murdered.

She moved away from the door, and as she undressed
and prepared for a shower, she considered the situation
as coolly as she could.

Jay dead . . . He had been so filled with energy and
the desire to do things that it was hard to conceive of
the idea that he was gone.

COMMENTS: Dad left behind a bewildering array of revisions of
this particular story. In trying to create a single coherent vision of his

best ideas, I have combined the most complete material from five of the nine or ten drafts into the version that you have just read.

All of these drafts seem to originate from a very short short story, one that seems like an autobiographical vignette, called "By the Ruins of El Walariah," first published in *Yondering, The Revised Edition*. It is merely an amusing conversation between a Moroccan boy and a young traveler, a man like Louis might once have been. It contains no hint that it ever could or would attempt to transform itself into a thriller.

I can only assume that was this story's original incarnation. It is the simplest version, and stylistically it feels like a part of the "*Yondering* era," stories that Louis wrote in the 1930s and '40s before his mainstream career took off. At some point later on, he seems to have gotten the strange idea to turn that particular story into a treasure-hunt adventure.

The next step in the evolution of this narrative seems to be the following concept, one that does not use either the Moroccan (El Walariah) or Turkish (Istanbul) locations. These notes read:

> Ali Brogan is a bit of the flotsam of the Middle East. He lives by his wits, and usually lives well, but occasionally he fails to come upon the needed opportunity.
>
> He knows a multitude of things. Most of it is highly useless knowledge, and he has a horror of work. Wherever he is, he gets along, and always with a weather eye for the chance.
>
> In Samarkand he overhears a conversation about a rug . . . a very rare rug, indeed, and woven into it is a map indicating the presence of a buried treasure.
>
> Let's say Ali sees a man killed and finds the rug. He carries it off, then an attempt is made to buy the rug from him. He studies the rug with great care, can find nothing, only the design in the center

strikes him as a bit off pattern (in one corner, rather) and has a faintly familiar appearance.

He goes to a woman who knows most things and discovers to whom the rug belonged, and gets some of the story from her, an old lady. One thing she says rings a bell.

The elderly lady with whom he deals was once married to a nobleman of Turkish or Arabic background. . . . She was an adventuress, but a shrewd and beautiful woman in her youth. Now an old lady with little money left she is still the grand dame, and still as gifted in her way as always. Ali has an admiration for her which he cannot keep secret, and he gives up his own profit for her.

Perhaps the design on the rug gives a map of a ruined building outside Samarkand. He is a crook who is outsmarted by his own sentimentality.

That idea led to a draft of the story that is much more like the chapters of *The Golden Tapestry* that you have just read. It included the characters of the shepherd boy, the mysterious and beautiful young woman, and some Bad Guys who want something she has. This draft was, like "By the Ruins of El Walariah," set in Morocco. Subsequent versions, however, make the jump to Turkey and incorporate Hannibal's treasure and the whole cast of characters; in fact, there is very little difference between the next nine drafts. Dad made small adjustments, the timing of some of the events, figuring out how to best establish certain bits of information, and that is about it. In one draft, Ballantyne is named Baliran and he experimented with some different names for Jay, the Maharajah of Kasur.

He wrote one of these drafts in the first person from Ballantyne's point of view ... then realized that was a mistake, that he needed to allow his audience to witness a number of scenes where Ballantyne could not be present. The first-person perspective made the delivery of that information difficult, and led to some extremely awkward expositional dialogue.

There were so many rewrites that I could see the storytelling begin to deteriorate; even as he got certain aspects of the plot nailed down, he began to take others so much for granted that he glossed over them, probably because he knew them too well by then. Louis did not like rewriting for this exact reason—unless a writer truly enjoys revision (and he did not), too many drafts can suck the life out of a story before it ever gets going.

It is very rare to see Louis sweating a bunch of little details like he did in these drafts. Usually, he was very self-assured about what he was doing and forged ahead with certainty. Even though he gave up on *The Golden Tapestry*, it seems like this is a pretty solid concept. Ultimately, he did get all those troublesome details nailed down in one version or another, and as you will see, he had a version of the entire story mapped out. Possibly Louis's biggest issue when it came to rewrites was that he didn't bother to do a careful analysis of the strengths and weaknesses of each draft. That, combined with the lack of a secretary (or a word processor!) to quickly shuffle all the good bits together, may have caused some of these story concepts to be left behind.

The bulk of these "Istanbul drafts" seem to have been written in 1960 and '61, the same era when he wrote the first version of *The Walking Drum* and tried to develop several other ideas to break out of the Western genre. Only one novel, *Sackett*, was published in 1961, and it ended up being a lean year. That was also the year I came along, and Mom and Dad were forced to move because their apartment building didn't allow children.

Eventually, they bought a house, and it's my guess that the financial pressure of the failed attempts to broaden his style, then my being born, plus the down payment on the house was what pushed him to accept the deal to write the novelization of the movie *How the West Was Won*, which came out in 1962.

At some point it seems Louis tried to sell *The Golden Tapestry* as a motion picture, no doubt feeling he could afford to go back to it if he had a buyer set up. No deal was ever made, but at least we will get the benefit of being able to read a treatment that suggests how the story might have developed and then ended if he had written the full novel.

As you read through the treatment below you may notice slight differences from the chapters of prose Louis wrote. Although the outline allows us to see what the overall structure of the story would have been like, I believe it was written fairly early in the process; the outline gives us the best overview, but the two chapters of prose you have just read are an indication of how he would have continued to work out the details in a more complete and sophisticated fashion.

THE GOLDEN TAPESTRY

Outline of a Novel

CAST OF CHARACTERS:

BALLANTYNE: He knows who is bribing who from Delhi to Istanbul, from Cairo to Samarkand . . . he knows where the power and influence lie, and who to see about getting things done.

His father was an Irish-American adventurer who came out to the Middle East with a bridge construction company and stayed on as an oil prospector. His mother was a Eurasian girl of good family, and Ballantyne, except for a few short periods in the States and in Europe, has grown up in the East.

His experience has been varied and colorful; he speaks a dozen languages, most of them fluently; he knows the argot of the beggars and the thieves; and he has wires out to all parts of the East where the only secrets that exist are the ancient ones. The bazaars, the coffee shops and wine shops teem with gossip.

At thirty-three he is good-looking, rugged, quick to

make a fast buck or a fast lady, and is a good man in a fight, but a better one at talking himself out of them.

He makes his living by acting as liaison man for oil companies in their dealings with Arab sheiks and other tribesmen, as a local contact for motion-picture companies, for archaeologists, etc. Occasionally, when he noses about old ruins he comes up with a fine head, a plaque, or a vase . . . and he knows who will pay best for what he has found.

He speaks fluent Turkish, Arabic, Hebrew, Hindi, Persian, English, and French; he speaks a smattering of Russian, Chinese, Bengali, German, and Greek.

They know him in Aleppo and Isfahan, in Kashgar, Srinagar, Damascus, and Bagdad as a fast operator, but one whose word is good, whose courage is unquestioned.

He has had frequent dealings with LEON DECEBILUS.

VILLETTE MALLORY: Born in Pawhuska, Oklahoma, on a ranch, she was singing on various radio stations in the vicinity when only fourteen; at sixteen, passing as older, she was a model for Neiman Marcus in Dallas; at seventeen she had gone to New York and had become within a few months one of the best-paid models in the country, her income had moved up to five figures, and she was known as "The Incomparable Villette."

She is beautiful, bright, and quick in conversation, and she knows how to take care of herself. Even with all her glamor and the romance that has become attached to her name she is a very regular gal who has never forgotten where she came from.

She has been courted without much success by an assortment of international playboys, visiting nobility, Texas millionaires, and the usual names that make up cafe society.

She had met the Maharajah of Kasur, a sportsman noted

for his polo playing, race driving, etc., but a very regular guy who lost most of what he had when Pakistan split
with India, and who divided much of what remained among
relatives and some old family retainers.

Villette is not in love with him, but she does like
him very much and they have become engaged. He has told
her, and at first she believed he was joking, that he was
not worried about money. He said he had a rug that would
make his fortune . . . a prayer rug.

Villette knows a good deal about the world and about
men, but she has never encountered the kind of trouble
represented by LEON DECEBILUS.

LEON DECEBILUS: Tall, strong, and with a superficial
polish that quickly disappears when he grows angry. His
voice grows rough, his language changes.

"Decebilus" is a name he uses; his own name is unknown, and he himself may never have known it. His na-
tionality is equally indefinite, except that he comes
from the Levantine coast.

He has been a thief and a pimp, a smuggler and a runner of guns and other contraband. He has but one loyalty,
to himself, is egocentric and cunning. He has the shrewdness developed from practice and from the peoples who
live in the marketplace. He is a completely ruthless man,
totally unimpressed by beauty. He still operates a chain
of whorehouses throughout the ports of the Eastern Medi-
terranean, and women mean nothing to him. He takes them
when he wants them, discards them when he wishes.

Villette, accustomed to coping with men without too
much trouble, finds herself completely at a loss with
him, a thing she does not sense at first.

Decebilus is interested only in money, and over the
years, through murder, blackmail, and a series of fast
operations he has become a financial leader in the Near

East. He owns a line of decrepit freighters and tankers,
a small airline operating in the Middle East, and various
other enterprises.

He uses bribery, threats, and blackmail to get what
he wants, but being absolutely ruthless and willing to
kill or destroy anything in his way, he is a man feared
wherever he appears.

He is handsome, dresses with great care in suits tailored in London. His outward manners and good taste are
visible everywhere except that he constantly wears three
large rings on his right hand, two on his left. His good
taste in clothes is an acquired thing. . . . Personally
he would prefer something more garish, but he has
learned. Only in the rings is this aspect visible. Yet
the veneer is thin. When angry the change is shocking.

RASHID: A goatherd who is twelve years old going on
forty; young in one sense, he was never young in another;
he has listened well over his few years, and has observed
the comings and goings of men. He will have more to do in
the story than the brief outline of the action indicates.

MUSTAFA BEM and BARBARO: Sharp tools for the cutting
hand of Decebilus, they supply his "muscle" when he does
not wish to be involved.

YUSUF: An old man who has lived long in Istanbul and
for whom life holds no mysteries. He knows much of rugs,
the rugs of Persia, Turkey, Bokhara, India, and China . . .
he knows the myths and legends woven into the rugs, even
some of their origins, for each rug is itself a puzzle,
and the motifs may be borrowed from China that appear in
a Persian or Turkish rug, or vice versa. Long ago his
family were retainers of the Maharajah of Kasur, and like
him, he is a Moslem.

HAMID: A cool, hard-bitten, and thoroughly honest police officer; formerly of the Army, he knew Ballantyne in
Korea, where the latter functioned as an intelligence officer and liaison man because of his command of languages. They mutually respect each other, but Hamid has
always been a little suspicious of his friend. Hamid has
a complete dossier on Decebilus but no opening for an arrest. Hamid is, however, more than a mere officer of the
police . . . he is a liaison man between the police and
the national government.

YACUB & KHALID: Father and son, who know the secret
of the rug and have searched for it as have their fathers
and grandfathers before them.

ZAIDA: Who has her own ideas about Ballantyne, Decebilus, and the rug. She is dark, slender, exotic, and is
brought into the picture by Decebilus but decides to
double-cross him and get the rug for herself.

LOCALE:

Algiers, Casablanca, and Hong Kong have been the subject of successful motion pictures, but Istanbul, formerly Constantinople, has never been used as it should
have been. The harbor, the Golden Horn, the Bosporus, are
indescribably beautiful and photogenic. The Old City,
with its ancient walls which still stand, its mosques and
minarets, is romantic and exciting.

During spring, summer, and fall the air is usually
startlingly clear and the sky blue as it only is in the
Greek islands, southern Italy, or Istanbul's vicinity.
The average temperature in July and August is 72 degrees.
Istanbul is 16 hrs. by air from New York, 5 hrs. from
Paris.

The best view of the Golden Horn, long famed as one

of the most beautiful harbors in the world, is from the
cemetery at the end of the bay.

The city is divided into three parts: the Old City,
and then across the famed Galata Bridge over the Golden
Horn is the modern city, and some old suburbs. Across the
Bosporus (the fare across by ferry is about five cents)
lies Asia.

Pop. about 1,200,000, and a mixture of all nationalities in the world. The city was founded in the 9th century B.C.

The Istanbul Hilton is the city's luxury hotel, new,
bright, and smart. The Parc used to be the lushest spot
in Europe and was a hangout for correspondents and adventurers. In the Chez Afrique, a subterranean nightclub off
the Street of Spices, von Papen used to meet his secret
agents. Every street has its own story; many of them have
thousands of stories.

The Seraglio Palace, which used to be the harem of
the sultans of Turkey and the Ottoman Empire, is now a
museum. It is a maze of rooms and passages, and part of
the chase sequence in this story takes place there. It
covers acres and acres of parks and buildings, is picturesque and exciting.

The Sunken Palace is one of the ancient cisterns
built beneath the city (miles of these still exist, most
of them forgotten long ago) to supply the city with water
in time of siege. This one looks more like a vast cathe-
dral than a cistern, and has 12 rows of 28 columns to
hold the vaulted roof, 336 columns in all. But this is
only one of the cisterns. It still contains water, and
part of the chase takes place there, by boat and torch-
light.

The Grand Bazaar has 92 streets and thousands of
shops selling everything in the world. Not so mysterious-
looking since the fire of some years back, but still an
interesting place, always crowded and busy.

The Tin Village is a collection of shacks and huts built of old sheet metal, oil barrels, packing cases, etc. Gypsies live there.

The Gulf of Izmit and Eski Hissar is roughly fifty miles from Istanbul by a good road.

The Pandeli, mentioned in the story, is a romantic place in the Old Town, and the best food of the Turkish variety. There are a lot of good eating places in town. The Abdullah, also mentioned, is very good and considered the best in town.

Istanbul is a hotbed of intrigue, and visitors are there from every country in the world. The Turks are a hardy, rugged people who have fought the Russians many times in their history and any Turk believes he can whip any four Russians and is quite ready to prove it. Their government is friendly to ours and has been so for a long time.

The Istanbul Hilton is located in the heart of the city in a lovely park, and alongside the lobby is a prom-enade overlooking a garden terrace, a reflecting pool, swimming pool, cabanas, tennis courts, and the gardens.

There are a lot of theaters, good music, etc. The city has nearly 500 mosques, some of them extremely beau-tiful. There are miles of good beaches, and the place has a romantic flavor all its own.

BRIEF OUTLINE OF ACTION:

BALLANTYNE discovers the body of an old man in a worn black suit on the shore near Eski Hissar, and the man has been murdered by three knife wounds in the kidney. This use of the knife is a trademark of MUSTAFA BEM, the right-hand man of LEON DECEBILUS, formerly known as "Dice," a name he would like to forget. Decebilus has in the past been a thief, a panderer, and a murderer. . . . He is now a shipping magnate and financier.

Few recall his criminal background, or that his success was founded more upon blackmail and murder than upon financial cunning. The few who do remember prefer to keep silent.

Ballantyne waits among the ruins and sees a Renault come along the goat track. Mustafa Bem gets out and talks to RASHID, the goatherd, asking about a blue car with a woman in it. Rashid professes to know nothing, and they leave.

The boy comes over and after some talk with Ballantyne, introduces him to VILLETTE MALLORY.

VILLETTE was to have met her fiancé, the Maharajah of Kasur, in Istanbul, but he was killed in a plane crash en route. She has beautiful clothes, and almost no money. She is living on her jewelry, which she has pawned bit by bit, and other than that has only a rug, a prayer rug given her by the Maharajah, who told her to keep it at all costs, that it would make them rich. She had thought of the rug as more of a good-luck piece than anything else but there have been several attempts to take it from her and she is no longer so sure it is only that.

The only person she knows is an old man who keeps a shop in the Grand Bazaar, known as YUSUF, and her fiancé has assured her that he is trustworthy. She has no one to turn to except him, and he is a relatively poor man.

Ballantyne, a fast operator where a buck is concerned, has arrived at some conclusions of his own, which explains his presence among the ruins at Eski Hissar. Actually, he knows nothing of what is going on except that something is happening. He has learned a few things and drawn some conclusions.

The Maharajah, an internationally famous sportsman, suddenly canceled, without explanation, an all-important polo game on the eve of the game, and took a flight for Istanbul.

The plane exploded in midair over Iran and the Maharajah is killed. There is some doubt about how the plane came to explode.

Leon Decebilus, long known to Ballantyne, arrives suddenly in Istanbul and occupies a suite opposite that of Villette Mallory. Heretofore Decebilus has always stayed at the Parc.

A beat-up old freighter, owned by Decebilus, has come from Greece in ballast and is anchored in the Golden Horn; it is not attempting to load a cargo but is instead waiting. . . . Why?

The Maharajah, who lost his estates during the split between Pakistan and India, is nearing bankruptcy, but before flying for Istanbul assured his creditors they would all be paid in full within the month.

It is obvious that the Maharajah expects to come into money in Istanbul and that Decebilus is aware of it.

Rumors are coming through on the grapevine, but nothing tangible. Not until Rashid spoke of it had Ballantyne heard of the rug.

Always keenly aware of any opportunity to turn his hand to making a fast buck, Ballantyne discovers that Villette is driving to Eski Hissar each day, and begins to haunt the place to meet her, and to discover what she is doing there. It is an unlikely place for such a girl to be.

Villette has lunched and dined with Decebilus, and Ballantyne warns her about him. He asks if she does not think it strange that he was so quick to arrange a meeting on arrival. She replies that men always meet her when she arrives anywhere, and if they did not she would change her perfume . . . or her coiffure.

She doubts his warnings until she hears him mention the dead man on the shore. She recognizes the description as that of a man who had come to the hotel and tried to buy the rug from her . . . a fact she had mentioned to Dece-

bilus when the man followed her to her meeting with Decebilus at the Abdullah.

She had mentioned it . . . and now the man was dead.

She doubts the connection but she is uneasy. She
agrees to lunch with Ballantyne but she will also see
Yusuf . . . whom Ballantyne also knows.

Ballantyne observes that Villette is followed to Istanbul and to the hotel by a man in a battered Volkswagen
whom Ballantyne later recognizes as having a strong re-
semblance to the murdered man.

Following his policy of pushing the opposition until
they make mistakes, Ballantyne promotes trouble between
Mustafa Bem and the man in the Volkswagen, whom he correctly supposes is son to the murdered man.

Villette meets Decebilus for dinner, but though she's
discounted Ballantyne's suspicions she is wary when the
subject of the rug arises and Decebilus suggests that to
avoid future trouble she dispose of it. In fact, he would
buy it himself.

When she refuses, he drops the matter. Later, speaking as a "friend," he warns her.

Ballantyne, meanwhile, has been visited by Hamid, the
police officer. It turns into a fencing match. Hamid
likes Ballantyne but does not altogether trust him. Hamid
also has received the rumors Ballantyne has been getting.
He is alert to something going on.

Villette returns to find her suite ransacked.

Hamid then appears to ask about the death of the Maharajah. They are cooperating with the Iranian authorities in the investigation. Hamid inquires about her
association with Decebilus.

She meets Ballantyne at the Pandeli and she is followed to that place. Evading their pursuers they go to
Yusuf's shop and find him murdered, the shop a shambles.

As Ballantyne and Villette are about to leave the

shop, Mustafa Bem and Barbaro appear. Ballantyne keeps
them occupied while Villette escapes with the rug, which
the searchers had failed to find.

Thoroughly frightened, she narrowly eludes a man who
grabs at her, escapes down an alley, and hiding in a
doorway, sees three men consult, then dash off in separate directions.

She is stalked along the Step Street, and people seem
to be watching her or pursuing her everywhere. At last,
frantic with fear, she runs into the Tin Village. Around
her are people who look at her with utterly emotionless
eyes, strange faces, savage faces, empty faces. At last
she falls, and is helped up . . . by Ballantyne.

They are stalked through the cisterns, through the
Sunken Palace, and then by a secret way under the Sera-
glio Palace itself. Coming up inside, they manage to join
a party of tourists and file out with them. They get to
Ballantyne's car and escape into the country, driving to
Eski Hissar.

From a point near Hannibal's tomb they stop, take the
rug, and open it for study. It is late afternoon.

The secret of Hannibal's treasure is woven into the
rug. Ballantyne studies the pattern, explains something
of the symbols, many of them very ancient, as he goes
along. Yet he cannot solve the problem. Somewhere here
there is a key.

Villette recalls that Yusuf's hand lay on the rug,
which he had simply spread on the floor amongst many others instead of hiding it, as he lay dying. Was it accident that his hand lay at a certain position? Or had he,
in dying, tried to tell them something?

His hand had lain upon the lamp hanging in the prayer
arch of the rug.

Carefully, they examine it. The treasure, they know,
is the treasure of Hannibal, and that it is somehow connected with his tomb at Eski Hissar. . . .

And then they see. The design woven into the rug, the design of the lamp, is also the key to the treasure, for it is the design of the ruined walls that lay scattered below them!

And plainly indicated is the place of the treasure.

Excited by their discovery, they start running down the slope toward the ruins.

Rashid is gathering his goats, but he ignores them. They call to him, but he walks on, never turning his head.

Warned by the boy's actions, they stop. It is too late.

Having lost them in town, Decebilus and his men returned to where the old weaver had tried to contact her. They step from the ruins, and they have guns.

Ballantyne tries to bargain. Let them go and they will give up the rug. Decebilus is too shrewd. He knows the rug holds the secret, woven into it long ago, and if he is willing to forfeit the rug, Ballantyne must have solved the mystery of the weaving.

Decebilus has no intention of struggling to solve a problem when a man who has the solution is in his hands. He has a counter offer: their lives for the treasure. Suppose they found it, he argues. What could they possibly do with it? How would they move it? How could they dispose of it without exciting the cupidity of those with whom they dealt or corrupt officials?

Gold is very heavy, and people are curious. Decebilus offers here some comments on treasure-finding that are rarely considered. Most people at one time or another have thought of finding a treasure, yet few of them have gone beyond that to decide what they would do if they found it.

The government of most countries would take half; some countries would confiscate it all. They would have to transfer a large amount of gold and gems into Istan-

bul, and like any large city, it is filled with thieves.
What then?

On the other hand, Decebilus explains, he is equipped
to cope with the problem. He has underworld means of dis-
posing of the loot; he has the force necessary to guard
and protect it; he can use methods they as reasonably legitimate people dare not use. He has a ship and a crew
prepared to handle it. He has a truck nearby to take it
to the loading dock in a fishing village, and he has
means of persuading the curious to be less so.

Ballantyne, realizing that Villette is in worse danger than he himself, tells them where to dig. They dig,
uncover a stone slab, remove it, enter an underground
chamber.

It is an ancient temple, prepared for worship. A
Phoenician god faces them from a dais. In niches in the
wall are four slightly smaller replicas. In the center of
the room there are twelve large amphorae lying piled in a
bunch.

Mustafa Bem calls to Decebilus.

They go to the opening and look. It is not yet dark,
although the sun is down. Standing on the slope are forty
or fifty people. They are the villagers, the friends of
Rashid, and they stand very silently, watching.

Decebilus is furious. He demands of Ballantyne who
they are, and Ballantyne can only guess. "They are my
friends," he said, "and they want no trouble, but they
are prepared for it."

It is a Mexican standoff, and Decebilus knows it. If
he starts shooting he will kill some of them, but he will
also raise such a turmoil that troops will be rushing
down from Istanbul, his ship stopped, the treasure confiscated.

He bargains. Ballantyne will let him take half. They
argue. Finally to save the villagers from a fight that is

not their own, he agrees to let Decebilus go with eight
of the amphorae, if he goes at once.

Decebilus departs and Rashid comes.

Villette comments that they have some of it, anyway,
but Ballantyne replies that they actually have it all!

THE TREASURE:

After his defeat by the Romans, while they sought him
everywhere, Hannibal escaped to the island of Crete. He
brought with him some large jars that were heavy and were
kept sealed and guarded. These were believed to contain
his treasure.

When the Romans discovered his hiding place he
slipped away from Crete to the Gulf of Nicomedia, where
he lived in a fishing village. Discovered again by the
Romans in 183 B.C., he killed himself rather than face
capture, and his treasure was never found.

For our story purposes, the treasure could have always been kept inside some hollow Phoenician idols (also
the gods of Hannibal's Carthage) outside his door.

A weaver of rugs, following a legend handed down in
his family for generations, found the treasure room at
Eski Hissar, but took only a few pieces away with him.

Arrested in trying to sell a gem, he was imprisoned
and after a while, because he was a weaver, was put to
work. He refused to tell the whole story, claiming he had
found only a few things buried in a ruin miles from Istanbul. After a while, he was believed, but he was kept
busy weaving rugs for the Ottoman Turks. Into one of the
rugs he wove the secret of the treasure, and into four
other rugs he wove a key that only his own family would
understand.

He died without knowing his son had died before him,
and his daughter had been sold into slavery in India. A

beautiful girl, she was taken into the harem of one of the Maharajah's family. With her she took the secret of the rug and a bracelet that had once belonged to Hannibal.

The Maharajah of Kasur's great-grandfather had finally found what the rug was, but not until Jay had they found anyone who could read the secret, and he read it too late.

COMMENTS: I believe that, had Louis continued on with this novel, he would have improved it considerably. The treatment you have just read seems to have been a fairly "quick and dirty" attempt to make a sale to a movie studio. If Dad had pressed on with this project, there would have been more development of the backstory between Decebilus and Ballantyne, and certainly some sort of mano a mano final fight between them. The arrival of the villagers at the finale feels like a cop-out intended to wrap up the treatment so he could get on to the next project. It is not the sort of thing that Louis ultimately would have gone on to actually write in a book.

Given that Decebilus discusses the difficulty of unloading a treasure, I suspect that Louis would have realized that Jay, being a fairly wise man, had worked out how to transport and dispose of whatever he finally discovered. Perhaps Jay had even been intending to use Decebilus in this capacity but Decebilus double-crossed him by planting the bomb in his plane once he decided (erroneously!) all he had to do was grab the rug from Villette. It is also clear that, unless Louis was planning to rewrite the beginning yet again, Villette knows more than she is letting on. The story starts with her spending part of several days at Eski Hissar. That indicates she already has a general sense of where the treasure is buried.

Louis left behind notes that suggest part of the secret is how the ruins look as the light changes toward the end of the day. It's not just that the pattern of walls is woven into the rug; the shadows they cast are also a part of the weaving. He also included a good deal of information on rug-weavers' knots, so much that I began to think that the ultimate trick in a story like this would be to have a certain thread that could be picked out of the rug and then pulled. This would unravel the section around the rug's archway lamp, leaving behind a different design . . . the one that showed the location of the treasure. I became so enamored with this idea that I added the line where the weaver mentions his family's secret knot. I may not be done with this story. We'll have to see.

At another point in his notes, Louis seemed to consider the idea that two different groups might be searching for the treasure, one a bunch of crooks, the other with political motives. . . . I believe this idea came before he conceived of the Decebilus character. The "political" group might have created a way of using the treasure for a higher purpose, as well as a method of unloading all that precious metal in a world that was still on the gold-exchange standard.

As was his way, Louis included a pep talk for himself in his notes:

Make this a suspense story in line of The Maltese Falcon, but make it deeper, better, a fine love story, a story of background and suspense, a sexy story.

Make the love affair gay, lighthearted, two people at an outpost of the world, both skating on thin ice.

Make this a definitely superlative book, something completely out of the ordinary. Discuss books, politics, painting, jewels, beliefs, folklore, magic, etc.

Make this something really fine. With a great suspense yarn and a beautiful love story. Make the writing something very special.

A final comment on the one thing about this story that I have never been able to figure out. It is this piece of the opening line:

He lay on his face in the wet sand, a tall old
man in shabby clothes, and looking down at the body,
Ballantyne knew that it had begun again but this time
he did not know why.

"... *knew that it had begun again* ..." It's a great opening and
Louis definitely had something particular in mind. Initially, I thought
"again" referred to the bombing of Jay's plane—chronologically, that
is the first death related to the plot—but now I'm not so sure. At a
guess, taking other drafts and notes into consideration, "again" may
imply Ballantyne suspects that those who got too close to the treasure
were being bumped off by someone guarding it . . . maybe an individual, maybe a secret group, who didn't even really know what they
were guarding. Perhaps Dad realized later on that having the hero
know too much in the beginning of the story wasn't going to work all
that well and started to pull back from that concept, or at least from
Ballantyne's knowledge of an ongoing plot or series of murders.

LOUIS RIEL

The First Three Chapters of a Historical Novel

CHAPTER 1

He stood upon the street in St. Paul and watched the people go by. Here he was a stranger, a lonely man with an aching in his heart that he did not understand. He wanted the nearness of people, but something within held aloof, feeling the difference within himself.

This was Minnesota, and off to the north lay his own land. Yet even here he glimpsed the blanket-coats of the métis, the half-breeds from the northern prairies and rivers, his own people.

For years they had been coming south to St. Paul or St. Cloud for their trading. This was the United States, and the cities of Canada lay far to the east over some rough country that made crossing a struggle. It was so much easier just to come south, to travel with the Red River cart caravans or to take the steamboat on the Red.

People brushed by him. He shifted his valise to the other hand and walked up to the door of the Merchants Hotel. He opened the door, catching the old familiar smell of the place: the stale cigar smoke, the warm, close air of the lobby.

This, at least, remained the same. The worn leather settees, the brass cuspidors, the buffalo head upon the wall. As a child he had once come to this place. To a boy from the vast plains this seemed a mysterious and somehow magical place.

He paused inside the door, letting his eyes grow accustomed to the change of light.

"Louis? Is it you? Mon dieu, but how long it has been?" It was Ambroise Lepine, a welcome face in a city of strangers.

"Ten years."

"Well, you have your father's look. More handsome, I think, and broader in the shoulder. He was a man, your father."

They sat down at a table and stared at each other, amused and curious, Lepine the woodsman and Riel the scholar. Lepine wore a coat made from a Hudson Bay blanket, typical of the country, Riel a plain, black, neatly cut suit.

"You are not a priest, then?" Lepine said. "Not a priest after ten years of study?"

"I am a religious man, Ambroise, but toward the last I believe the good fathers were worried. I doubt if it is in me to become a priest."

"Was it money? We could have found it. For a son of your father, nothing would be too much."

"My mother needs me. You know that better than I, for you have been here. I have done little for her, and there are the girls, my sisters. I worked for a lawyer in Montreal but the pay was very poor. Besides . . ."

"Besides what?"

Riel was embarrassed. "I was homesick."

Lepine nodded. "I know. A man cannot go far wrong

when he is close to the trees, the rivers, and the plains.
After all, Louis, we are a part Indian, you and I."

Riel's smile was twisted. "I have had cause to remember that, Ambroise."

Lepine put down his pipe and reached for his glass.
"It is better that you have come back, Louis, and better
that you are not a priest. We need you."

"Is Mother well? She never writes of herself."

"She is well, I think." Lepine shook his head in awe.
"She is a woman, your mother. But she does need you; it
has not been easy for your mother, and now with the
surveyors--"

"Surveyors?"

"Have you heard nothing? Men have come from Ontario
who survey right across our lines. They say we own nothing, that the whole land must be resurveyed and reallot-
ted.

"They say this to us! Three, four generations we have
lived on this land. We have built our homes, cut hay in
our meadows, fished in the streams, and trapped for fur.
Old men have died here and young men have had sons.

"I reached out and touched a tree and it is mine, it
has grown with me, as has the grass beneath our feet. I
drink from a cold stream, smell the pines and the grass
warmed by the summer sun. I turn the sod and see the corn
grow where the seeds fell. . . . And now they say the
land is not ours, that we are only métis, we are nobody."

"You have spoken to the Company?"

"The Company is no more. The Company is selling out,
it is leaving us. The Hudson Bay Company was our father
and our mother and now it goes from us."

"But who is to govern? The Company administered the
land. It has been the government. What will be done?"

"Who knows?" Lepine spread his hands helplessly.
"Some say the Queen does not want Prince Rupert's Land,

that Canada does not want it, but Louis . . . those men from Ontario . . . I think they want it. I think they mean to have it, and that is why we need you."

"Me?"

Lepine looked down at his huge hands. "I can lift anything, Louis, anything I can take hold of, but words do not come to me. You are your father's son, and when in the old times there was trouble, we went to your father, the miller. It was he who led our fight for free trade. It was he who went to Ottawa to speak for us. He was a man of words, as you are."

"You have spoken to the governor?"

"Mactavish is an old man, and he is ill. He is tired now, and soon will leave us. I do not believe he likes what is happening, for he has always been a just man. A stern man, but just."

Louis Riel was silent. The love of his people for the land was no small thing. They had not come to get rich and get out. They knew nothing of politics or land specu-lation, for they were a people of the earth, of the for-est, the lake, and the stream. They walked where the grizzly walked, and hunted the elk for meat on its own pastures. They knew the whistle of the marmot and where the beaver built his dams.

When the Company first sent its men west to trade with the Indians, many of them, French, English, and Scottish, married with the Indian girls, and from them came a different people, a fine, strong people. They were woodsmen and canoemen by birth, natural horsemen, confi-dent hunters.

Louis Riel was himself one-eighth Indian; the rest was French, Irish, and Scandinavian. Yet he was consid-ered a métis, a half-breed. He had borne the designation with pride, never really thinking of what it meant to some until . . .

"We must talk of this, Ambroise. I have been gone too

long and have missed much. In Montreal there are rumors,
sometimes, but to Montreal this is a far and savage land.
They know nothing of us, and care less."

"They know of us in Ontario. They hunger for our
land." Lepine got to his feet. "I have much to do, Louis.
You are going home now?"

"I have no money, Ambroise, and cannot go empty-
handed. To have an education is one thing, to have money,
another. In Montreal I could save little, then like a
fool I stayed overlong with friends in Chicago. I was
like a child. My money just seemed to melt away, while I
dined and talked with friends."

Lepine chuckled. "It is the way of money. They make
the coins round so they can roll. But when did a métis
save money?"

"I kept hoping a way would open for me, Ambroise. Out
here there is little need for educated men."

"Bah! You can do anything, Louis! At St. Boniface you
were the brightest of the lot."

"I had too many questions, Ambroise. There were books
to read, and I read them, but it worried the fathers that
what I saw in the books was not always what they saw, so
I did not become a priest; but what is a man to become
who studies to become a priest and then is not a priest?"

Lepine chuckled. "He becomes a politician, Louis.
Come home; help us. You know them, these men of the cities. You know their minds."

The big man scowled, but it was worry, not anger.
"Louis, men come among us and say disturbing things. You
will meet them in Pembina, when you go north. One of them
is an American who has no legs."

"No legs?"

"From the waist up, he is magnificent. He has a special saddle, this one, and you should see him ride. It is
a miracle that he rides, but he does."

"What about him?"

"He wishes to see Rupert's Land a part of the United States. He wishes us to sign a paper to the United States asking them to govern us."

"We are Canadians," Riel objected. "We are not Americans."

"Agreed. But do we not have more in common with the men of Dakota and Minnesota than with Ottawa? When we ride north from here, where is the line between us? The color of the grass does not change, nor does the air have a different smell, or the wind blow in a way other than it does here. God made no line upon the earth; it exists only in the mind."

"We are British subjects," Riel objected. "We should remain so."

Lepine nodded unhappily. "So I believe. I believe it in my belly, but I have no words to answer the men from Pembina. They say the Queen does not know we are here, and they say the men in Ottawa wish to please the voters in Ontario, so they will give our lands to them, and who are we to object? They say Ottawa will not listen."

"They will listen, Ambroise. We must send somebody to talk to them."

Riel was silent, thinking of what had been said. "You spoke of men who would resurvey the land? Who are they?"

"They come from Ontario, most of them. They are Protestants."

"There are many Protestants, Ambroise. The Company was Protestant, and we got along with the Company."

"I do not believe the Company had any religion but fur. They treated us fairly . . . most of the time." Lepine grinned cheerfully. "And we treated them fairly . . . enough of the time. These men are not the same."

"They have a leader?"

"A man named Schultz. He is a Swiss, I believe. A very big man, very strong . . . but not so strong as me, I think." Lepine hesitated, no longer joking. "There is

MacDougall who says he will be a king out here. And there
is Dennis."

"MacDougall I know of. There are others?"

"There is Scott . . . Thomas Scott. He is a loudmouth
and a troublemaker. He gets along with no one, but he
hates Catholics, Indians, and métis. He says we are
dogs."

"He said that to you?"

"Not to me, nor does he say it where I am. If he did
I would squeeze him . . . so," and he closed his huge
fist.

When Lepine had gone, Louis Riel stayed at the table.
Only a few men remained in the lobby. Two were talking in
a desultory fashion of the wheat crop, and across the
room a big man was telling of a cattle drive he expected
to meet in Rapid City.

"Longhorns," he was saying. "They're big and they're
mean, but they could walk across the world. These come
from Texas. Last year, in '68, nearly three hundred thousand head came over the trail from Texas to Kansas!"

Riel was scarcely listening, for his thoughts had
gone back to his last meeting with his father, who had
been returning from a business trip as Louis left for
school in the East. They met on the trail, and none of
the words they had to say to each other had anything to
do with what they were thinking.

The bond between them had been strong, but unspoken.
Why had he not told his father he loved him? Why had he
never said it aloud? Yet his father had not said the
words to him, either.

How could he guess the father he loved would die
while he was away at school?

Yet when the news came it was his mother of whom he
thought. She had always been strong, original, and with a

great appreciation of the amusing. Never while her husband was alive had she had to exert her strength or her
will, for Louis Riel the elder had been a forceful man,
although quiet, lifting his voice rarely, his hand never.
He had given off a feeling of strength, of quiet assurance, and his mother had drawn upon that, and been all
the more warm and loving because of it, there being no
need to expend elsewhere the strength she herself possessed.

His was a strong heritage. Was he worthy of it? Was
he half the man his father was? Or a quarter the person
his mother was known to be?

The Merchants Hotel was old, born with almost the
first breath of St. Paul, and over the years it had become a hodgepodge of logs, lumber, bricks, and stone with
all the various repairs and additions. During the late
summer and fall rooms were scarce, but Louis Riel went to
the desk and asked for John Dodge, the clerk.

"I would like a room," he said, "and I should like to
stay for a while."

Dodge hesitated, puzzled by the half-familiar features. "Have we met before, Mr. . . . ?"

"Riel . . . Louis Riel."

"Of course. I knew your father. Knew him well." He
glanced over the register. "Yes, yes. I think we can find
something for you."

"Thank you, sir. I will be also looking for employment. If you hear of anything I would appreciate it."

"Of course. Yes, I have a room for you, and Mr. Riel?
Do make yourself at home. Your father was very helpful on
many occasions and your people have been coming here for
years."

"Thank you."

He went up the stairs to the room. A bed, a dresser,
a white bowl, and a pitcher filled with water. Two tow-
els, a washcloth, and a bath at the end of the hall.

He put his valise on the bed and removed his coat, hanging it over the back of a chair. When he turned about he found himself looking into the mirror above the dresser, at a reflection which regarded him seriously.

Wavy hair, a high forehead . . . He had been called handsome, which he was not. Five feet ten inches with shoulders so broad that he appeared shorter. He was physically powerful without wanting or trying to be. He had always been strong, yet curiously, he had never been healthy.

He shrugged. A man could not dwell on such things, but must get along with what was to be done.

In this almost bilingual town--for so it was at the moment--there should be a job for him. At this season of the year the influx of French-speaking trappers and traders was great. Each year the great caravans of Red River carts came down from the north, and after unloading their freight, prepared to load up again for the trip back.

Many Indians came as well, but he spoke several dialects so they would present no problem.

He stared at his reflection. At St. Boniface he had been considered a brilliant scholar, and so attracted the attention of Archbishop Taché. Because of him he won his chance to attend school in Montreal.

There he had done well despite the greater competition, first in his class many times, often second or third, rarely fourth.

What had gone wrong? At what point had he lost his desire to become a priest? Or had he ever desired it? Was it not simply that it offered the only road he knew to an education?

Reluctantly, he admitted to himself that he had never considered himself priestly material. There was too much in him that was impatient, restless, demanding.

Was he ambitious?

He walked to the window and stared out at the gathering darkness. No, he decided after a few minutes, he was not really ambitious. He did not want wealth. Security for his mother and sisters he did want, and his own lot sufficient enough that he was himself not a case for charity. Searching himself, he found no need for luxury or power.

Yet he did want something.

He had come from a land where all things were useful. A man had an ax to cut wood, a plow to break the soil, a canoe with which to travel lakes and rivers, traps to take fur, a pole or a net for the catching of fish.

Everything must be useful, so it followed that he himself must be so. A priest was a useful man, a necessary man. So, if not a priest, somehow he must become useful and necessary.

He removed his vest and hung it over his coat, then taking off his shoes he lay down on the bed, clasping his hands behind his head. Then he prayed.

Prayer had been his custom since childhood, but he did not always kneel or bow his head. He prayed when he felt like prayer . . . yet that, too, left him uneasy.

Was he actually talking to God through prayer? Or only to his better self? Did it matter?

That was always his problem: He questioned all things, even his own decisions, his own plans.

He did not lack faith. He had never lacked faith. He was, and had always been, a deeply religious man, yet he was a reasoning man as well, with a naturally cautious, judicious, measuring attitude of mind.

His eyes remained closed when his prayer ended, but his thoughts drifted like a soft wind toward his northern land. The land he loved, the land that was home.

His eyes opened to reality. He must find work. He must have something to take home, even if it was ever so little.

Tomorrow he would look. He knew a few people by name,

and had friends from the north who had traded here. He would find something.

He sat up on the edge of the bed, suddenly worried. What right had anyone to survey land the métis had held for generations? What was happening up there?

If the Hudson Bay Company was leaving, and no other government stood by to take its place, what would happen to his people?

The métis numbered only a few thousand, and if The Bay no longer controlled Prince Rupert's Land, which was virtually all that lay between Hudson Bay and Lake Supe rior west to British Columbia, then hordes of people from the east or from the United States could rush in and deluge his own people, taking their land, their privileges, their all.

Lepine, he realized, had been more than merely worried. The big man had been frightened.

CHAPTER 2

It was wet and cold in the morning streets. A late storm had blown down from the north, pouring rain upon the town, but he turned up his coat collar and walked along, unminding of the rain. He walked slowly down to the river and looked at the swollen waters.

This was the Mississippi, flowing away from here to the south, toward a sunny land he would never know, for it was not his river. His river was the Red River of the north, flowing out of the United States into Canada, flowing through one of the most fertile valleys on earth.

When he returned home it would be along that river by steamboat, for the Red River carts would soon be a thing of the past. He remembered those great caravans and the wild, screeching, caterwauling sounds that had come from those wooden, ungreased axles. . . . One of the caravans had numbered as many as five hundred carts, and the sound of them could be heard for miles.

He must go home. He must hear the troubles of his people, and if necessary he must speak for them. As his father had been before him, he would be their voice.

First . . . a job.

When he found one it was in a store selling dry goods and hardware, a store to which the métis came, and to which more of them came when they discovered he was work-ing there. They brought not only their trade but gossip as well, and he needed the one as much as the other.

Again, several times in fact, he heard the story of the surveyors, and always they spoke of Schultz . . . John Christian Schultz. Not a surveyor, but one who coop-erated with them, possibly even invited them to make their surveys.

He was a doctor, a storekeeper, and a Swiss. He de-tested Indians, Catholics, and the métis. "Bastards," he supposedly called them, "the misbegotten sons of riffraff and savages."

Whether Schultz actually said such a thing Riel did not know, but it was widely quoted and widely believed.

He had been behind the counter but three days when a lean, dark man came in and stood about, waiting until Riel was alone. "You are Louis Riel?"

"I am."

The man glanced quickly right and left. "Come across a man from up your way. He was buyin' rifles."

"It is a country where all men are hunters," Riel re-plied mildly.

"This man wanted a hundred rifles for delivery at Pembina. He was gettin' them through some of them whiskey-peddlers at Fort Whoop-Up. He said somethin' about showin' a bunch of breeds who was boss."

"Why do you tell me?"

"Heard you was a breed, although you surely don't look it. I'm half-Sioux myself, an' just figured you should know."

"Thank you," Riel said, and the man left.

One hundred rifles . . . It was a lot, yet the métis could muster several thousand if need be. If there was someone to call them out and to direct their actions.

There had always been rough characters along the border, men who would lend themselves to any action if the price was right, or if there was a chance of loot. The Fenians, too, had been talking of invading Canada again. They were an Irish organization inspired by hatred of all that was British.

Of course, they had been talking for years, threatening and blowing off steam, yet there were hotheads among them prepared for any desperate action, and if there was an invasion there would be violence . . . and his mother and sisters were there.

The thought disturbed him. What if some such an attempt were made? Who was there to stop it? If the Bay Company was stepping down, who would act? Who could act?

There was no one.

The métis were men accustomed to the quick, iron discipline of the buffalo hunt and the fur brigade. Such groups could move like a well-oiled machine, but so far as he knew they had no leader, nor any plan of action.

Such lawlessness as was known in the mining and cattle towns of the American West had never existed in Prince Rupert's Land because of the Hudson Bay Company. From the beginning The Bay had complete authority, and it was there first, firmly established and in command before there was any possibility of others coming into the country.

Their authority had been complete, and from their decision there was no appeal. Without The Bay no supplies

were to be had, no ammunition, food, or liquor available.
Access to these things depended on conformity to a pattern of behavior that suited the Bay officials. They also
offered the only market for furs west of Montreal.

Any westward movement had been held in check by that
desolate wilderness that lay between Hudson's Bay on the
north and the Great Lakes on the south, and particularly
that area north of Lake Superior.

If one wished to migrate westward it was far easier
to go to America, as many were doing. The Ohio, the Missouri, and the Platte offered easy access to the heart of
the plains country and the mountains that lay beyond.

There was talk of a railroad that would join British
Columbia to eastern Canada, but thus far it was no more
than talk, and most of those who knew the land ridiculed
the idea. The easiest way to go west, or even to Rupert's
Land, was to take the Grand Trunk Railway from Toronto to
Detroit, then westward to Chicago and La Crosse, Wiscon-
sin. From there it was a short ride by steamer to St.
Paul.

He shook his head irritably. It was madness. All men
needed some restraint, for few could restrain themselves.
If there was no government there would be anarchy, and he
was a man who believed in order.

If Rupert's Land was abandoned by the Bay Company and
no other government existed, settlers might rush in, and
he could see fighting and confusion, for none of the inhabitants of Rupert's Land would relinquish their lands
without a fight. Yet if the area was to become a part of
Canada, it should be as a province, with its own government and proper representation at Ottawa.

Several days passed. He was paid, and carefully put
aside all but what was needed for the bare necessities.
He was doing well at his job. His quiet dignity and re-
serve were perfectly suited to selling to the métis, In-

dians, or settlers. They came seldom to town, but one and all they loved shopping, fingering the materials, wandering through the stores and trading posts to see what was available.

He knew his people, and he let them look, offering suggestions only when asked or when there seemed some hesitation; at other times he simply listened to them talk.

Between the store, the hotel, and a boardinghouse where he ate most of his meals, he was gradually coming to understand what had happened in his homeland, and what seemed about to happen.

The fur trade was no longer as bountiful as it had been, and although there were buffalo, even they seemed to be thinning out. The great profits the Hudson Bay Company had once known no longer existed, and the problems were increasing. The Bay, wisely, was stepping out to avoid an impossible situation.

Lepine came around to the hotel when several weeks had gone by. The big leather chair creaked when he dropped into it. "Louis? When do you come home?"

"Soon, Ambroise." Riel leaned his forearms on the table. "Have you heard any talk of rifles? A lot of rifles?"

The big man looked up. "I have heard such talk."

"Who would want so many rifles? Who do they plan to shoot?"

Lepine leaned forward. "Look, my friend, you must have forgotten your homeland. Think, man, is it not a prize worth taking? Do you think those who talk of confederation are thinking of anything but our land?

"Who cares about us? We have no voice in Ottawa! We are scattered people on a far frontier, and those who

would take our land from us have voices to speak for
them. I think you had better come home, Louis, and see
what can be done."

"Do you think there will be fighting?"

"Louis, they have sent surveyors, and we have stopped
the surveyors. I do not think they intend to be interfered with again."

"I want no fighting."

"There need be none. But we must have someone to
speak for us. There is enough land for all, but we wish
to keep that land we have. . . . Let them take other
land.

"However, there are some who threaten violence. That
Orangeman named Thomas Scott is a troublemaker. He had
trouble when he worked for Snow on the road they are
building, and he threatened Snow. He is forever starting
fights and threatening to kill people."

"He is a leader?"

"Only of a few like himself. He has no intelligence.
He is a child. He worries me because he could start trouble. He could begin trouble where there need be none.

"Then there is Schultz. Schultz uses Scott, and Scott
follows him as much as he will anyone, but Schultz is no
fool. He is very intelligent, but I think he has no
scruples. . . . I think he would stop at nothing, but
that is only my idea."

Riel was silent and worried. If there was trouble--
and certainly all the ingredients were there--his mother
and the girls might suffer. Also, his people were regarded by many Easterners as people of no account. They
had had a great hand in building the country, in gathering the furs, laying out the trails. Without them there
would have been no Hudson Bay Company, and no opening of
the West for many years. But in Canada, as in the United
States, the Indian was regarded as an obstacle to be

brushed aside, with only a slight claim to the land on which he lived. He had heard such arguments in Montreal.

The white man was taking the land, using it. Just as the Indian had taken the land from those he found when he came, other varieties of Indians or aborigines of some kind. From the beginning of time it had been so, a weaker people displaced by a stronger.

In England the Celts had pushed back the Picts, the Angles and the Saxons pushed in their turn, and then there was the Norman invasion.

Yet this was not conquest. Rupert's Land for so it had been called for many years--was being sold by the Hudson Bay Company without any thought for the rights of those who lived there.

There was no question of fighting for what was theirs--it was simply being sold out from under them. Of the open lands, well and good . . . but what of their homesteads? Their villages?

"I will want a place to stay, Ambroise. My mother will be crowded, with the girls growing up. I would not be a trouble to them."

"I will speak to Schmidt. I think he has room enough to spare. He is a good man."

"He is. And I would like that."

He remembered Schmidt. They had been in school together and he was an easy man to be around, one who did not intrude upon another man's thoughts.

Mentally, he counted his money. The sum was small, but soon he would be paid again, and he owed very little.

He would go north. He would take the steamer.

"Tell me about Schultz," he asked.

Lepine hesitated, then said, "You will have to meet him, to hear him. He used to operate a newspaper, The Nor'wester. Ran it four years, from '64 to '68. He's anti-métis, he's for annexation, and he thinks we've nothing to say about it. Near as I can get it, he was born around 1840 and started to practice medicine when he was twenty, but he's been so busy with his store and the newspaper that he's had little time for medicine except what he prescribes over the counter.

"He was thrown into jail when he refused to pay a judgment the court declared against him, and he simply broke out and stayed out, defying them to move against him.

"Whatever he says, Louis, do not take him lightly. He is an ambitious man and he refuses to be balked by law, custom, or anything that gets in his way.

"There's a man named Mair who is or was living in his home who is a very able journalist. Some of his writings about this part of the country have been getting into the Toronto papers. Of course, he's preaching the Schultz side of things."

Lepine hunched his shoulders and folded his hands before him. "He is one of a small group," he explained, "who wish to set themselves above all others. They would like to bring to us again what our fathers escaped in coming to America. They want a small aristocracy, Schultz and his friends, to be the ruling class. He has frankly said that when Rupert's Land, or Assiniboia as it is called, becomes a part of Canada, he will rule."

"He and MacDougall?" Riel said wryly. "I think we will have too many kings, when all we want are citizens."

He sat silent, brooding. There were too many complications, and he wanted simplicity. He wanted only to be home, to see his mother and sisters, and to find a place for himself.

"It is all right, Ambroise," he said, finally. "I shall come home now."

CHAPTER 3

He stood on the street before the Hayward Hotel in
St. Cloud and waited for the stage. A dozen others waited
beside him, one of them a fat, amiable man with an elk's
tooth on his watch-chain.

"The Northwest'll be part of the United States soon,"
he was saying, "and that will solve problems for them as
well as us."

A lean, sour-faced young man glanced at him. "Where'd
you get an idea like that? Do you suppose the British
would let all that country slip through their fingers?
Besides, you don't know how the people feel about it. It
is their decision."

Riel glanced at him. The man was perhaps thirty, or
even younger. In the hotel lobby he had seen him reading
Vico, a writer on the philosophy of history too little
known.

"Sure it's their decision!" The fat man waved a hand.
"But how else could they decide? Most of their trade is
with us; lots of them have relatives this side of the
line. You just wait until the U.S. government moves in--"

"It will not 'move in,' as you say." The young man
was impatient. "Do not be misled by such windbags as Alexander Ramsey and his like. Grant will have no part of
it, nor will any of the others. There will be a lot of
hot air over it, and then nothing will happen."

"Nothing will happen?" The fat man's tone became
shrill. "You just bet something will happen! Those French
Indians up there will rise up! They'll want to be American citizens! Why shouldn't they?"

"Perhaps they will wish to remain British subjects,"
the young man said mildly, "and there is no reason why
they should not."

"You a Canadian?" the fat man demanded suspiciously.

"I'm a Vermonter," the young man replied, "and in Vermont we tend to look at realities. There will be fears north of the line and a lot of shouting south of the line, but nothing will happen, believe me.

"I have talked to several senators, and they do not want it. We have had our share of trouble with the war, and we want none with England. We would rather have a friend north of the line than a suspicious enemy, and we have enough to do with what we have."

"You just wait and see! I happen to know there's a movement up there to join up with us, and then there's the Fenians--"

"A bunch of hotheads," the Vermonter said.

"They'd better join up," the fat man argued. "I happen to know there's some as expect to get rich up there when Canada takes over the government. The only chance those folks have is to join us.

"This outfit I'm talking about, they figure to grab title to most of that farmland, and if there's trouble they'll have support from the Army--"

"I doubt it," the Vermonter said. "Anyway, that's no hide off my nose as long as we're not involved."

"You'll be involved. You take them métis, they're mighty fine rifle shots, and they can outwalk, outride, and outshoot anybody around. They'll stop anybody tryin' to take over, but then they'll come to us for help. You'll see."

Riel was irritated. They talked like children, at least the fat man did, but he supposed there were many who felt as he did. Yet how right was the Vermonter? He glanced at him thoughtfully, and the Vermonter caught the glance and winked.

"How about you?" he said, with an amused glance at Riel, but speaking to the fat man. "Will you shoulder a rifle and get into a fight for Rupert's Land?"

"Me?" The fat man was startled. "I am not a fighter, I'm a lover. I'm just telling you what will happen. I happen to know--"

"Nothing . . . just nothing at all." The Vermonter's smile took the sting from the words. "You make a mistake, sir. Those who talk of Rupert's Land becoming a part of the United States are indulging in fantasy. No sober, serious student of affairs would have anything to do with it, and most of the citizens are well pleased to have the late war ended and to get down to business again without going off on tangents.

"Grant is a serious man. Despite his cronies, he is no fool. He will lead us into no foreign adventures. You will see that all this talk of annexation is so much wind."

The fat man was not persuaded, but Riel had not expected him to be. Personally, his opinion was that of the Vermonter. If some of the border Americans and promoters wished to indulge in foolish dreaming, that was their affair. He was sure neither the government in Washington nor the rank and file of citizens had any such idea.

He wanted no part in the discussion. He simply wanted to be seated in the stage and moving toward home. He waited, shivering a little in the predawn chill, and when the stage finally drew up he was the first aboard, taking a seat on the far side, where he relaxed and closed his eyes.

Despite the fact that he was at last on the road home, he was uneasy. What would he find there? What would he do himself?

When the stage stopped at Sauk Centre he got down to stretch his legs. He had been very young when he had come this way before . . . or had it been exactly this way? He scowled, trying to remember.

Whether or not he had come exactly this way, the town
had a flour mill, obviously new. There was a blacksmith
shop, a lumber mill, a store, and a saloon. When they
left Sauk Centre their way took them over rolling prairies dotted with clumps of oak and poplar, with occasional lakes or sloughs.

From Lake Osakis they took a road cut through the Big
Woods to Alexander, and then on to a night station with a
log stockade, called Pomme de Terre.

"Riel?" the stage driver said confidentially. "Better
sleep in your clothes. The bugs will eat you alive."

It was good advice, and he took it, but even so the
bugs did their best, and their best was far too good.

They crossed the Otter Tail River above its junction
with the Bois de Sioux and turned west to avoid the al-
kali and came at last to the Red River and halted at Mc-
Cauleyville, opposite the fort.

There was no room in Nolan's Hotel, but Nolan advised
he sleep in the hay-barn. "Damn sight better, anyway," he
admitted frankly. "They're sleepin' four an' five in a
bed, and some of them snore something fierce. If it were
me, I'd take the hay."

Riel shrugged. Why not? He had slept in hay before
this, and enjoyed it.

The restaurant was crowded with a rough, casual crowd
of would-be settlers, farmers, drifters, and trappers. He
found a place at the table and helped himself to the
trays of food that were continually refilled. The meat
was good, the gravy and potatoes even better.

"You goin' north?" his neighbor asked.

"Yes . . . to Fort Garry."

"Me, too." The man was a burly, affable sort, roughly
dressed. "I want a piece of that land. They say the soil
is deep, rich, and black."

"Are you a farmer?" Riel asked politely.

"Hell no! I'll just grab onto a piece of it an' sell it to the first one offers me a good price."

"How do you propose to get a piece of land?"

"How? Just take it. How else?"

"What of the people who live there?"

"You mean the Indians? Hell, they don't own any land! They just drift across it. A few years from now they'll all be settled down to farming. At least, the smart ones will."

"They probably enjoy the life they are living," Riel suggested.

"So would I. That there's a good life, but it isn't practical anymore. Times are changing, and a man, Indian or white, who won't change with them just doesn't have a chance.

"Look, there ain't no way to avoid it. Folks want land, and one way or another, they'll get it. Down here in the States, for example. How's the Army going to stop people? Tell them they can't go any further? They'll slip by at nighttime. Shoot them? The public wouldn't stand for it.

"Sure, the Indians kill a few here, and a few there, but there's always more a-coming. Look at the Little Crow massacre. The Indians rose up when the Army was away fighting in the Civil War, and they killed nigh onto a thousand men, women, and children; now there's twice as many living there. They just keep comin'. It's land hunger; folks want homes, a chance to improve their lot.

"I like the Indian way, myself, but it surely isn't practical. The Indian lives off wild game, wild seeds and roots, and in the same area that it takes to feed a hundred Indians, you can be plowing and planting and feed fifty thousand by the white man's way."

"I hear much of that land is lived on by the métis," Riel offered mildly.

"The half-breeds? It don't make no difference. From what I hear they are a shiftless lot."

"But good with their rifles. Most of them have been hunting all their lives, and are dead shots."

"Well, that's another kind of thing. Me, I don't want any land that belongs to somebody else. There's plenty that stands empty. But I'm only one, and there's men right in this camp who don't care who they ride over. They aren't much worried about the breeds, because they're scattered and they won't stand together. They've got no leader."

"Americans?"

"Some of them. A good many are likely Canadians. Most of them don't care if the American government takes over or the Canadian, just so they get in, and get in they will.

"But, hell . . . look around you. See the big black-bearded one by the end of the bar? He's a Russky, and that man next to him is a Swede. Used to be a sailor. There must be fifty Scotsmen in this crowd, and twice as many English. . . . You can't just call them one thing or another.

"They tell me that once you've seen that land--"

"I have seen it."

"You have?" The man's interest quickened. "Is it as pretty as they say, or is that all talk?"

"It is one of the most beautiful lands under the sun," Riel said quietly, "and it has everything--deep soil, good grass, timber, lots of running water, lakes, ponds, game . . . especially game--and that's why I think the métis will fight."

"Look," the man protested, "maybe they will, but whether it is the Canadians or the Americans in charge, they stand to lose. The Hudson Bay Company sold out and nobody could care less about the breeds. The Bay owned the land. The breeds just lived on it, so what title can they have?"

"They have lived on the land for generations," Riel replied. "It is theirs by right of possession. In many cases The Bay upheld their right of ownership."

"Maybe . . . maybe." The man shoved back and got up. "Nice talkin' to you. My name's Graham."

"Mine is Riel . . . Louis Riel."

"French?"

Riel smiled gently. "Yes, it is, Mr. Graham. I am a métis."

The _International_ was lying a hundred miles from Fort Abercrombie at Frog Point.

At breakfast Graham came around and straddled the bench beside Riel. "You catchin' the boat? If you are you're welcome to ride with me. I got one of those Red River carts and I'll be pullin' out in maybe thirty minutes."

"Thank you. I will appreciate the ride."

Graham glanced around. "Can't carry more than you and one more. Get your bag and slip away. Meet me down the road maybe two hundred yards into them trees. All right?"

Riel glanced after Graham as he walked away. For a moment, he hesitated, then shrugged. The man seemed honest enough, and probably was. He wanted no trouble, but if attacked, he felt himself strong enough to handle any one man.

Borrowing a cord, Riel hung his bag from his shoulder and walked out from the settlement as though starting to hoof it. If anybody noticed, they apparently did not care, for there was no comment. Soon he was lost in the oaks and giant cottonwoods along the river.

He had walked almost three hundred yards and was prepared to give up when a voice called, "Hold up there!"

Glancing quickly to his left he saw a Red River cart

drawn by a single horse waiting in the shadows under a
tree, but well hidden by brush.

"Climb in." Graham glanced around apprehensively. "If
they guessed I had me a cart hid out there'd be fifty men
wantin' a ride to Frog Point," he explained, "and some of
them I've known for a while. Seemed to me, you going home
and all, that you might need the ride most of all."

"Thank you."

Creaking and groaning, they pulled out into the muddy
road.

"You've ridden this way before? I mean in a cart?"

"I came down from Fort Garry in one, a whole caravan
of them."

The carts, with two giant wheels, were made entirely
of wood cut from the forest. No oil could be used on the
wooden axles, for it caught the dust and sooner or later
the axle would "freeze" in place. The sound of such a
cart was like what one imagined a tortured banshee would
sound like.

"Been wet," Graham commented. "You being from this
country know what that means."

Riel nodded. It meant mosquitoes . . . and mosquitoes
in such clouds they had been known to kill a horse or an
ox that was left tied and unable to escape. Mosquitoes so
thick they drove both men and animals wild in their efforts to escape.

"Got an oilcloth. If it gets too bad we'll tie the
horse behind and cover cart and all with the oilcloth. It
won't keep 'em out, but it will help some."

Prairie chickens flew up and away. Within the first
mile after leaving the forest they started a dozen cov-
eys. The groaning and screaming from the wheels was such
that it precluded conversation, and Riel was just as
pleased. He wanted time to think, time to get the feel of
the country once again.

They met no one. Once, off in the distance, they
glimpsed a buffalo . . . perhaps two.

"Don't see many this far east," Graham commented.
"Getting mighty scarce."

They stopped to eat at Georgetown, then moved on,
then camped alongside the road, but it was just a brief
rest, and then they were moving once more. The steamboat
would not remain long, nor would there be another for
some time.

Graham seemed tireless. Twice, for brief periods he
handed the reins to Riel and dozed, but the horse needed
little guidance, and just a slap of the reins every now
and then to keep him moving. The trail wound in and out
of the brush, allowing glimpses of the river from time to
time through the willow, chokecherry, and cottonwood that
lined the stream.

Finally, they caught a glimpse of white through the
green. It was the steamboat. The International was tied
to the bank, moored to a couple of large trees, and already crowded with passengers.

To Riel's surprise, Lepine was one of them. The big
man moved to him at once. "Got to talk to you," he said,
low-voiced. "Trouble's brewing."

They stood together in the stern near the huge
paddle-wheel.

"What is it, Ambroise?"

"Some of this crowd are landing at Pembina. Listen to
them when you get a chance. They're all going north after
land . . . our land."

The International backed slowly out of her berth
along the bank and swung into the current. The big stern-
wheel reversed itself and slowly the steamboat began to
edge upriver, gaining speed.

One hundred and thirty feet long, the <u>International</u>
drew but two feet of water. Already a veteran of seven or
eight years upon the river, she showed the harshness of hot
summers and the bitter cold of winter when she lay idle.

The green banks slipped away behind them, now and
then permitting a glimpse of the prairie beyond. There
were many twists and turns in the river, so actual progress in miles amounted to very little.

Riel walked aft and stood watching the great wheel
turning, crystal drops falling back into the water. For
two hundred years the Hudson Bay Company, under a charter
granted in 1670 to Prince Rupert and his associates, had
ruled the vast territory known as Rupert's Land which lay
east of the Rockies to the shores of Hudson Bay.

Not that their control had been unlimited, for in
1783 a group of "free-traders" had combined to form the
North West Fur Company, and there had followed for nearly
forty years a bloody rivalry.

In 1812 the Earl of Selkirk planted a colony upon the
Red River, a colony of Highlanders displaced from their
own land in Scotland. They were viciously attacked, and
many, including the governor of the Hudson Bay Company,
were shot down.

Later, the earl imported portions of two bodies of
foreign troops, marched them west, and took possession of
Fort Douglas. They in turn were attacked, and peace was
not finally resolved until the two companies merged to
leave only the Hudson Bay Company in the field.

The inhabitants of what was called Assiniboia were
not all métis. Many were retired Hudson Bay Company factors and servants, others their descendants, often of
mixed blood. Aside from occasional disputes over religious matters the colony was singularly peaceful, considering the time and the place. Now all that was to change,
and Louis Riel paced the deck, hands clasped behind his
back, considering what might be done.

Graham found him on the top deck. "Looking for you,"
he said mildly. "You'd better go ashore at Pembina.
That's my advice for whatever it's worth. You listen a
mite. There's talk to be heard there that'll teach you
more about your country than weeks of living in it."

"Where do you stand, Mr. Graham?"

For a moment, he seemed to be thinking about it. Then
he said, "I'm not a well-off man, Riel, not at all well-
off. I'm an American, but there's little choice, seems to
me, whichever side of the border a man decides on.

"I'm looking for land, and I'll be looking there, I
imagine." He paused a moment. "But I'll look for unsettled land, and that's more than most of them expect to
do."

COMMENTS: Louis Riel went on to lead two resistance movements
in Canada, seeking to preserve the rights of the métis people. He was
elected three times to the Canadian House of Commons, though he
was never able to attend due to being forced to live in exile in the
United States. One of the most controversial figures in Canadian history, he was executed by the Canadian government for high treason
in 1885.

Growing up in North Dakota with a father who had spent a good
deal of his life in Canada, Louis L'Amour was raised on stories of
Louis Riel, debates on his sanity, and discussions of French versus
British and Catholic versus Protestant Canadian identities.

The idea for this book was suggested to Louis by Governor William L. Guy of North Dakota in 1972, and fairly quickly a motion-
picture production company jumped on board, taking an option on
Louis's yet-to-be-written novel. Dad went and did something like this
every once in a while, and it nearly always got him into trouble.

He loved making the deal, or the idea that he *could* make the deal (he'd struggled for so many years), and there was that part of him that always figured it would be easy. And often it was easy, when he'd had time to get the whole story settled enough so he could write with a minimum of conscious thought. In this case, he seems to have optimistically assumed that he could research, plan, and write this book just about as fast as he might have written a story he'd had in mind for years. The further he got into the research, the more interesting yet more demanding the story became, and the more he realized that the schedule was simply not going to work. Almost as soon as he started writing he was offering to return the option money. In a letter to his movie agent he wrote:

> I have to take my time on these projects. I have worked very hard and given a lot of time to this one and look forward to completing it, but I simply can't work with demands being made on me for pages or such things. I am sorry. I would like to have completed it in the time specified, but new materials kept developing and new aspects of the story that deserve consideration.
>
> The story is a very involved one, with many political ramifications and many characters. I have turned up a manuscript written by one of the major participants, and some letters, that have been permitted to my view in confidence by a Canadian reader. It has made it necessary for me to backtrack and revise some of what I have written, and make it essential for me to rewrite several portions of what I have done. There is no doubt as to their historical accuracy and they permit a greater understanding of the material.
>
> However, that is beside the case. This is a book that in many ways resembles a jigsaw puzzle with bits and pieces that need to be fitted with care. It is not a simple, straight-line story, and cannot be written as such. It is utterly fascinating material

and the characters are remarkable, and of course, the
events led at least to the formation of the province
of Manitoba, and to other wider effects.

 If I am wanted at all it is because I approach my
work with a feeling for history and a sense of its
overall meaning. I would be contemptuous of my readers and of the history of Canada if I were to hurry
this through.

 I insist on returning the complete $5,000 myself.
I want no strings attached.

By "the complete $5,000" he means that he did not expect his
agent, Mauri Grashin, to return his 10 percent of the fee. Louis would
pay it all back himself.

 Some unknown element, however, seems to have kept this deal
puttering along, because these comments start showing up in Louis's
journal two months later:

 October 11 1973--I am working on LOUIS RIEL, and
occasionally the first Sackett, to take place in
Shakespeare's time. The Riel book is an irritation. I
want very much to do it, but Kathy [Kathy L'Amour,
Louis's wife and my mother] is right and I should
never take on such jobs. I agreed to do this, and I
prefer to write on what excites me at the moment.
This does not . . . at the moment.

 November 7 1973--Working on the Riel book; I want
to write it, but not now and because of the commit-
ment, I must. I like to write what takes my mind at
the moment, and to write swiftly upon what excites me.

On the third of December he finally returned the option money,
writing:

 I want to write the book but to be free of dead-
lines. Kathy happy, and I also.

Louis eventually did end up using Riel in a more limited way in his novel *Lonely on the Mountain.*

Here are a few more notes:

Open with action.

RIEL - suffered from the handicap of being a fair man. His loyalty to the Queen and to his people did not waver. He wished to do the best for the latter without in any way failing in loyalty to the Queen.

Had he been a fanatic he would have had no decision to make. Rebellion would have been his course; he could have been more dynamic, he could have given unlimited scope to his speaking, he could have and would have resisted the Canadian Army, and might have stopped their advance.

His fault lay, if fault it is, in being a reasonable man. He hesitated at points where a fanatic would not. Yet, considering the situation, his end was inevitable.

His vision of lost opportunities brought him back to seek a victory when the time was past.

LLANO ESTACADO

The Beginning of a Western Novel

CHAPTER I

As they say in that song, my hat was throwed back and
my spurs was a jinglin'. I was sittin' up in the middle
of that old paint pony of mine and headin' for the same
horizon I'd been riding for these past two weeks, with
nothing changed.

That country was so flat out yonder I seen a prairie
dog come out of his hole against the horizon and he
looked so big I thought he was a bear. It seemed like an
awful lot of nowhere and I was fresh out of grub and down
to my last couple of swallows of water.

Supposedly, somewheres up ahead there was a buffalo
wallow where after rains the water gathered, and that was
supposed to tide me and my horse over until we could find
us a water hole.

Nevertheless I was young enough so's trouble didn't
seem like nothing more than sweat off my neck, and I was
riding free and lonesome with the world all to myself. Or
so I thought.

Next thing I knew something hit me spang, and I heard

a shot. I went off my horse a rolling into the dust and
somehow I'd had the good sense to grab for my Winchester
when I left the saddle. Maybe it wasn't no good sense a-
tall. It was pure-dee luck or some kind of instinct. Anyway I hit the dirt and by the time I quit rollin' I seen
some dude come from behind a little throwed-up dirt and
leggin' it for my horse.

Well, I wasn't about to see somebody ride off on my
horse and leave me out here. A man caught afoot where I
was would be a sure-enough dead man, so I rolled over
again, come up on my elbows, and got off a shot just as
that gent hit leather on my saddle.

My shot missed him but burned the pony's neck and he
went buckin' off across the prairie with this man not
down in the saddle yet, and believe me, that paint could
buck! He done a good job and throwed that hombre sky-high
and when he came down he was settin' and the horse was
gone a-flyin' off across-country and there we was, both
afoot and miles from anywhere.

My hand just naturally worked the lever on my rifle
and she spat an empty shell and taken another one in the
chamber. I looked at him settin' there cussin' and I held
that rifle on him and said, "I never shot no man cold
turkey afore, but I'm about to."

"You fly at it," he yelled. "We ain't got nothin' but
a little time, anyways. You damn fool. Had you left me
alone on that horse one of us could of had it, anyway.
Now we're both dead!"

"That was my horse," I said. "I was alive and headin'
for more days of living. You was afoot out here and as
good as dead."

He got up off the ground and I seen he didn't even
have him a six-gun. His holster was as empty as my belly.
Right then I should have started using what good sense I
had, allowing as how I had any a-tall, but I never paid

it no mind. I was sore, and I was fixing to shoot that
man.

"You say that was your horse," he said. "How do you
figure?"

"I ketched him myself right out of the wild bunch and
broke him to carry," I said. "That makes him my horse."

"Well, I say you just had him prisoner. He was his
own horse. You had no more right to him than me. He was
runnin' wild when you caught him, and he was runnin' wild
when I jumped him. I say he was my horse."

Such a boneheaded reasoning just throwed me there for
a bit and then he said, "You goin' to shoot or just stand
there? I'm gettin' tired of waitin' for it."

"Oh, shut up!" I said, disgusted. "You talk too
much!"

"If you ain't goin' to shoot me," he said, "we'd better start pickin' 'em up an' puttin' 'em down. I mean, we
ain't gettin' no closer to grub or water just standing
here while you run off at the head. Let's walk."

"What the hell?" I said, disgusted. I fell in alongside him and started to walk. He kept looking at my
rifle. I also had a six-shooter.

"Rifle gettin' heavy? Want I should carry it for
you?"

"Are you crazy? I'll carry my own piece."

"It's goin' to get mighty heavy, give you a mile or
two," he said cheerfully. "You'll be glad to let me tote
it afore sundown."

Well, we hung up our jaws and took to walking, which
no cowboy ever likes very much. By the time we'd gone a
couple of miles that rifle was getting heavy but I wasn't
about to let him have it. If ever I saw a man who was a
coyote this was him, right here alongside me.

We walked maybe six miles before we stopped to look
around. I don't know what for. That West Texas Panhandle

country they call the Llano Estacado or the Staked Plain was just about the flattest country on earth, and there was an awful lot of it.

I was commencing to spit cotton and he was already past that, but he was so mean and contrary that I didn't seem to make him no mind. He just didn't care. All he wanted was me dead and my rifle and gun-belt, and I was dedicated to the proposition that he would get neither.

Finally, the sun went down. Darkness comes almighty soon in that country but there were stars coming out and unless I was much mistook there would be a moon some-wheres further along, so we just kept puttin' one foot ahead of the other right on into the night.

The stars faded and the moon did come up and out yon-der where it was good and black the coyotes began to howl the moon, talking it up across that flat country. A time or two this gent kind of eased over toward me like he had it in mind to jump me, but I laid it down to him.

"You ain't much comp'ny and without you, I'd have been puttin' my feet under a table right down with a pot of coffee to drink, so you just step back an' keep your distance or I'll be walkin' alone."

"You scared!" he sneered. "You're as big as me. What do you say we fight, winner take the guns?"

"I got the guns. You want to fight you just take off into the night and wrastle with evil or your conscience," I said, "admittin' you have one, which I doubt."

"I was Christian-raised," he protested. "I was a gospel-shoutin' Methodist from the south. Methodists going to rule the world someday. They believe!"

"You sayin' Baptists don't? I'll have you know, I am a Baptist, least I was raised one, an' proud of it."

"Don't take much to make some folks proud," he said, and I lifted a hand at him, but he stood his ground. "You Baptists ain't got a chance out here," he sneered. "You say to get baptized you got to go down into the water."

He waved a hand. "Where's the water you can get into? You ain't got a chance to baptize nobody so there's not going to be any Baptists in West Texas or anywhere this side of the Pecos."

"What d'you know about the Pecos?" I demanded, trying to get away from a losing battle. I surely didn't know how the Baptists figured to work it and didn't feel up to speaking for my church, not having enough know-how. Truth was I hadn't been to a church but once in three, four years since I left home and that time was because I seen a yellow-haired girl goin' up the steps. Turned out she was meetin' some gent in a store-bought suit with his hair slicked down and no chance for a dusty cowpoke like me.

"I know it ain't but two or three times a year you'll get water enough to baptize anybody, even there," he sneers, and I can't argue with him because I never seen no Pecos. All I know is it's there, somewheres yonder across the horizon.

"I seen the Pecos," he said, "and the time I seen it last I was fetchin' for it and up ahead I seen a cloud of dust. I figured it for Indians, maybe, or a herd of cows, but when I came up to the river I seen it wasn't."

"What was it?"

"Fish," he said, "swimmin' upriver, huntin' for water."

After that we didn't talk much and it came to be mighty tirin' out there. He kept falling back and I kept urging him on as he seemed to be gettin' weaker and weaker by the minute. Finally I was so dry I couldn't talk and I left off yellin' at him. I just kept slogging along and next time I looked back he was nowhere in sight, but it was still moonlight and I could see a little way. I stopped and tried to yell but couldn't make a sound above a whisper. I walked on, into the night, more than half-asleep, right on my feet. I stumbled a time or two, but it was the need for sleep more than anything

else, and I was fairly walking in my sleep when suddenly
there was a whisper of something behind me and I made to
turn. Something crashed down on my skull and the last
thing I recalled was dust in my throat, which was already
dry enough.

It was the sun brought me out of it. The hot sun on
my back.

I rolled over; the sun hit me in the eyes and it
hurt. I struggled up, my skull throbbing, and slowly it
all came back to me.

My rifle was gone. My gun-belt and holster were gone.
Even the few coins in my pocket were gone and a letter I
had offering me a job on a ranch near Wagon Mound, that
was gone.

Worst of all, he'd taken my boots.

Those boots didn't come up to much. They were old and
about wore out, but they were all I had, and he knowed
it, and a man without boots wasn't going to get far.

Only I was.

Right about then I was mad enough to spit had I anything to spit with. I seen his tracks plain enough, and
started after him. What I figured to do, him having the
rifle and six-gun, I didn't know.

Suddenly I seen something. I seen a man on a horse.
At first I thought I was dreaming, for a body could stand
in one place and look off across the country for three
days and still see nothing, but there he was, maybe two
miles off, setting easy in the saddle. I yelled, whooped,
and hollered, and nothing come of it.

Anyway, all my whooping was in my mind because I
couldn't raise a sound above a whisper.

He disappeared and then maybe ten minutes after, I
heard a shot. It was afar off, but I knowed what it was.

That skunk who knocked me in the head now had him a
horse.

I fell down, I got up, then fell again. Somewhere
along there I got kind of light-headed but I kept walking. Something sobered me whilst I was lying on the
ground one time and when I got up I seen some tracks.

They were buffalo tracks . . . old ones, leading off
to the southwest.

For a moment I studied them, then walked on. Few minutes later I come on some other tracks, looked like wild
horse tracks, three or four of them, and they too led
southwest.

Now in that country one direction is as good as another unless there's water. I turned around halfway and
started off. I walked on, following those tracks, and
then they turned west again and all of a sudden the earth
split wide open in front of me and there was a canyon the
like of which I'd never seen, and in the bottom of it was
green grass, even a few cottonwoods and willows. Trouble
was, the side was sheer for maybe thirty feet and there
looked to be nowhere to get down. Now that didn't make
sense, because those buffaloes and wild horses couldn't
fly. I scouted for their tracks, found them, and found a
break in the cliff.

A half hour later I was sprawled on my belly, drinking water.

CHAPTER II

Altogether that canyon was hundreds of feet deep,
just the first thirty was sheer rimrock, and after that a
steep talus slope, partly grass-covered, to the bottom.

When I had drunk a little water I splashed more on my face and chest and sat up and looked around. From where I sat there was a little mesquite and a few willows, further along some cottonwoods.

Getting up, I started following the creek bed, only I ran out of water within about thirty yards, so I stopped and walked back. This here canyon was a hidden place, although how far it ran, I had no idea. There were horse droppings around, and plenty of buffalo tracks. The horses were mostly unshod, although there were two or three wearing shoes; all of them, and I could tell by their tracks, were running loose now.

If a horse is ridden, or even with a herd, they keep to a direction, but these were just wandering, grazing, taking a bit here and there.

From where I stood I could see maybe a quarter of a mile of the canyon, up and down. I had taken another drink and then walked on down the canyon. Knowing where the water was, I could always come back.

Rounding a bend helped none at all. From that point I could see almost a half-mile further, but there was nothing in sight. What I needed most was a weapon, something more than my belt-knife, which was all I had. Luckily, that had been fastened to my pants-belt, not the gun-belt. That polecat had not taken the time to undo two buckles.

First off, I was right glad to have come upon water, but I was sorry to lose my horse and my arms. Somehow or other I was going to have to rig something to carry water in, because this place I'd come upon seemed to be plumb lost and alone and maybe nobody even knew of it but me and some Indians.

Suddenly, I seen movement!

In one step I was out of sight in the brush, but watching. What I saw was horses, three or four mustangs that came out of the willows, where they'd probably had a

drink at some pool. One was a kind of dusty-gray, fine-
looking horse, maybe three or four years old. Although it
was some distance off it seemed to have a brand on it, so
it might have been saddle-broke sometime. Now if I could
just get my hands on that horse . . .

Two or three more showed up. Likely it was safe
enough for them down here, and certainly there was plenty
of water and grass, both scarce items up on the cap-rock
at this time of year.

Kind of easing myself out from cover, I just stood
there and let them see me. One of those mustangs pulled
up sharp when she spotted me and she blew through her
nostrils and just stared, ears pricked. Me, I stood rock-
still, letting them get used to me.

The wind was gentle, from me toward them, so they'd
caught a whiff of me too. I thought that branded horse
stood a little longer than the others, and seemed interested. "Hiya, boy!" I called, and I walked out a few
steps. The others had started drifting off, not spooked,
but being careful, yet the one still lingered.

"I think somebody treated you pretty good sometime or
other," I said aloud, "somebody you're missing, maybe.
Well, I'm friendly."

Moving a couple of more steps, I just stood there,
and that horse actually walked toward me a little,
stretching its nose in my direction. Putting out a hand,
I walked toward it, although I was still a good hundred
yards off. It turned and walked, then trotted away.

"Given time," I said, "we could get together."

The trouble was, there wasn't going to be time. Water
I had, but I'd no food, and if I didn't starve to death
then some Indian would come along and take my hair.

Among the willows and close to a cluster of big old
cottonwoods I found a place to bed down. It was smooth
grass, there was water close by, and plenty of firewood
around. Gathering sticks for a fire I startled a rabbit,

but it was gone and away in an instant. I also saw some deer tracks. Somehow I'd have to rig some snares, or starve to death.

All the while I kept a sharp eye out for people tracks, but found no sign. Of course, moccasin tracks do not make much impression and rarely last long. A boot heel can cut deep and sharp and the track may last for weeks, even months if in a sheltered place.

There wasn't much point in my making a fire even if I could manage it. I'd nothing to cook and doubted the night would be that cold. Also, it might attract unwelcome visitors. Still, what visit would be unwelcome?

Something else came to mind. If that horse yonder had known and liked a man or woman before this, he must be familiar with campfires, and much as horses like the wild, some of them were people-horses, they just naturally liked to be with people as many a dog likes it.

Not that I was fooling myself. The chances of me catching myself a horse was about one in a hundred. With any horse but that one, one in a thousand. Yet I had it to think about and I'd done some mustangin' as a youngster and knew something of how to trap wild horses.

If I did catch one I'd need a rope. If I could find an old campsite there was just a chance I might find a piece of cast-off rope. Maybe a dozen times I'd come on such things where somebody threw out a busted rope and just let it lay, or left a piece of it tied to a tree.

One thing I knew. If I got out of here at all, I'd have to use my head. There wasn't any kind of settlement within a hundred miles in any direction, and in some directions, like north or south, it was more likely two to three hundred. Not that I knew for sure, but I knew enough to know I wasn't going to walk out of here and make it.

Things surely didn't shape up so good for me. Here I was twenty-two years old, worked hard all my life

punchin' cows around Beeville and then down Uvalde way,
going up the trail from Texas to Abilene with a herd of
mean steers and just short of town by two days' drive I
tangled with an ornery old Mossy Horn from down in the
brush country and he hooked me in the side, tore me up
some, and busted a couple of ribs and a collarbone. By
the time I was up and around again my outfit had gone
back to Texas and I was broke.

All I had was my saddle and a sore-backed bronc the
boss left me. Whilst I was mending its back healed so
when I got on the street I had a horse, anyway. A cattle
buyer taken me on to ride herd on some stock he was holding on grass about twenty miles west of Abilene. When he
sold his steers I had twenty dollars coming.

Standing on the street with that twenty dollars in my
pocket I saw a young woman come into town riding a neat
little filly and they surely did make a picture. She was
settin' sidesaddle, the way women-folks rode, and she had
a gray riding outfit on.

Right alongside me a girl about fourteen stopped. She
was walking with her pa, a gray-haired man with a white
hat and a neat black suit. I heard this girl say, "Oh,
Pa! Isn't she beautiful! I wish I had a horse like that!"

"She is beautiful," her father agreed, "and if we
stay here I'll buy a horse for you."

That woman on the horse rode up and got down right
close by and the old gentleman stepped over to her and
said, "Ma'am, I will give you a hundred dollars for your
horse."

"Oh, no! I'd never sell her!"

"Two hundred?"

"I am sorry, sir. She is not for sale."

Well, it seemed to me like opportunity was knocking.
I taken off my hat. "Sir," I said, "an' Miss? For two
hundred dollars I'll find a more beautiful horse than
that one and break him gentle."

The man looked at me out of cool blue eyes. "There are very few horses I have seen west of the Mississippi for which I'd pay two hundred dollars," he said, "and that horse wasn't worth it, but my daughter wanted it."

Now I looked like pretty much of nothing. I was wearing a pair of striped store-bought pants with a blue wool shirt, a buckskin vest I'd made myself, boots with run-down heels, and a .44 Colt on my hip. My hat was battered and had been stitched with rawhide along the crown to hold it together. Moreover, I was just nineteen then, and looked it.

"Sir, I been holding some cattle out yonder on the plains, and a time or two I had to ride out west huntin' strays. Well, I seen the prettiest little horse out yonder you ever did see, proud, high-headed, and built like a dream. You should see that horse move! I started them a time or two just to see him run."

"What color was he?"

COMMENTS: The Llano Estacado, sometimes called the Staked Plain, is a high plains area covering a good deal of western Texas and eastern New Mexico. One theory about the name was that it was so flat that early travelers used stakes driven into the ground to navigate across its expanse and to find water. Though cairns (piles of rock or debris) and possibly stakes may have been used as guideposts, it is more likely that the name came from the look of the mesa-like edges of the plateau, which resembled palisades or a stockade.

It's very likely that the canyon that our narrator discovers is Palo Duro Canyon, in which the JA Ranch was established in the 1870s. Louis's early experience with this general area came when he got a job skinning dead cattle on the Elwell Ranch, near Lubbock, Texas, in the mid-1920s. Later, his family traveled across the Staked

Plain to reach eastern New Mexico, where they worked for some time.

The line about how the "polecat" took the letter containing the job offer near Wagon Mound suggests how and where the two men may eventually meet up again. It seems utterly in character for this conniver to take advantage of that particular opportunity. It's also amusing to see Louis write an exchange about Methodists and Baptists. Dad was raised Methodist, though "gospel-shoutin'" was the last thing his family seemed to be!

I'm not sure what the "polecat" used to shoot our hero out of the saddle. Certainly the next time we see him he does not have a firearm and the narrator doesn't seem to have been shot. Maybe he dropped the gun later when the horse was bucking, or maybe Louis or a good editor would have gone in and changed that section to make it a thrown rock. Obviously, the hero isn't terribly injured, and I think it would have been funnier that way; his pride is wounded, not his body.

SHELBY TUCKER

The Beginning of a Western Novel

We hadn't seen them for a long time, but we knew they were out there. We were belly down in the grass on top of a knoll and the sun was hot. We could smell the dusty grass, we could almost taste it, and above us was the wide sky, brassy with sun and heat.

It was mid-afternoon and the earth had the smell of death, because in all the world there was no help to come for us, nor anybody to ask after us or know that we had gone.

We were four men and a girl, all that was left of Mellin's wagon train, we five surrounded on a hilltop, and around us were vast and empty plains as we lay waiting with the taste of fear in our mouths.

There was Tuthill, Constanatus, Pike, and me, Shelby Tucker. And there was Laurie Connor, seventeen and pretty, already a wife and already a widow, her tall young husband dead on the charred earth of the wagon circle.

Out there in the grass were thirty Kiowas, wanting
our hair, and some of them fixing to die.

Twenty miles east of us the wagon train lay scattered
and burned, a dead thing that had moved with life, its
voices stilled, its heart no longer beating. The low rum-
ble of wagon wheels and the creak of saddle leather were
gone, and without them the world was empty, for these had
been the song of our days.

Fifty-six men and women gone, and more than twenty
children, their blood emptied to the grass, their homes
to go unbuilt . . . and we, the last of them, pursued to
this place of ending, to this hot and lonely hillside in
the long grass.

We settled ourselves down, nothing to see but the
wind, nothing to feel but the sun. The rifle was hot in
my hands.

Nine of us had made a break for it when the last
charge came, but four had died before they reached the
draw. It had been Pike spotted that draw--Pike, who
never went into a place without knowing a way out--and
in the rush of the Kiowas after loot and scalps, we got
away.

Until they found our trail.

"Hold low, kid." Pike looked over to me. "An' take
your time. They'll be comin' soon."

"I'll be all right," I told him, and I would. Pike,
he was a great one for giving advice, but a good fighting
man. I was glad he was with us.

The four of us squared to the compass in an old buffalo wallow, with Laurie under the high edge and out of
harm's way. When I took my hand off the rifle to wipe it
dry of sweat on my shirtfront, Laurie was looking at me,
her eyes big and dark, so I smiled at her to keep her
gumption up. After a moment, she smiled back.

Goes tough on a girl to lose her man that way, al-

though to my thinking Lafe Connor was no catch. The Con-
nors were a feuding outfit from the high hills, West
Virginia folks . . . and Lafe a trouble-hunting man. If
that Kiowa brave hadn't taken him it was like to have
been Pike or me, for he was pushing us, time to time.

Laurie was folks . . . mighty sweet girl, liked by
all. Pike, he had been giving her the eye when Lafe
wasn't around, but she paid him no mind.

They came then, just a whisper in the grass, crouching low and running. My Spencer took the first, hitting
him in the notch below the throat.

They were coming from all around and I could hear the
others firing. An Indian loomed suddenly, scarcely beyond
the muzzle, and I felt the gun jump in my hands but had
no memory of squeezing off. The heavy slug went into his
head over his eye and he was dead before he hit the
grass.

Then they were gone, and there was an acrid smell of
gunpowder. One suddenly came out of the grass trying to
get further away, and my bullet split his tailbone. He
went down . . . a bloody hand flew up, and I heard a low
sobbing in the grass down there, then nothing more.

Pike turned his face around. There was blood on his
temple. "Get any?"

"Three."

"Two," he said, "I got two."

"One," Tuthill said, "and maybe another."

"Four," the Greek spoke quietly, "all dead."

Pike looked at him. "Figured you were new to this."

Constanatus shrugged. "They are like Turks. I have
killed Turks and Russkies since I was a boy."

We waited then, not thinking of water, not thinking
of anything. We had hurt them . . . worse than expected,
no doubt. They would be arguing now, planning another attack. But ten down . . . that was shooting.

A cool breeze moved in the grass, and high near the

sun a buzzard swung in wide, slow circles. Of us all, he
was the one sure to win.

We had two horses when we slipped away during that
final attack at the wagon train. Laurie rode, and the
others of us took turns. We made fast time, but not fast
enough. The Kiowas had stampeded our horses first thing,
and even if we drove them off we were footloose in the
midst of everything and nothing.

My mouth was dry and my head ached with a slow, dull
throb. Lying there close to the ground I watched an ant
working, felt a dry blade of grass brushing my cheek.
When I looked around, Pike was watching Laurie and I
could see the woman-hunger in his eyes.

Pike was a blond, lean-waisted, tough-walking man
with scars to his hide. He wore one gun in sight and a
hideout gun under his shirt. We met in Natchez-Under-the-
Hill, him nigh to thirty, me just pushing nineteen. We
teamed up, neither of us talking much.

Men walked shy of him, all but Lafe Connor. There was
trouble coming between them, and we all knew it. Pike
fancied himself with a handgun . . . and in Ash Hollow,
on the way west, he had killed a man.

The sun declined and a low wind stirred the grass.
The Kiowas came suddenly out of the sun moving with the
wind, and they came shooting.

My first shot laid along the grass tops into a big,
dark-skinned man. He went down, and I came up, shooting
the Spencer from the hip. A Kiowa screamed . . . another
fell. Behind me there was a thud of a bullet striking
flesh, and I met the last Kiowa with an empty gun. But
the muzzle jerked up hard to the soft spot behind his
jawbone and his head jerked back, his scream choking on
blood and dying with the dull thunk of my rifle butt
against his skull.

Then there was quiet upon the grass, wind stirring
and the sun low across the plains.

Tuthill was gone. He took one through the chest and one high through the shoulder, but dead. The Greek was kneeling and Laurie working at a bandage on his right arm. You could see the shock in his eyes.

Pike sat up and rolled a smoke, looking at me. "You an' me now, kid." His face looked gray, but the old hard light was there, and I was glad again that it was Pike, for he was a fighting man.

Not talking, I got Tuthill's rifle and loaded it, took the ammunition off his body. Then I loaded the Greek's rifle. When I put them down I took out my Bowie. It was razor-sharp.

"Watch for me," I said. "I'll be back."

Then I rolled over the rim of the wallow into the grass. Behind me Laurie called my name and I heard Pike swear, but I was belly down on the ground and moving through the grass.

Pike, he figured himself for an old-timer, but me, I'd lost my parents when I was eleven on the Overland Trail, and lived three years with the Shoshones. At fourteen I was driving a freight wagon on the Santa Fe Trail and fighting Apaches in the Mogollons.

The Kiowas would know we'd lost a man . . . might figure there was two gone. And they knew Laurie was there. They wouldn't be expecting me down among them, and the Shoshones had taught me how to move in grass.

Sweating, I was, and the dust from the grass itched my skin. Flat down I moved, snaking along until I saw brown skin, a startled face, a voice starting to scream. My hand choked it off at his throat and the knife went in twice, fast and slick. In and out, and I held his throat until he was dead. Only sound his heels kicking in the grass.

You can bet they heard it, though, and wondered. Then I was moving on . . . only now I had a bow and the arrows.

The next one I saw was a dozen yards off across a
little cut in the slope. The Shoshones had taught me to
use a bow, too. The arrow went into his kidney and he
screamed, leaping up and dragging at the arrow-shaft. My
second went to his throat. . . .

A long time I lay still then. The Kiowas would be
trying to figure what had happened. They were superstitious and they would not like this happening among them.
One reared up as if to see and Pike's Sharps put him
down.

After a while I snaked it back to the wallow and
rolled over the rim. Laurie, she looked at me big-eyed
but Pike, he said nothing.

Not for a while. Then he said, "I think they've
gone."

"I think so, too."

He looked to me again. He had me figured for a kid
from the farms. "What happened out there?"

Me, I shrugged. Pike looked at the bow and the quiver
of arrows. "Find a dead one?"

"He was dead when I took these off him."

When dark came we started out, walking. Then we found
four Indian ponies waiting for riders that would never
come. We mounted up and rode west, and Pike, he began si-
dling up to Laurie.

"Lafe's gone," he said. "You should have you a man."

Laurie said nothing, just looking between her pony's
ears at the low stars.

Me, I said nothing either, leading that spare horse.
It was no time to be talking to that girl. If she had a
lot of love for Lafe Connor it could surprise me, for he
was a hard, unfeeling man. Nevertheless, he was a short
time dead and she had been his wife.

"We'll make it fine," he said, "you an' me. Good country west of here."

She said nothing at all, only I could see the white of her face, looking to me.

"Leave it lay," I said.

Pike's head came around, sharp. "My business, kid."

"Give it time," I told him.

He said nothing for maybe a hundred steps, and then he agreed, "Maybe you're right." But, he added, "She might's well get used to it."

Darkness lay soft upon the land, coolness on our faces, and miles fell behind us with the turning of the stars and the night-walking moon. We'd no water, nor any food, and where there was water there might be Indians. Yet when the sky was gray behind us, I saw a fringe of darkness in a low place . . . trees.

Dark trees and the smell of water. We moved toward them, taking it easy. A dozen cottonwoods, bunches of willows, and a pool. We drank, and we filled empty canteens, and Pike looked at Laurie. "We'll bed down here," he said.

Her face was pale in the vague light, her eyes large and frightened. I did not know what she was thinking. Only I said, "No."

Pike looked at me again, and there was nothing nice in the look. "You crossin' me, kid? Once too often."

I just looked at him. He could sling a gun, all right, but so could I . . . and I had, an' more than him. Only he knew nothing of that.

"Ain't safe," I said. "We got to move. This here place is a Comanche water hole." I lied then. "I seen their tracks."

He stood silent, not liking it, but not wanting to fight Comanches, either. Kiowas were bad enough. Comanches were worse . . . much worse.

We took out, riding west again, the rising sun at our
backs, holding to the hills just below the ridges, keeping from being sky-lined, yet staying where the going was
easy. All morning we rode, and Laurie, she was dropping
in the saddle, she was all in.

"We got to rest, kid." Pike was looking around. "Comanches or not."

"Place up ahead. Water in a cave."

Pike looked at me again, funny-like. He was puzzled,
taking me as he did for a kid green to the West, and I'd
never told him different.

First thing I saw was that twisted paloverde. Then
the white gash in the cap-rock. We rode over the lip, the
horses taking it easy-like, then down a long path toward
the bottom of the canyon, but before we were halfway down
we made a sharp double-back amongst some broken chunks of
the whitish rock. The cave was there, like I remembered
it, half-concealed by brush.

Pike looked at it, big enough for us and horses, too.
He walked in, then came back. He looked at me, his hands
on his hips. "How'd you know this place?"

"Camped here once. More'n a year ago. This here is
border country. Comanches east, Apaches west. Not many
ride through here."

Laurie almost fell when she got out of the saddle,
and I caught her. "Here!" Pike said. "I'll help her."

"She's already helped," I said, and guided her inside
the cave to where she could sit down.

Pike, he was almighty quiet while we unsaddled our
blankets and canteens, along with the extra rifles. The
horses we staked out on grass near the cave, after letting them water at the pool inside.

Out of the corner of my eye I saw Pike shift his gun
a little, and he started over to me. Turning around before he got to me, I said, "Look." He stopped, squared

toward me, his feet apart. "This girl is tired. She lost her man. It ain't right to start pushin' her. Let it go for a while."

"You keep your advice to yourself. She's done been married. She ain't no baby."

"She's waitin', though. She makes up her own mind, in her own good time."

"Maybe you think she'd choose you?" he sneered.

"Might be."

For four long counts I let that stand, keeping him on edge. Then I said, "Pike, you're a first-class fightin' man. Without you, neither Laurie nor me would be here. But without me, neither you nor Laurie would be here, either. There's a sight of country west. I know that country. I like you, an' I don't want trouble, but if you can't use your head, an' if you want to die, have at it."

He didn't like none of it. He stood there, his eyes cold, trying to figure what was behind my talk. It was not easy to fit this into the picture he'd made of me, but he was no fool.

If we started shooting, one of us would die, maybe both. And it was me knew the country. He swore and turned sharp away, but I knew it was not over, just a sort of a truce-like.

COMMENTS: Okay, a classic L'Amour beginning, except ... what happened to the Greek guy? He was kind of a badass and he was just winged. But that's why some of these stories were started over and over again; as Louis discovered where the story was taking him, he would adjust and adjust until it was ready to go all the way to the finish. Or he'd discover that the story just wasn't ready to be told and he'd move on to something else. In the next iteration, the Greek would probably never have been there, or would have died in the fight. As in so many other endeavors, getting the beginning right was critical to the way he worked.

This character Shelby Tucker should not be confused with Edwin Shelvin Tucker. Ed Tucker appears in Louis's novel *Tucker* and the little jewel of a short story that the novel was adapted from, called "Cap-Rock Rancher" . . . one of my all-time favorites.

CITIZEN OF THE DARKER STREETS

The Beginning of an Adventure Story

Bangkok is the place . . . two a.m. the time . . .
and across the street in the dark maw of an alley waits a
lean wolf of the streets . . . with a knife. He is waiting for me.

It is hot and still and in the fetid air there is a
lingering smell of dust, overripe fruit, sweaty bodies,
heat, and opium. . . . . It is the smell of the tropics,
the smell of Bangkok, of Makassar, of Pondicherry. It is
the smell of death.

Behind me, drawn back into a shadowed doorway, is a
hulking brute with huge hands and powerful shoulders. He
has been following me, and like his slat-ribbed comrade
across the way, he has slowly been edging me away from
the principal streets, readying me for the kill.

My name is Martin Cross, they call me "China" Cross,
and my home is anywhere in the world.

Somewhere in town there is a girl, a beautiful, lus-
cious girl, with a golden-tan body like something out of

a lonely man's dream of paradise, a girl lost and frightened . . . and in danger.

So here I am, citizen of the darker streets, by-
stander in the alleys of dingy commerce, spectator in the
theater of iniquity, a searcher for things lost . . . a
man looking for a girl in a town where girls are a dime a
dozen. China Cross, the man who finds things, that's me.
Paintings, matched pearls, rare volumes, hidden wills, the
rarest of rate stamps, strange wild animals from the deep-
est jungle, and even lost and frightened girls in Bangkok.

China Cross whose life right now isn't worth a
plugged peso or a shot of cut gin. A man whom somebody
had spotted for what he was before he had his feet off
the dock, a man who is never supposed to see the light of
another day.

Sweat trickling down my stomach, sweat trickling between my shoulder blades, sweat greasy on my face, it is
two a.m. and the only way open for me is toward the rice
mills and the wharves, toward the narrowing streets and
the dark slips where sampans bob on the slow swell of the
harbor waters.

Out of the doorway I move and behind me moves the one
man, across the street the other. Ahead of me there is a
narrow and odorous alley and they are pressing me toward
it. Somewhere out on the water sounds the deep-throated
blast of a steamer, and then in the alleyway before me
there is movement, a quick rush of bare feet on paving,
and there is no time--knives flash, and my shoulder hits
a door in the wall near me. The latch gives way and I
fall inward into deeper, more velvety blackness, and as I
fall my hand goes to my shoulder holster and my .380 automatic jumps, a shell casing taps the wall then the
floor and my ears are ringing. The door is empty again
and I hear the moaning of a dying man who wished to kill
but did not think to die himself.

This is a sort of warehouse, a dark place haunted by
the ghostlike smells of the thousand cargoes once stored
here. I weave among the bales, finding and feeling my
way, using my fingers for eyes. Behind there is movement
again. . . . My hand lifts a latch, the door closes
softly behind me. I feel for a bar and find it. Carefully
I place the bar across the door. A stairway leads into
upper darkness.

The air is close and hot and I climb. My shirt
presses damply against my chest and at the head of the
stairs I pause, aware of life around me . . . the stirring and breathing of many bodies, a whisper of movement,
a deep sigh, the sickish-sweet smell of opium and of
long-dead smoke . . . a smell of living bodies in thick,
close air.

Moving, I stumble over legs. A faint voice is plain-
tive with protest. . . . These are coolies waiting for
another day of labor--the loaders of ships, the carriers
of bales, sodden with opium and working only for a bowl
of rice, a dried fish, and the dark stuff of the poppy's
heart which brings them escape from hunger, misery, and
life.

Behind me there is a splintering. . . . The door is
open for the air stirs faintly. Trapped.

Through the bodies, over them, stumbling, suddenly a
vacant place among them and an idea . . . Swiftly I
strip, glad that my body is bronzed by sun and wind.
Naked to my shorts, I tuck the legs up until I have only
what looks to be a breechclout, and then I lie down among
them . . . among the collapsed bodies and among the in-
sect life that accompanies them. . . . I lie still,
clutching my pistol beneath my body, waiting.

A light flashes and plays over the room, over the
bodies. There is a stirring and a growing chorus of complaint. It is a huge loft and over a hundred men are
sprawled about. A low voice says, "I don't think he came

up here." And a reply in the music of Malaya, "If he did,
he went out. He is not here now."

The flashlight snapped off; feet murmur on the
stairs. Rising, I listen, then climb into my clothing. My
hand feels for my gun to be sure it is still with
me. . . . On the floor a man stirs, whimpering softly like
a sick child in the night . . . and then I move away.

Day was a vague promise over the temple towers when I
was once more in my room. After a shower I stretched out
on the hard bed of the tropics and stared up at the ceiling beyond the mosquito netting.

Who had alerted them to the fact that I was searching
for Gwen Moran? Or could these have been casual thieves?
Or someone who suspected me of being an American agent,
spying on the local Communist allies? Most of all, I wondered, where was Gwen Moran, the girl whose lovely face
had been living with me since the pictures arrived a few
hours before?

A friend of my father's had known that I was in
Macao; his cabled offer had reached me there. Five thousand and all expenses if I could bring her home safely.
Pictures and details were to go by air and would be
awaiting me in Bangkok.

Gwen Moran had been one of a party of five. She had
come ashore from a world cruise . . . and had disappeared
from her hotel later, leaving a note that she had fallen
in love and would be married at once . . . a cable to her
father to the same effect. Not to worry, details later.

Silence, then, and nothing more . . . silence, until
one night an agonized cry for help over the shortwave . . .
A man in Los Angeles, idling over his set in the morning's small hours, caught the call . . . another in Ma-
nila picked it up. A frightened girl begging for help, a
call cut quickly off.

American officials could learn nothing. Local reports
were that she had run off with a man, perhaps had flown
to Singapore. The following morning my own inquiries
began. I only knew two things--she had access to a shortwave set and her kidnapper could hire killers. Both indicated wealth, perhaps power.

The shortwave clue cooled swiftly--it could have been
no known set in the vicinity of Bangkok. So I gathered
the details. Gwen had come ashore with her party and they
had stopped at the Oriental, an excellent and respectable
hotel near the river, a cooler location than my own stopping place. The party had consisted of a man and wife in
their early fifties and the three girls in their twenties. They had gone to the Chez Eve for dinner.

Gwen attracted immediate and appreciative attention.
She danced with a French Colonel, with the local director
of an American firm, twice with former American flyers.
And she had talked briefly with a man in the shadows at
one side of the floor.

Nobody knew what was said or who he was. Returning to
her table, Gwen made no comment. Local officials knew
nothing more. . . . I fell asleep mulling over the few
known facts.

At noon I awakened suddenly and swung my feet to the
floor. My tongue was thick and my brain was foggy. The
lethargy left by sleeping through the hot, still morning
deadened my muscles. By the time I'd shaved and showered
I felt better, so I went around to the Chez Eve and
perched on a bar stool.

In Bangkok, this is the place to go. It is a nightclub, a restaurant, an odd combination of the American
and Eastern. Seated on one of the chromium bar stools, I
ordered a long, cool Myrtle Bank Punch and began to study
the situation.

A man walked up and straddled the stool beside mine.
He was enormously fat with a tiny mouth and three chins.
A waxed mustache perched on his lip and he had a high
forehead from which the hair waved back gracefully. He
smelled of expensive perfume and his large, intelligent
eyes met mine in the mirror back of the bar. He smiled.
Because of the perfume I viewed the smile with some skepticism.

From an inside pocket he drew a leather wallet, carefully extracting five neat, new hundred-dollar bills. He
placed them carefully on the bar between us, and atop
them he placed a plane ticket for Los Angeles.

"California!" His voice held a fluted overtone. "How
lovely at this time of year!"

Extracting a long, slim cigarette from a gold case,
he offered the case to me and when I declined, returned
it to his pocket and signaled for a drink. He fitted the
cigarette into an ivory holder. "So much cooler in California, Mr. Cross. Have you been there lately?"

So he knew my name. The bartender came and spoke with
respect as he took the order for a drink.

"Not lately," I said, "and I've no plan to return
soon."

He lit his cigarette, smiling wisely. Then he touched
the money lightly with his manicured fingers, moving it
toward me. "A good-bye to Bangkok, then a quick
flight . . . Ah, how I envy you!"

"There's the ticket," I said, "and there's the cash.
They are yours, aren't they?"

He shrugged dismally. "They are a present, Mr. Cross.
A present from someone who wishes you well. Someone who
would like to think of you sunning on the beaches of faraway California instead of encountering the risks of life
in our dark and lonely streets. Oh, I'm sure, Mr. Cross,
that you would find it so much more healthful if you were
there!"

"Pick up the money," I said quietly, "and tell whoever you work for to deliver Gwen Moran to me not later
than midnight."

His face stiffened and he put his cigarette down
quickly. "I know nothing of this Gwen Moran," he said impatiently, "but you are a fool! A miserable, interfering
fool!" He hitched his fat behind off the stool and
straightened his coat, but before he could speak again my
left hand shot out and the fingers went down inside his
collar. Closing my fist I bent my knuckles hard against
his Adam's apple. He gagged and gasped, his eyes bulging,
his hands fighting wildly to tear my fist away.

Pulling him close I said quietly, "Don't call me a
fool, Fat Boy"--nobody had noticed us; the bartender was
deeply engrossed in a flashy brunette down the bar--"just
go tell your boss what I said!" I jerked him toward me to
get him off balance, then shoved back hard and let go.

He hit the floor on his fat behind. Heads turned and
the bartender hurried up toward us. My left hand held my
drink and I glanced at the bartender and shook my head
gravely. "Think of that! Only one drink, too!"

Fat Boy was rising awkwardly from the floor, and when
he straightened up his eyes were ugly with hatred. I gestured toward the money on the bar. "Yours," I said.

"Use it," he told me, low-voiced, "use it, or by
the--!" He jerked his coat down and bustled out.

The bartender looked at the money and then at me. I
picked up the bills. Who was I to look gift horses in the
teeth? Then I held one of the century notes in my fingers
and glanced up at the bartender. "That guy," I asked.
"Who was he?"

The bartender glanced at the century note. "His name
is Siatin," he said. "He's secretary to some big shot. Or
right-hand man for him."

"What big shot?"

He hesitated, not liking it much but liking the money

more. "Banjak," he said, and he spoke the name in a low
voice.

"And who," I asked, "is he?"

He hesitated again. "Everybody knows him," he said.
"He's from an old family in Thailand, but a very unpopu-
lar family. Lately"--he glanced right and left, wiping a
glass--"they say he's dickering with the Reds. But he's
got money, he's got power, and there's men working for
him who'd cut your throat slick as a whistle."

The century note was folded and slid over the counter. He palmed it. "You watch your step," he said warn-
ingly.

"Thanks." I got up and straightened my coat a little.
"My name," I said, "is Martin Cross. I'm looking for Gwen
Moran, that American girl who disappeared. If you hear
anything, let me know."

"Yeah." He put the glass down and picked up another.
"That Banjak," he said softly, "he's completely nuts over
blondes."

Banjak's name was a sure way to ring down a curtain
of silence, I soon discovered. But here and there a ray
of light filtered through the curtain. He had an import-
ing and exporting business . . . largely, rumor said, oil
and rubber to Russia and Red China . . . and tin. He had
an estate on the Mekong on the Indo-Chinese border, plus
a house in town, a huge, ancient, rambling place. From
that estate a man with a launch could get to Indo-China
in five minutes, to Burma in a matter of two or three
hours, to Red China in but a little more.

It was almost dark when I entered the Chez Eve again,
and when I found a seat at the crowded bar I ordered a
bourbon and soda from the same bartender. He glanced at
me, nodded slightly, and said, "Nice to see you again,
Mr. Cross. Some men were looking for you."

"Thanks," I said, catching his expression. Whoever had been looking for me had been anything but friendly, I could bank on that.

Over the bourbon and soda I contemplated the situation. If it was true that Banjak was active in supplying the Reds, a shortwave set would be an asset, and it might be either here or on the Mekong. And one thing was certain. If Banjak had gone so far as to kidnap an American girl she was either out of the city or extremely well guarded.

A man came into the room and walked across and slid onto a stool beside me. He was a sallow man with hollow cheeks and a lank, unhealthy frame. His eyes were large and luminous, his features a mixture of Eastern peoples. He ordered a drink and under his breath said, "You are Mr. Cross? You search for the young American lady?"

"That's right." I kept my own voice low.

"I can take you to her," he said softly, "but quickly, or she will be taken away."

"To the Mekong?"

"Who knows?" He lifted a shoulder. "If you will come, it is outside the door, and stop for nothing. You have frightened Banjak, and a frightened Banjak is dangerous."

It could be a trap or it could be the lead I wanted. "Your interest is what?" I asked him.

He lifted his drink and speaking around the edge of the glass, he said, "Nothing . . . except that the lovely lady looked very sad, and what I am not strong enough to do might be done by another, such as you."

He finished his drink and walked outside and I followed him after a minute or so. He was standing near a palm and when he saw me he started to walk away, going very slowly. I followed at a reasonable distance, which he seemed to want. . . . The street was brightly lit, but not for long. . . . He turned into a dingy byway between two buildings and issuing out on the street of the Bampon

Boon Building . . . then he began to hurry. Soon he
paused and lit a cigarette and I joined him.

"We go faster now," he said, gesturing at an antique
car standing by the curb. It was something hatched in a
remote period probably not long after the Spanish-
American War, if anybody remembers when that was. Sur-
prisingly, the motor purred like a contented tomcat and
when I climbed in we moved smoothly away from the curb
and down the street.

"I am a clerk," he explained, "a seller of jade in a
shop. Miss Moran had come to my shop to buy jade and she
was followed there by a man I knew. He approached her,
and she was very sharp with him and when she talked again
to me I showed her a bit of jade and warned her about
this fat man . . . that he worked for a powerful man who
served a country that was very dangerous, that she should
join her friends at once and stay with them."

"And then?"

"She asked that I escort her to the hotel with her
purchases and my employer permitted me to go, but we were
followed there."

"By whom?"

"It is said you have met Siatin. It was he."

Suddenly the car slowed, driving down a long avenue
lined with trees. This was not exactly a street, and not
exactly a country lane, but it resembled both. Turning
the car, suddenly he stopped under some trees and got
out. Set well back in a huge garden was a vast, rambling
old mansion.

"It is the house of Banjak?"

"Yes, and what you will do now, I do not know."

"Watch me," I said.

Stepping into the street I started for the gate. My
idea was to go right up to the house, demand to see the
girl, and if she wanted to come, take her away. There was
a chance in a hundred it might work or that I might at

least find out if she was still in Bangkok. If that
failed, then I could take other steps. They had started
the rough stuff, but I would avoid it, if possible.

There was an iron gate between stone columns and it
was standing open just a little. There was a small hut
for a gate tender but he was, fortunately, nowhere in
sight. I entered and walked swiftly up the gravel drive.

At the huge double door, I pulled a bell cord and
waited. The doors opened finally, and a tall man in a long
coat stood there. He wore a small round cap on his head.

"I want to see Banjak," I said.

"I am sorry. He is not here." The servant started to
close the door but I put my shoulder against it and
stepped in. He backed away from me, his eyes wary but not
frightened. "I have said he is not here. If you persist,
you shall have trouble."

"I was born to trouble," I replied shortly. "You will
tell him I am here. If not him, tell Siatin. But it's
Banjak I want to see."

Siatin stepped into sight from a doorway concealed by
curtains. His fat jowls were set and hard now, and there
was a light in his eyes that was anything but promising
for my future. When I started to step by him the servant
put up a hand as if to stop me and I swung him aside.
Face to face with Siatin, I said, "Where's that girl? I
want her and I want her now!"

Before he could speak, there was a slight movement
and on the steps at the end of the hall was a huge man
clad in a white silk suit with a green sash. He was built
like a Turkish wrestler, and he came slowly down the
steps. He paused a dozen feet away, his black eyes utterly cold.

"You wished to see me? I am Banjak."

"I have come for Gwen Moran."

"I have never heard of her." He spoke calmly, his
eyes level.

"You're a liar." I said it flatly. I was in this as deep as I could get now, and my only chance was to push on through. Anyway, I hate to take a pushing around. This man had tried to have me killed, and he had kidnapped an American girl. In my own way, I, too, could be ruthless. "Gwen Moran is here or in some place of which you know. I want her now. And if I don't get her at once, I'll take steps."

He smiled, a faintly supercilious smile, yet impatient, too. "What steps?" he sneered. "Your government will do nothing. It would be bad for propaganda. There is nothing you can do. Nothing at all."

It was coming up in me and I could feel it. I wanted to take a swing at this big lug. Stifling the impulse for the moment in favor of sometime more opportune, I said, "I've no intention of calling in my government. They have too many problems to bother with something I can handle myself."

"You think well of yourself," he said shortly. "Now leave, or I'll have you beaten and thrown out."

"Why don't you try it?" I suggested. "What's the matter? Are you a yellow rat aside from being a stealer of women?"

He didn't like it. He didn't like it even a little, and he liked it less that Siatin and the servant stood there listening. His face darkened with angry blood and he took a catlike step forward, then stopped. "Siatin," he said, "have him beaten and thrown out." Deliberately, he turned and started for the stairs.

If I was thrown out now--but I wasn't going to be. Not without a fight.

With a lunge, I started for him. Siatin and the servant both sprang for me, but they were too slow. Head down, I rammed Banjak in the behind and at the same time grabbed his ankles and jerked up, hard. Grabbed in that way, a man can only fall on his face, but he strikes headfirst. Banjak came down hard, only the soft carpeting on the stairs saving him from a cracked skull. I went over him, and up the stairs.

The servant was fast but not eager, and Siatin much too fat and slow. I made the top of the stairs with time to spare and glanced swiftly both ways. Somewhere far off in the huge old building I heard a bell ringing.

Now that I was in the house I meant to stay. That bell was calling help, I knew. But with luck they would not find me. The left side of the house opened onto the garden, so I turned left, but then circled around by a passage that led across the building and ducked into the first door on the right side.

It was a cozy room lined with books. On the stand was a cigarette, still smoking. There was also an open book. Evidently it was from here that Banjak had come. I crossed the room to another door, and opening it, stepped into a bedchamber. Crossing that, I passed through an ultramodern bathroom into a larger chamber that was empty. Behind me somewhere, I heard a door open.

COMMENTS: The mention in this story of the nightclub Chez Eve and the fact that Gwen was seen dancing with a "French Colonel" suggests that it might have been written prior to the mid-1950s, when the French were forced to leave Indochina. Chez Eve opened sometime in the 1940s and was famous as one of the few air-conditioned public places in Bangkok. Louis's comment about "American flyers" is probably based on the fact that two of the partners who owned the Oriental Hotel were pilots from the USA; a number of others in the expatriate community were men who had been with the wartime OSS. Although I do not believe that Louis was ever in Thailand, he did make several stops just to the south, along the Malay Peninsula, prior to World War II, a somewhat similar environment.

Obviously, Dad was still finding his way with this one; but it was shaping up to be a fun story and I wish he'd continued it. I'm especially intrigued by Louis's mention of his protagonist's father. Heroes with important, and still living, fathers are somewhat uncommon in L'Amour fiction. I really wonder what he was planning to do with that relationship, or if it was just a way to get Martin Cross involved.

The next story is also set in Bangkok. For a while, I wondered if returning to write about this city was due to the influence of a pair of Thai brothers my mom and dad met in the late 1950s. They originally came to Southern California to go to college, and have since become virtual cousins of ours. We have now known four generations of this prestigious Thai family. Yet both "Citizen of the Darker Streets" and the next title, "Where Flows the Bangkok," feel more like they come from an earlier period, after World War II, but before 1958 or so.

———————————————————

WHERE FLOWS THE BANGKOK

A Treatment for an Adventure Story

Kip Morgan leaves a tramp steamer in Bangkok looking more like a beachcomber than the man he is looking for, the drifting ne'er-do-well nephew of rich old Miles Vaughn, who had died leaving several millions and no relatives but Jim Vaughn. After several months of drifting from port to port, Morgan has finally arrived in Bangkok, aware that this was the last place Jim Vaughn had headed for--twenty years before.

After making inquiries around town, Morgan, unshaven and in battered whites, drifts into a waterfront night-club, where he finds a cool, self-possessed-looking girl he has been told about. He tells her he is a detective from the States looking for a man named Vaughn. She leaves him abruptly.

Following her, an attempt is made to kill him, and after a street battle, Morgan takes shelter from his hunters in the loft of a warehouse, where a hundred or so opium-drugged coolies lay sprawled, sleeping. Stripping off his coat and shirt he lies among them, and is so

tanned that he is passed over in the rather cursory inspection.

Getting back to his hotel, he falls into bed, and in
the morning, freshly bathed and shaved, wearing fresh
clothes, he starts to follow his one clue--the girl's peculiar reaction to his comment.

The girl is one Etta Bryan, an entertainer in a
nightclub, and she has lived in Bangkok most of her life,
coming there as a child from Gorontalo, in the Celebes.
Listening to her sing, he sees another watcher is one of
his pursuers from the evening before. Now, Morgan is a
tough man himself, and doesn't relish being shoved
around. He starts for the man, and the fellow ducks out
the door. Following, Morgan finds the man laying for him
and they slug it out. The police come and the man escapes. Etta Bryan will still not talk to him.

He waits to follow her but several tough men with
guns close in. Morgan is taken to a waterfront shack,
where a bruised and battered man awaits him. This, the
man with whom he fought, is Shanghai Charley. He slaps
Morgan across the mouth. "So, Detective, you are lookin'
for me, are you?"

Morgan tells him he has made a mistake, that the man
he is looking for is much older, a man named Vaughn. Jim
Vaughn.

"Jim Vaughn? What you want with him?"

Morgan explains about the estate, and Shanghai Charley smokes thoughtfully. Then he apologizes for the slap
and the trouble, explaining that he himself is wanted in
the States, and has no intention of going back or being
taken back. He also tells Morgan that Vaughn is dead.
Then he asks, "This Vaughn now? If he had a kid, wouldn't
the kid inherit?"

Morgan learns that Vaughn had fathered a child. That
he had settled down at last in Bangkok, had married the
daughter of a planter, and they had lived for years.

Charley claims he can produce the child. For a price.
Five thousand dollars.

The following day, Morgan does a little investigating
of his own, then comes to meet Shanghai Charley, who
tells him Etta Bryan is the child. That Vaughn was her
father.

At Etta's home, she shows him several pictures of Jim
Vaughn, including one taken with the dead uncle. She
shows him a marriage license--Jim Vaughn and his wife--
she shows him a watch, a ring, and a few other possessions to prove her claim.

Still unsatisfied, Morgan goes to a Sister, who tells
him some facts and hands him several papers. Then going
to an old man, he learns from him that Etta Bryan had
come to Bangkok from Gorontalo, all right, but that Jim
Vaughn had gone after her, and had brought her back with
him.

Shanghai Charley insists she is the child, but Morgan
nevertheless believes Charley is attempting a fraud . . .
that he knows something about the child but is attempting
to substitute a stooge of his own. Despite that, Morgan
is attracted to Etta.

Charley is obviously worried. He will not leave the
house, tries to hurry the decision through, tries to get
money from Morgan, even gets into Morgan's room and attempts to rob him while he is asleep. When caught, he
laughs it off, then insists again that Etta is the right
child. That it is no trouble for Morgan--why not take her
back to claim the estate? He can, he says, furnish depo-
sitions to attest to her birth.

As Charley has underworld connections everywhere,
Morgan has no doubt of this, but he believes that for
personal reasons Shanghai Charley would like to see Etta
get the money.

Returning to the house, he accuses them both of

fraud, and tells them what he has learned from the Sister at the convent--that the child was not a girl, but a boy!

Then Charley, obviously in a sweat of fear, asks him again for money, offers to forward evidence later as to who the child is, evidence to prove there has been a mistake.

Disgusted, Morgan goes to the door to leave. Two men lunge in, firing. Shanghai Charley goes down, killing one man as he falls, and Morgan gets the other. These are the men Charley has defrauded and the ones he has been trying to escape.

Dying, Charley begs Morgan to take Etta anyway, explains that he had planned to blackmail her into paying him large sums after she got the estate, but to take her--that she's a good kid, and was the daughter of an old friend of Jim Vaughn's. Much as he would like to, Morgan refuses.

Charley then asks to see Etta. Morgan sends her in, and leaves them together with a mission priest who is a doctor.

Called back, Charley tells Morgan that he has made his point. That he has married Etta, making her <u>his</u> heir. When Morgan wants to know what that means, Charley explains that <u>he</u> was Jim Vaughn's son!

He hands Morgan the papers, birth certificate and a passport, to prove it.

COMMENTS: Kip Morgan was a character Louis first introduced in the somewhat comedic short story "The Dream Fighter." Kip then evolved over the course of several stories from a boxer into a private detective.

Occasionally, Louis would write treatments, like this one, when he was trying to sell ideas or even finished stories to motion-picture or television companies. But because this draft is so roughly sketched out I think it's more likely an example of Louis writing a treatment for his own use, as a trial run for a full-fledged story. He did this very rarely because it was nearly the same amount of work as writing the story itself.

Perhaps this theory explains the origin of some of the other treatments in this volume . . . that they were written more as creative experiments than sales tools. I have always hesitated to make that assumption, knowing that Dad disliked having a tale too completely worked out before he really started writing. But he would have had to learn that lesson at some point, so maybe what we are looking at is part of the learning process.

It is also interesting to see both the city of Bangkok and the scene where the hero hides in the opium den show up again. I suspect that this fragment was written before "Citizen of the Darker Streets," but that is only my intuition; I have no evidence.

Certainly "Where Flows the Bangkok" has a lot of aspects that need to be improved, but that is one of the reasons to create a treatment: to allow the writer to confront the story and see where it leads.

————————————

VANDERDYKE

The First Three Chapters of a Historical Novel

CHAPTER 1

Icy wind fluttered the small flame and the firelight danced the shadows on their faces. The night was bitter cold, and the tiny fire struggled bravely to put out a warmth that died almost at the edge of its flame. But these were men strange to comfort, men grown harsh in the harshness of the winter wilderness.

Jeblish Mun, lean and hawk-featured, poked a small stick into the fire.

"He wants you dead, Van. He was makin' war-talk, general-like, but when he spoke of you he was most pa'-tic'lar, and he spoke clear, with no nonsense to him.

"He said, 'I do not want him taken--I want him killed. I want to see not his scalp but his <u>head</u>. I want to look into his dead eyes. Then I can be sure.'"

"Give any reason why he was favoring me?"

"None that would hold water. He made it out you were the King's enemy in these here woods, but it surely seemed like there was more to it, the way he spoke."

"Jeb?" Vanderdyke looked up from under his brows from

where he lay beside the fire. "You'd best not go back. I
think you've played out your string around Detroit."

"Kin o' got that idee m'self."

"Did he have a name? Who was he?"

"Never heard no name, an' I didn't waste around
tryin' to find out. Names don't cut much ice, no way. He
was a tall man, on the thinnish side, but thin like a
whip or a steel blade. Wore one o' them powdered wigs
like they wear down to the settlements. Described you to
a T. Gave me the shivers, like somebody steppin' on your
grave. He really wants you dead, Van."

Vanderdyke sat up, hunching his shoulders against the
wind. It was cold . . . cold, cold, cold. Even to him it
was cold, and he had not slept under a roof a dozen
nights in the year.

"Who was there?"

"Couple of dozen Senecas, some Onondagas, and a Mohawk or two. I seen some Cayuga around the fort, so if
it's Iroquois you want, they're all there. I could fairly
feel those eyes right in the middle of my back. I taken
out. Cold as it was, I never waited for daybreak. I just
up an' skedaddled while I had my hair."

In the black forest the low wind moaned, and the
river-ice cracked and strained. The first warm days would
break up the ice and start it downriver. But it would be
a late spring.

Vanderdyke was uneasy. For three days he had waited
within a mile or two of this place, waiting for Jeblish
Mun, Henry Slack, or one of the others to rendezvous
here. The longer they stayed in the area the greater the
risk, and now that Jeblish had come he wished to move.

"Be war before snow flies again," Jeblish commented.
"The Injuns know it, an' I feel it in my bones."

"I will be crossing the mountains, Jeblish. I am
going to the settlements."

"What can you tell them they don't already know?"

"I want to see what's happening, and I want to talk to George Mason. He's a canny man, and busy as he is with his plantation he knows all that's happening."

"Comes to fightin', they ain't got a chance back there. Out here on the frontier it's mostly us an' what Injuns they can get to fight for them, but over yonder it'll take an army, which they ain't got.

"Anyway, the Colonies are always wranglin' with each other. Can't agree on anything, so how could they get together to fight?

"Far's that goes, New York, Boston, and Philadelphia are just about as English as the old country. Why, to hear them talk in Detroit there's dances ever' night, and they're dancin' with our girls!"

"Don't worry about it, Jeblish. If trouble comes they will do what needs to be done, and those girls may like to dance, but when trouble comes they'll stand with us."

"Who would lead them? Even if those city fellers could stand up to gunfire, who would lead them? Who could lead them?"

"There's been some talk of Charles Lee. He served in the British Army, I think. There's Montgomery, and of course, Old Put."

"Aye, there's them. Had my choice it would be that young colonel from Virginny . . . the one who was with Braddock. Don't recall as I ever heard his name but he surely didn't run when the shootin' started. He was ridin' back and forth, rallyin' the boys to fight. He didn't scare worth a hoot."

"Washington. He's a planter and a surveyor. Been out on the frontier a good bit."

"Injuns still talk about him. They missed so many shots at him they say he's got a charmed life. That there's the best excuse for poor shootin' I ever did hear."

Jeblish took a coal from the fire to light his pipe.

"Him havin' frontier experience an' all, I can't figure why he didn't tell Braddock he couldn't fight Injuns the way you'd fight Frenchmen."

"A colonel of militia," Vanderdyke explained dryly, "does not tell a general of regulars what to do or how to do it. He listens, and speaks when he is spoken to . . . if ever."

Vanderdyke drew back the ends of several partly burned sticks to begin killing the fire. "We'd best move. We've been in one place too long."

They kicked dirt over the fire, what little they could find that was unfrozen, then added snow. The light died and the shadows took over. Into them the men vanished as if they had not been. The wind moaned and blew a few leaves across the campsite. Where they had been there was nothing but darkness and the cold.

The forest was thick, then scattered, with here and there a meadow. Twice they crossed streams on ice, and finding a place where the snow had been swept from the ice by the wind, they traveled downstream where they would leave no tracks.

Jeblish turned from the ice at a place where there was no snow and led the way back through thick forest to a cave under a bank. Back inside the cave, which had a hole overhead that had been used in ancient times to let smoke escape, they built a small fire.

"Found this place one time. Never seen no Injun sign around. I laid by some wood a couple of years ago; nobody never used it. Either this is one the Injuns missed or they fight shy of it."

They were not talkative men and now they were cold. Huddling over the fire, they gradually warmed, and the small cave grew less icy.

"You'll be stopping with Lint?" Jeblish asked.

"Aye. I'll pass the word to him. He's one man alone
and he'll need to be watchful."

"That lad of his is coming of size now."

"Aye, and Artemus has a good wife. He's a canny
farmer, so they should do well."

Jeblish grunted. "We seen many such, you an' me.
Where be they now? Scalps dryin' in some Seneca long-
house."

"But they keep coming, Jeblish. They will never stop
coming as long as there's the promise of free land. The
French are better traders, and they get along better with
the Indians, but trade never settled a land. You need
people for that."

In his mind he went over the route he would follow.
More and more the people of the frontier were turning to
horses, but like the long-hunters, he preferred to travel
afoot. By shank's mare, as they put it.

A horse kept a man traveling along a trace while a
man afoot could go anywhere. A man left fewer tracks and
wearing moccasins as the woodsmen did, their tracks were
scarcely to be seen except by a skilled eye. A horse
might be faster but day in and day out a walking man
could kill a horse, for the man had the greater endur-
ance. A woodsman such as Jeblish or himself could run for
hours on end without giving it a thought.

"Figured to scout south," Jeblish commented, after a
while. "You figure it's war?"

Vanderdyke shrugged. "Who knows? Most think it can
still be worked out, but there's others, like Sam Adams
and Tom Paine, who think the time for talk is past."

"Figured it might start back there when the Boston
Massacree happened."

"It was nothing but a drunken brawl. Some idlers on
the way home began to pelt the British soldiers and somebody tired of it and fired a shot, then they all fired.

"I didn't blame the soldiers one bit. After all, men

were killed with sticks and stones for thousands of years before a gun was invented. Anybody who pelts rocks at a man with a gun is a damned fool and if he gets shot it is no more than what he should expect."

"Maybe they thought them guns weren't loaded," Jeblish commented.

"Then they were doubly fools. I am as loyal a patriot as any man, and I think the soldiers were within their rights. So did John Adams, who helped defend them in court."

"It'll be war," Jeblish said. "I seen it comin' for a long time, an' my pa before me, he seen it. Spoke of it. The King's laws weren't made for no such land as this, nor for no such people. They never worked west of the mountains, and not very well east of them. Trouble was, Parliament could never get it through their heads that things were different over here."

"They've gone against their own laws," Vanderdyke agreed.

"Made a nice, neat little package, that English island did. All the land held by the King an' a few lords an' gentry. Everybody knowin' his place the day he was born.

"Oh, I ain't sayin' there wasn't some as got out of it! There was . . . one way or t'other. But it would not work over here where there was land forever. If a man doesn't like where he is he just picks up an' fetches hisself west. If folks don't like the government they just move away."

"I know. You and me, Jeblish, we grew up hunting for the table. If we didn't shoot our meat we didn't have any, but over in England only the King and his lords could hunt. Nobody had a gun but the gentry, and no use for one if he did have it. Here everybody has a gun and needs it to live by. If we ever have a country of our own, we can protect it, from foreigners or from rabble alike."

"That's right. If an Injun or somebody comes a-
huntin' trouble you might call a constable or the Army.
But likely they just get there in time to look at the
body and maybe chase who done it. I don't want a government what's going to act without reason, but I don't
think I should have to take a chance of dyin' just to
give it to them."

Vanderdyke shook his head. "I'm thinking a government
that rules an armed people needs be . . . well, polite. I
figure that's one way of saying it. They'll learn. Soon
enough, the King's men will learn."

Wind guttered the small fire. Vanderdyke drove two
stakes into the hard ground and lay chunks of wood
against them to make a reflector. Rising, he went around
the bend of the cave and out into the cold. Glancing
back, he could see no firelight or moving shadows. He
gathered wood, shivering in the icy wind, and went back
inside.

Jeblish rambled on, suddenly talkative, but Vanderdyke was thinking of how long it would take to cross
the mountains and return again, and of what might be
gained by cutting across country. He had learned from
bitter experience that leaving a trail was always dangerous.

Traces were not where they were by accident but because long use had proved them the best routes. Most of
them had been begun by the buffalo; now one never saw a
buffalo east of the mountains, although when he was a boy
there had been buffalo even there. To deviate from trails
meant a man could get tangled up in swamps, mountains
without passes, and other time-consuming obstacles. Yet
the traces were where the Indians would be, and where
spies would be watching.

Nobody knew exactly what was taking place across the
mountains. There might be fighting by this time, and it
would be wise to move with care and approach no settle-

ment without carefully scouting the area. There were many Loyalists, men and women who held to the King and Parliament against all else. Many of them good people, too.

Most of those living in the Tidewater area believed things would be worked out and settled peacefully. As for Vanderdyke, he was skeptical. With another administration, perhaps, for there were many in England who were sympathetic to the Colonies; but whereas others understood the situation, George III was both stubborn and ill-advised.

There were those in England who believed the Colonies were also striking a blow for greater freedom at home, but there were others who wanted the Colonies to pay for their own defense, and with these Vanderdyke was inclined to agree. The difference was that he believed the army to defend the Colonies should be recruited there, and they should not have to pay for British Regulars whom they did not want.

"You comin' back this way?"

"Further south. I may cross by the Cumberland."

Jeblish added two sections of heavy wood to the fire. The wind scarcely reached them here, and there was a chance the fire would last throughout the night.

"Got no family," Jeblish said, after a while. "Just as well, times like these." He banked the fire a little. "Had me an Injun girl one time. Fine girl. Never was no better."

"What happened?"

"She was a Huron. Whilst I was off on my trapline the Iroquois come. Killed her, our youngster, and half-dozen others. They taken the hair of her an' the baby." He spat into the fire. "Taken me two year, but I got their hair back. Opened up their grave and put it with them."

"No parents?"

"Me?" Jeblish added a small stick to the fire. "I

reckon they was good folks. Injuns kilt them, too. That
was away back. Neighbor girl, she found me in the bushes
an' hid with me. We traveled alone through the woods for
eight days, gettin' us to where folks were.

"Eight days in the woods with a baby-child! An' sometimes I figure I done a few things! That damn-fool girl
was nigh thirteen when she done it! I tell you, Van, if
this here country, with folks like that, don't breed a
race of <u>men</u> there's something wrong! Women-folks . . .
they can do the damnedest things, if they're of a mind
to!"

"What happened to her folks?"

"Kilt. Same time as mine. There was nineteen in the
settlement--she told me that when I was older--nineteen,
all kilt dead."

Before daybreak, their fire smothered, each went his
own way. Vanderdyke started off at an easy trot. The path
he followed was little known and rarely used even by Indians, yet it did not pay to take anything for granted.
He ran along with long, easy strides. He knew the spring
where he hoped to arrive by the time the sun was at mid-
sky, and it was some twenty-five miles away. He had often
run as far in the morning and an equal distance in the
afternoon. The biggest problem was moccasins, for they
were constantly wearing out. A fact that enabled a knowing man to identify the tribe of the Indians who had used
a camp by the type of moccasins they wore, for each was
somewhat different.

He had three hours behind him when he stopped again
to look and to listen. Long ago he had learned to trust
his instincts and now he found himself uneasy.

Deliberately he turned from the trace and went into
the trees. What had alarmed him he did not know, but he

realized the senses often perceive things of which a man
is not consciously aware. In this case it might have been
a faint smell of wood-smoke, a sound, or something distantly glimpsed during one of the moments when he crossed
a ridge or hilltop.

He moved now like a ghost, careful to avoid branches
or the rustling of leaves. He suspected whatever it was
that disturbed him was some distance away, yet he moved
warily, pausing often, keeping his eyes and ears alert.
He was careful to leave as little sign of his passing as
possible, knowing how little an Indian needed.

Again he paused, merging his body with that of a huge
old hickory, standing perfectly still, only his eyes moving, seeking, searching. The dampness of fog lay upon the
trees and shrubs, an icy fog that had settled all about
him. He was some distance from the river now--

A faint clink of metal on metal, but not close by. In
the stillness of the frosty morning, sounds carried for
some distance.

He was well armed, carrying two pistols for close-
range work and his six-shot carbine. This was a weapon
designed by John Dafte, in London. The six shots were
carried in a cylinder that must be revolved by hand. The
gun had been designed and built in small numbers more
than a hundred years before, but his was scarcely nine
years old, built by a skilled gunsmith from an ancient
weapon Vanderdyke had inherited from a Dutch ancestor.

With modifications introduced by the gunsmith, the
weapon had been much improved and was accurate up to two
hundred yards. After that it became a chancy thing, although he had scored hits up to three hundred yards. It
was shorter than the long rifles of the Kentuckians, and
much lighter in weight than the muskets used by the Army.

He waited, listening. For a time he saw nothing,
heard nothing. He was about to step out when his eyes

captured a movement along the trace, of which he could
see only a little.

Somebody, or something . . . there! Two men in buckskins, travel-stained and soiled, behind them a British
officer in his red coat. Then the Indian . . . a Mohawk!

Two more Indians . . . He looked again to make sure
his senses were not deceiving him. . . . Two women.

Women? White women? Here?

Both women were riding horses and behind them were
several pack mules, then four redcoats and two more
Indians.

The women's hands were free and there was no evidence
they might be prisoners.

Slowly they drew closer, and he stood rock-still,
waiting. To move might be fatal, for the Mohawks missed
nothing.

These were no simple pioneer wives. The women were
dressed for travel, but the elegance of their costumes
could not be disguised, despite the fact they were far
from civilization, far from any house or settlement.

Who were they? Where could they be going?

He was no more than thirty yards off the path and if
he was glimpsed they'd be all around him in seconds.

He held his breath . . . waiting. . . .

CHAPTER 2

A cabin in a moonlit clearing, a barn adjoining, the
skeleton rails of a corral, and the snow-covered haycocks
with the black wall of forest all around.

A wagon standing alone, the tongue pointing upward
like a finger gesturing for silence.

Nothing moved but the thin trail of smoke into the
sky, a frail bride for the wagon-tongue. Nor was there
sound, no breath of wind, only silence and the cold
stars. A smell of wood-smoke on the still air, and then a
shadow that moved under the edging trees.

Inside the cabin a man reclined on a black bearskin
before the fire, propped on one elbow to hold his book's
face to the firelight, a big man in a rough, homespun
shirt, a rifle beside him on the puncheon floor. The man
read slowly, moving his lips with the words.

On a bed built into a corner his wife lay sleeping.
There was a table, two benches, and a chair made by cutting off one side of a barrel halfway down and building a
seat into the barrel's middle.

A candle in a pewter candlestick stood on the table,
but it was unlighted. Candles were for visitors, if and
when, for stoppers-by were rare. Like the wagon-tongue,
it stood straight and listening, for awareness was the
price of existence.

In the half-loft where the children slept, young
Jacob Lint was awake. He stared up at the rough timbers,
thinking of the snow on the roof and of the dark woods
beyond the clearing's edge. The Iroquois were on the war-
path and revolution was brewing in the Colonies.

He had never seen the Colonies to know them, although
he had been born there. He had never seen a schoolhouse
and a church but once, nor had he ever seen a store. He
thought of these magical, faraway things, often with
longing. The only other children of his age he had seen
had been the Elders. . . . That was two summers ago when
they came through, going west.

Pa turned the page and the whisper of it could be
clearly heard. Pa turned half over to reach for a stick
from the wood-box when they heard the owl hoot.

Jacob saw his father pause in mid-movement, listen-

ing. Very gently then, he put the book down, marking his
place with a shred of bark. He took up his rifle, glancing toward his sleeping wife. He got up in one fluid,
easy movement and moved to a place near the shuttered
window. The owl hooted again, somewhat closer. Jacob Lint
saw his father put the rifle down close to his hand and
draw his knife.

Horrified, the boy stared, his mouth dry. Indians?
Every settler lived in fear of them, knowing inevitably
they would come. Was this it? Was it now?

They had lived long at peace with the Indians, but Pa
had warned him that Indian ways were not always the white
man's ways, and they might take offense at something that
seemed insignificant to a white man, and kill them all.
Agreements had been made, but Artemus Lint knew, and so
warned his son, that such agreements were not considered
binding on those who did not like them. The old chiefs
made agreements, young warriors broke them, and both were
within their rights. It was a rare chief who spoke for
all his people; as with the white man, there were always
dissenters. Those who did not wish to accept a treaty
simply ignored it.

At the Lint cabin they had fed Indians, shared with
them what small store they had, but the Indians took it
as their due with no appreciation of the hard work it
took to grow. The white man was despised for his planting, for that was squaw's work and only fit for squaws.

The Indian was inclined to despise the white man because his traders were always looking for furs. Obviously
the white man was a poor hunter or trapper or he would
catch his own fur. Artemus, a quiet man with a quick
sense of the feelings of others, had soon learned several
Indian languages and spoke easily to them. He knew that
for the most part the Indian considered the white man in-
ferior and looked upon white men with haughty disdain.

There was a faint scratching at the door. Jacob saw
his father sheathe his knife and take down the bar and
open the door. The bar itself was a weapon, deadly in the
hands of a man skillful in its use, and Jacob had seen
his father use it on a white renegade.

The latch-string had been drawn in through its hole
so the latch could not be lifted at night, but when Artemus Lint lifted the bar, the door swung open and a man
glided swiftly in. The door was closed and the bar
dropped in place. The boy saw only movement melded into
movement and the man was there, beside the fire.

The newcomer put his rifle down and took his powder
horn off his shoulders and hung it on a peg near the
rifle. That rifle had drawn the boy's eye at once, for it
was unlike any he had seen before.

"You're welcome. There's meat and bread."

"All's well here?"

"No trouble."

"It will come. I have seen them."

Artemus went to the sideboard. "Milk?"

"It is a good drink."

"Aye, there's many prefer ale, but we've none of it
here."

"My father had cows. I grew up on milk."

Jacob's father added fuel to the fire. It was the
first comment he had ever heard, from anyone, about the
family of Vanderdyke. He was a man of whom no one knew
anything, nothing of who he had been, nor of whence he
came.

Men who knew said he was the greatest woodsman of
them all, and they were not men who were free with com-
pliments. If he had a place he called home no one knew
where it lay, nor if he had kinfolk anywhere at all.

Vanderdyke ate his meat and bread, then drank almost
a pitcher of the milk before stretching out on the robe
before the fire.

He reached over and got his rifle, putting it down
beside him. He opened his eyes once. "Seen some Senecas.
Six, eight miles back."

He was asleep then, and Jacob Lint looked down from
the loft at the long, lean body, the deep chest and powerful shoulders. He looked to be even stronger than Pa,
who was considered a mighty man.

Jacob saw his father put the mug on the sideboard and
the milk into the cool-hole under the floor. Then his father removed his moccasins and stretched out beside his
wife, pulling the buffalo robe over him.

Buffalo were scarce now, and Jacob had seen but
three, all at one time. That was over a year ago. The Indians said there once had been a good many and there were
still a lot of them south of the Ohio, in Kentucky.

When he awakened in the morning Vanderdyke was squatted by the fire. "Stay close to the cabin," he was advising, speaking to Jacob's mother, "and keep the boy close.
He's old enough to keep a good lookout, and to shoot if
he has to."

"Artemus will be out in the field," she said.

"Yes," Vanderdyke said. "He came here to build a
home, to plant fields, and to make a life for his family
and himself. He must get on with it, and you'd have it no
other way."

"Times are hard," she said, wistfully.

"They always are," Vanderdyke commented. "There never
was a perfect time, and there never will be. You hear of
golden ages and glorious times, but they were only so for
some people, and even for them it was only some of the
time.

"The way to go, ma'am, if you'll take my advice, is
to enjoy the minutes and the hours. Enjoy now, not some
distant day when things may get better. Maybe they will,

but it doesn't really matter. You've a fine son, so watch
him grow and become a man. You've a fine husband; enjoy
your time with him.

"Maybe if a body works hard enough and keeps a-going,
he'll make life easier for himself and his family.
Chances are war, taxes, and storm will take a part of it,
and maybe all, but those times you have together, those
quiet hours, nothing can be better.

"I've known men that wished to be drunk, that wished
to have a woman, who wished for this and for that, and
all the while, all around them there was so much that was
theirs for the taking."

He got up. "I've spoken my piece for the morning, and
I reckon I'll drift along now. It is a long way to the
settlements."

"The settlements!" She sighed, drying her hands on
her apron. "Will I ever see them again?"

He smiled. "More than likely, but you'll find the
only difference is there's more to want, more to spend
money on. Maybe you live a little more comfortably--"

"I'd just like to sit and talk with another woman."
She looked at him, her eyes wide. "It's been two years
since I have had a woman to talk to. I don't want to talk
about anything particular, just about folks and cloth-
materials and how to fix this or that."

"I know." He put a hand on her shoulder. "Folks will
be coming by, but pioneering . . . well, ma'am, it's hard
on women-folks.

"I'll be back this way . . . maybe next year. I'll
fetch you something from a town. Something . . . I don't
know what."

"I'd be pleased," she said gently, and watched him
away across the field and into the trees.

A moment he was there, and then he was gone, and that
was Vanderdyke.

Jacob spoke of it later, to his father. "It's his

way. He's a kindly man. A lonely one, I think. Maybe
somewhere he lost something . . . somebody."

"He stays nowhere long. He's like a ghost in the
woods. He shows up, then he's gone, and never a leaf
stirred nor a ripple left behind."

"How does he do it, with the Indians about?"

"He does it. Odd thing about Indians, Jacob, most of
them would kill him in a minute and carry his scalp with
pride, but they'd miss him. They are warriors and they
love a good fighting man. The Iroquois hunt him, and yet
they sing songs about his bravery and the things he has
done."

Mady Lint stood in the doorway after Vanderdyke was
gone. She loved her husband and wished for no other man,
yet she sensed the loneliness in Vanderdyke and her heart
followed after him.

"He needs someone," she said aloud.

"You speaking of Vanderdyke?" Jacob came close to
her.

"Yes. Everybody needs somebody, Jacob. We're lucky,
you and I and your pa. We have each other. Maybe in time
you'll have a baby brother or sister."

"I'd like that, I reckon," he said.

His eyes were on the woods, and he was remembering
what Vanderdyke had said, that he was old enough to be a
good lookout, and it was something he had already
learned. It was Pa he worried about, out in the field
plowing, and having to give most of his mind to his work.

Ma had told him the story of how she had married his
father, but he never tired of hearing it over again. Her
father--Jacob had to remember it was his grandfather--had
been a prosperous man: owner of a store and a gristmill,
a deacon in the church, and a member of the town council.

She could have married up, as the saying was, for
young men were courting her who were well-off, but after
she met Pa there was nobody else in her thoughts.

He had come into the store on a day when she was helping, and he brought furs and hides to trade. She handled the trading with him, conscious that he was watching her always. She was flushed and excited, but not so much that she did not deal sharply with him on the furs. They were, she noticed, beautifully dressed.

"I've come a far piece," he had said, speaking suddenly and with no preliminaries or wasted time, "and I'm a woodsy man. I've neither house, nor land, nor cow, but there's land aplenty where I ketched my fur, and a cold spring hard by. I've the hands and the skill to build a house, if you'll abide with me."

She looked up at him, right into his eyes, and her pa said, "Madeline, I--"

She was not listening, although she heard the words coming to her as from another time, another age. "I will abide with you, Artemus. I have been waiting for you to return."

He just looked at her.

"Three years ago," she said, "in our church of a Sunday morning. You'd come from the woods then, too. I tripped on the step and would have fallen but your hand caught me. You were so strong, yet so gentle."

"There's a boat going down tomorrow, if you're of a mind to come."

"What is it like, Artemus?"

"It is sleeping on pine needles and cooking over a fire. It is trees so large you cannot believe in them, and lost meadows with no foot upon them, ever. There are streams nobody has named, and a far, far land of beauty that stretches on forever.

"Of a winter the nights are bitter cold, and time to time there's Indians, some friendly, some not. It is no easy land in which to abide, and mayhap you'll grow old before your time, but there is richness in it and beauty, and wherever you are, I shall be close by.

"You will have no fancy clothes and for a long time there will be no meetinghouse, nor anybody to attend one. There will be times you will yearn for the voice of a stranger, no matter whose, but the soil under your feet will be deep and rich, and you'll have mist rising off the river, the sound of a paddle dipping, and the smell of the forest.

"You will be shaping a new land for those to come after. You will see your own house built and say how you wish it to be, and there will be corn growing where none ovor grew boforo."

"I will come with you, Artemus. Is it to be in the morning, then?"

"Before light," he said.

She took off her apron. "I had best go across to the parson then. He will be wishing to speak his words."

"Madeline?" Her pa was worried now. "It is a hasty thing to do."

"Pa," she explained, her hand upon his sleeve, "I knew three years ago if he came back from the woods and had no woman of his own that he would be the man for me. If you will be telling Mama, I will speak to the Reverend Goslin."

And that had been the way of it. Madeline had never been one to back and fill or flutter her mind over things. She saw what she wanted or knew what she would do and went promptly about it.

She told Jacob later how she had listened to every word she heard spoken about Artemus Lint, and there were words from time to time in those three years while she grew to be a woman and waited for him to come back. There had been talk around the store, for no country is so big that a man is not known for what he is. They spoke of him as being a fine hunter and trapper, a good, steady man who took a drink but did not make a thing of it, and who saved his money.

She had put by a little of her own, knowing the man she wanted would probably never have wealth, although she meant to see him well-off, in time. She had been sewing and stitching, too, and no doubt her mother saw it and wondered somewhat, but Ma was a woman who kept her own ideas and did not talk them about.

Jacob liked hearing the story. He knew this was their third cabin. The first cabin Artemus sold because he did not like neighbors crowding him, and the second cabin was burned by Indians while they were away, visiting. Artemus had never liked it because it was too far from the spring.

This, the third cabin, was by far the best, and with Jacob's help Artemus had put in five acres of corn, two of barley, and an acre of vegetables. Hunting had been good and they'd jerked enough meat for winter. Soon they would be harvesting corn, but the root crops were already dug and stored in the cellar . . . most of them, at least. Jacob was nine years old now, and worked beside his father, dawn to dusk on some days.

On this morning Jacob went to the fields with his father, driving the old muley cow his father had trained to draw a cart. They had begun picking corn; the shucking would come later. Each walked on a side of the cart, picking the ears as they went.

At mid-morning they stopped for a breather and Madeline brought cold water from the spring and a turnover for each.

"Pa? Who is Vanderdyke?"

Artemus had his mouth full of gooseberry turnover and he finished chewing before he answered. "He may be the best long-hunter there is. Nobody knows how far he has gone to the westward, to the north or the south. Folks say he never misses with that rifle, but he often carries a bow and arrows, too, and he is equally good with them.

"By name he's a Dutchman, and some say he came from a

Dutch settlement in New York State. There's Indians who
say he's no man at all, but a 'wind-spirit'. "One story
is that the Senecas killed his family and when his pa was
dyin' he gave Vanderdyke his rifle-gun and his hatchet
and told him to get away.

"Some Indians say he's always been here, like the
hills and the streams, that he belongs to the land. One
thing seems sure. He's a loyal man of this country, and
will fight for it.

"He's wary of the Iroquois because he believes they
will join the British against us if it comes to a fight.
They fought beside the British against the French, and
war will give them an excuse to wipe out such folks as we
are who are moving toward the frontier.

"One thing is sure. The Iroquois are a strong, fighting bunch of Indians . . . conquerors much like the Romans were.

"When the French first came into this country the fur
trade routes were controlled by the Hurons, enemies to
the Iroquois. The French wanted fur so they naturally
sided with the Hurons, and the Iroquois never forgave
them. At first, because the French had guns, the Iroquois
took a whipping, then they traded with the Dutch at New
Amsterdam for guns. Then they really started to move.

"They nearly destroyed the Hurons, wiped out the Neu-
trals and several other tribes. For a hundred years they
were almost continually at war, and were feared from the
St. Lawrence to the Tennessee, from the Atlantic to the
Mississippi. What they haven't subjugated they have destroyed.

"Do not fear them, son. Respect them, however. They
are a shrewd folk, uncommon fighters, and never to be
trusted because they do not think as we do, nor have the
same standards or beliefs."

Jacob Lint remembered that morning. They had worked
steadily, stripping ears of corn from the stalks, and

from time to time his father paused, stretched, and took time to look all about, usually while drinking or seeming to drink from the water-jug.

That afternoon the cart was not half-full when suddenly he said, "We will go in now."

"But Pa, the corn--!"

"Can wait." Artemus spoke sternly and handed the lines to his son. "Drive right to the barn now, and do not stop."

Artemus picked up his rifle and swung his powder horn easier to his hand. His face looked stiff and strange; only his eyes were alive. "When you get to the house, leave the cart in the barnyard and go in. Close the shutters and bar the door."

"Pa?"

"No questions. Move along now, but don't seem to hurry."

Jacob Lint was scared. He felt his heart pound with slow, heavy thumps, and his stomach had gone all hollow. What had Pa seen? Or heard? Fear choked him, but he kept his eyes straight ahead while his father walked alongside the cart.

Often his father had warned him that when told to do something he should never pause to ask why or argue, but just to do what he was told. In an emergency it was best to act quickly and with intent.

Never had the barnyard seemed so far away, never had the old cow plodded more slowly. He wished he had his pa's shotgun. He saw his mother come to the door to throw out dishwater, saw her stop and shade her eyes toward them, then go quickly inside. When they came into the yard the shutters were closed and Ma was filling two buckets at the well.

Turning the cow into the barnyard, Jacob got down to loosen the traces.

"Don't bother with that. Get into the house."

There was no sign of anything, no unusual movement.
Taking one of the buckets from his mother, he followed
her into the house. He took down the shotgun.

His father stood in the barn door. He caught a movement at the edge of the forest. Four Indians stood there,
in plain sight. One of them suddenly lifted his bow and
loosed an arrow. It struck, quivering, in the doorjamb of
the barn.

His father did not move. He simply waited, his rifle
in his hands. Another arrow flew, this one into the casing above his head.

"Why doesn't he shoot?" Jacob cried out.

"That is what they want. If he shoots his gun would
be empty. Once he fires, they will charge. He could not
reload in time."

She was very calm, but her eyes were large and she
was very pale.

Opening the door a crack, Jacob showed the muzzle of
the shotgun, and no more. He glanced toward his father,
and he was there, his rifle ready and easy in his hands.
How could he be so calm? So steady? He glanced toward the
Indians, and they were gone.

"Why have they gone? Were they afraid?"

"No, Jacob. They are not afraid. Nor do they wish to
die. We were ready for them, and your father could not be
frightened into firing, and they knew that when he did
shoot he would kill at least one.

"Knowing that, they just went away. They will come
again, and again, hoping to catch us off guard." She put
her hand on his shoulder. "You did the right thing,
Jacob. You may have made the difference, because when
they saw your gun muzzle they knew two might die, and if
they killed your father, you could still reload and fire
again."

"Why do we do it, Ma? Why doesn't Pa take you back to
the settlements?"

"He doesn't suggest it because he knows I would not go. This is the life he has chosen and I am his wife."

CHAPTER 3

Vanderdyke's route was south, then east. Deliberately, he avoided the traces, traveling a route roughly parallel to them so as to leave no obvious signs of his passage. It was slower, but safer, and he was never a man to take an unnecessary risk.

This was mingled hardwood and pine forest, and his travel-stained buckskins merged well with the trunks of trees, pine needles, and mottled hillsides, where some snow had melted, leaving patches of gray-brown or yellow grass and leaves.

Crossing a long hillside he came upon an old buffalo trail. The woods buffalo who had frequented the area in the past were somewhat larger than the plains buffalo, and the paths they made were easily followed. Always they held to the contour of the hills and found the best crossings of streams.

By midday he had put thirty miles behind him and found a place on a rocky brush-and-tree-covered hillside where he could rest and see the country over which he must travel in the next few hours.

The noonday sun was warm and he had a sheltered place where he could enjoy the sun without being seen unless man or beast approached within a few feet, which was unlikely as the spot he had chosen was difficult to approach and far from any beaten track.

Leaning back against a rock, his rifle across his knees, he studied the country before him while he considered the travelers he had seen the day before. For hours

their presence and probable destination had been nagging
at his consciousness, yet he dared not let his mind wander in a country so dangerous.

Two men, obviously women of some importance, traveling with an escort of British soldiers and Indians, but
traveling away from any known British fort.

He had back-trailed them for a short distance in
order to establish the hoofprints of their horses clearly
in his mind. Now he knew he would know those prints wherever he saw them. All the horses had been freshly shod,
evidently with this trip in mind.

Had he been less close to the cabin of Artemus Lint
he might have followed them to see what he could learn;
at the same time he knew how risky that might be, for the
Mohawks were shrewd and cunning woodsmen and it would not
be long before they would become aware of his presence.
It was just as well he had let them go. Yet their presence disturbed him.

He broke off a corner of the journey cake Mady Lint
had given him and then a piece of jerky. He slowly chewed
the venison, enjoying its flavor. The place where he sat
was a hundred feet or more above the floor of the forest,
and he could see the breaks in the mass of trees that indicated where streams flowed, and here and there a
meadow. In one of them he could see a deer feeding.

The leaves of the hardwoods had long been gone, but
their gray branches intertwined to shield the forest
floor below that canopy of boughs. There was a scattering
of evergreens, too, mostly pine.

A slow, lazy hour passed during which he rested, doz-
ing in the warm sun and storing energy for the long drive
ahead. Such relatively safe places as that where he now
sat were few and opportunities for rest were rare.

When he had rested for a little more than an hour,
Vanderdyke started along the slope, then into the deeper
woods. Once under cover he crouched near a huge old dead-

fall and listened. If anybody had seen or heard him they would come along, hunting him. He remained unmoving, all his senses alert. After a brief time, when he heard no sound, he continued on.

The way he had chosen would take him south and east across the mountains and into Virginia. The nearer he came to the mountain passes, the closer he would come to trouble.

Although there were those who still spoke of the New World, Europeans had been settled along the eastern seaboard for more than one hundred and fifty years. The British colonies expanded slowly but persistently, and those who pushed to the farthest frontiers, building homes in the outer wilderness, developed a sense of independence and self-sufficiency that left them impatient with rulings from the mother country or by the governors of the Colonies appointed from England, rulings that often had little to do with living conditions on the frontier.

Far more important than the ruling powers in the Colonies to the man on the frontier were the Indians. The problem of the Indian was present and immediate, and they met sometimes in friendship, often in hostility. There was right and wrong on both sides--both white man and Indian had liars, boasters, and outright villains numbered among them; they also had good men, trying hard to achieve a natural and easy relationship.

No two peoples ever met less likely to understand one another than the white man and the Indian, and in those beginning years patterns of behavior were established that were to persist down the years.

Vanderdyke, who had lived with both peoples, had from his first day on the frontier recognized the difficulty. The basic conceptions and beliefs of the two peoples were totally dissimilar.

The word "Indian" is as loose a term as "European."

There were Indians who differed as much as would a Finn
and an Italian. The Indian was thought to be a stone-age
man, but there were stories of greater civilizations to
the west and south, civilizations that some white men,
with their obsession with architecture and written language, might have to take more seriously.

Although the nature of some tribes was often seen as
stoical, the better one knew the Indian the more one
learned to recognize emotion and expression. He was vola-
tile, demonstrative, and had a fine sense of drama. His
code of chivalry, while different from that of the white
man, was just as demanding in its way . . . and, in all
likelihood, the Indian was more faithful to it.

But only some had anything like the white man's feelings or traditions regarding the ownership of land. An
Indian rarely thought of owning land in the usual sense
of the term. Certain areas were regarded by him as his
hunting grounds, but much depended on the tribe or nation
being strong enough to protect such an area. These areas
were often expanded by war, or were severely contracted
in the same way. The concepts of formal boundaries and
absolute possession were an alien way of thinking to an
Indian.

When the white man first appeared among them, whether
on the first landings or elsewhere in the country, he was
generally looked down upon by the Indian. Both peoples
were guilty of this, and in this they were quite similar.

The Europeans' knowledge of the proper way, the
Indian way, of doing things was either slight or nonexis-
tent. These failures were seen as weakness and ignorance.
Of course, the white men had weapons that were superior
in certain ways, and their tools were even better. Yet in
other cases European equipment lacked much. For traveling
rivers and streams the canoe was superior to the cumber-
some boat; for life upon the prairies the tipi was superior to any tent the white man owned.

But few Indians understood the source of the white man's equipment, the technological progress that it indicated. Few understood that even the greatest cities in the Americas were but frontier outposts to the civilization of Europe. And, as much as alliances with the American tribes had been useful to the white men, the larger the white population grew, the more self-sufficient it became and the less it needed the Indian. The days in which the red man could assume superiority over the whites were dwindling rapidly.

Vanderdyke came to the path for which he had been watching. He glanced both ways, then at the trace itself.

No tracks . . . nothing less than weeks old, at least. This was an ancient path, made first by buffalo or perhaps even the hairy elephants of even older times. Vanderdyke, who knew a little of many things, knew such creatures had existed, and they had been described to him by Indians. No doubt those Indians had never seen the creatures, but they had been told of them, and had shown Vanderdyke some salt licks where the bones and tusks were to be found.

Vanderdyke had killed his first buffalo between the Great and Little Kanawha when he was much younger, and was tolerably familiar with the country into which he was now going. There were various Indian trails, all of them former buffalo paths, and of them two of the most important led one to the head of the James, another to the head of the Potomac.

Before him the valley he had been following narrowed to a ravine, from which a small stream issued. He squatted under a rhododendron and studied the opposite slope with care, then the slope right below him. There was a scattering of growth, much of it only bare branches now. Atop the opposite ridge he could see a little snow blow-

ing. The wind was picking up, and if wise he would be
tucked into a new camp well before sundown.

A fallen log had left a bare space beyond it where
there was no snow and he walked that way, reaching a
cluster of pines where he stopped again to look around.
Although he had heard no sound, he was uneasy . . . perhaps because he heard no sound.

He was about to start on again when he caught a movement from the tail of his eye, and instantly held himself
still.

There was nothing to be seen, yet the movement had
been on the hillside not two hundred yards off. Even as
he looked a chunk of snow fell from a branch, disturbed
by something that had passed.

He brought up his carbine, holding it ready in his
hands. When he caught the movement again, it was slight.
A shoulder, or what appeared to be a shoulder.

He waited. Suddenly down the slope he caught another
movement. This was the back of an Indian, a Mohawk he
suspected, who had just moved into sight. He was on Vanderdyke's side of the trail, less than fifty yards away.
Both Indians were watching or waiting for something that
was coming along the creek bed below.

This part of the country was, so far as he was aware,
claimed by no one. The Shawnees had moved away, the Dela-
wares had been here, but now it lay empty, although
hunted over by several tribes.

Three Indians appeared suddenly in the creek bottom.
Even as his eyes caught them, he saw another Mohawk high
on the ridge behind them. Obviously an ambush, and the
three Indians in the creek bed below were the quarry.

He stood up suddenly and stepped from the trees,
knowing the movement would be observed. The Indians
looked up and he waved his arms. There was no need to
shout.

As instantly as he waved he had stepped back into the

trees. When he looked again the three Indians in the creek were gone.

Turning swiftly, he darted along the slope, escaping to a farther clump of pines, knowing his own life was at stake now. From below he heard a shot, then another one. He saw an Indian cross over the ridge, getting away. In all there had been at least five of the attackers, and only three Indians in the creek. Yet the attackers had no desire to close with their enemies.

Vanderdyke doubted if the Mohawks had seen him, for their attention had been concentrated on their quarry, but he dared take no chances.

Five against three? Vanderdyke was almost sorry he had warned them, for if the three were fighters it might have been a battle worth seeing.

That men might have been killed down below did not distress him overly much. They had been lying in wait to take advantage of the travelers and got no more than they'd expected to deliver. Men of the wilderness knew that death was always with them, at their elbow forever. Men killed and were killed, just as with the other creatures of the forest. He had heard it said that only man killed without need, but that was untrue. Those who said such things had never seen a henhouse after it had been invaded by a weasel. The blood of one chicken might satisfy his hunger, but it was rare he left any chicken alive.

Long since, he had come to terms with life and knew that when death came he would meet it as might any bear, wolf, or other wild creature.

The Indian, of whatever tribe, was a wise fighter. He fought when he believed he could win, and if he could win without risk to himself, so much the better. He was none the less brave because he would kill without warning, for if challenged to fight he would almost always do so. His standards were simply different than those of

most white men; there was no more treachery in him, nor
no less.

Now the three Indians he had warned came into an open
place and stood still, so he stepped from the trees and
did likewise. He recognized them for what they were . . .
Kickapoos.

A small tribe, but one noted for fierceness in battle. Now he knew why the attackers had not wished to continue when their surprise failed.

The Kickapoos had been relentless in their resistance
to all efforts by white men to win them over. They had
fought the French consistently, had been attacked by the
Sioux from the west and the Iroquois from the east, and
had resisted both. They had raided Iroquois towns as far
east as Niagara, for they were noted also for their wandering. The name "Kickapoo" was derived from an Algon-
quian term, Kiwigapawa, meaning "he who moves about," or
"he who wanders."

His rifle was loaded and ready but he wanted no trouble. "They were Mohawks," he said. "It was a trap."

"Kickapoo no white man friend," one of them said.
"Why you do this signal?"

"The Kickapoos are great warriors," Vanderdyke replied. "I would not see you killed without a fight."

"You are Vanderdyke."

He was not surprised. He had spent much time with
other tribes; his description might have gone from village to village, from tribe to tribe.

"I am Vanderdyke."

"You go?"

He gestured with his free hand. "Beyond the mountains. I go to warm myself at the fires of wisdom."

"You find wisdom there?" One of them sneered.

He shrugged. "As it is with you, some are wise, some
are not."

"You have much enemy."

He smiled grimly. "The Kickapoo has many enemies, too. A man is known by his enemies," he added, "and some enemies of mine are your enemies also."

"The French?"

He shrugged again. "I do not know the French. They are not my enemies. The Iroquois are. I do not seek enemies," he added. "I wish to be no man's enemy. I am content to live in the forest, and to hunt."

He lifted his left hand, palm toward them. "Now I go. I am your friend."

"We do not ask for friend."

Vanderdyke smiled again. "I did not <u>ask</u> for friend, either. I say I am friend to Kickapoo."

A step backward put him under the trees, another step and he was gone. They stood still, looking after him, and he left them with no sound, going as a ghost goes, fading into nothing.

———————————— LT ————————————

COMMENTS: Below are some of Louis's notes on a story about the Vanderdyke character. It is likely, however, that these notes were written years earlier. The story you have just read seems to be aimed in a different, more sophisticated direction. As with a number of other entries in this book, it is written in a form much like a motion-picture treatment with a fairly thin "mid-century Hollywood" plot and characterizations. Whether he was at one time considering "Vanderdyke" as a motion-picture sale or not, this treatment is just the earliest sketch, the bare bones of an idea, which had not yet developed to the stage where the villain's motivations were completely explored or explained.

VANDERDYKE learns of a mysterious enemy he has among the British forces; strange to him, the man ob-

viously has power and influence, is a strong, dangerous man. The man is notorious for his cruelty. His
position is uncertain. Although not an officer, he is
seemingly obeyed by other officers. The sources of
his power are not obvious.

Later, VANDERDYKE visits Gov. Patrick Henry and
meets a young girl there who is a guest at a neighboring estate, but often in the Henry home.

VANDERDYKE hears the man who is his enemy spoken
of in most flattering terms, but expresses his own
feelings frankly. The girl listens to him and is obviously intrigued by his words, or by him.

A wealthy woman and her daughter are also present, and announce their intention of going to visit a
relative near the frontier. VANDERDYKE advises
against it, but they are indifferent to his words and
plan their trip. They have a guide and a young man
who is going with them; the latter is very conde-
scending to VANDERDYKE.

He leaves on a further mission and in the woods
encounters the wealthy woman, her daughter, and
the two young men, one of them an acquaintance of
VANDERDYKE's, as well as a party of Indians accompa-
nying them. The guide invites him to accompany them,
but insists they go to an Indian village a short distance off where there will be food. They arrive at the
village and find it deserted, so at the guide's in-
sistence proceed onward to a stockade, where they
find all gone but a lone priest and an Indian boy.
They advise the party to escape while they can, but
the wealthy woman insists she is too tired to go on,
and their guide has assured them there is no danger.

Suddenly a band of Indians led by white men de-
scend upon them; they are taken prisoner, with the
exception of VANDERDYKE, who has mysteriously vanished. The leader of the attackers is furious with

the guide, but when by questioning he discovers who
the woman is, he is somewhat appeased.

When a company of British soldiers invade the
area the Indians and bandits mysteriously disappear.
Leading this group is VANDERDYKE's enemy, who, posing
as the rescuer, is very affable and pleasant. He en-
tertains them all very graciously, and the only skep-
tic is Van's friend, who sees the whole affair as
something of a charade. Yet neither the woman nor her
daughter will believe him, and he warns them to say
nothing to their guide. The woman does so, however,
and the young man is taken prisoner, taken away from
them as a "troublemaker." The Enemy then suggests
that he will be unable to get them through the Indians around them without help, and he will need from
each of them some identification so he can prove to
the British they are indeed prisoners. They provide
the identification.

Shortly after the renegades and Indians are seen
near the stockade by the young man, and the Enemy
makes preparations to move out.

The woman and her daughter are convinced VAN-
DERDYKE is the cause of all their misfortune and the
girl then says she has seen him near the stockade,
talking to the young man.

The other young girl, who had been traveling with
them, but who had remained very much in the background, has very little to say, and is not present
when a plot is laid to seize VANDERDYKE. Using the
girl as bait, they do catch him, and for the first
time he comes face to face with his enemy.

VANDERDYKE is to be tortured by the Indians and
here the woman and her daughter object. She is refused, and when she angrily objects again, the Enemy
knocks her down with a blow from the flat of his
hand.

Furious, the daughter threatens what will happen
when help comes, and he tells them no help is coming,
that he has used the objects they gave him to prove
they were dead, and no hope is held out for them.

Horrified, they hear him tell them that when he
is through with them they will be given to the Indians, traded into the far west, and if ever found
again, they will not be recognized, that the savages
have their own way of dealing with such cases.

VANDERDYKE and his friend are to be tortured then
burned at the stake.

The other girl gets into the cache of whiskey
left at the fort (its presence known to her only
through a drunken renegade's babbling) and when the
Indians are drunk, she liberates VANDERDYKE, and he
takes them away with him.

Under the stockade there is a secret cache of
powder, also, and in leaving, he explodes it.

An attempt to stop him is made by the Enemy and
there is a fierce hand-to-hand fight which arouses
the Indians and renegades, but VANDERDYKE'S FRIENDS
have arrived also, and they escape at last.

A few days later, he accompanies Patrick Henry
and some others to a ball and there he encounters the
woman and her daughter; both cut him dead.

The other girl does not.

VANDERDYKE: a legendary frontiersman, his exact
role uncertain, a mysterious man who moves through
the forest like a ghost, feared by the Indians, admired by others, loved by some. He has fed the hungry, treated the sick, helped the helpless. He is a
dead shot and a fearless fighting man of great
strength and skills. He seems to have never been anywhere but the forest, is as much a part of it as any
wild creature. He appears, then disappears.

A patriot, he carries news to Henry and his comrades of impending trouble on the frontier. The Iroquois are being supplied with ammunition, there is
trade with them going on with the seeming consent of
the British government, and a shipment of powder,
shot, and whiskey has been attacked by other Indians
and now no one is sure of where it is.

PATRICK HENRY has told VANDERDYKE to either capture or destroy that powder and shot as well as the
whiskey.

This is a mission, also, to discover what is happening on the frontier.

There are many stories of his youth, of his reasons for being where he is, none of which can be
clearly substantiated.

AUGUSTA GOSLEN: A widow in her forties, an attractive, opinionated woman who has always had money,
and is socially ambitious. From a lower-middle-class
family she married into merchant money. Her husband
had invested heavily in American business and property, so much against her will, she had come to America to see what she owned and if possible to sell it.
She has no idea of conditions on the frontier and insists on going to the area where her land is. She has
been assured by CHRISTOPHER SKITTLE that there is
nothing to fear, that he will have adequate help, and
excellent guides.

The plan is to get the widow and her daughter to
a remote place in the woods and there hold them for
ransom while taking all they possess.

The arrival of VANDERDYKE poses a problem until
they learn that his head is wanted, and they plan
to kill him also. He senses what is about to happen
and slips away into the forest. His friend,
WILLIAM FOX-FOUNTAIN, is left behind, which does

not dismay him as he is interested in Augusta Goslin's niece.

    One of the aspects of frontier life that this story flirts with is the
differences between the early, colonial-era relationship between Europeans and Native Americans, and what came later. Early on, there was
much more of a balance of power and a sense of cooperation. Not only
did Indians give some instruction to whites on how to survive in
North America, but they were also important political allies to the
Europeans. As long as European powers fought with one another
over their American possessions, and as long as the Colonies were not
free from their British, Dutch, French, and Spanish masters, the various tribes were valued for their ability to side with one group of
whites or another. Though, as is mentioned in this fragment, both
Indian and white did a good deal of looking down on one another,
they could also cooperate in a way that benefited both parties. It was
a situation that did not survive the creation of the United States without dramatic changes.

VANDERDYKE: NOT ONLY THE
WOODSMAN BUT A MAN GIVEN
TO CONTEMPLATION.
  "OURS IS A DIFFICULT WORLD,
FOR FIRST A MAN MUST DO —
HE MUST BE — WE HAVE NO
TIME, IN MOST CASES, TO CON-
SIDER WHAT WE DO, NOR IF WHAT
WE DO IS WHAT SHOULD BE DONE."
  "OURS IS A LIFE OF ACTION.
TO FIRST HAVE A FIRE THAT WE
MAY NOT FREEZE, AND WE HAVE
NO TIME TO THINK OF WHAT
THE FIRE DOES BEYOND GIVE
HEAT, NOR WHAT IT BURNS.
  "WE BURN WOOD, RARELY
CONSIDERING WHAT OTHER
USES THERE ARE FOR THE
WOOD - WE BURN COAL ALSO
YET WHAT ELSE MIGHT WE NOT
MAKE FROM COAL?

> "YET HE WHO TAKES TIME TO THINK OF SUCH THINGS MAY DIE OF COLD BEFORE EVER HE REACHES A CONCLUSION.
>
> "~~WHAT I HIT~~
>
> "IF SUDDENLY I AM ATTACKED BY AN INDIAN, I HAVE NO TIME TO CONSIDER THE ETHICS OF THE THING. THE FIRST CONSIDERATION IS TO EXIST, TO CONTINUE TO BE.
>
> "PHILOSOPHY IS A PURSUIT OF LEISURE, AND TO HAVE LEISURE A MAN MUST HAVE BOTH SUBSISTENCE AND PROTECTION.
>
> "VIEWPOINTS DIFFER, HE WHO VIEWS LIFE FROM AN ARMCHAIR HAS NOT THE SAME VIEWS AS HE WHO CROUCHES BESIDE HIS SMALL FIRE, CLUTCHING HIS WEAPONS.
>
> "WE HAVE DONE HARM TO THE INDIAN, BUT WE ARE SIMPLY THE INSTRUMENTS OF CHANGE.
>
> "HUNTERS HAVE ALWAYS RESISTED PLANTERS. WHEN TWO CULTURES COME FACE TO FACE THE MORE EFFICIENT WILL INEVITABLY SURVIVE — AND THEY ARE NOT NECESSARILY EVIL BECAUSE THEY ARE VICTORIOUS.
>
> "NO MAN NOR ANY RACE OF MEN CAN BE ISOLATED AND INSULATED FROM CHANGE. IDEAS ARE CARRIED ACROSS SEAS, MOUNTAIN RANGES AND DESERTS.

Material to be considered for use in "Vanderdyke."

In some of the other notes that Louis left behind there is a slight indication he intended Vanderdyke to be a descendant of his character Barnabas Sackett. However, I am far from certain that he wrote any of these pages with that in mind. ... He may have later decided that would be his direction if he ever returned to finish this story.

MIKE KERLEVEN

Notes for a Crime Story

COMMENTS: This next set of notes shows you what it looked like when Louis was trying to "break" a story. "Breaking a story" is not a term that Dad would have used, but it is how screenwriters refer to the process when they are experimenting with ideas and trying to discover the fundamental building blocks that will allow a concept to become a fully fleshed-out script or movie, or whatever. I've never figured out if the term refers to breaking a story down into acts and scenes, or breaking it open to see what is inside, or even breaking it like it is an untamed horse. . . . My personal experience is that all of these examples are accurate!

Anyway, to discover the pathway into the story Dad would usually use an interesting incident or twist to set it off, then he would try to follow the potential narrative from there. This is a good example because much of the time this sort of work was simply done in his mind.

```
        Mike Kerleven arrives in town; he has lost all
    his luggage and it is Sunday. He succeeds in getting
```

some help from the hotel manager, buying the bag of a
man who ducked his bill.

Mike has bought clothes the evening before, but
had forgotten the traveling bag. In the bag that he
buys he finds singularly little. There are no
clothes, except that is, for a couple of neckties,
a pair of socks and a dirty shirt. There are a few
other odds and ends, including a razor (unused) and
a bundle of clippings, all concerned with fatal
accidents and apparently having no connection.
There are several other clippings and a couple of
ticket stubs.

Mike is curious. The various articles in the bag
represent a strange character, and he becomes obsessed with the idea, and very little evidence he
has, that the man is in some way connected with these
fatal accidents. Making an inquiry about the man, he
finds there was a fatal accident in the hotel on the
day he vanished.

Possessed of a little money, he begins the effort
to trace down the owner of the bag.

Problems: How to bring the killer in and still
keep him a mystery. How to introduce other characters.

Mike believes in telling about his belief,
hoping in time to attract the killer to himself,
also to make other people cautious. He finds, after a
time, that the killings center about a certain area.
There are occasional variations, but it seems the
killer has returned again to certain spots where it
is easy to find someone walking alone and to dispose
of them.

Mike is making friends.

1. The murderer is not known as a "name" in the
   story, not until the very end.
2. The murderer must be tracked by his habits, feelings and desires.
3. His character must develop for the reader as it
   does for the investigator, bit by bit, slowly he
   pieces together a man.
4. In his room, behind a curtain, Mike has a jigsaw
   puzzle of the man. There are two charts. One is
   the figure of a man. His size is pieced together
   by various clues. The socks, the shirt. His
   tastes, feelings and reactions are placed upon
   the neighboring chart.

At times changes are made as new evidence
comes in.

Clues: He stayed several days in the hotel and
paid his bill each day.

He stayed several days, yet the razor is unused.
Therefore, he had another razor or went to barber
shops.//Investigate barber shops.

He likes music, good music.

Bit by bit he forms a physical picture of the man
on one side, and a psychological picture on the
other.

Mike follows down various leads, and steadily
builds up the character of his man.

And he becomes obsessed with his figure and does
not realize until too late that one of his new
friends fits it to perfection.

Several friends must be introduced. The murderer
has become aware that he has someone on his trail.
That after several years of successful killings, he
at last has an antagonist. He draws his follower near
in order to watch him better. He begins a bloody

game. He tries to trap him into accidents. He tries
to trap him into arrest for a murder.

The puzzle is first interest. Then the building
of suspense.

The feeling of horror must be brought in, the
helplessness of the victims; the killer who is not
even suspected; the accidents that no one believes to
be murders; the complete lack of motives.

Mike must find a man who:

1. Is much alone.
2. Likes good music.
3. Has good taste.
4. Abhors the poor, crippled and unpleasant.
5. Who has private income (obviously doesn't work
   because of times of accidents).
6. He draws nearer and nearer to the criminal. And
   his danger increases, bit by bit.

Mike goes, in the beginning, to the police. He
meets there a detective lieutenant, who scoffs at his
ideas. Yet Mike goes to him again, then meets him casually. And the detective begins to wonder, then to
believe.

At one time Mike suspects this detective. At one
time he even suspects himself. He proves to himself
that he could have committed the first crime, and
several of the others. His tastes are somewhat similar. He meets the detective at a concert. He begins
to wonder. The detective suspects him also.

Then he and the detective work together. The detective gathers material, and they work toward a
given end. The detective suggests to Mike that he
himself may become a target of the killer. But, if

so, the murderer must deviate from his rule. Thus far
he has just roamed hither and yon in search of easy
victims, off a bridge, under a train.

Decisive clue: a theater stub torn around the
edges. In the bag he finds one curiously torn, then
finds another. The victim has ripped the murderer's
pocket loose in the struggle. Then, in a theater, he
sees the man he has become friendly with tearing just
such a stub!

STAN BRODIE

The First Four Chapters of a Western Novel

CHAPTER 1

His eyes opened upon fear. He lay facedown on an ill-smelling bed in a small, bare room with the first edge of daylight showing around the drawn window-blind. Directly before his eyes was a boot . . . a boot with a leg in it.

He lay perfectly still, his eyes open but his mind empty. Slowly his thoughts gathered focus.

The leg belonged to a man, and the man was dead.

How did he know that? Or was he only surmising? No matter. He did know it. He was sure of it. Close to his face was a fist, his fist, and clutched in the fist was a knife-hilt, the knife gripped for stabbing. For striking down.

He had not moved and he did not move now, yet there was a sudden awareness in him, a realization of danger, a crawling horror of being trapped, of being caught up in something he did not understand.

The man whose leg he saw was dead, the upper part of his body out of sight at the foot of the bed. Without a doubt he had been killed by the knife that Stan Brodie now held, and he was alone in a room with the body.

He knew he had killed nobody, nor had he ever wished to kill anyone, but it was obvious that his good character and good intentions were not known to the people in this town and it would be taken for granted he was the killer.

Murder meant hanging, with or without a trial.

He sat up quickly, the bed creaking. His head ached abominably, his mouth tasted foul, and when he tried to stand his brain spun. He tiptoed to the window and lifted the edge of the blind.

An empty alley, gray in the first vague light of dawn. Western towns were early towns and in a matter of minutes this one would be awake and alive.

He looked quickly around: a small, square room with a bed, a chair, a bureau and washbasin, a white crockery basin, and a pitcher of cold water.

He put down the knife. It was bloody.

The hat on the floor was his. No gun-belt, no rifle. On the bed where he had been lying in a drunken sleep . . . nothing.

He looked at the dead man. Three narrow slits in the back of the vest where the knife had entered, very little blood.

One side of the man's face was visible. It was Bud Aylmer.

Bud Aylmer, whom he had met three days ago at a desert water hole, seemingly an easygoing, drifting cowhand who rode in out of nowhere and was going nowhere that he mentioned. Now Bud Aylmer was dead, struck down from behind by the knife that killed him . . . but why?

He had been killed for the gold. They had robbed a stage and the stage had carried twenty thousand dollars. The robbery was supposed to be a lark, simply to scare

the stage driver, after which they'd all ride into town
and buy him a drink.

Neither Bud nor Stan had known about the gold. At
least he had not known about it and did not believe Bud
had either. What of the other man, he who proposed the
idea? Stan Brodie thought that over and decided the other
man had known and that he had planned to kill the stage
driver from the first. He and Bud had been suckers,
damned fools.

He had a fire going and Bud was making coffee when
the stranger rode up to the water hole. He was a tall,
high-shouldered man with a swarthy face and a large beak
of a nose. His eyes were intensely black and cold.

He had a bottle of whiskey and Bud was ready enough
for a drink. As for Stan Brodie, he was no drinker, but
as Bud said, why not one to keep them company? He had
that drink, and then another.

There was no time to think of that now. He had to get
out and get out quickly. He put on his hat, stepped to
the door, and looked around. An empty hall, an open door
a dozen steps away, and the gray light of dawn on a dusty
street.

Taking one last, quick look about the room, he
stepped into the hall and closed the door behind him. He
had taken three steps when the door opposite his own
opened and a girl was standing there, wide-eyed and
frightened. He touched a hand to the edge of his hat to
her, and went into the street.

No horses stood at the hitching-rail; the street was
dusty and empty. Wind scurried a bit of paper into the
corner of a building and somewhere a rooster crowed. Tug-
ging his hat down he turned toward the livery stable.

Why had that girl stared at him like that? Had she
heard something during the night? Who was she? What was
she doing in that cheap rooming house for drifters?

He had killed nobody, but how could he prove that?

How did he even know that? He had known Bud Aylmer but a few hours. He could not prove that, either.

He saddled his horse in the shadowed stable. As he reached the stable door there was a man standing there with his hand out. "Mister," the man said, "that will be fifty cents."

He thrust his hand into his pocket, and his hand stopped. The pocket was stuffed with coins. His fingers felt among them for a fifty-cent piece . . . found it. He handed the half-dollar to the hostler. "There," he said, "and thanks."

He started to mount and the hostler said, "Mister?"

Stan Brodie turned, his skin crawling with apprehension. "You dropped this," the hostler said, and handed him a gold eagle.

He walked his horse outside, ducking his head at the door. Turning his mount he rode down the street at a walk, and his heart pounded when he realized he had turned the wrong way, a way that would take him right down the main street, with all the risk that implied.

Suppose that girl down the hall had opened the door of his room and seen what lay there?

He held the horse to a walk until he cleared the edge of town, then let it canter for a half-mile, then a dead run for a quarter. Seeing where the herd of thirty or forty head of cattle had crossed the road, he turned into their trail and followed it for some distance, heading down into a maze of ravines.

Of Bud Aylmer he knew nothing but his name. He had a fire going when Bud rode up. "Join you?" Bud had asked, and Stan had said, "Light an' set."

Bud picketed his horse after stripping its gear, then brought a loaf of bread to the fire. "Ain't got much," he said. "This an' some coffee."

"Coffee's on," Stan said. "I've got some bacon."

The third man had come along a few minutes later,

made as though to ride by, then swung his horse over to
the fire and joined them. He added a can of beans and a
fistful of prunes. Then he produced the bottle.

Stan Brodie was no drinker but he knew good whiskey
when he saw and tasted it. This was good. Unaccustomed to
drinking, Stan took only a sip, but the big stranger
smiled at him. "Don't worry, friend. Have at it."

Stan grinned. "Good stuff," he said, and took a hefty
swallow. His stomach was empty and he felt the jolt of
the whiskey at once.

The stranger got Bud's name, the first time Stan had
heard it. He turned to Stan. "Call me Tex," he said.

"Well then, call me Montana," Stan said.

They ate, then they had another drink. Looking back
Stan could see how Tex had guided the conversation.

It was not until they had still another drink that
Tex suddenly chuckled. "Got a friend drives stage through
here. Rides empty most of the time. I've got a notion to
give him a scare."

"How's that?" Aylmer asked.

"Oh, I dunno. Maybe put a sheet over my head an' play
ghost . . . only I don't have me a sheet. Be fun at that.
Tom is sure a scary one. On'y thing he's scared of is
ha'nts and holdups, an' I don't reckon he's seen nary
one."

"Knew a feller stuck up a stage one time," Bud said.
"They done it just for the fun of it. For the excitement.
You know, they'd been out on the trail pushin' a herd of
steers up Kansas way and they was plumb bored, an' they
seen this stage . . ."

They ate, drank, and discussed the humor of scares
and being scared, each one coming up with a story to
tell. Under the influence of the liquor and amused by the
idea of a practical joke, they accepted Tex's suggestion.

"What the hell?" Tex said. "Let's do it! Give him a

good scare an' then ride into town an' buy him a drink.
Be a real lark . . . like Hallowe'en."

The trouble was the stage driver was not scared. He
grabbed for his six-shooter.

Tex shot him, grabbed the express-box, and they fled.
Half-drunk they raced away, sobering quickly in the
chilling awareness of what they had done.

When they pulled up, Aylmer said, "Tex, you shot that
driver. You killed him."

"Hell, he was fixin' to kill us! You seen his gun
come up!"

"This was s'posed to be a lark, a game, sort of. We
didn't bargain for anything like this."

Tex shrugged. "Well, we done it. Might's well divvy
up an' skip the country."

"I want no part of it," Aylmer said.

"Me neither," Stan agreed. "I'm no thief."

"You sayin' I am? I wasn't alone back there. But
what's done is done." Tex scowled at him.

"I'm only sayin' this was a damn-fool notion and we'd
better return the money and light out . . . fast. That
man's dead an' that could mean a necktie party."

Tex shrugged. "Well, maybe you're right. It wouldn't
do for us to get caught with this stuff. I'll tell you
what. We'll ride into town, leave the stuff, have a
drink, then get the hell out of the country."

It had made a kind of sense at the time and neither
of them had a better idea.

Tex indicated a saloon as they rode in. "Let's have a
drink and get the lay of the land," he suggested. "Then
we can decide where to leave the gold."

Tex seemed friendly with the bartender and they all
had a second drink on him. That last drink evidently car-

ried something special because Stan recalled nothing more until he awakened in the rooming house with Aylmer dead on the floor.

Why had Bud Aylmer been killed? Had he awakened and caught Tex leaving with the loot? Or was there some other reason? The fact remained that whatever the reason, Bud was dead.

Looking back it was easy to see that Tex had planned the whole operation. Obviously he had known about the twenty thousand in gold the stage was carrying, and he had simply picked up a couple of gullible drifters and talked them into helping him. He had then killed Bud and stuffed Stan's pocket with gold, evidence enough to hang him for both the killings.

Stan Brodie turned from the trail where several cows had crossed it and followed their trail along a ridge until he could look over the country. He disliked sky-lining himself but this was not familiar territory and he needed to put some distance between himself and town.

He followed a game trail marked with fresh tracks of a deer. He was no more than five or six miles from town but well away from the usual trails.

Nothing was to be gained by riding without destination, and if he got out of this predicament it would only be by using his head. From time to time he glanced down his back trail and kept aware of the country around while trying to assay his position.

Nobody back there knew him. He had been seen by that girl and by the hostler. No doubt some of those in the saloon the night before had seen him, but how many would remember him he could only guess. Nor did he know how he had gotten into that room where he had found himself.

Tex had not known his name, nor had Bud Aylmer, so he had that much going for him. Yet as soon as Bud's body was found they would be looking for anyone connected with him.

Obviously Tex had planned for him to be found in the
room with the dead man, a knife in his hand and loot from
the stage robbery in his pocket. There could have been no
other reason for stuffing his pocket with a couple of
dozen gold coins.

Thinking of that, he counted the money for the first
time. Twenty gold coins of twenty dollars each. Four hundred dollars that would buy him a rope necktie if they
were found on him.

He had eighteen dollars of his own money and the hostler had seen him drop a gold coin so he would keep the
oldest and most worn piece. He began looking for a place
to cache the rest.

Rounding a corner of a bluff he saw a huge rock, tall
as a three-story building. Momentarily out of sight of
any trail, he dismounted and climbed up to the rock, hiding the money under a pack rat's nest in one of the wind-
worn hollows.

He climbed down, dusted his pants, and turned to his
horse.

A rider was sitting there, holding his horse's reins.
He was a tall man with close-set eyes and a coarse face.
"What you doin' up yonder?" he asked.

Stan Brodie took the reins from his hands. "Never
could pass up one of those honeycomb cliffs," he commented. "Always figured there should be something hid in
them. Too obvious, I guess."

"Find anything?" The small eyes probed his.

"Oh, sure! Pack rat's nests, one hawk's nest, and a
place where there was fresh bobcat sign. I came down
fast. I got no wish to tackle a bobcat on a cliff-face."

He mounted. "One time I did find some pots, and when
I told some Eastern dude about them he offered to pay me
to show him where they were. He said some folks study
them."

"You mean them ol' clay pots like the Injuns use?"

"Uh-huh."

"That makes no sense. They're just pots for storin' water, grain, an' such. Anyway, what did them Injuns know?"

"Maybe, but he give me twenty dollars to guide him. Only a few miles, too. Easiest twenty bucks I ever made."

They rode on, the stranger lagging, seeming in no hurry. Soon the stranger pulled up. "I been thinkin'. I've got no grub for a long trip. You headin' west?"

"Uh-huh."

"I'd better stock up. See you."

The stranger swung his horse and started back. Stan stared after him, glad to be free of him yet worried as to what he might say back in town. He might also stop to look over that honeycomb cliff, just for luck.

The morning was hot and still. Heat-waves danced over the bunchgrass levels where the cattle grazed . . . a few cattle.

A lonely, empty land, and he was unarmed. Tex had taken both his Winchester and his Colt. He needed a gun. He had never killed anyone and did not want to . . . not even Tex. Gun or no, a man who wanted to kill could always find a way. Defending yourself, however, that was often a last-minute thing and a gun would be good to have.

He had seen too much killing in his time. All he wanted was a quiet place where he could work and save a little.

He rode on into the morning, rode until the sun was high. Sweat trickled down his face and into his eyes. He looked back. Nothing . . . nothing yet.

Finding a dim trail leading off to the east and north, he followed it. When he had gone a hundred yards he tied his horse to a clump of brush and taking off his boots walked back in his sock feet until he reached his turnoff. The tracks he had left were vague. He took his

hat and fanned the dust until the tracks showed almost
none at all. Backing up, he did the same thing further
along, then returned to his horse, brushed off his
tracks, pulled on his boots, and rode away.

Was that a dust-cloud?

He had been a fool to take those drinks. He had no
head for liquor and had never cared for it. Tex made it
all seem like a joke until suddenly that driver was dead
and it wasn't funny at all. If they caught him they would
hang him.

When that stage driver reached for his gun Stan knew
it was no lark. That driver hadn't been amused. Then Tex
shot and the driver tumbled into the dust.

Tex had known right where to look for that box and he
had gone right to it, paying no mind to the driver he had
said was his friend. Of course, that had all been a lie.
Bud and him . . . they were fools. But he had never heard
of anybody escaping hanging because he had been a fool.

He slowed his horse. No use killing the poor beast
because he was running scared.

Something shadowed the land, far ahead.

Hills? Trees? A ranch? No matter, for there was apt
to be water and he was already spitting cotton . . . or
would have been if he could spit. The horse needed water.

He glanced at the shadows behind the brush. Almost
two hours past noon. The shadow ahead began to take shape
and it was all three things he had suspected: low hills,
trees, and a ranch.

When he came up to it the house and barn proved to be
low buildings made of flat stones taken from a ledge behind the barn. There were a couple of corrals, no horses
or cattle, but there was a well.

He rode into the ranch-yard and swung down. There was
water in the trough, some green moss in the bottom of it,
and there was a pump. He trailed the reins and began
pumping. He expected to have to prime the pump but it was

not necessary. Clear, cold water gushed into the trough.
With a gourd dipper that hung from the pump, he drank,
then drank again.

He pumped the trough full, keeping an eye on the
house. There was neither sound nor movement. Was it
empty?

Stan Brodie pushed his hat back on his head and,
holding the dipper for another drink, he looked carefully
around. No sign of life, no dogs, no stock, yet the pump
had been recently used.

The leaves of the cottonwoods rustled and the sound
brought him to realization. He was still not far enough
away for safety but his horse had been hard ridden and he
knew it needed rest. He led the horse to the stable.
There was fresh hay and he forked some into the manger.
He stripped off the gear and left the horse free to eat
or to roll in the dust of the corral. If anyone did come
he wanted to appear unworried and unhurried.

He took a handful of hay and rubbed the horse down,
talking to it as he did so. A man had to talk to somebody
and most cow-horses received a lot of confidential chatter which they were in no position to repeat. That was
one thing about a horse. You could say almost anything to
it as long as you treated it decent.

Walking outside he sat down on the bench that circled
a huge cottonwood. The soft wind stirred the hair over
his damp brow. It was good, good to stop if even for a
little while.

Stan Brodie was twenty-two and had been an orphan
since he was nine. He had never had anything like a home
since his folks passed on, but he knew what a home could
be like.

Once when he was eleven a man needed a boy to do some
chores around the place, but when Stan arrived the man
was not yet home so the maid showed him into the parlor

and warned him, "Now just you set, and don't you touch anything."

He had seated himself on the very edge of the sofa, holding his cap in his hands. The carpets were deep and soft, and there were pictures on the wall and some glass-doored bookcases holding books in red and gold or black and gold leather. There was a lamp with a fringed lamp-shade and the room was all red plush, so quiet that his breathing worried him.

Finally he tiptoed over to the bookcases and read the names on the books. Scottish Chiefs, by Porter; Lord Halifax, Gentleman, whose author he couldn't make out; Pilgrim's Progress, by John Bunyan; and The History of the Five Indian Nations, by Cadwallader Colden. He was staring longingly at the books when a man entered.

"What is it, boy? What are you looking for?"

Guiltily, Stan had stepped back quickly. "I . . . I was just looking at the books, sir."

The man was pleased. "Well . . . I haven't many. About thirty, I'd guess, but I've read them. Most of them several times. Can you read, boy?"

"Yes, sir. I can do sums, and I can write. I went to school in the orphan asylum."

"Orphan? You've no parents?"

"No, sir. Not that I know of, sir. My mother died when I was nine and my father was off somewhere and nobody knew where to find him. I ran away from the asylum, sir."

"Why?"

"I wanted a job, sir. I wasn't getting anywhere in that school."

He had worked for Alec Winters for two months, cleaning up the yard, cutting grass, sawing wood, and exercising his horses. Then Mr. Winters got him a job herding cattle.

Not that he was a real cowboy. He had to be sure that no cattle strayed and to bring them into the big corral at nighttime. He stayed with the job all summer and when he left Mr. Winters he had seventy dollars. He put ten dollars in his pocket and hid the rest in his belt at a place where the stitching was broken.

Two men grabbed him as he left town. Peterson was an itinerant laborer of doubtful background, the other man he did not know. One held him with his face in the dirt while the other went through his pockets. They found a little more than seven dollars because he had bought a pair of shoes.

"Where's the rest of it?" Peterson demanded angrily. "Winters paid you seventy dollars."

"No, sir," Stan lied. "There was the deducts. He deducted some for this, some for that. There was no more than ten dollars left when he got through."

They did not want to believe him, but they did. Deducts were a common experience and more than one workman had found himself broke at the end of a job. There were deductions for time lost, for tools broken, for any excuse an employer could find. Why should Winters have treated this youngster any different?

They argued, slapped him around a little, but he held to his story. Then they let him go, telling him to keep going and that they'd beat the life out of him if he came back and told anyone.

He kept going.

That was in Illinois. In St. Louis he cleaned boots and shined them, in Louisville he was a printer's devil. In eastern Kansas he helped with the harvest, and in Fort Smith he worked for a printer again, delivered newspapers, and swept out a saloon every morning before opening time. He earned two dollars a month from the printer and fifty cents a month from the saloon-keeper, but he actually found the equivalent of four or five dollars a month

in the sawdust on the saloon floor. Or he did until the
saloon-keeper found how well he was doing and began
sweeping his own floor.

When he was fourteen he joined a cattle drive that
had been turned west short of Baxter Springs and drove to
Abilene with it. He drifted south when the cattle were
sold and joined another drive starting near San Antonio.

He drove an ox team from Westport to Cherry Creek,
Colorado, tried placer mining, worked on other men's
mines, swung a sledge driving spikes on a railroad, and
then one night he helped a drunken man home.

The man's wife was a plain-faced, pleasant woman who
took her husband and put him to bed. She glanced criti-
cally at Stan. "Should I know you?" she asked.

"No, ma'am. I'm Stan Brodie. I've been laying track
for the Denver and Rio Grande. Your husband got a bit too
much and asked if I'd help him home. I never saw him before."

"You're a good lad. Will you have a cup of coffee?
That's the least I can do."

"Yes, ma'am. Your husband was talking to me for some
time, ma'am. Said some mighty fine things about you."

"He's a good man. He just can't handle whiskey. He
never could. Mostly he stays away from it but when he
starts . . . What worries me is the paper."

"Paper?"

"We publish the _Bugle_. He does it all, but without
him we'll have nothing and now we're apt to lose it all."

"But he'll be sober in the morning."

"Not him. He will be drunk for weeks, if I know Tom.
We can't afford it."

Stan put down his cup. "Ma'am, I could run your newspaper. I have done it before."

When morning came he appeared at the newspaper office, which was below the rooms where he had taken Tom
Hayward the night before. Mary Hayward opened the door

for him. "It isn't much," she said, letting him in. "Can you handle a Washington handpress?"

"Yes, ma'am. I used one in Fort Smith."

"There's the type. Most of it is there. There isn't enough of the letter 'k' so Tom's been using 'q' in its place. Most of our readers are used to it by now."

"All right, ma'am. In Fort Smith we didn't have any 'f' and we made do with 'ph.'"

"The paper is due out tomorrow and I am afraid he doesn't have anything done. There's a few items he's set up over there, mostly local news. The patent-medicine ads are set." She looked worried. "There will be a lot of space to fill, I'm afraid."

"Yes, ma'am, there nearly always is. Don't you worry about it." He held out his hand. "You might give me that key. I've got to run down the street for a few minutes."

Gebhardt was sitting over his breakfast in the Stockman's Restaurant where Stan had known he would be. He dropped into a seat opposite him.

"Gep, do you still have that St. Louis paper I saw you with?"

"It's over in the wagon. Mighty handy out on the road to have a paper around. Why? D'you want it?"

"I need it. That paper isn't more than a week old, is it?"

"Week? Why, that paper is just two days old! Got it from a Pony Express rider."

"Can I have it?"

"Sure enough. You'll find it down on the left side of the seat."

Stan picked up the newspaper and glanced over it on the way back to the office.

Inside, he sat down and read through the last few copies of the _Bugle_, capturing the essence of the style used by Tom Hayward. Then he set up the type for a story on the candidacy of Ulysses S. Grant for president lifted from the St. Louis paper.

He found another story on a speech by Schuyler Colfax, who was to be Grant's running mate, on payment of the national debt in gold.

He also included a brief item to the effect that an organization calling themselves the Jolly Corks had formed a new organization to be called the Benevolent and Protective Order of Elks. He also reported the robbery of a train at Marshfield, Indiana, by a gang reported to be the Reno brothers.

Stan remembered that day and those that followed. Most editing was done with scissors and a paste-pot, newspapers borrowing liberally from each other but careful to give credit. Where additional space had to be filled, he added bits and pieces from memory, a poem by Lord Byron, and an historical question about the name of the great-grandson of Cleopatra who became emperor of Rome.

He chuckled, remembering that. Nearly every subscriber had written in wanting to know who the emperor had been and how it happened. "Caligula" had been the answer and historical or sporting questions had become a regular feature of the paper from that day on.

He was startled from his reverie by the sound of horses' hooves . . . a lot of horses. He started up, then suddenly realizing he could not run, he removed his coat quickly, folded it, rolled up his sleeves, grabbed a bucket, and started toward the house.

They rode in and drew up sharply, dust swirling about them. "Howdy!" The man wore a star, as did one of the others. "Mind if we have a drink? We're huntin' a killer."

"You don't say?"

"Held up the stage an' murdered his partner, but we'll get him. He ain't gone far."

"I've seen nobody." He gestured toward the well. "There's water, and I've just pumped the trough full. Help yourselves."

"He didn't come this way," one of the posse volunteered.

"This was the closest water so we circled around." He looked at Stan again. "Do I know you?"

"I haven't been around long," Stan said. "Just came in to help out a little."

"Well, they can use it. Carrie's all right but she's not up to all she has to do. I hope you can help her, son. I hope you can."

He heard the buckboard coming as they led their horses to the trough. He felt his mouth go dry.

Several of the men had remained in the saddle. His own horse was unsaddled and in the stable. He was trapped, his stomach gone hollow, his heart beating with slow, heavy throbs.

The buckboard came up in a clatter and a rattle and swung into the yard. A pair of matched grays driven by a girl. A girl with red hair and freckles.

The girl from the hotel.

CHAPTER 2

The red-haired girl's eyes were upon him. Her surprise obvious.

"I'm sorry, ma'am," he heard himself saying, "I haven't done much yet. But I'll get to it."

"I guess we interrupted, Carrie," the man with the

badge said, "comin' up the way we did. But I'm glad
you've got some help until things get straightened out.
If there's anything we can do . . ."

"No, Mr. Blake," she replied, "Stan will take care of
things. I have an idea he will prove to be the best hand
we ever had. If he doesn't," she added, smiling, "you
will be the first to know."

"'Day, ma'am. We'll be ridin' on."

"I think you must be, Sheriff. There's been a hanging."

Stan felt a chill finger run along his spine. He
stood very still. "They caught a man in town, and he'd
been spending that new gold . . . like that stolen from
the stage. When they searched him they found a lot of it
and, well . . . I believe they were kind of hasty."

Blake's face showed angry impatience. "Damn it, I--!"
Then he looked to her. "Sorry, ma'am, but they should
have held him for trial. This here lynching has got to
stop."

He swung his horse and rode out, followed by his
posse.

For a moment Carrie and Stan simply stared at each
other, then she said, "Put up the horses. Then come into
the house. I think we should have a talk."

She got down from the buckboard before he could move
to help. She looked straight into his eyes, a cool,
searching glance.

She was pretty, he realized suddenly, very pretty.
The few freckles only made her more attractive. He had
always liked girls with freckles, anyway.

He took the team into the shadowed recesses of the
stable and stripped off the harness, hanging it on hooks
left for the purpose. He took his time, trying to think
it out.

Where did she stand in all this? Why hadn't she given
him away? How had she gotten his name? Was this her

ranch? What had she meant when she added that comment to the sheriff that if he did not pan out he would be the first to know?

He could saddle up and run, but his direction was the way the posse had been searching, and if he left here now there would be questions, too many questions.

He dried his hands on his pants, wiped the sweatband of his hat, and started for the house.

Coffee was on and it smelled good. When he removed his hat and stepped into the house there were two cups and saucers on the table along with bread and butter and some cold slices of meat.

"Sit right down," she said, "I'll be only a minute."

He sat down carefully, holding his hat in his hand. It was a cool, pleasant room with window curtains, rag rugs on the floor, and a couple of oval, tinted pictures on the wall. One was of a man with a round head and a collar that was a size too large, the other a dignified-looking woman with her hair done up on top of her head except for three curls on each side of her face. They looked like all the other pictures of people he had ever seen.

There was a Bible on the table, a big, square old-fashioned Bible with heavy leather covers. There was a coal-oil lamp and in the corner some shelves with books, about twenty of them, and some stacks of Godey's Lady's Book. The room was neat, clean, and quiet.

In a moment she came in, poured coffee, and sat down. She looked across the table at him. A pretty girl, he thought again, but a stubborn one.

She smoothed her skirt over her lap, then she lifted her cup. "The first thing you must understand," she said, "is that you are my prisoner."

"What?" He was not sure he had heard right. "What did you say?"

"One word from me and you would be arrested, perhaps hung. I shall not give that word unless I must. If you do your work properly and conduct yourself correctly I shall not give it."

"I have done nothing," he said, which was a small lie. He had participated in a holdup, even if it had been done without criminal intent.

"That is no concern of mine," she said primly. "That would be for the courts to decide . . . if it ever got so far. My concern is this ranch. My father has been injured. It will be weeks before he is able to work, and it may be months. In the meantime, I have you."

He did not believe it. He stared at her, shocked. "Now see here," he began, "I--"

"You see here! As you noticed, the sheriff is a friend. So is every man on that posse. So are many of the people around here. If you leave before I permit you to leave, or if anything happens to me, you will be caught and hung . . . hanged."

He studied her for a minute. "You know," he said, "you're not a very nice girl."

She flushed to the roots of her hair, but her chin lifted. "My character is not under discussion. Each day until you understand the situation here I shall lay out your work. Each day I shall expect a report that the work has been completed.

"The weather is good. You will sleep under that farthest cottonwood. When you are on the home ranch you will have your meals here with me. You will attend strictly to business. From time to time there will be visitors. Talk to them as little as possible and perhaps I can keep you alive."

"What about wages?"

"You--? You speak to me of wages?"

"Yes, ma'am. I will want wages. Slavery has been out-

lawed in this country. I shall want thirty dollars a
month and found, payable at the end of the month. If you
don't want it that way, turn me in."

She stared at him, uncertain whether he was bluffing
or not. His features were bland, unreadable. Suddenly uncertain herself, she wavered. Then she said, "I see no
harm in that. If you were not here I should have to pay
someone else.

"Also," she continued, "I shall want your gun. You
will not need one here."

"I have no gun. I have no firearm. Neither rifle nor
pistol. They were taken by the man who murdered Bud
Aylmer."

Obviously, she did not believe him, but before she
could speak he said, "Please think back. You saw me in
the hotel. If I had been carrying a weapon you would have
seen it."

He finished his coffee and stood up. "If you have no
further need of me, I'll be going. In the meantime you
might list the things that need to be done."

He went outside and stopped in the morning sunshine.
He should get out of here, get as far away as he could,
yet he was certain she would do just as she threatened
and Stan had no doubts about that sheriff--he was a tough
man.

Her name was Carrie . . . Carrie what?

What kind of a spot had he gotten into, anyway? How
long did she expect to hold him here? Until her father
returned? And what if he never got well?

Stan Brodie, he told himself, play it cool, play it
smart, and when the chance comes . . . run!

He had never been given to idleness, and the presence
of work was the occasion for work. He started by repair-
ing the corral gate, which needed fixing. Then he forked

hay to the horses. The hay started him wondering. It was good meadow hay, and the meadows spoke of low ground, possibly water. He had seen little water coming here and most of the range closer to town was indifferent, at best.

He led out his horse and saddled up. As he tightened the cinch he looked across the saddle at the house, and she was standing in the door with a rifle in her hands.

"You wouldn't be thinking of leaving?" she suggested.

"Just thought I might ride out and see where that hay came from. If I am to be of any help I'd better get acquainted with your range."

He rested his hands on the saddle. "You know, if you're going to keep an eye on me you'd better ride along. I might just decide to take out of here."

"There's the sheriff," she replied, "and that posse. Then there's that rough crowd in town who might want another hanging. I am not worried about your leaving."

She lowered the rifle. "Ride north two miles. That point of rock with the white streak of quartz in it marks our corner. Then ride east for six miles or just about that. You will see a hole in the rock, high up. That's the Keyhole. Everybody around here knows it. Ride south four miles to Two Cabin Creek and about a quarter of a mile further on you will come to our line fence. Then come back here."

"Sounds like quite a layout."

"It could be. If you see any riders over toward Two Cabin, stay clear of them. They won't be friendly."

"May I ask why?"

"They want the water in Two Cabin. They settled over beyond there knowing they couldn't make it without our water and knowing it belonged to us."

Stan Brodie considered that. "What happened to your father?"

"His horse fell with him."

"Where's the horse?"

"We had to destroy him. He broke his leg."

This was a wide and empty land where the short-grass plains ran up to the mountains and lost themselves in the open mouths of the canyons. Yet it was a deceptive land, for viewed from afar it seemed only one vast plain of gently rolling hills with here and there a butte or mesa standing stark against the sky. Riding over it one found that the plains and rolling hills were cut by shallow canyons and the dry streambeds that ran only in the hours following heavy rain.

Stan Brodie had punched cows in just such terrain, and rode warily. Without a gun he felt naked and exposed. He had climbed somewhat and the grass seemed greener, due no doubt to some pattern of prevailing winds and rainfall. Miles away he could see what he was sure was the Keyhole, the rock Carrie had mentioned.

There were a few longhorns mingled with some of the whiteface cattle they were beginning to bring into the country. Dipping into a grassy hollow near an arroyo he came upon the ruins of an adobe house, gutted by fire. A lean-to barn some distance away was also burned . . . Indians probably.

Suddenly a buzzard flew up, then another. He rounded a turn in the arroyo and before him lay the remains of a dead horse. Two more buzzards flew up and he drew near. This must be Carrie's father's horse.

Buzzards had been at work on the carcass, but the forepart was little damaged. He glanced at the broken leg. It had been a bad break, offering no chance to save the horse. He was about to ride on when something else caught his attention. Swinging from the saddle, he walked back.

Across the front of the horse's leg right above the break the skin was broken, a straight-across gash that had cut to the bone. The animal must have run full tilt into something, maybe the bottom wire of a fence, tripping the horse and throwing the rider.

He returned to his horse and mounted, but he did not ride away. That horse had ridden into something, a taut wire it looked like, yet such a wire in a canyon like this was unlikely. He looked around, studying the rocks and the ground.

Whatever tripped that horse had to be close by. No horse was going far with a leg like that.

He wished he had a gun.

He walked his mustang down the canyon, then pulled up. A lot of hoof tracks . . . This must be where the horse had fallen, then it stumbled up and hobbled around.

The horse would have been killed when they found Carrie's father.

What _had_ that horse tripped over? Had Carrie guessed that the horse tripped?

No wire.

The canyon widened a little and there was a cove on each side. He walked his horse over and checked one cove. Nothing. In the other he found the tracks of two horses and the stubs of cigarettes smoked by men who waited here. One of them smoked his cigarettes tight and small.

But were those tracks and cigarette stubs left before or after the accident?

He glanced back toward the dead horse, out of sight now. Walking his horse, he studied the rocks on both sides of the small canyon.

Turning, he strolled back down the canyon, keeping his horse beside him. One wall of the rocks was honeycombed and pitted, and suddenly he saw what he had been expecting: a place on the edge of one of the holes where something had chafed the rock.

Squatting on his heels, he glanced into the shallow

hole. It joined another hole not over a foot away. A wire
had been run into one hole and out the other, then tied
to itself outside the holes.

He stood up and glanced directly across. A juniper,
squat and gnarled, stood just opposite. Walking over he
could see where something had scratched the bark.

He walked back, brushing out any tracks he might have
made, then mounted. Someone had stretched a wire across
the canyon at that point, then somehow, by a shot or some
other means, had startled Carrie's father or the horse
into a run. Hitting the wire he had spilled over, breaking the horse's leg and injuring himself.

Stan glanced around quickly. He had better get away
from here, and fast. Quickly he turned his horse into
some deep sand in the bottom of the arroyo where no de-
fined hoofprints would be left, then he climbed out of
the arroyo and lost himself along a hillside covered with
juniper. It was scattered, but in places it was quite
heavy. He was barely under cover when he glimpsed three
riders. Reining in, he waited in a clump of five thick
juniper trees, watching the riders.

He had never been one to decorate bridle or saddle
with flashy ornaments and he was glad for that now, for
they picked up the sunlight and could be seen for miles.
The three riders came along up the hill on a line that
would take them within fifty yards of where he sat.

There was no escape. The best thing he could do would
be to sit still and hope they did not see him.

Stan Brodie was without illusions. Nothing in his
twenty-two years had given them fertile ground for breed-
ing. Still, he had his own dreams and aspirations, and
none of them included being killed. He had no enmity for
any man but trusted few of them.

If these riders did not ride for Carrie they had no
business being where they were, and if they had no business there it was likely they would not wish to be seen.

He had no loyalty to Carrie. She had taken advantage of his seeming guilt to use him for her own purposes, and he had no choice but to go along until he could choose a time for escape.

What he wished to avoid was getting in deeper while he waited.

He was positive an attempt had been made to kill her father, and if it had not succeeded it was not for lack of trying. The attempt was sufficient to convince him they would stop at nothing . . . and here he was, unarmed, and within easy rifle-shot of them.

He spoke softly to his horse, whose ears were pricked toward the oncoming riders.

That these men were among those who were trying to get Carrie's water he had no doubt, and they would assume he was a spy.

He had made a fool of himself once and he did not intend to do so again. Every time he had gotten into trouble it was from keeping bad company . . . but how was he to know about Tex? Yet, he admitted, he had known. He had not trusted him from the first. It was the whiskey that mellowed his doubt of the man.

The man they hung in town? Could that have been Tex? Possible, but unlikely. It was more likely that stranger he met on the trail had gone back, looked, and found the stolen gold Stan had hidden under the pack rat's nest.

Yet Tex could still be around. Certainly, he had known that bartender.

The riders turned sharply away from him and began to spread out. Then for the first time he saw that several head of whiteface cattle had come into the open below him. The three riders rode toward them and hazed them off toward the west. That they were Carrie's cattle he could not doubt, but he was unarmed and men who had killed once would not hesitate to do so again.

With the cattle drifting west the three turned back

and rode up the hill toward him. Suddenly one of them
pulled up sharply and called out.

Stan swore bitterly. They had found his tracks. One
glanced up the hill toward the clump of trees, then
scanned the side of the hill to right and left.

Abruptly they turned and rode down the hill. Stan
mopped his brow. Of course, they did not know if he was
still up here, nor would they guess he was unarmed.

And that gave him an idea.

CHAPTER 3

When he rode into the ranch-yard Carrie came to the
door. "Supper's ready."

A thought came to him that was disturbing. "When you
drove up in the buckboard you called me by name. How did
you know it?"

"I heard somebody call you that in town."

Now a gentleman did not call a lady a liar, but that
simply was not true. Nobody in town knew his name. Tex
and Bud had only known him as Montana, a name he had
given himself on the spur of the moment. So how could she
have known?

"I saw three riders," he commented at supper.

"On our ranch?"

"Yep."

"Did you order them off?"

He gave her a wry smile. "Three armed and unpleasant
men? And me without a gun?"

She was irritated. "Well, perhaps I was foolish.
You'd better wear a gun. Get yours out and carry it."

"I don't have one."

She started to reply angrily, then stopped. "But if you don't have a gun, then how--?"

She was wondering how he could have held up the stage, and he saw no harm in letting her wonder. "I don't have a weapon of any kind," he said, "but this knife." He put his hand on the haft.

"That man . . . the one they found in the hotel . . . he had been killed with a knife. They found it."

He drew his own. It had an eight-inch blade and had a nice feel but it was obviously more of a working knife than one that would be chosen to kill a man. "I still have mine," he said quietly.

That she was disturbed and puzzled was obvious. Evidently this information did not conform with what she had believed.

"We have rifles," she said.

"All right, I shall carry one."

For a few minutes they ate in silence. There was an occasional crackle from the fire, and the subdued rattle of knives, forks, and dishes. It was pleasant, that he admitted, and she was a pretty, in fact a very pretty girl. A very pretty girl who now held him captive.

He finished his coffee and pushed back from the table. "You'd better let me pick out a rifle. Those men were running off your cattle today."

"I'll tell the sheriff."

"All right, but I doubt if it will do any good. They won't have the cattle where they can be seen, or if seen, be tied to them. Let me take care of it."

"You?"

"I'm slave labor, don't you remember? I'm the man you blackmailed into working for you."

She flushed angrily. "Don't be like that! I needed somebody, I--!"

"And I was handy, is that it? And I didn't have any

way out?" He turned and looked at her. "What about you, ma'am? A woman can use a knife as well as a man. You were in that hotel, too!"

For a moment he thought she would strike him. He waited, but she simply stared at him, her eyes hot with anger. After a minute he said, "Better let me have that rifle, ma'am. And some ammunition . . . a lot of it."

"They'd never believe you."

"What?"

"I mean they'd never believe you saw me in that hotel, and they'd never believe I killed that man."

"Did you?"

"Of course not! I did not even know there'd been a killing until somebody found the body. I heard them talking of it downtown."

"And thought of me."

"Who else?"

He shrugged. "All right. I am a possible suspect and I know I did not do it. You are a possible suspect and you say you did not do it. So what became of the man who did it?"

"Who would that be?"

"A tall, high-shouldered man with black eyes and a lean look about him."

Carrie got to her feet and picked up the dishes.

"There must be many such men. Anyway, he is probably gone."

She took the dishes to the sink, then turned on him.

"Do you wish to leave? I won't report you to the sheriff."

"No." He went to the rifle rack. They were good guns. There was one Winchester there of which he liked the feel. He took it in his hands and held it for a moment. Then he replaced it in the rack.

"Take your pick," she offered. "There are two or three pistols in the drawer at the foot of the rack."

He opened the drawer. There was a gun-belt and holster there, then two six-shooters, an Army Colt, and a newer Remington.

He took out the holster and belted it on. It felt good around his waist, too good.

"I'll take the Colt," he said, his voice cold. He took the Winchester down. "And this rifle. I am sure your father won't care."

"Do you really mean to stay? There'll be trouble, I know."

"I'll stay for a little while," he said. Now, more than ever, he wanted to know what was going on . . . a part of him had to know. "When will your father be up and around?"

"Three weeks, I think. Three weeks at least."

"All right. You can count on me until then."

Outside in the darkness he shifted his bed to a hollow among some rocks. No use to advertise the place where he slept. He touched the gun, then drew it. For a moment he stood holding the pistol, then holstered it. "Stan Brodie, you'd be better off a-runnin'. Curiosity is what killed that cat, isn't it?" he muttered.

The guns he had taken were his own, taken from his room the night Bud Aylmer was killed.

CHAPTER 4

The place he had chosen to sleep was on a small, rock-covered knoll some fifty yards from the ranch house but overlooking the area. There were fifty or sixty boulders scattered across the top of the knoll, ranging in

size from the size of a barrel to twice as large. Between
them were grassy hollows free of stones. In one of these,
where he had merely to turn his head to see the house, he
bedded down.

Once he was settled, he kept an eye on the house, but
his mind was busy, and there were a lot of questions to
which he had no answer. What he should do was cut and
run, yet if she called the sheriff there was small chance
of him getting out of the country before they caught him.
They knew the area far better than he.

How had his rifle and pistol, apparently taken from
the room the night Bud was murdered, showed up here?

What had become of Tex?

Carrie had obviously not been aware that the weapons
he chose to take were his own. Who had access to that
house other than Carrie and her father?

Off across the hills the coyotes began to yap. It was
a familiar sound and one he had never found unpleasant.
He lay, hands clasped behind his neck, thinking.

The stars overhead were very bright, and the night
was cool. He listened, vaguely aware of movement . . .
cattle? He wanted no part of this mess. He wanted to get
away, but he suspected the sheriff or some of his posse
were already a little suspicious--after all, where had he
come from so suddenly? And there were a few people who
could place him in town.

He awakened suddenly, having no memory of falling
asleep or of even being sleepy. It was morning.

Getting out of bed he gathered his bedding and rolled
it carefully, stowing it in the corner of the stable he
had taken for his own. Carrying his rifle he went to the
house, where smoke was coming from the chimney. As with
many such ranch houses there was a basin at the back door
and a towel hung on a nail near a small hand mirror fastened on a board.

He shaved in cold water, turning occasionally to look

over the hills around the ranch. If he was going to be in
the saddle so much he would need more horses, which
brought another thought. If this was a working ranch,
where was the saddle-stock?

He wiped his feet at the door and went inside. His
breakfast was on the table, obviously just put there for
it was hot, although there was no sign of Carrie.

Drawing back a chair, he seated himself, then feeling
something under his foot, he glanced down.

Mud . . . soft mud . . . several crumbs of it and one
good-sized piece that might have fallen from the edge of
a boot.

Somebody either was here or had been here, somebody
who had recently stepped in mud that had not had time to
dry. He ate his bacon and beans, a couple of slices of
home-baked bread, and then finished his coffee. The only
place he remembered seeing any mud was near the horse
trough. There might be a track.

He got up from the table, pushing his chair back and
purposely making some noise, but Carrie did not appear.
Was the visitor still here? Or had Carrie been outside
herself?

He went out, closed the door behind him, and dumped a
little water in the basin to rinse off his fingers. In
the mirror he studied what he could see behind him,
shifting position for a better view.

Nothing . . .

He went to the stable and saddled his horse, leading
it outside. As he walked up to the trough he glanced in
the mud. Somebody had deliberately scuffed a foot across
the mud, smearing any track that might have been left.

Stan Brodie swore softly. What was going on here,
anyway? Her father was in the hospital . . . so who had
been here? A lover? Despite himself he was suddenly jealous. Then he laughed for being so foolish.

What was she to him? A girl he knew and worked

for. What was he to her? A drifting, probably no-good
cowhand.

He shoved his rifle into the boot and stepped into
the saddle. He was not going to let them see him scouting
for sign, but he intended to do just that. He meant to
find out what was going on.

In the meantime there was work to do. He found a few
steers and drifted them back away from the Two Cabin
area. All morning long he rode, stock was scarce and he
wondered how many had already been stolen.

Several times he saw tracks of small bunches of cattle, usually driven by two or three riders. Those he
found he turned back. The range was in tolerable shape
and that in the area around the Keyhole was the best. Beyond it was wild country.

The sun was straight up by the time he reached the
Keyhole so he rode into as much shadow as there was near
the rocks, picketed his horse on a patch of good grass,
and climbed up the rocks. He had neglected to fix himself
any kind of a lunch and Carrie hadn't fixed one for him,
so he was hungry, but he had often been in that fix. Settled down with his back to the rocks, he studied the
country.

Stan Brodie was not a big man, being a shade under
six feet and rarely weighing over one-sixty, carrying
most of it in his chest and shoulders, which was partly a
result of driving spikes on the railroad and work with a
pick and shovel.

In the orphan asylum one of the men who supervised
them had liked to see them fight so he would tie gloves
on the youngsters and let them go to it. Stan was often
whipped, until he realized that the boy who just kept
coming usually won. So he began to simply pile in swinging, throwing punches until the other boy began to back
up. After that Stan usually won. Here and there in the

years that followed he had picked up a little more know-how as to fighting and survival.

The other day they had found his tracks and lost them, but they had been curious, maybe a little worried. A guilty man can find a lot to worry him in something he does not understand. Well, that was something he could do. He could worry them.

From his position he could see over quite a lot of country, and it could save him miles of riding. He spotted several groups of cattle feeding on slopes or draws over toward Two Cabin. These he would drift back away from the borders of the ranch as he had done the others.

Coming down off the rocks he mounted and rode back to the south and west, pushing cattle ahead of him. Once, in the distance, he glimpsed a rider, but he could not make him out, and disappearing into a draw the man vanished from view.

When he came within sight of the ranch he swung around it in a wide circle. He could see no horses at the hitching-rail nor at the corral. He picked up the old tracks of the posse coming and leaving, and almost a mile further along, the tracks of another horse that had gone to and returned from the ranch. He glanced at the sun. Almost an hour before sundown. Turning his mount he walked him along the trail of the lone rider. He followed the trail into the low hills until he came to a small spring with a trickle of water that sub-irrigated a meadow below it. Here he found where another rider had waited, smoking many cigarettes, until the visitor to the ranch returned. They rode off together.

He studied the hoof tracks so he would know them if he saw them again.

Carrie was setting the table when he came up to the door to wash his hands. "Who are those fellows over at Two Cabin?" he asked.

"I don't know them all. There's the Tutler brothers, Brockey and Red Fitz Tutler. There's Shang Hight, and a man named Trainor. They are a bad lot, and I doubt if any of them is using the name he was born with." She paused. "Stan, be careful. If they killed Pa, they would kill you. Of course, they did not kill Pa, but they tried, and they would have."

He offered no reply, but seated himself at the table. She filled his cup. "Where did you come from, Stan?"

"I'm a drifter," he replied, "just a loose-footed saddle tramp."

"I don't believe that. You sound like an educated man, sometimes."

"You'd be mistaken. Most of my education I got in an orphan asylum or a newspaper office."

She brought food to the table, and sat down opposite him.

"If I were you," he said suddenly, "I'd be very careful, and be sure your father is well guarded."

"Guarded? He's in the hospital, such as it is."

"His fall was no accident, you know."

"Of course it was. His horse fell with him, that was all."

"Your father's horse," he said, "was tripped by a wire stretched across the canyon."

"What? I don't believe it."

"Anybody who took the trouble to look could see where the wire cut the skin on the horse's leg. I found where the wire was tied. Somebody came down out of the rocks and took up the wire while your father lay there on the ground. He just let him lie, thinking he was dead or dying."

"You mean somebody tried to kill him?"

"It's obvious, isn't it?"

"I'm not going to leave."

"Then you'd better get ready for a fight. I doubt if

they will wait until your father is up and around . . . if it is the place they want."

"Do you doubt it?"

He shrugged. "I'm just a passing stranger, ma'am. I don't know anything about you or your father. But somebody tried to kill him and I think they will try again."

"Can you stop them?"

"Seven or eight men, maybe? That's asking a lot from a man you only got to stop by using blackmail."

She flushed. "I was all alone, and I needed help. Maybe it wasn't nice of me but--"

"You've got other friends," he replied quietly. "Get them to help you."

"Other friends? Why, I don't--" She paused. "What do you mean by that? What friends?"

Stan did not reply. For a moment there was silence and then she said in a somewhat lower voice, "I don't know what you mean."

He stood up. "If you will excuse me? I am quite tired."

She looked up at him, wide-eyed and embarrassed. Then she stood. "Oh, by the way. You spoke of reading. We have a few books if you'd like to read them."

"I would, indeed. However, I doubt if a campfire that would provide enough light to read by would be good for my health. Not if you have as many enemies about as I believe."

"You could come in here. I wouldn't mind."

"All right, but not tonight. I believe I should be outside. I had the distinct impression," he added, "that someone was around last night."

He stepped outside and closed the door behind him, then moved along the wall to the corner before stepping into the shade of the big tree. He remained there for a moment, listening.

Every instinct he possessed warned him that something

here was radically wrong. Unless the ranch had had a lot
more cattle until recently but they'd been stolen, it had
too few to be a worthwhile operation. To make ranching
pay they'd need to run at least six hundred head, and if
they had half that they were lucky. The herd was a mixture of Hereford and longhorns but the latter predomi-
nated . . . and where were their horses?

Was the operation simply a cover for something else?
But if so, why have him around?

The answer to that seemed obvious and unpleasant, for
the only reason he could imagine was simply to have him
here as a suspect in case anything went wrong.

The place he chose for his bed that night proved a
bad one. He slept restlessly and awoke irritated with
himself and his situation. He was getting nowhere here,
and it was time for him to get away, to move on. He had
lost enough time in drifting and it was the moment to
make a decision as to where he was going and just what he
intended to make of himself.

He shook out his boots, knocking a centipede four
inches long from one of them. He swore and tugged the
boots on, then got up and looked around. The prairie was
a uniform mixed green and brown, the hills rolling, the
sky somewhat overcast.

Taking his rifle he walked down to the house and
washed his hands and face. Carrie put her head out of the
door as he threw the water from the washbasin into the
yard. "Come on in. It's ready."

First good thing he'd heard all morning. At least, he
told himself, the cooking was good. He started to turn
away toward the door when he looked again at the small
mirror. It was held to the log wall by bent-over nails.
He turned two of them aside and, taking down the mirror,
dropped it into his pocket.

This morning it was pancakes and eggs. Where she had
gotten the eggs he could not guess but obviously there
was somebody around the town who had chickens. He ate
them with pleasure.

Sitting back, he looked across at her. "You set a
good table," he admitted.

"My father likes to eat, so I had to become a good
cook."

"How's he doing?"

"He's still unconscious." He glimpsed the worry in
her eyes. "He must have fallen very hard."

"Or was slugged on the head before he could get up."

She stared at him. "You don't believe that?"

"I believe it's likely." He hesitated, then said,
"Where's the riding stock around here? I need a fresh
horse now and again."

"Oh! I didn't think! I've been so worried, I . . .
Stan, there's a place about a mile west of the Keyhole.
It's a small valley there and there's some water in it
and we've fenced the ends. The walls are steep enough
so that's all we have to do to make a corral that has
about sixty acres. We have a dozen head of horses in
there.

"Catch up the gray or the Appaloosa. There's a dun
there who's the best horse of the lot but nobody can ride
him since my brother--" She broke off, then added, "Ride
him if you can, but he's mean."

Finding the valley was easy enough, and they had a
nice place for holding stock. A small, isolated valley
kind of tucked into a corner of low hills, and the grass
was good. I roped the gray and saddled it, meanwhile
keeping an eye out for trouble.

An idea had been working itself around in my mind for
some time but whether it would work or not would depend

on how many of the cattle gathered by the Tutler brothers and their friends were longhorns.

Now a longhorn is no ordinary cow-beast. A longhorn is a wild animal, as much so as any elk, buffalo, or deer. Even though occasionally rounded up and herded by men, they remained wild, very skittish, and likely to stampede on the slightest provocation. A sudden whiff of a wolf-hide, the drop of a tin pan, a shot . . . many things might cause a stampede.

A Hereford, or whiteface, was less likely to stampede, but if one started the rest would go along with the crowd. There was no way I could tackle that bunch of land-grabbers head-on, but there were several ways I might give them trouble. The first thing I had to do was to worry those longhorns. They were probably nervous enough but I'd leave nothing to chance.

So far as I'd been able to see they had altered no brands. They had simply drifted cattle over to range they claimed, and as cattle often strayed far afield nobody could then move in and brand whatever cattle there were.

Until now they had been doing all the scaring and the threatening. If all went well we would see how they liked it when somebody put a saddle on their own horse.

Mounted on the gray I scouted their camp. There were

COMMENTS: Yes, that is exactly how this story ends! Its beginning has something in common with the "suddenly out of place" situation found in Louis's novel *The Man Called Noon* and it also harkens back to a few of his noir or crime thrillers from the days when he was writing for the pulp magazines.

Like "Borden Chantry" and several of Louis's other stories, this looks like it is headed toward being a melding of the mystery and

Western genres. I can never quite figure out how they did it, but Louis wasn't the only writer who tried to create and solve mysteries in just one draft. I had a couple of conversations with novelist Tony Hillerman about how to pull this off, and it's not easy. However, as in quite a few of the works in this book, I think Louis finally got to a point where he needed to do some more figuring before he continued. Here are a few lines out of his notes on this story:

> Somebody seems to have visited the ranch during the night.
> What was CARRIE doing in that cheap hotel where Bud Aylmer was killed?
> Where are CARRIE'S cattle? Where are the horses? Why are the horses kept some distance from the ranch house?

Some of these questions may simply have been things that Dad figured he'd better clarify, but others may have been intended to be part of the mystery. Your guess as to which is which is as good as mine.

_____

JACK CROSS

The Beginning of an Adventure Story

CHAPTER I

The name is Jack Cross, John Cross, if you want to be
particular, and I'm a guy in need of a fast buck. So I'm
standing on the Avenida de Almeida Ribeiro in Macao with
ten dollars in my pocket and a .45 Colt in a shoulder
holster.

Sure . . . I'm broke . . . but this is my backyard.
Or it used to be, 'way back before the war. They knew me
here in those old days, and they knew me on Malay Street
in Singapore, in Shanghai's Blood Alley, and on Grant
Road in Bombay . . . and in a dirty little bar in a back-
street of Bangkok there's a guy who holds mail for me.

Profession? Well . . . what can I say? I'm a guy who
has been around, a guy who knows most of the answers but
is quite sure he doesn't know them all. I'm a guy who can
use his mitts, a guy who can handle a rod, and I've run a
machine gun a couple of times in wars that didn't belong
to me.

Beginning? Maybe there was never a beginning, and

maybe there was a map of the world hanging on the wall
when I was born. Maybe it was reading Jack London and
Stevenson and Conrad. More likely it was a melody of foreign names, the sound of names that rang little bells in
my brain, or great gongs. Names like Bangalore, Gorontalo, and Taku Bar.

Way down in my guts there was something that liked
the sound of those strange and far-off places. Samarkand . . . Makassar . . . Kuala Lumpur . . . Chit-
tagong . . . the Malabar Coast . . . the Banda Sea.

Education? Mostly the kind you get from learning what
to do when somebody stabs a fast left for your mouth or
when a guy comes at you with a shiv or sticks a rod into
your belly.

The kind of education that enables you to take a
Browning apart in the dark and under fire, or tells you
how to tell the feel of gold from silver, or how to con a
ship through a reef-strewn sea somewhere south of the
Line.

Sure, I've read a book. In fact, I've read a lot of
books, read them in the aimless, casual way of a man who
loves to read and loves books for themselves. I've read
them in fo'c'sles and bunkhouses from Magallanes to the
Yukon, read them all, Plutarch, Thucydides, Homer, and
Shakespeare, from the classics to the fast action magazines, and found plenty of interest in all of them.

What did I want from life? The sound of bow wash
about the hull . . . the slat and slap of empty sails on
a dead calm sea . . . the smell of copra and tar and musk
and the acrid smell of burning camel dung.

Sure. And temple bells and elephant gongs, the hot,
excited bodies of tan-skinned girls . . . the feel of a
Colt butt bucking in my hand . . . the solid thrill of a
hard punch landed . . . the knowledge of far-off places
and seas untracked and unmarked . . . the smell of opium

in the Shanghai "Trenches" and all the fierce, hard,
lonely, beautiful intoxication of living all of life that
I could get hold of.

Put it down in your book that I'm an unreconstructed
savage, that I'm born out of time, that the Spanish main
is gone and the free companies are gone and that Drake
and Hawkins and even O'Reilly and Christmas have passed
the way of all flesh. But put it down, too, that there's
always a war somewhere, always a fast buck to be made,
and always a man or a woman who will take a chance when
the going is rough. And put it down that the old spirit
isn't dead yet, and that if tomorrow, in spite of all
those boys who are still babies at eighteen, if tomorrow
somebody said they would need a crew to build a bridge
on the moon, they'd have the office jammed within an
hour.

Put it down that I'm a fool, that I'll find my finish
someday cursing my luck on some lonely reef in the wash
of a weedy sea, or in some barroom with a knife in my
back or some lead in my guts . . . but put it down that
when that day comes I'll have lived. I'll have seen it
all, known it all, and tasted it all.

So it's been . . . and so it was last night when I
heard that sampan paddle chunking astern of the
freighter, the freighter that had been my home for the
past three months.

It was past two a.m. and the ship was dark except for
the anchor light forward and a bulb by the gangway where
the night watch was loafing. We were due to put out to
sea shortly after daybreak and I was restless. Standing
beside the rail looking at the lights of Macao, I heard
the paddle moving in its locks.

Then I saw the sampan not far off the stern, and just
like that my mind was made up. He came at my low call and
waited alongside. So I got my gear and lowered it with a
heaving line then went down beside it.

It was an ugly part of town where he landed me and an
ugly hour of night, but I'd landed in a lot of towns and
this was no worse than many. Finally, I found a sleepy
rickshaw coolie and shook him awake.

So I was on the beach again . . . like that first
time, so long ago in Shanghai. Oh, those had been the
good, hot, wonderful days! I'd landed there with forty
cents, had a fight in the ring for a few bucks, a fight
won quickly. . . . Then there was the matter of some guns
up the river in piano boxes, and of a man who ended his
career with his head on a piece of pipe. . . . There was
a poker game up the Yangtze near Yichang with twenty thousand dollars on the table at one time. . . . There had
been jai alai games and horse races and dog races. . . .
And then there had been some tribute silk smuggled from
the Forbidden City in Peiping in the darkness of a rainy
night and sold to a Greek with a sweat-soiled collar. . . .
There had been dinners at the Del Monte, and dancing with
Rose Marie of the Lido . . . the Peach Blossom Palace and
there had been trips to that Venice of China, Hanchow.

There had been songs and laughter and stories told,
and there were fights in the streets and there were dark-
eyed Eurasian girls and sad Russians and turban-wearing
Sikhs and a fortune teller who failed to tell his own and
there was a dark night and a dark street and a time when
two good British seamen jumped into a fight to help me
and were killed for their pains . . . but several of the
Chinese rivermen died, too, and I came away with a bloody
coat and a half-dozen minor cuts and a gun in my pocket
that I forgot to use . . . which comes of fighting with
your hands until it is second nature to think of no other
weapon.

And those wonderful hours of talk over wine or whiskey, talk of the names of which history never speaks, the
men like General Lee Christmas, Tracy Richardson, Tex
O'Reilly, One-Arm Sutton, Rafael de Nogales, Larson of

Mongolia, and Rajah Brooke, and other names that echo
down the brassy halls of warlike memory.

These were the men of whom we talked for these were
the men of our kind . . . and some of them were there
among us.

So I was back again . . . back on the beach in the
Far East and north of me there was war . . . and all over
the East there was a stirring and moving of new forces
rising . . . the Malays, the Chinese, the Tamils, the
Bengalese . . . all of whom were feeling their own urge
to freedom, to throw off the old shackles of colonial
government, to remove the burden from the white man (who
relinquished that burden bitterly), and to look around
with a new awareness. But it was my East, the place I
knew best.

The fingers of dawn felt their way down the quiet av-
enues of Macao, life began to stir again and the working
citizens began to go about their business. I found my way
to a seaman's hotel and checked in, and after breakfast I
started making the rounds.

Haig . . . he might be in Macao. The last I'd seen of
him was before the war and probably he had been recalled
to service. Giacomo . . . where was he?

It was past noon before I saw a familiar face. I was
behind a table in a little bistro on a side street off
the Avenida when he came in . . . Jimmy Pak Lung.

He turned quickly when I started up and then his face
smoothed out and he came to me, his grin spread wide, his
hand out. "John!" he said. "You're back!"

We gripped hands and stared at each other and I never
felt better. Jimmy was born in California, but nobody
would have guessed he was anything but Chinese. He could
play the cynical denizen of a treaty port or a wide-eyed
rube from the interior, but he had all the mannerisms of
an American, too.

So we talked, and the hours went by, and then he
said, "You want to make a spot of cash?"

"Who doesn't?"

"You've been up-country in China. I know a man who
wants to go there."

"Now?"

"Right now. And he's got money, plenty of money."

"What's he after? He's not a Russian, is he?"

"He's a Yank, like you. I don't know what he's after,
but it smells of money."

So there was talk of this and that again, and finally
back to this American, Jonathan Spurr, who wanted to fly
into Red China at a time when Americans were hated by
many and especially by the government. It was just such a
trip as appealed to me . . . full of risk, yes, but a
quick reward too.

So we went to see him, this Jonathan Spurr. . . .

He rolled a fat cigar in his lips and he looked at
me, and he didn't like what he saw. I've read that look
in the eyes of too many men before this and didn't like
it any better from him. I'm a big guy, six-one and an
even two hundred pounds, but I carry no scars and your
average punk who has never been across the street from
home thinks a tough man should swagger and talk out the
side of his mouth and act hard. It always irritates me
because I've licked fifty guys who were just like that.

"You've been to Kansu?"

"Yeah."

"Ever hear of Choni?"

"I've been there."

That surprised him. He looked at me with more respect
and some doubt. That I could understand, for Choni is one
of the most out-of-the-way places in the world. Wars and
revolutions had passed and repassed over China without
ever touching it.

"Are there any white men there?"

A test question. "There was. A missionary, some kind of a Scandinavian. He'd been there a long time."

"What were you doing there?"

When he asked me that I just looked at him. "We're talking business, not history," I said.

He didn't like it and I didn't give a damn. This guy was used to throwing his weight around, used to being obeyed. He would be hell to get along with until I'd broken him in . . . and I was ready to start just anytime.

"Could you take us there? In a plane?"

"Who," I asked, "is 'us'?"

"There will be four of us. The plane will carry eight and some freight. It's an amphibian."

"For enough money I'll take you any place you damn well please."

He rolled his cigar in his fat lips. "I've heard you were tough. You don't look it."

It was a stupid remark. The remark of a fool or some romantic girl who has never been out of her home circle. "And what," I asked him, "does a tough man look like?"

"I know one when I see one."

"You're fortunate. It will save you a lot of trouble while you're looking for one." I got to my feet. "Look, friend, you'd better not tackle this sort of deal. You're not going to be up to it."

My hat was in my hand and I started around the table toward the door.

"What's the matter?" he demanded. "You walking out?"

I turned back. "You may know a tough man when you see one but to me you assay like a forty-eight-carat sap."

His face got red and he started to say something he would have been sorry for--after I'd hit him.

Then from behind me was another voice. "Take it easy, Jonathan. I think this is our man."

He came into the room, a lean-bodied, older man with

cold gray eyes and white hair. His face was weathered
with the fine lines at the corners of his eyes that come
from looking at too many hot suns.

"No man can talk to me like that!" Jonathan Spurr
was a big wide-beamed man and he came blustering around
the corner of his desk. He came around the corner of
his desk and I stood there waiting for him, knowing how
much I was going to enjoy it. Maybe he saw something of
it in my eyes, maybe some little sixth sense of caution
warned him he was running into trouble. Anyway, he slowed
down.

"What's the matter?" I asked him. "Don't you want to
lose some teeth?"

"Forget it!" It was the older man. "Take it easy,
Cross. Spurr's just on edge, that's all. This is a big
deal and we've got to keep our heads."

Spurr mopped his face. "All right," he said, more
quietly, "let's forget it. No need to go off half-cocked.
If you've been in Choni you're just the man we want."

Right then the door opened again and a girl walked
into the room. She was a blonde with a golden tan, and
lovely blue eyes with a hint of Hell in them.

She came right up to me, and Spurr said, "Mr. Cross,
my niece, Joan Iveson. And Doc Pardee, a friend of Joan's
father."

"How do you do, Mr. Cross?"

"Better," I said, letting my feelings show in my eyes
with an overcoating of insolence. She stiffened a little.
"Much better."

Then I turned away from her and said to Spurr, "All
right, lay it out for me. What's the score? What's in
Choni that you want bad enough to risk your life to get?"

"Research," he said. "I'm doing some research into
the--"

"Nuts," I replied shortly, "save that for somebody
who will believe it. Talk turkey with me or get yourself

another boy. You never went after anything in your life
unless there was money in it."

That he didn't like, either, but he chewed on his
cigar and then Pardee said, "Go ahead and tell him. He'll
have to know anyway."

"Joan's father had an uncle who was a missionary in
western China. He saw something very valuable in a remote
place. We're going after it. We're going to bring it
back."

He rolled his cigar in his lips and looked at me. "I
want a man who knows that country," he said, "and one who
can handle a gun."

CHAPTER II

"It will cost you," I said, "it will cost plenty. Is
there enough up there to pay for the trip?"

"There is," he said, "and more."

"Know anything about that country?"

"A little. We looked it up, studied it in books and
magazines." Then he indicated Joan. "And she has her
great-uncle's notes. He was very accurate as to details."

"That will help. As for the books and magazines, few
of them can give you anything that will help in that
country. In the first place, nobody out here knows what
has happened back there. Not even me. Choni has lived
under the rule of a hereditary prince for many years, and
maybe it still does. It is an out-of-the-way valley green
and lovely, and not too easy of access. But the Reds have
been getting in everywhere so they are probably there,
too."

"We expected that. However, we heard that a little

money . . ." Spurr rubbed his fingers together sugges-
tively.

"Maybe. Money used to buy almost anything in China,
and with some of them it will yet. But a true Communist?
Forget it. Money won't work and whatever you bring with
you they can take by force. Any plane that can make it in
there will be especially valuable."

"We've thought of that. That's one reason why we want
a man who can handle a gun."

"Is what you want right at Choni?"

"No . . . it is beyond Choni."

Beyond . . . mountains and gorges, high, cloud-
piercing peaks, black canyons, trackless and lonely,
boiling rivers of black water laced with white. The
strange, bleak, lonely land lost in the interior of a
vast continent. The very thought of it made me stir restlessly, for it was that sort of thing that had drawn me
back.

That vast and lonely land where Tibet meets Sinkiang,
the land of the Kun Luns, the Altin Tagh, the Chang Tang.
A land of lonely ice lakes and forbidding mountains, the
land of the white bear and the snow man, the land of the
Lolos and the Ngoloks. A bitter, savage mountain fastness
where the outside world was a rumor and nothing more,
where the wars and dynasties of China were only travelers' tales and the doings of the outside world were misty
legends, faintly known and altogether, to those people,
unbelievable.

A land without roads . . . a land of camel trails or
yak paths . . . a land of passes and mighty mountains, a
land where the highest peak on earth might be and yet nobody could say for sure whether it was or was not . . .
fantastic, mysterious, remote.

"Beyond Choni," I said musingly, "that's the loneli-
est place on earth, excepting, perhaps, the Antarc-

tic . . . and even less known." I looked up at Spurr, for
I had seated myself and he was still standing. "What is
it you're after?"

He hesitated, brushing the ash from his cigar, studying the ash as if to read the answer there. Doc Pardee
stirred a little and then said quietly, "An idol of gold
encrusted with gems. It is in a long-forgotten temple,
unknown and lost. Charles Iveson actually saw it."

"You're sure of that? It wasn't just a legend he repeated?"

"He saw it," Joan said, "and he described it in detail. He even brought home two large diamonds from it.
The money from their sale paid for my education."

"It's worth a fortune," Spurr said.

"It belongs in a museum." Joan spoke almost on top of
his words.

Right there was the problem in a nutshell, not to
mention that it really belonged to the locals. The communists wouldn't value a religious artifact but they certainly weren't going to hand it over to foreign thieves
either. None of that was my problem, I intended to have
money in the bank before we took off.

"Alright, you said four would go? Who are the others
besides you?"

Jonathan Spurr nodded at Pardee. "Doc will go, Joan,
and Bob Landes."

"Joan?" I was surprised. "You want to go into that
country?"

She smiled, her eyes bright with excitement. "I
wouldn't miss it for the world!"

"That's no place for a woman," I said, "and the less
of a load we have, the better. I don't see any sense in
carrying excess baggage."

"I'm not excess baggage!" she flared angrily. "I can
cook, I can shoot, I know first aid, and I've flown a
plane! I'll do my part!"

Doc Pardee smiled. "Also," he said quietly, "she has the location of the temple. The rest of us only know it approximately."

That settled that. I know better than to argue with a woman when her mind is made up. Besides, she'd be nice to take along. Right then she must have read my mind because she looked at me, her eyes cool and carrying a challenge. "Bob Landes," she said, "is my fiancé!"

Jonathan Spurr and Pardee were eager to talk about it. Spurr began telling me about the plane, and I listened, then nodded toward Jimmy Pak Lung, who sat quietly by the door. "Jimmy goes along," I said.

Spurr stopped abruptly. "Nothing doing," he said, "we can't afford the weight."

"You weigh twice what he does," I said, "so suppose you stay behind? You or this Landes guy?"

His face got red. Jonathan Spurr did not like me. He was not going to like me under any circumstances. "Landes," he said, "is a fine rifle shot, a skilled woodsman, and a very useful man aside from being Joan's fiancé. I," he added grimly, "am running this show . . . and financing it."

That I would have bet on. Leave it to the Jonathan Spurrs of this world to have money . . . no matter what they have to do to get it.

For that matter, I was in no position to speak myself. I suspected myself of some ethics, somewhere along the line. If my methods were not always strictly legal, there was at least a sense of fair play . . . as long as they played fair with me. But I was not a disciple of the "turn the other cheek" school. In my book it was every man for himself when the playing got rough. I had my own feelings about Jonathan Spurr, and a good hunch that he did not intend to share any more of that gold than he could help. And then he brought up the key consideration.

"How much," he asked, "will you want for this?"

It made me smile because I knew I was going to hit him where it hurt. "Five thousand," I said, "in cash and on the line . . . and twenty percent of the take."

Jonathan Spurr's face and neck grew red. For an instant he could not bring himself to speak, or lacked for words. And he was not the only one. Both Joan and Doc Pardee were staring at me as if I were insane.

"Preposterous!" Spurr flared. "Why--!" He stopped, then turned abruptly. "All right! Forget it! We'll get another man!"

That made me smile. "Spurr," I said, "you're a chuckle-headed idiot. You ask a man to risk his life flying almost four thousand miles over enemy country, in danger every minute he's out of Macao.

"You ask him to go into a country where any man is a fool to go unless at great profit, even in peacetime, even when the people are friendly. You won't find anybody else who is crazy enough to go; furthermore, if you go around talking about it the government here won't let you take off with gas enough to get you there. They want no trouble with Red China.

"And I might mention this: You won't find anybody in Macao who knows Choni. If there's one man in the city who knows of the place, I'll pay off any bet you'd like to make. And you seem to imagine you can fly in there, pick up this idol, and fly out. You'd better think it over, and think it over a lot."

So I started for the door, and then hesitated, Jimmy at my elbow. "You've exactly five hours to change your mind. I'll be having dinner at the Hotel Central and you can find me there at that time. Furthermore, I won't bargain: Five thousand in my hand when the deal is closed . . . and twenty percent of the take. I'll pay Jimmy."

We walked out and closed the door after us. Jimmy chuckled, then shrugged. "Well, it would have been a mean

trip, anyway," he said cheerfully. "We'll find something
else."

"We won't need to," I said. "They'll meet our terms.
You wait and see. Who else could they get?"

He was silent a few minutes, and then he said slowly,
"One way they could get it--just one other way. They
could go to Shuksan."

That stopped me. "Petro Shuksan? He's here?"

Jimmy looked at me seriously. "Yeah, I should have
told you. He's not only here, he's the biggest operator
in town. He's got a hand in everything."

Petro Shuksan was a half-caste, half-Portuguese and
half-Chinese, and a renegade in any language. He had
been, when I first knew him, a petty thief and a runner
for a waterfront girl-house. He had graduated from that
to smuggling, thieving on a larger scale, and running a
house of his own. On one occasion over at the Nine Islands I had slapped him until his nose streamed blood and
his lips were smashed. That was for trying to kidnap a
girl I knew.

Since that day his hatred for me had been a living
and ugly thing, and if he was a big wheel in Macao then
I'd better get out of town or kill him, but fast.

"It was the kidnapping," Jimmy said, "of Dr. Lu. He
arranged that, and it was he who notched his ear and received the money. He dealt with the Japanese during the
war. He trades with Red China now, and he has great influence with them. If he learns of what is planned he
will not hesitate to warn them or to come in himself."

So there it was. A man like Shuksan could have another man killed by a simple word or gesture. And in
Macao it would mean nothing. That he would find whose
palms to grease was certain, he would grease them gener-
ously. And in my own pocket was a lone ten bucks.

There was no avoiding the issue. Shuksan was the
worst enemy I had in the world and the years that had

passed would not have dulled that feeling in the least.
He would never be satisfied until I had suffered for the
beating I'd given him. Every minute I was in Macao was a
danger.

"He'll know, Jack," Jimmy said. "You'd better stay
away from the Central. The place is full of his spies.
Get your gear from the hotel and move out to my place.
He doesn't like me but he doesn't watch me, either."

"Tonight we go to dinner at the Central," I told him,
"and after that, we'll see."

The hours between were not wasted. Jimmy Pak Lung
briefed me thoroughly on the events since our old Shanghai days, and we went to look at the plane, then stirred
around among the dives, talking to this person and that
person.

No, Haig hadn't been seen since the war. Last anyone
heard he had been a colonel in the British Army in Burma.
Giacomo had remained in Shanghai for the first year of
the Japanese occupation and then he had vanished.

"Killed?"

"No" my informant said, "I don't think so. He went
back inland somewhere."

Everywhere we heard rumor of what went on inside of
China. There were purges . . . rewards were given for de-
nunciation. The call for political purity was being used
to repay old grudges . . . to prevent being denounced by
others . . . to gain favor.

Yet beneath the surface old China went on as it always went on, and I was satisfied that when the present
furor was over China would have absorbed communism as it
has absorbed all religions and all philosophies. In the
end communism would be turned out as they were, as something distinctly Chinese. A hundred years or so of nearly
continual war had driven the Chinese to welcome almost
any stable government. Chiang had failed in twenty years
to bring reform or any real change to the great mass of

the people; now they seemed ready to let the Communists try.

"Shuksan," I commented later to Jimmy, "would take them, but good. He'd keep it all for himself."

"But do they know that?"

No, they did not, that was the rub. And Shuksan was a glib talker, just the sort who would know how to handle Jonathan Spurr.

Nevertheless, I went ahead with my planning and thinking the thing out. Of course, it was no trick to realize the main problem was the matter of gasoline. The plane could not fly there and back without refueling, and there was no gas that I knew of in Choni.

"Jim," I said, "remember that field outside of Tak-wan? I wonder if it could still be used?"

Pak Lung shrugged. "Could be. I was in there once--it was in '46. It had been deserted for months, then." He started to get up. "I could find out. I know a guy . . . he was a Nationalist flyer. He deserted to the Reds, didn't like them and got out. He's in town."

"See him, then meet me at the Central for dinner . . . at eight." He sauntered to the door, a slim, shabby young man in a soiled drill suit. "And ask him what he knows about Meitsang."

Jimmy was curious. He looked at me, quick and interested. "In the Min Shans? What's there?"

"You ask him; don't volunteer anything. If he knows anything, he'll talk. Just get him to tell you about it."

Jimmy Pak Lung went out and I sat there alone in his room. And when a man is alone there is no reason to kid himself. I was a sap, of course. I was a worse sap than Jonathan Spurr, because I knew better. The Red Chinese were eager to lay hands on any American illegally in the country. A spy trial would fit into their propaganda program very nicely right now.

In another sense, it hinted of disloyalty to even

make the effort, for it could deal the USA a political blow. Wryly, I reflected on what would be said. The fact that I had a reputation could give the State Department their out. I'd fought for cash in China before . . . and I'd been a smuggler. And they could drop the whole thing--Spurr, Joan, and Doc--under my cover.

On the other hand, and this I considered seriously, I might learn a good deal. I'd been an Army man, and renegade or not, I was a Yank. Maybe I was out to make a fast buck, but not at the expense of my own country. I might find out a great deal if I got out safely. If . . .

It depended on so many things. Leaving here would be the first one, for the town was full of spies. All planes departing in that direction would be reported. If we were sighted flying inland they would send fighters after us. If there was any hitch in our refueling we would be dead ducks, and as for getting out again . . . The whole operation was insanity.

Who was I to talk? Sitting here with ten dollars in my pocket and a dinner ahead of me that would cost at least that. If they failed to show and talk business I was a goner. This had to go through.

The room had grown dark as I sat there thinking. Starting to rise, I stopped suddenly. There was a man loitering outside, staring at the building.

Relaxing in the chair, looking out the window, I watched him. He hesitated, lighted a cigarette, then leaned against a lamppost.

This was it then: Shuksan was suspicious. Or was it somebody else? For some other reason?

My eyes strayed to the dial of my watch--it was past seven and time to be moving. When he turned his eyes from the window I came out of the depths of the chair and slid into my shoulder holster, then my coat. There was a back door to the alley. . . . I turned that way, searched the alley with care, then stepped out into the night.

    Flattened against the building, I waited. Nothing
moved. I went to the end of the alley, looked around and
saw nothing. And then I stepped out into the open street
and walked quietly away. And I was smiling.
    This was my backyard. . . . I was home again. . . .
The street smelled of ancient fish, of dust, and the re-
membrance of heat, but I was back. . . . This was
Macao. . . . This was living.

COMMENTS: This fragment is related to "China King," the story
fragment that you will read next. That is not to say this one was written first, but they probably were created within a few years of each
other. Mentioned here is the "tribute silk" caper that makes up the
backstory of "China King." Both stories have a foundation in the era
of chaos that reigned in the Far East before and after World War II.

    Louis often had his protagonists express a litany of odd jobs and
experiences. This was always a general refelection of his own life and
varied employment history but in a few cases, this being one of them,
the list held even greater resonance. Occasionally, Dad mysteriously
suggested that he returned to the Far East after his first trip in the
mid-1920s. Supposedly, a few of the details mentioned in this story—
jumping ship with forty cents in his pocket, a fight in the ring for
some quick money, inside knowledge of the fake arms sale that ended
with the con man's head being impaled on a pipe driven into the gravel
of a Shanghai parking lot—were events from his life. The latter incident is more specifically described in the short story "A Friend of the
General." In my opinion, the jury is still out regarding the veracity of
these tales. What is more likely true is the story about the fight between the British seamen and the Chinese river pirates. I know that
Dad was in Shanghai for four days and that story sounds like something that might well have happened along the Huangpu waterfront.

    A few of the people and places mentioned here might be familiar
to the soldiers and sailors of the time. "The Trenches" was a tough

neighborhood of dope dens, gambling houses, and brothels outside the control of the Europeans who ran the International Settlement, or Treaty Port, of Shanghai. Del Monte's was a popular nightclub in Shanghai, as was the Lido Gardens ballroom. Notoriously—or perhaps mythically—beautiful White Russian women (the "Whites" fled Russia to avoid the "Reds," or Communists, after the revolution of 1917) were paid to dance with the male clientele at many of the clubs. Sikh bodyguards from India were hired to chaperone these girls, and "taxi dancers" were, supposedly, only there to dance. Of course, the White Russian women of Shanghai were also some of its most legendary prostitutes, so the rules may not have been as cut and dried as all that.

Lee Christmas, Tracy Richardson, Edward "Tex" O'Reilly, Francis "One-Arm" Sutton, and Rafael de Nogales were all famous mercenary soldiers, though not all in the same part of the world or at the same time. Frans August Larson was a missionary and explorer who managed to travel through some very remote parts of China, Mongolia, and Siberia. Most notably, James Brooke became the first "White Rajah" of Sarawak (an area of North Borneo) when he was given the territory by the Sultan of Brunei for his help in putting down piracy and a rebellion. The Brooke family ruled Sarawak from 1841 until conditions during and following World War II forced them to cede the country completely to Great Britain. All were Europeans who sold their abilities, often violent ones, in the hinterlands of Asia and Latin America.

"Haig" is not just a character in this fragment, but a man Louis claimed to have known, a British intelligence officer in China who had become a Buddhist and was an opium addict. There is a good deal of crossover between potentially real and totally fictional versions of this man, some of which occur elsewhere in this volume. While I have done my best to separate what is true from what is not, there is no way to tell how much truth, or fiction, there is to many of these stories.

From references in the text this seems to have been written in the early 1950s, when the Chinese Communists were still solidifying their hold on the western sections of the country. Louis did spend some time in China prior to World War II and his brother was there right afterward as part of Ambassador Patrick Hurley's mission just before the Communists took over in 1949.

It is interesting, in light of all the Red Scare paranoia of the time, the horrific drama of China's Great Leap Forward, and then the Cultural Revolution, to see that Louis's predictions about Red China have turned out to be, at least so far, correct:

> . . . I was satisfied that when the present furor was over China would have absorbed communism as it has absorbed all religions and all philosophies. In the end communism would be turned out as they were, as something distinctly Chinese.

Dad had great confidence that China would emerge from its Communist period in a manner that was both prosperous and fundamentally Chinese. He didn't think the totalitarian idealism of communism stood a chance in the long run when compared with the Chinese interest in doing business with the rest of the world.

CHINA KING

The Beginning of a Crime Story

When I opened the door he was sitting there with a gun in his hand. He was a lean and evil man with a scar on his cheek that had not been there when I saw him last and the stench of unwashed clothes about him. There was another scar on his upper lip which I had reason to remember. My fist put it there in a brawl on a ship's deck one hot night off the mangrove coast.

"It's been a long time, Jack," he said, grinning at me, "a very long time."

If there was any change it was not for the better. He was older, of course, and his tongue-tip kept touching the thickness in his lip where the scar was. That wasn't a good sign.

"How'd you get in?"

"A few years ago you wouldn't have asked that. You'd have known." The smile left his lips and his eyes veiled a little. "Ask me what I'm here for and I'm not going to like it."

He was an inch taller than my six-one, though a good

thirty pounds lighter. But I made no mistake about China King. Even without the gun he was no bargain in any kind of fight.

"Want a drink?" Ignoring the gun, I crossed to the sideboard.

"Sure," he said, "just so I watch you mix it."

When he had a bourbon in his hand he took a sip, then grinned. "Taste, kid. You got it. But you always had it. Clothes, liquor, and women."

He chuckled then. "Whatever became of the Malay babe you picked up in that place on High Street? When you moved in there I figured you were due for a throat-cutting. Her old man was a big muck-a-muck up in the Federated States."

"We got along," I said. "We got along all right."

This was trouble, real trouble. Nor was it anything I had coming to me. China King and all like him were a thing of my past, my drifting days. That was over now, and I wanted no part of him. When a man drifts from port to port and lives as he can, he meets many people, good and bad. China King was poison.

"Nice place you got, kid. The first time I met you was in Shanghai. You were broke and on the beach."

"All right." I was a little irritated. "What do you want, China?"

His face changed as if he'd been slapped. His thin shoulders hunched and there were ugly lights in his eyes. "You know what I want! I want fifty thousand dollars! I want it right here in my hand, an' don't try stallin' me!"

"I haven't got fifty grand and never had it."

Something in my voice made him look twice at me. "It had to be you!" he said angrily. "Only two of us got out alive."

"Maybe."

"What does that mean?"

"What about Forbes?"

"That limey? He's dead. I killed him."

Opening a drawer in my desk I put my hand in. "If it's a gun," he said, "I'll kill you."

"It's a magazine," I told him, and took it out. The magazine was more than three years old. The picture I showed him was a group of three men . . . three top-flight business executives representing three separate airlines celebrating a merger into Trans-Orient. The man on the right was the new president of the company, Paul Greenway.

China swore. "How could I have missed? I had him dead to rights."

"You didn't get me, China. And you had me right where you wanted."

"You." There was no bitterness in his tone. "You were always a fool for luck."

Fifteen years can be a long, long time. And the Far East was a wide world away and in those days it was a place to make a fast buck. Gunrunning, pearl poaching, smuggling, buying and selling the stuff big ships couldn't afford to handle, looting, gambling . . . fifty ways to make it and a hundred to lose it again.

Seven of us were in on the deal, seven men from all over the world and every man out for himself. We were lifting tribute silk from the Forbidden Palace in Peiping and peddling it to a Greek who sold it again in India. It was not stealing . . . not in the usual sense. We were under orders from a Chinese official; ostensibly the money went to buy guns but that was none of our business. Only we made our share in the process.

Up to a point, we did. The Chinese decided on a dou-ble cross . . . cutting out the Greek and the rest of us once the pipeline was set and the connections made. When we brought out the second load they were waiting for us with guns.

It was a hijack. A good old Yankee-style hijack. Only
it didn't work. It didn't work because we were a suspicious lot of lads, and all of us had been around a little. We knew what the score was, and when that dark boat
moved in alongside and they ordered us to stop, we took
our time.

We knew the voice: It was our Chinese official. We
would have stopped for nobody else. Then we saw three men
rise out of the waist of that boat with tommy guns. We
were ready for trouble, and even as they opened fire we
dropped flat and heaved three homemade grenades into
their laps.

That was it. One of our boys copped it. He was
gone before he hit the deck, and a Chinese boatman with
him.

Six of us left, and a load of silk.

We never stopped, just kept going down the coast. We
didn't go near Shanghai and we avoided Hong Kong. We went
to Macao, made a quick deal, and we were sitting on top
of three hundred thousand dollars.

Three hundred thousand dollars . . . six men from nowhere. Forbes was an Englishman, he had been chief mate
on a Chinese steamer line but did too much smuggling on
his own hook. There was the Portugee, a beachcomber named
Finley, a little rat named Joe Hollinger, China King, and
me. Fifty thousand apiece, if we all lived. If some of us
died, there would be more to split.

That idea came to all of us, I think. For myself,
fifty grand was plenty, more than I'd dreamed of having
at this stage of the game, but I knew the rest of them.

"We'd better get away from here," Forbes advised.
"There's too many in Macao who have wind of this."

So it was Hong Kong we started for, and Hollinger
opened the game. He picked a fight with the Portugee and
before anybody knew what had happened, the Portugee was
on his knees with his gut ripped open. Hollinger was

short, mean, and ready for trouble. "He asked for it," he
said, and I slipped the safety off my Colt.

Five men and nobody felt sleepy. We were off Tingkao
village in the approaches to Hong Kong when the lid blew
off. Who started it I never knew. Suddenly, everybody was
shooting at once. Forbes shot Hollinger and China King
shot at me, and I did some shooting, too.

Somebody splashed in the water, and then I went over
the side myself. The water was shallow in that wide sandy
bay, and I got to shore. There was another shot, then silence . . . but I did not go to Hong Kong. Instead I went
to Canton and from there flew to Shanghai . . . and
safely in a room in Shanghai I counted my money.

When everybody started to shoot, King shot at me and
I went into the bottom of that boat, stuffed my shirt
with money, and went over the side. They thought I was
gone when King shot, and they were busy killing each
other. My take was seventy thousand. . . . I neither knew
nor cared what happened in the junk, but it was pleasant
in Europe that spring, and from Paris I went to Rome,
then to Nice and through North Africa. I was broke when I
got back to the States, but it had been worth it.

Hollinger, Finley, the Portugee . . . they copped it.

"Somebody got away with the boat," King said. "It had
to be you or him."

There was no need to mention the seventy thousand.
"It was a long time ago. It's best forgotten."

He sneered at me. "I ain't forgettin' it. I'd figured
it was you," he scowled, "but you never drank nor gambled
them days, an' I know you hit the beach in the States
flat busted. You never drank enough to wet a man's whistle. You couldn't have gotten rid of three hundred grand
so fast."

He was right about that. Even seventy thousand had
given me trouble.

He got up and poured himself a straight shot of bourbon. "I think I'll see Forbes."

"I wouldn't," I said. "I'd lay off."

He left me then, and after a while I went to bed. But
I couldn't sleep. Forbes had always impressed me as a
cold-blooded proposition, and certainly he had done his
share of the shooting, but whatever else had happened,
that was past. He had gone on and made a place for himself in the world and I couldn't let him look into the
eyes of murder without a warning. So I rolled over and
picked up the telephone.

It took me more than an hour to get to him. When I
did his voice was brusque and impatient. "Yes? What is
it?"

"Greenway, if your name used to be Forbes, I just
want to say that China King is in town. He wants to see
you."

His hesitation was brief, then he said in a quiet,
perfectly cool voice, "This is Paul Greenway. My name was
never Forbes. I do not know any China King. Good evening."

So I went to sleep. If he was not Forbes he had something to wonder about. If he was, he knew what was in
store for him. No matter what happened, the burden was
off my shoulders.

Two nights later I came up to my door and dug for my
key. My hand stopped there and I listened.

My radio was playing, and louder than I usually play
it. Somebody was in my apartment, and that could only
mean it was China King.

At first I thought about calling the cops. Then I
shrugged and opened the door and stepped inside. It was
King, all right, only he wasn't sitting on the divan

waiting for me. He was lying on the floor and he had been shot twice in the stomach. What he failed to get that night off Tingkao he had now, a bellyful of it.

And so had I.

There was no gun, but I had a very good hunch. Opening the drawer of my desk I looked for my pistol. It lay just where it had always been. I sniffed the barrel. . . . It had been fired.

There could have been a lot of men who wanted to kill China King, but I did not believe more than one of them was in Los Angeles . . . and trust Greenway to have known about me, and to have guessed who the call was from.

Sitting very still in my apartment with a dead man at my feet, I tried to remember all I had known of the man we had called Forbes.

It summed up to very little. We called him a limey, but whether he was actually English or not, I did not know. We had met in Shanghai the way drifters do meet. None of us had known the others well. I'd known the Chinese who got us all into it, had seen King, Finley, and Forbes around. Forbes was a cold-blooded fish, a good poker player, and a cool head under fire. He would be a dangerous opponent, and now, of the seven, only two remained.

Knowing something of the man, I knew he would have an alibi; I knew also that he would have arranged to point this killing definitely at me. It was not enough that it be clear, but there must be no mystery to invite inquiry, and I was the only one who could point a finger at Greenway.

The only one . . . In that case I'd be better off dead, from his viewpoint. Dead, I could not talk. Dead it would appear that either I had shot King and killed myself, or had been wounded and died later, or was killed by a friend of King's or the police.

Hence, his best bet was to kill me. The man I had known as Forbes would reason just that way.

How much did he know about me? That would be important now. What would he decide that I would do upon finding the body of King?

Call the police? Or remove the body to some other place? He would suspect me of the latter move. If that was so, and if he wanted to kill me, then he or his killer would be someplace near my car, which was parked in the space behind the apartment house.

COMMENTS: This is a much more interesting story fragment than it may seem on the surface. The underlying idea, that a group of desperate characters, near strangers to one another, perform a dangerous or illicit act in order to gain a "treasure" and once they do can no longer trust one another, can be found in more than a half dozen of Louis's stories and novels. These include "What Gold Does to a Man," "Desperate Men," *Kid Rodelo* ("Desperate Men" was the short story that became the novel *Kid Rodelo*), a couple of story fragments here in *Louis L'Amour's Lost Treasures*, and the best of all of them, the short story "Off the Mangrove Coast," to which this piece has certain connections. It will also show up as a subplot in Louis's soon-to-be-published first novel, *No Traveler Returns*.

The basic idea contains elements of B. Traven's classic *The Treasure of the Sierra Madre*, but in "Off the Mangrove Coast," Louis added a brilliant refinement: It's not much of a treasure. The fact that there really isn't enough money to go around increases the likelihood that one of the men will try to kill the others for the chance to get it all.

Was there some element of this story that was true to Louis's life? Is that why he returned to this plot over and over? He did tell some stories to this effect, but so far, I have no way of knowing if they actually happened. One thing that appears in this story that is true is that he did run into a man named Joe Hollinger, both at sea and with the Hagenbeck-Wallace Circus. And, it seems, a knife was Joe's preferred weapon.

This is also a sequel of sorts to the story fragment titled "Jack Cross." The "silk caper" mentioned is referenced in both stories, and the time period seems right. At a guess, "tribute silk" was silk either given the Chinese emperors in tribute or intended to be given as tribute to allied governors or heads of state. Possibly stock of this silk remained in the Forbidden City for some time. The other oddball crime mentioned here is "pearl poaching," which probably refers to sneaking into Australian territorial waters without the appropriate permits and diving for pearl shell. Before cultured pearls, the real market was for mother-of-pearl from the inside of the oyster (it was used for many of the things we now make out of plastic, like buttons, combs, and the keys on musical instruments). The pearls themselves were so rare that it was a waste of time diving in the hopes of finding one. However, if you were in the mother-of-pearl business and earned a living from the thousands of oysters you brought up, the pearls themselves served as a windfall profit.

Contrary to what one might think from reading some of the overtly macho material Louis wrote, he was a fairly mild-mannered guy. He had great presence, but certainly by the time I came along, he had little to prove in any way other than just trying to be a good writer. Though he could certainly tell adventurous tales about his life, he was a gentle man who could inspire that same gentleness in others.

———————————

TAP TALHARAN

The Beginning of a Western Story

He made camp where the rising sun found frost on the hill, bedding down under a clump of aspen that lined a small hollow on the slope. He was dead tired with the miles behind him, and when the picket pin was driven in he fell into his blankets and slept.

The next thing he knew was a boot in the ribs and a harsh voice, "Get up out of that! Get up, I say!"

His gun was hanging on an aspen near his hand but one of the three men had been thinking of that and held a shotgun on him, grinning as if to say that he should go ahead and try it.

Tap Talharan sat up. "What's the matter?" he asked mildly.

He was in trouble. He was no pilgrim and he knew it when he saw it. These were hard men, riding a hard way, and no give to them at all.

"We want no saddle tramps on this range." The man was slab-sided and hatchet-faced. "Get on your horse and get out of here."

"Look," Talharan said mildly, "I rode all night. I'm dead beat. I've been asleep maybe thirty minutes. When I've had some rest I'll be moving."

"You'll move now."

"What's the trouble? I don't even know you, or the country. Why push me out?"

The stocky man with red hair was a fighter. He had a broad, tough face and scarred knuckles. He packed a gun but a man could see he liked to fight with his fists.

"You can leave now," he said, "or be buried here."

Talharan walked to his saddle and grabbed it. When he was cinched up and had his blanket roll he belted on his holster, but they had taken the gun.

"Give me my gun," he said.

The big man just looked at him and the wiry, sallow-faced one snickered.

"I've had that gun a long time," Talharan said.

"You've got thirty seconds," the big man said, "thirty seconds to start moving. You get no gun."

Talharan looked at him a slow five seconds and then stepped into the leather and rode away. He rode steadily for fifty yards and then slapped spurs to the buckskin and took off. Talharan realized then that he was mad.

He was not a man who often became angry. It had been several years since he had last lost his temper, but he needed sleep and he did want that gun.

When he reached the crest of the ridge he looked back and could see the three riders sloping off across the country, following a trail diagonally opposite his own. In the distance a thin trail of smoke pointed a questioning finger into the sky.

Talharan was three days unshaven, and four days tired, and had but six silver dollars in his pocket, but he turned toward the smoke that suggested a town.

    *   *   *

Two hours later he had walked his horse down the dusty street to the livery stable. The buckskin was dead beat and had to rest. And Tap Talharan was no man to kill a good horse. He walked up to the livery stable and found he had arrived late.

The redheaded man was sitting on a bench at the wide stable door. There was an older man beside him but the redhead did the talking. "When you don't know a country," he said, "it takes a longer time to get places. Now you keep moving."

Talharan looked at him. "You're pushing me," he said. "Why?"

The redhead grinned at him. "Maybe we don't like your looks. Maybe we just don't like strangers. Maybe we don't want your horse eating our grass. Maybe we think you'd live longer if you kept going."

Talharan nodded. "Maybe you're right about that last item. Trouble is, I'm a most stubborn man."

He walked his horse down the street and saw the sallow-faced man loitering in front of the general store, and the big man in front of the saloon.

"Well, Buck," he said, "this looks like a closed town. And it isn't much of a town, either."

He rode steadily west until he saw the churned-up ground where a number of cattle had been driven across the trail. He turned there and lost his hoof tracks amid those of the cattle and the riders who drove them. He followed the trail across the prairie into a grassy bottom where a small stream found a winding way among the trees. Entering the stream he doubled back, riding toward the trail he had left until he found a clump of willows. Entering the willows he pushed on until he found a bare space that was open. There was a little grass there, and he picketed the horse again and stretched out in the sun.

* * *

Voices awakened him in the late afternoon. The buckskin was standing with its ears pricked and he whispered to the horse to prevent it from nickering. The buckskin flicked an attentive ear and relaxed. Tap Talharan sat up and listened.

His camp in the willows was not fifty yards from the trail, but these men were off the trail and closer.

"The gun has seen a lot of use." It was the voice of the redhead. "Who do you think he was?"

"A drifter . . . saddle tramp. Just as well to get rid of him."

"I don't think you have," Red was saying. "Look, Talbot. You took his Winchester and his Colt. I don't think he would leave without an argument."

"He's gone."

"I thought at first he might be one of the Macken Boys."

"Don't be a fool. Johnny Macken was the last of them and he was killed in Texas. The old man's alone now."

"He's a tough old man."

"He was tough." Talbot was speaking. "Now he's just old."

When they had passed along, Talharan got up and looked at the sky. It was about two hours by the sun until nightfall, so he saddled up. The buckskin had done well by the grass within the small clearing, and now he drank from the stream.

Talharan had a deep hunger within him, but knew there would be no food for him in the town. If you could call a store, one saloon, a post office, and a stable a town.

Macken had been the name. An old man named Macken. The name sounded some memory deep within him but he could not place it; however, the name Johnny Macken did mean something. Macken had been a Texas Ranger, killed fighting rustlers the year before, and a good man, by all accounts.

Talharan took a long drink of the cold water and then got into the saddle. Macken had an outfit, and the chances are it was back behind him . . . back where he was camping when they came on him first.

Their pushing him out of the country made no sense unless they were afraid he was going to work for Macken, against whom they must have some sort of plan. If Talharan could find Macken then he might get a real meal and a gun. Looking for him was not smart, but Talharan had never thought of himself as very smart. However, he was stubborn to the point of mild insanity. And he did not like to be pushed. When pushed he was inclined to dig in his heels.

He circled widely, getting a feel for the lay of the land as he did so.

Under the late afternoon sky the hills lay tawny with autumn, and through the cresting pines gold fingers of light found their way, but already the valleys were gathering shadow. Tap Talharan rode warily, enjoying the cool of the evening, but realizing he would ride warmer with a filled holster.

On a far, high slope some cattle grazed and the land lay empty between, and then when he topped out on a new ridge Tap Talharan saw a cluster of shabby buildings lying at the end of a long sweep of a magnificent valley.

Twice he saw M Bar brands on cows and decided this must be the Macken brand, so he rode on, walking his horse to approach slowly. The sky was painting its clouds for sunset before he rode into the ranch-yard.

Several horses were in the corral, good stock. The place looked down-at-heel and needing a handyman around, and he went into the yard and hallooed the house.

"All right," the old man's voice came from the open doorway of the barn, "speak your piece, and while you're talkin' keep it in mind that this here's a .56-caliber Spencer."

"Mr. Macken"--Talharan drew a foot from the stirrup and hung his knee around the saddle horn--"I'm a wandering man. The last few weeks I've come a far piece on mighty low rations, hunting the sun and of no mind to stop where there'll be snow.

"Last night I rode all night because I bedded down for a couple of hours' sleep in the sunshine.

"Three men came along, a man named Talbot and two others. They kicked me awake, took my rifle and six-shooter, and told me to get out of the country.

"Mr. Macken, those men have trouble with you. Of its sort and kind I'm not familiar, but I've a mind to do something about what they've done to me."

"You'd be safer to keep riding."

"You are right. But I've a fat streak of meanness running through me that makes me want to see those men again when I am standing upright with a gun belted on."

"You're a fool."

"I'm a hungry fool. How's for some grub?"

The old man came from the stable with the Spencer in the hollow of his arm. "Nobody ever left this ranch hungry. Come inside."

When Macken opened the door, light streamed out, and the kitchen was warm and cheery with the smell of baking, and there were curtains at the windows and a cloth on the table, and then Tap was removing his hat hurriedly, for there was a girl there, too, a girl with sandy hair and green eyes.

"I am Ruth Macken." She held out her hand and Talharan took it and looked very foolish. "Sit down," she continued. "I was just putting supper on the table."

Tap looked at her and turned quickly away to the washbasin, where he washed his hands and face, then slicked down his hair.

"You're riding the grub line?" she asked.

Talharan was riding it, all right, when he had a
chance, but admitting it to a girl like this was something he could not do. "No, ma'am." He remembered the six
silver dollars. "I can pay.

"It was the frost that did it, ma'am. When the first
frost came to Montana this year it came early, and when
the frost comes, I ride. So I threw a hull on my horse
and started south."

She went about putting supper on the table and when
she had seated herself, Macken looked across the table at
Talharan. "They've been driving cattle at night, driving
them across my land, and I would not have it. There were
other trips at night, too, times when they rode fast and
hard, cutting across to the breaks along the river."

"You work the place alone?"

"There were two hands, but they ran them off."

"The sun is brighter down Arizona way, but if you'll
have me until the trouble is over, I'll abide."

He went outside when the meal was over and forked hay
to the stock in the corral. There was work to do around
the place and he stayed with it until sundown.

When the red arrows of the sun shot into the high
clouds, he saddled up and rode away, and glancing back,
saw Ruth Macken watching him, and he thought how pleasant
it was to see a woman standing in the doorway, seeing him
go. Yet it left an uneasiness on him, and for a moment
there was a feeling that Arizona was far away and he had
better waste no time.

Lights were in the windows of the saloon when he
rode into town. There was a lantern over the door of the
livery stable, and two more inside, hanging from the roof
beams. Tap drew up outside the stable and saw the hostler
sitting there on the bench. "Where's Red?" he asked
mildly.

The old man drew on his pipe, it glowed briefly, and

after a moment he said, "I've seen your kind before, and you belong nowhere. Ride on. . . . There's country you haven't seen."

Tap Talharan considered that in the slow way he had, and knew the old man was right. This was not his fight. He should look upon his guns as the chance of the trail; they might as easily have been lost fording a stream. He should ride on. It was safer, and there was nothing at issue here.

He shifted in the saddle, and the words he spoke came unbidden. "You are one hundred percent right, but there's something else. They began trouble with me, took my guns when I was asleep."

"It isn't reason enough."

Talharan remembered the girl in the doorway, and he remembered the quiet way she had, serving the food, and the direct way she looked at him across the table.

"A man has to stop somewhere," he said, and walked his horse toward the saloon.

Behind him he heard the old man say, "He's alone, but not for long."

Tap tied his horse at the hitch rail and felt the emptiness in his stomach that he remembered. It was still possible to get into the saddle and ride on. Yet he mounted the steps, knowing he was not a brave man, and a little curious about what bravery really was, and then he opened the door and went in.

It wasn't much of a place. A sheet-iron stove, two tables and some chairs, and a short bar not over eight feet long. Red was sitting at a table and there was a bartender behind the bar. Two men sat quietly at a table nearby and he knew them for small ranchers like Macken.

Red looked up at him and grinned and Tap walked over to the table where he sat, and Red's expression changed, a flicker ran through the muscles of his face, and he

started to get up. Tap remembered the way they had come
on him asleep and he swung a long right that caught Red
rising and knocked him back over his chair.

Red sprawled in the wreckage of the chair and stared
up at Tap, and then started to gather himself, and when
he was almost ready to get up, Tap kicked him in the
solar plexus. Red grabbed at Tap's leg, too late, retched
violently, and then Tap reached down with a big hand and
jerked him to his feet. He pushed him away and swung at
his face with both hands, and the big fists smashed dully
in Red's features, and the blood started from a broken
nose and smashed lips.

Red pawed at him with weakened hands but Tap slapped
them down and, reaching over, took Red's gun and dropped
it into his own holster.

Coolly, he pushed Red against the bar and hooked a
hard right into the man's stomach, and let him fall.

"You didn't give him much chance," the bartender said
mildly.

"He made his own rules," Talharan replied, "about
daylight this morning."

Boots sounded on the steps outside and the door
opened. The big man was the first inside and the sallow-
faced one followed after.

Talbot saw Red lying on the floor, struggling to
rise, his face bloody. He stopped and he turned partway
around and saw Tap Talharan. Red's pistol was in his
hand.

"I've got a gun, Talbot. You can drop your gun-belts,
or you can die right here, it don't make no matter to
me."

Nobody moved or spoke. A moth fluttered about the
coal-oil lamp, and Talbot stood darkly against the light.

"You've got the drop," Talbot growled. "Give me a
break."

"Just what you gave me this morning? You drop your
belts, both of you. I'm not going to count, I'm just
going to start shooting."

The other man's hand went to his belt, and very deli-
cately he unfastened it and let it fall. Talbot hesitated, not liking it, the hot fury showing all through
him. Reluctantly then, he unfastened the buckle and let
his belt fall.

Talharan moved them back and gathered the gun-belts.
He took the guns and thrust them behind his belt, and
coolly, taking his time, he removed the shells from their
gun-belts and shoved them into his own pockets.

"Now put your money on the bar."

Talbot started to speak, then stopped. None of the
ranchers moved to protest.

They piled it on the bar, some thirty or forty dollars. Talharan gestured at it. "Pour them each a drink,"
he said. "And one for Red. Talbot's buying."

When the glasses were filled, Talharan said, "Now
drink it. This one is for luck. Just toss it off."

Talbot looked at the whiskey and started to speak,
but Tap said quietly, "You booted me in the ribs this
morning, Talbot. I could kill you for that, like you
threatened to kill me. Now drink up."

He sat down then, and when the bartender had filled
their glasses again, he had them drink again.

An hour later they were drunk, and unable to walk
straight. The sallow-faced man was the first to pass out,
and Red was the second. Talbot lasted another hour, and
it was close to midnight when he slumped to a sitting position on the floor.

Talharan gathered up the change and put it back in
Talbot's pocket. Then he stopped and picked the big man
up and carried him outside, the ranchers and the bartender watching. He tied Talbot in his saddle and did the
same with each of the others. Then he released the horses

and tied the bridle reins to the horn of the saddle on each one. With a hat he slapped each of the horses over the rump . . . only taking time to slip a Winchester from the scabbard on Red's horse.

The three horses clattered off down the trail, their drunken riders bobbling in their saddles.

Tap Talharan walked back inside. "Sorry to have kept you open," he said.

"Worth it," the bartender said.

COMMENTS: A careful reader will recognize Ruth Macken's name. This is not intended to be the same character who is the resourceful widow in the novel *Bendigo Shafter*. That woman would have been married to a man named Macken, whereas this one seems to be the daughter or daughter-in-law of the man who owns the ranch. This is simply a case of Louis reusing a character name he liked.

THE DARK HOLE

The Beginning of a Crime Story

CHAPTER I

There were deer tracks in the dust, and nothing more. Dia was gone.

He hesitated, looking around into the gathering dusk. She could not have gone far. He called . . . and his voice echoed, then lost itself lonesomely against the far walls of the canyon.

It was unlike her to walk away, and she had been tired. She had remained behind to rest while he took an exploratory walk up a branch canyon. He could have been gone no more than ten minutes . . . or fifteen.

He called again, and the echoing voice made him cringe inwardly, for this was a place of silence.

The meadow was shadowed and still with the late evening. There was sunlight upon the mountains, but in this deep hollow it was gone. The parched grass was matted and yellow, offering concealment for nothing larger than a fist.

He called again and yet again, but there was no answer, no sound, no faint reply.

He paused before the boulder where he had last seen her. Her tracks were there, where she had walked up and seated herself. He could see where she had shifted her feet several times, but no sign of her leaving.

Dia, his gentle, fragile Dia . . . gone!

But where could she go? He called again, mounting worry giving rein to irritation.

Then he saw something else. A small, circular spot in the dust, such a spot as is made by the toe when one rises and suddenly turns.

Ho lifted his eyes and looked to where hers must have looked. He was staring at a dark finger of woods. A finger of dark trees pointing at the rock on which she had been seated.

Dia had risen suddenly--something had moved there, something that startled her. But Dia was not easily frightened. Slender, fragile, yes . . . but with courage.

What then?

He walked swiftly, half-fearfully because of what he might find. He was careful to walk wide so as to obliterate no tracks. He paused within the shadow of the trees, straining his eyes to see.

It was darker here but he could make out fallen trunks, a few boulders. . . . He searched among them but there was nothing, simply nothing at all.

Dia was gone.

He called, and his voice lost itself down the empty canyon.

It was twelve miles to the nearest town. Seven miles to the ranch through whose gate they had come to reach this place. He called again, and yet again, walking beneath the trees. It was dark, yes, but light enough to see her body if it had fallen here.

Her body.

His throat tightened.

Then relief flooded over him. Why, what a fool he

was! Knowing it would be too late to go on farther into The Dark Hole, she had simply started back toward the car, knowing he would soon catch up!

Wheeling about, he started back, disgusted with himself for his foolishness. He set out the way they had come, then began cutting a zigzag trail to find her returning tracks. He was good at reading sign and at times had followed deer for miles. . . . But there were no tracks.

Only the tracks they had made as they neared the place, that was all.

He stopped again . . . and called. His voice echoed down the canyon toward the outer world, and there was no other sound. Somewhere, far off, a nightbird called.

Could she have gone on, up the canyon, deeper into The Dark Hole?

Perhaps she felt that she moved too slowly for him, and had gone on. She knew his curiosity about this place, and that he would not want to go back when they were so close to seeing the end of it. It was unlike her. . . . He hurried on across the meadow and started up the narrowing canyon again.

It was darker here, and there were many water-worn boulders, some of them gigantic. He stumbled up, calling again.

His wife was gone. Dia was gone.

Suddenly, he knew. He could not find her. She was certainly gone. He must go out to the ranch at once, call for help, get the sheriff out here with a searching party. It was too late and he could cover too little ground alone. She must have gone away, started away. Possibly she was lying in some crevice now, hearing his cries, her own voice lost to weakness.

No tracks . . . Now there was a star in the sky. The cliffs had turned to edges of solid black against the pale cloudless gray of the oncoming night. Under the

trees where he had searched for Dia there was ominous
darkness now. Fear clutched at him.

"Dia!"

His voice rang out against the cliffs, echoed down
the canyon and up the canyon in twin voices, weakening
with increasing distance. "Dia, Dia, Dia . . ."

But only his own voice called into the silence, and
only his own voice answered, and there was no other
sound; there was nothing, not even the wind.

Magill forced himself to think. He forced his mind to
be cold. He ruled out fear and doubt. He fought to abandon emotion. To think.

She had suggested waiting. After all, he would be
gone only a few minutes, and she _was_ tired. When he was
exploring he was always overeager and sometimes he forgot
that others lacked his enthusiasm and his physical condition. Yet today he had remembered not to hurry, to think
of Dia, to take his time.

He considered the situation. After all, he was a
thinking man. It was through thought that Man had risen
above the beast, yet at the first sign of fear, of panic,
of danger, he was apt to stop thinking and to act
blindly, instinctively. And man could in most cases no
longer trust his instincts. If he was to find Dia, he
must think.

The canyon's line was roughly east and west. To north
and south were cliffs that would be difficult to climb,
even for him. Nor could she have climbed them in the time
he had been gone. Therefore, she must have gone down the
canyon toward the car, or up the canyon and deeper into
The Dark Hole.

He looked down-canyon for tracks and found none. He
had looked up the canyon and found no tracks either. Nor
had he seen any tracks leaving the rock where she had
been seated.

The canyon leading into The Dark Hole was narrow and

almost floored with boulders. Only at the side, sometimes along one wall, sometimes along the other, was there room for a path.

A path that was a game trail, nothing more. The walls of the canyon were not rock, although there was much rock in them. They were of cretaceous formation, but almost sheer, reaching up for all of seven hundred feet to the rim.

There was some brush on the cliff, sparse stuff, mingled with poison oak. In the canyon bottom there was a mixture of trees, dark pines or oak, with an occasional cottonwood. Once, halting to gasp for breath, he paused beneath a cottonwood.

He called again, "Dia!" It was incredible that she could disappear, but disappear she had.

He stood alone in the bottom of this narrow crack in the earth. He was in the middle of California, but he was utterly alone. There were cities not far away, crowded with people; there were intervening villages, farms, homes. . . . Yet he was alone, all, all alone. And Dia was gone.

There was danger where there were people, but here there were no . . . But how did he know? Could he be sure they had not been followed? That some unseen madman had not lurked under the trees? Possibly some creature of feeble mind but great strength? He had heard of such things.

Yet he had seen no tracks. Not even so slender a girl as Dia could leave without tracks. And he had followed the trails of rabbit, deer, and wolf.

He was gasping and bathed in sweat. He had a horrible feeling that she might be in desperate trouble, that he might be running away from her rather than toward her. Perhaps she was held silent by some criminal who even now was watching him. But that was imagination. He had no reason to think such a thing.

He started on, then stumbled and fell. He got slowly
to his feet, his hands torn by the gravel. He was
scarcely conscious of the pain. It was then he thought of
a fire.

He would go back to the meadow and build a fire. She
would see it and come to him . . . if she was alive.

He gathered wood. There was plenty of it--no fire had
been built in this place for a long time. He put sticks
together, and soon had a blaze going. Under other circumstances it would have made a peaceful camp. He was a
quiet man, interested in wildlife, in trees, shrubs . . .
open country, mountains, and forest. He had always lived
quietly. Violence had no place in his life.

The flames leaped up as he added dry sticks to make a
bright blaze. A big fire, that was what he wanted. Yet he
was careful, even now, to keep it from spreading. He let
a little circle of grass burn off around the spot, letting it spread only a few inches at a time. Soon he had a
border of blackness where no chance spark could ignite
the dry grass if he had to leave the blaze.

He gathered wood in a pile. He moved away from the
fire, listening. There was no sound but the crackle of
the flames. He paced anxiously; he waited. He thought of
a thousand things. Nothing made sense. Dia would not wander off by herself. She never had; she wasn't the type.
She would have waited for him. That was just it--none of
it made sense.

His Dia gone . . . It was impossible.

Footsteps.

He came quickly to his feet and sprang away from the
fire. "Dia!" His voice rang. "You've . . . !"

It was not Dia. Three men had walked to the edge of
the firelight. One was the rancher, Rorick. The other two
were strangers, but one was obviously a forest ranger.

"Don't you know you can't build fires in here?" The
ranger's voice was patiently angry.

"It's for my wife. She's gone."

"Gone?"

"Lost, I guess. I left her sitting here. . . ." He started to explain, trying to talk coolly, to remember everything.

"But that's ridiculous!" The ranger was irritable. "Where could she go? In this canyon you can go up and you can go back. Unless she could go up the wall."

"She wouldn't do that."

"There was a girl in the car with him," Rorick said, "a pretty little thing."

"Look," the ranger insisted, "if your wife came up here with you she's got to be here now."

"You passed my car?"

"It was empty."

"You passed no one?"

"Wouldn't we have mentioned it?"

"Then she must be up in the canyon, if she isn't dead."

Their eyes all turned to him, startled. The ranger's eyes seemed to grow more intent. Or had he imagined that? "Why would she be dead?"

"I've been yelling. She would have answered, wouldn't she?"

The search lasted two hours. There were four of them now and they walked abreast up the canyon to the head. They found nothing . . . or almost nothing.

The head of the canyon was a cliff down which water fell during heavy rains. The rocks there were polished and smooth. There was, nowhere, any sign of Dia.

Returning, they stopped at one place. It was a fresh slide. The ranger, whose name was Bronson, threw the beam of his five-celled flashlight up the slide. It was still somewhat damp.

"After sundown," Rorick said, "or maybe an hour before. The sun would have dried it out."

"Maybe." The ranger walked around the pile and studied it with his light. "The sun only reaches the bottom
at midday. That's why they call it The Dark Hole."

They lingered, and Magill shifted from foot to foot.
Dia . . . where was Dia? Somewhere out in the dark, Dia
who never wanted to be alone, who hated to be alone. She
was out there, somewhere alone in the dark.

"Do we have to stand here?" His irritation was in his
voice. "My wife may have fallen somewhere. She may be
suffering."

Bronson straightened, brushing off his breeches, taking his time. "Mister," he spoke slowly, carefully. "Your
wife did not come down the canyon. She isn't, so far as
we can see, up the canyon. If she was alive, we would
have found her."

"I don't think so anymore. If she was dead we would
have found her. We've been over every inch of this canyon."

Bronson nodded. "That's right, mister. We have been
over every inch of it . . . almost."

He stared from one to the other. "What do you mean?
Almost?"

"We've been over every inch of this canyon," Bronson
repeated, "except what's under that rock pile!"

CHAPTER II

Bronson turned away from Magill and began gathering
material for a fire. The third man helped, and after a
minute or so, Magill did also. He felt numb . . .
shocked. He could not look toward the debris but kept his
eyes averted.

Rorick conferred quietly with Bronson, then started

off into the darkness. They could see his light bobbing down the canyon for several minutes, then it disappeared.

The third man was short, stocky, and quiet. "My name is Don Matthews." He moved over beside Magill.

"Mine is Magill. Morgan Magill."

The forest ranger was squatting beside the new blaze, feeding it with fuel. He looked over his shoulder at Magill. "Not the Morgan Magill? Who wrote the book on tropical birds?"

At Magill's nod, Bronson turned back toward the fire, vaguely disturbed. If that was true, then what he had been thinking would be absurd . . . or would it?

He had read the book, and loved every page of it. Here was a man who not only loved birds, knew them well, and understood them, but who could write.

Yet how could one tell? Murder came to the most unlikely places. Considering this big, quiet, easy-moving man behind him, he decided that Magill must be around thirty-five, possibly a year or two younger. And he had been around a lot. Exploring for birds in Borneo, New Guinea, Halmahera, Indo-China and Brazil. Looking for rare birds and studying their habits.

"Been married long?" Matthews asked.

"Four . . . almost five months. We met in Honolulu on my way home. Dia was there on vacation."

They waited, keeping the fire going. At last, Magill could stand it no longer, and moving to the rock pile he began lifting away the larger rocks. Steadily, quietly, he worked. Finally, the others joined him. By the time Rorick returned with shovels, all the larger rocks had been moved.

Carefully, taking their time, they began work with the shovels. There was no chance, nor had there ever been any chance of finding anything alive under that pile. Many of the rocks were large and they had come down with great force.

When the pile had become quite small, about to the limits of a small human body, they rested. Bronson rubbed his jaw and looked around uneasily, avoiding Magill.

For the first time Magill noticed the butt of a pistol sticking up out of Rorick's pocket. It had not been there when he left to go for the shovels. Magill lifted his eyes to Rorick and found the man watching him. He must have seen Magill's eyes on the gun. After a moment, without seeming to do so, Rorick moved back, farther from Magill.

Morgan Magill suddenly felt very tired. There was no coolness left in him. He was simply exhausted now, emotionally and physically. He backed up and sat down.

She was not under that pile. She could not be. Not his lovely, fragile, beautiful Dia. Not crushed and broken and . . .

More footsteps . . . He came to his feet instantly, tight with awareness.

No . . . they were not light-stepping feet, but the heavier scuff of men walking. Then a bobbing light and after a long minute two men came into the circle of firelight. One wore a badge on his coat.

"Hello, Bronson . . . Rory." He glanced once at Magill, then at the pile. "All right, uncover it."

The men went to work, with their hands this time. Magill sat very quiet, suddenly aware of a new tension, a new feeling in the air.

The sheriff . . . they thought he had murdered Dia.

He got swiftly to his feet and the sheriff turned on him, his eyes alert, his hand near the edge of his coat.

Magill flushed. How silly could you get? But he said nothing at all. Now they were down . . . Rorick got up.

"Nothing here, Sam." With the shovels they moved the last of the debris. There was nothing there. No Dia . . . nothing.

"She's alive then," he said. "She's got to be alive."

Bronson looked over at Rorick, frowning. "You're sure there was a girl in that car?"

The rancher was impatient. "Of course! I brought her a cup of water from the well. Gave it to her with my own hands."

"Then," the sheriff asked quietly, "where is she? Don't tell me she climbed over those seven-hundred-foot cliffs in the dark?"

Magill shifted his feet. "Sheriff," he said quietly, "it was not dark when I first missed her. It didn't become dark for almost thirty minutes. I looked under the trees . . . everywhere."

"You think she climbed out?"

"I think the idea is absurd. Dia did not like heights. At least, I could never get her to climb. Besides"--he looked around at their faces--"where could she go? And what would be the object of it?"

Nobody had any answer to that. The sheriff moved off to one side and held a low-voiced conversation with Bronson. Don Matthews remained beside Magill. He seemed sympathetic. "You were very much in love?" he asked.

"She was the only woman I ever loved. In fact, she was the only woman I ever knew very well."

"You must be well-off," Matthews suggested. "Those trips must have cost money. I've read a couple of your books."

"The trips didn't cost so much as you'd imagine. I came back from overseas with a little money saved. That paid for the first one. I sold a few articles, then I got a grant from a foundation and took the second. It was not difficult after that."

"Did your wife have money?"

"Dia? No . . . nothing. She had been a librarian somewhere in the Midwest before we met. We . . . we married rather suddenly because she was almost broke and if

she returned to her job we would be separated. I didn't
want that and neither did she." Matthews dropped to his
haunches and poked absently at the fire. Magill was a
handsome man in a rugged sort of way, but seemed more the
scholar than the explorer. Leaving Bronson and Matthews
beside the fire in case Dia might be alive and lost and
the fire might lead her to safety, the sheriff and Rorick
started back toward the ranch. The other man had disappeared somewhere in the darkness.

"Just relax"--the sheriff's name was Sam Gates--
"we've done all we can do tonight. By daylight we'll have
searching parties moving in from both sides. That's wild
country but we can cover it. If she got out of the canyon, we'll find her."

They returned silently to their vehicles and Magill
found himself back at the farmhouse. He paced the floor
restlessly, and finally, just as the sun was rising, he
fell asleep in a chair.

He awakened with a start. Instantly wide awake and on
his feet. He looked at his watch, but it had stopped. He
wound it, then checked with the clock in the kitchen.

The backyard was full of men. Not far from the window, which was raised a little at the bottom, was Sheriff
Gates. Rorick and several other men were standing with
him. "If you hadn't seen her," Gates was saying, "I'd say
she never existed."

"Killed her an' hid her body, if you ask me." The
speaker was a burly, unshaven man. "Plenty of places a
body could be hid. I figure that there slide was started
a-purpose. It was just a blind."

They all looked at the man. "How do we know," he continued, "she ever got as far as the Hole? We saw where he
left his car. There's plenty of canyons open off the

trail before you get to the Hole. Has anybody looked in
that old quicksilver mine? I say she never got to the
Hole."

Magill backed up and sat down heavily. The sleep had
cleared his mind, and he was a man who was accustomed to
dealing with problems. He was possessed of two facts of
which they could not be sure. He <u>knew</u> his wife had
reached the canyon, and he <u>knew</u> he had not killed her.
Therefore, where was she?

If her body had not been found, it was not there. The
only place where the earth was disturbed had been examined. Hence, if she was not there she had gone away or
been taken away.

Yet he had found no tracks and Dia would have been
unable to cover a trail sufficiently to deceive him. And
why should she wish to?

Suppose someone had come upon her suddenly . . . But
there had been no evidence of a struggle. Unless she had
been knocked unconscious. Little by little he began to
examine all the possibilities, all the situations that
might have arisen.

Again and again his thoughts returned to the slide.
Something had to start a slide. It could have been a coincidence, but it was almost too much of one. And it was
the only thing in the area that seemed in any way different than usual.

A woman had vanished . . . and there had been a rock
slide. Had anyone scouted the rim above the slide? She
might have been knocked out and carried up the cliff. That
might be accomplished by a man of unusual strength . . .
but it was improbable.

Turning his head he glanced at his reflection in the
mirror. He was a big man with rumpled light brown hair
and quiet gray eyes, but now those eyes had dark circles
beneath them, and his mouth looked drawn.

Dia . . . gone.

He remembered how they had met. It seemed like yesterday, and yet . . . in some ways it seemed a faraway,
impossible time.

He had devoted four months of his life to Halmahera
in the East Indies . . . Indonesia, it was now. He'd
spent most of those four months in the jungle, away from
the coasts, and without with any preconceived plan. He
had just started out with four native boys and rambled
from place to place.

Returning, he had decided to spend two weeks in Honolulu assembling his material. It would be more pleasant,
and he might take a few short trips to the more remote
islands and add to his knowledge and his collections.

For the first three days he had held to his plan. He
had worked hard, cataloguing his finds, spending his evenings planning for three trips among the islands . . .
and then on that never-to-be-forgotten morning he had
taken a walk down the beach.

It was not much of a beach. It was away from the pop-
ulated centers and actually, it was more of a picturesque
shoreline with, here and there, patches of sand.

She had come along the edge of the sea that morning,
her skirt whipping in the wind, her blond hair blowing.
She was walking toward him, oblivious of his presence,
and she was singing a tune in a pleasant, if untrained
voice.

She drew abreast of the rock on which he sat, and he
applauded. He grinned, remembering her embarrassment. But
they had talked, and although she had refused his invitation to lunch, she did agree to have dinner with him.

That had begun it. The two weeks fled by and he forgot the island trips he had planned. They lunched together, walked, danced, worked together. Once she
discovered what he was doing, she began to help him. She
knew a little of birds . . . not of tropical birds, beyond a few scattered and largely mistaken ideas about

parrots and parakeets, but the birds of her home state, and she had read several articles about penguins. However, it was her librarian's patience and organization that made the greatest contribution. She could understand the smallest difference in the most insignificant bird, and if she wondered that he was content to pass his life in such a way, she never mentioned it.

When the subject of marriage first came up, he did not exactly remember. It seemed to have been about the time she first mentioned leaving; by that time he was used to her and the thought of her going away dismayed him. Nor could he recall who had first mentioned the subject, but it had remained on their minds, and had come up again.

She had told him, frankly, that her money was almost exhausted and she must return to her job.

His response had been automatic. "Why not stay here with me?" He started to add that he would gladly pay her whatever she was earning at wherever she had been working, but somehow she had misunderstood him and the first thing he knew she was accepting his proposal.

Flustered, he started to explain, but there had been no chance, and as she talked happily on, he began to think of the advantages . . . a home, Dia . . . It was more, really, than he had ever expected.

Now, looking back, he was forced to smile at the way it had all happened. Dia . . . but Dia was gone . . . gone.

And he was accomplishing nothing. He must get out and join in the search. He glanced at his watch. It was not yet eight o'clock in the morning. He could not have slept more than two, possibly three hours. He had been awake thirty minutes at most.

He walked back through the house to the bathroom and washed hurriedly, then combed his hair. He was thinking

again of the problem at hand, and where to search. He would
work, as he always did, by himself. He knew where they had
been, knew exactly where he had last seen Dia . . . and he
would investigate that slide.

Perhaps she had rested a few minutes, then wandered
up the canyon. Frightened, she might have started up the
wall. Frightened by what? A snake . . . a skunk . . . a
steer . . . almost anything might have frightened her.
The slide might have started and she might have believed
it was easier to continue on to the top than to return.

Back in the kitchen he selected a cup and poured coffee. It was only lukewarm but he gulped several swallows,
then put it down and started for the door.

Passing the window he stopped abruptly.

They had something. He looked again. It was a scarf
of Dia's. . . .

A scarf . . . but Dia had worn no scarf!

He was a man who gave attention to detail, and he
could describe in detail what Dia had been wearing, and
there had been no scarf.

Yet the scarf was here; he remembered buying it for
her. The scarf was hers--and it was dark with the stain
of blood!

COMMENTS: The Dark Hole is in Kings County, California. Louis's
journal shows that he first visited the area in November of 1951. Indonesia, the country of Magill's ornithological studies, only came into
being in 1949, so it seems very likely that this was written by the mid-
1950s.

I like the character of Morgan Magill. He's a more normal guy
than a lot of Dad's heroes. It's amusing to see Louis commenting:

When he was exploring he was always overeager and
sometimes he forgot that others lacked his enthusiasm
and his physical condition. Yet today he had remembered not to hurry, to think of Dia, to take his
time.

    That was Dad. I think most of the memories I have of him when
we were hiking were from behind. Dad was always moving on, barely
waiting for whoever was with him. He might pause, but as soon as my
mother, sister, and I caught up, he would head off again. . . . If we
wanted to keep up we didn't take time to rest, we just kept plodding!

SAMSARA

Three Beginnings for an Adventure Novel,

and a Treatment

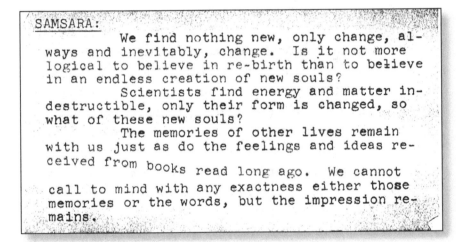

SAMSARA:
        We find nothing new, only change, al-
ways and inevitably, change. Is it not more
logical to believe in re-birth than to believe
in an endless creation of new souls?
        Scientists find energy and matter in-
destructible, only their form is changed, so
what of these new souls?
        The memories of other lives remain
with us just as do the feelings and ideas received from books read long ago. We cannot
call to mind with any exactness either those
memories or the words, but the impression remains.

A toe prodded me in the ribs. "Get up," a voice said,
"here they come again."

And then I was conscious of the sun's heat, and the
smell of blood, sweat, and dust. From afar I heard a
thunder through the earth, and grasping my broken spear,
I stood.

We could scarcely see them for the dust, and our
ranks were thin. I, who had stood in the third rank of
the phalanx, now stood in the first row. My spear, which
had been twelve feet long, now measured less than half of

that. My skull throbbed and the pounding grew louder and they came out of the dust, a solid wall of horsemen. To my left they crashed upon our points. There was a screaming of animals and men. A sword swept down and my shield shattered under the impact.

I saw the fierce glare of eyes, a face only half revealed because of the helmet, and as the sword lifted to strike again, I thrust upward with all my strength.

The point of my spear took him below the breastbone and went into him like a driven spike. We crashed to the ground. He swept a hand up, brushing back the helmet, and for the first time I saw his face.

His eyes were wide, his lips already pale with death, twisted with words. "Apollodorus! It is I--Rameses, your friend!"

My name was not Apollodorus and I had never a friend named Rameses, yet something stayed my hand. "My horse!" he gasped. "Get my horse . . . quick! There is a book--!"

That ended it. He died like that, leaving me staring at him, this man who seemed to know me as someone I was not. Still, the horse was there, and it was my prize, along with what armor and possessions the man had. But as I grasped the bridle, a hand reached over mine to take it, an officer of Alexander.

"The horse is mine," I said, gripping the bridle. "I won fairly."

"You shall have him," the officer replied shortly, "but first there will be questions."

"Forget it then. I want no questions."

The battle was over. I picked up a shield and a whole spear before leaving the field, for our leader looked with no favor upon a weaponless man.

As to the man Rameses, I despoiled him of a ring, and two bracelets from his arm. His sword was a handsome weapon with a fine, beautiful feel to it, so I chose it for my own. Then I walked away, but twice I looked back

upon him. He had been so sure he knew me, and even knowing he was dying he had sought to do me well. He had mentioned a book. I had nothing to do with books, but to
mention a book at such a time . . .

I wished for the horse. Not that I could do ought but
trade him, for I was a foot soldier.

Back at camp I cleansed myself with fresh sand, for
water there was none. I rubbed the sweat and dust away,
then hunted for wine. I had none, nor had Crates, the one
who had kicked me out there after I had been felled. My
head still ached from that one, or from something else,
for there was an uncertainty in me that I had not known
before.

The officer who had taken the horse came to me. "He
wishes to see you."

I was shocked, and frightened, too, for I knew what
might come of his displeasure. We who served him thought
well of him, for he was brave and wise in battle, a wiser
man than his father, whom I had served as a boy.

"Be quick--he does not like to be kept waiting."

He was sprawled in a chair just inside the door of
his tent where he could drink wine and watch the camp. I
had seen him like that before, and he missed nothing. It
was said that he had eyes and ears everywhere, and we believed it.

Alexander was a handsome man, arrogant and proud, but
as fine-looking a man as ever I had seen, and he wore
more gold than I had ever seen upon any man or woman.
Some said he wore it as a challenge to enemy soldiers. To
kill him and take what he had in battle would make a man
wealthy. My mouth watered at the thought, but I'd no wish
to kill him, only to serve him. As much as he appeared
the dressed-up one, he was a fighter. Few of us could
have stood up to him in even battle.

"What is your name?"

There was something in this that puzzled me, and I agonized trying to think what I had done that was wrong. But there was a curious look in his eyes. He was not looking at just a soldier, he was looking at _me_. Besides, he knew my name well enough. He knew the name of every man in his army, and always had.

"Carlax," I said.

There was movement behind me and I glanced around, though I knew I shouldn't, for when you talked to him you faced him.

It was the horse. They had led him right up behind me.

"Carlax," he said, "you fought well today. You fought very well, as you have always done."

He straightened in his chair and studied me; still dusty from the field he was. "A good soldier," he said, "and a fighting man. I have watched you. You do your job well--no recklessness, no heroics, just a good steady job. I like that in a man. We would win nothing if it were not for your sort."

He seemed to ponder, and then casually, he asked me, "Who was that man you killed? I hear he called himself Rameses, but I also know that was not his name."

"I never saw him before."

"He knew you. I saw it with my own eyes. I was there to see if the charge would break upon you spearmen, as it did. He seemed to know you well, and wished you to have his horse."

He studied me in a disturbing way. I did not like it and wanted to be away. He seemed to feel I was concealing something, and I had heard it said he had a way of sensing things unspoken. The man knew so much. Aristotle was his teacher, after all. Whenever there was no fighting he had a way of gathering the wise men around him . . . those from the land around . . . and he asked them many

questions, far into the night, prodding them to debate
with one another.

"He was sure he knew you. He called you Apollodorus."

"It is not my name."

"And he called himself Rameses, and that was not <u>his</u>
name. I have prisoners. They have looked at the body and
told me his rightful name. Do you wish to know what it
is?"

"What for? He is dead."

"Ah . . . ? Yes, of course. He is dead. And death
does come to us all, does it not? Too soon, sometimes."

He glanced around at Ptolemy. "A chair for our
friend. We have much talking to do."

Uneasily, I sat down. He sat there for a long time,
watching the camp bring itself into order. Crates would
be opening a bottle now, and slicing a haunch of mutton.
I was hungry, and ill at ease, wishing to be free of all
this. I did not know the man I had killed. . . . Did they
think I was a spy?

"You have served me long. How old are you, Carlax?"

"Twenty-nine, I think. I have been fourteen years a
soldier."

He was in a strange mood, silent, musing, yet there
was friendliness in him. "You fought well at the Cilician
Gates," he said to me, "and you prevented a fight at
Soli."

This was a surprise. My way was the soldier's way,
and I did what had to be done, not looking to be seen or
praised for it, unaware that it had been noticed.

"You did not think I had seen," he said, "but believe
me, Carlax, there are twenty thousand of you whose worth
I know as well as this ring." He tapped the heavy gold
ring with the red stone. "It is the commander's task to
know." He looked around at me. "Battles are won by men,
not by tactics alone."

The minutes dragged by. Wine was poured, and I drank, feeling better. Some of the tiredness left me. "You fought in the army of Philip," he said. "Did you know Aristotle at all?"

"When I came for the first time to the army," I said. "He had questions, that one."

He looked at me. "He asked you questions?"

"He asked me an odd thing: Had I ever been to Samothrace, or to Delphos."

He did not look at me now, but at the plain where the tents were pitched. "And had you?"

"No."

He shifted his seat somewhat, impatiently, I thought. "He was not one to ask the foolish question, Carlax. Why did he have questions for you at all?"

I shifted uneasily. "There was foolish talk. Some comrades of mine began it. We had come up to a mean village, a petty sort of place on a low hill beside a stream. I found a corner of wall . . . it was some ancient ruin . . . and I dug down and found a vase filled with coins."

The shadows had vanished; the fires were showing bright against the darkness. Still Alexander sat there, staring out over the plain. "Had you been there before?"

I hesitated. "No . . . no, never. Only . . . it reminded me of something I couldn't put a name to. As for the gold, well, I just tried to think where I might bury some gold. . . . It was a fortunate chance."

He was still silent, and after a long time said, "You can ride?"

"Yes."

"Keep the horse. You will not be with the phalanx any longer. I shall want you close to me."

He had said nothing about the book, but I knew that I was dismissed, and got to my feet, leading the horse away.

Out in the darkness, I stopped to think about what

had been said, but it made no sort of sense. Yet I could
not get the face of the man I had killed from my
thoughts. It stayed with me, open, smiling, as no dying
man's face was expected to be when he looked into the
eyes of the man who had killed him.

What had Samothrace, Aristotle, Delphos, and the discovery of a small vase of gold to do with this?

COMMENTS: Thus begins just one version of what is probably the
strangest story in this book—and in Louis's career. It was an idea that
he experimented with in different forms for nearly thirty years. The
story of a man, or a group of people who, at some point in their lives,
realize that they have been reincarnated and that the knowledge from
their past lives can be recovered. From generation to generation, these
reborn souls or identities have moments where they can recall those
lives and, if the conditions are right, find repositories of information
cached in order to help them remember more and move forward in
whatever plan fate has in place for them.

I do not possess every version of these manuscripts, nor a complete set of Louis's notes. Whether the other pieces were lost in one of
Dad's moves, thrown in the waste can in frustration, or suffered some
other fate I do not know. What I do know is that a few other fragments remain. Here's an alternate version where, instead of telling
Alexander the Great about finding the hidden coins, Carlax tells a
more mysterious story:

He sat there staring at nothing for several minutes, then he called to the man holding the captured
horse and told him to bring the saddlebags. But he
let them lie unopened.

"Tell me, has this ever happened before? Have you
been recognized by anyone else?"

"No," I said, and then hesitated. He waited expectantly, and I replied that there had been one other occasion.

"It was in Crotona, when I was a lad. I had come there for the first time that morning and a passenger aboard our ship wished to see the school where Cythogorus taught. So I took him there--I do not remember how it was that I knew, but I did.

"He was curious, and asked me many questions. He, too, said I looked like someone he knew."

"And . . . ?"

"That night he tried to kill me."

We sat long over our meal and the wine that followed, and he asked me many questions about myself. Yet what was there to tell?

I was a soldier. I had been a man of the sea from boyhood, but joined Alexander when he marched into Asia.

COMMENTS: When Dad wrote the majority of these drafts he was in his sixties, and I have often wondered if his work on *Samsara* may have been an attempt to confront his own mortality. He collected dozens of books on the subject of reincarnation and on the various religions and mythologies that dealt with the transmutation of souls. Although a spiritual man, he was not an adherent of any particular religion. I have often wondered if his interest in writing this story (especially, as you will see, since his efforts took so many forms) didn't come from some desire to feel that there was something beyond death, some continuation of the soul's narrative.

Below is a piece of either a series of notes or part of one of the various forms of this story that explains a certain amount of what Louis had in mind:

It is not surprising that some know and others do
not. Some men are content with a little knowledge,
others would not be content with all knowledge. Some
wish to know enough to get along from day to day,
some wish to know enough to progress in their particular field, but there are always a few who wish to
reach out, farther, and still farther.

Long ago there came a realization to such a man:
perhaps an ancient memory from some past life, perhaps a recognition of some other such as himself. He
approached the other, discussed the question, felt
his way carefully along until he knew that this man
also remembered. So a pact was made. An agreement to
find a way to meet again in some future life, to
share experiences, and to plan for the future. This
must have happened so long ago that when these men
planned to cache a few treasures against a future
life, all they could leave would have been a stone ax
or perhaps an amulet.

Over the years, over the centuries, a few such
men and women banded together, and from this derived
the Eleusinian Mysteries, and many secret orders
had their beginning in this desire to preserve this
esoteric knowledge for themselves in future lives,
and for others like themselves.

These people chose themselves and as a result of
their mystical experiences and thinking, planning,
and mental preparation they became able to control
the processes of rebirth, and they shared this knowledge among themselves. Few could pass on the new
knowledge, and fewer still had the discipline necessary to cope with it, or to use it. Some of the elect
died before they could effect plans for their future,
and after several such deaths or failures to locate
the repositories of knowledge, some of the elect forgot the old knowledge. In other places it became min-

gled with ineffective superstition and only the superficial forms of the practices were followed, and thus the effect was lost.

Each of the elect made it a practice to exchange knowledge with the others, but also to leave behind in some form the knowledge he had, and the knowledge that he would need in the future. Among the ancient Egyptians and some others it came in the form of murals on the walls of tombs, or tools and equipment, much of it fallen to dust, that had been left for the future. Many of the tomb robberies were done by the former occupants of the tombs, returned to find that which was needed for a future life.

Most of the elect deliberately court obscurity, and they learn very early to be wary of sharing any part of what they know, for skepticism, resentment, and persecution often follow.

COMMENTS: Now, here are two chapters of a very different version of the story, or perhaps simply the story of another incarnation in the wheel of many lives that the soul of our narrator has lived.

CHAPTER 1

When it began I do not know, nor in what land, for it was in a time before the names began.

The legend is that I myself was the first to understand. I, and the wise Adapa, although what name was his at that time I do not know. He was the second.

It began, we believe, with the memory of a spring.

Upon a certain day, in a time when all men wandered
in search of game and gathered nuts, roots, and berries
as they traveled, and when men had not yet learned to
plant seeds, my people had come to an ending.

There had been a great dying of plants and animals;
the sun shone hot each day and the clouds did not gather,
nor did the rain fall. Our band had taken up our few
things and wandered in search of food, in search of
water, and we had found nothing but more sun, more dust,
more pools of cracked mud.

The last of our food was gone, and only a little water
remained and many had come to sit and wait for death.

They said, "Why must we struggle when it is only to
die? There is no more grass, and there is no more water.
The time has come for dying."

Then I stood and pointed. "Yonder where lie the blue
hills there is water, and there will be food."

My people stared at me, their eyes wide with hunger
and suffering, their bodies thin and worn. Their will had
fled from them and all they wished was to lie still.

"Hills? Where are these hills of which you speak? We
see no hills."

"Yonder," I said, "another day only."

They did not, they could not, believe, but one man
looked at me, with understanding upon him, and said,
"This man has become the voice of a god--follow him."

They stared at him, and then at me, and they laughed,
a terrible laughing from raw, parched throats. "He? We
have known him from birth. What manner of foolishness is
this?

"He is young and we have watched him grow. He is not
the voice of any god. He is no more than any of us."

"One more day of walking," I said, "just one more
day. A green valley lies there with a stream that is cold
and swift. Wild sheep are there, sheep that have seen no
man, and wild cattle as well."

"How is it that you say this? Have you looked into the smoke?"

"It is there. Are you children that you lie down to die when water is near? Lie then, if you wish. I shall go on, and tomorrow I shall drink deep of the cold, cold water."

Taking up my spear and sling, I started forward, although my feet were sore from wandering, and my muscles from struggling on.

And they followed. . . .

The sun rose higher but we plodded on. The heat grew great and there was no green . . . only the vast sky, only the long grass bending before the wind.

They stumbled often, and sometimes fell, but they arose again and continued, no longer thinking, no longer planning, only putting one foot before the other in a kind of stupor, moving through the trembling air, their throats parched, their tongues drying within their mouths.

And suddenly there was a low purple line across the horizon, which only a few noticed, and of which they did not speak, thinking it born only of their desires, but after a while it grew larger, and they began to see these were mountains indeed, with peaks and shoulders and great ridges.

Now their steps quickened, and I, who had known, walked before them, pointing my way with my toes toward the distant loom of one opening jaw of hills.

No one stumbled now. There was a breeze from off the hills, a hint of coolness. Day began to wane and the glare of the sun departed. Still we marched, and then we could see trees, though only a scattered few.

"There is water?"

"There will be water. There will be much water," I said, "and there for a long time we will stay."

Into the darkening canyon we walked, and into a broad

open valley within the mountains, and they asked me,
"Where is the water?"

"It is there," I said, pointing, "beyond those
trees." And they ran ahead, and there were cries, and the
others ran, and there was a stream, running cold and
clear, and they drank the water, and then drank again.

A wild ox came down from the hills and stared at us,
head up, nostrils distended.

Choosing a rock I put it in my sling, and I swung a
mighty blow and the rock flew, striking the ox between
the eyes.

He dropped, and running forward I finished him with a
spear thrust. And after their thirst was quenched they
came to cut up the meat, and to eat it. Some was eaten
raw from hunger, and some was roasted above the fire.

The old man came to me, he who had said I had become
the voice of a god, and he said, "You knew."

"Yes," I replied.

"How did you know?"

I thought of that and said, "I remembered."

"Do not tell them so. Tell them you saw it in the
smoke."

"You wish me to lie?"

"Only to let them believe. How, they will say, could
he remember? Have we ever seen this place? Have we ever
come so far? And has he not grown up among us? What could
he remember that we could not?"

"I saw nothing. I simply knew."

"Perhaps that is the way of it," he said. "I think we
must be careful, you and I. People do not always like
those who are wiser than they; they do not like to believe that some know and others do not."

Something within told me this was wise, so when Pied
Bull said, "How did you know?" I shrugged and said, "I
did not know. It was a lucky guess."

Pleased, Pied Bull said, "I thought so," and he went
to tell the others.

Pied Bull aspired to be our chieftain, and was an arrogant man, a strong warrior but a man of small judgment
and much impressed with himself. He was among them now,
making little of my leadership in this case.

"It is well," the old man said. "Let them not know
too much."

His eyes turned to mine. "This has happened before? I
have seen it."

My reply was guarded. "Who knows?"

"Even as a child, you hunted with a warrior's skill,
and when you looked for berries, you knew where to look."

"It was my good fortune," I said.

"You remembered," he replied, "just as you remembered
this place. You have been here before."

"That cannot be." I hesitated, then said, "You know
my life. None of us have ever been so far."

He waited for a while and then said, "Sleep well tonight, but unless I am mistaken in the night you will remember other things. You are one of Them."

"Them?"

"Those who remember," he said. "Once when I was very
young the shaman told me there are some who remember, and
to be alert for them."

"And you think I am one?"

"I know it. I have known it these ten years."

"Long ago I might have heard this place spoken of, in
a time when I do not remember. Perhaps some hunter . . .
some visitor to our camps . . ."

"Perhaps." He got to his feet. "Eat," he said, "and
rest. We will talk of this again."

Eat, I did, but no rest came to me. Warily, I let my
eyes look about. Did I know this place? Was there more
that I could remember? I wiped the grease from my hands
upon the grass and went to the stream to drink again.

I drank, then took from my feet the sandals I wore,
and I bathed my feet in the cold water.

Hot water, I thought, might be better. Yet who had
ever heard of heating water for the feet? I had better
not think of that or they would know me for a fool.

When I had rested a little, my back against a tree, I
became restless to walk about. Taking up my spear and
sling I walked away among the trees, and then stopped
where I could look up at the walls of the canyon.

It was a wide canyon with meadows and trees, the
stream offering water. We would stay in this place, for
there seemed to be game. Everywhere I saw the tracks of
animals, but none of men.

And then my feet found a path.

It was a hidden way, a winding way among rocks and
old, old trees. How I came upon it I do not know, but suddenly it was there and my feet were walking it as if . . .
as if they knew.

The path led along one wall of the canyon but close
to the foot of the cliff, and it was a good way, a very
good way where one could come and go and be unseen from
the valley below. Then, I stopped.

Someone watched me.

Turning from the path . . . a path that left nothing
for the eyes to see except at great intervals when there
seemed to be places a little worn . . . I went into the
trees. Suddenly I saw Pied Bull.

"Where do you go?" He peered at me, his small eyes
prying and cunning. I shrugged my shoulders. "I look for
the droppings of game. I do not know if there are deer,
or more of the big oxen."

"You are a fool," he said contemptuously. "There are
droppings everywhere. I have seen them. And there are
tracks. This is a good place."

"Well," I said, "you are a great hunter. You would
know best."

He looked about, and his curiosity satisfied, he went away. He had not seen the path.

Yet . . . had I really <u>seen</u> it? Or did I see it because I knew it was there?

The way grew steeper; it wound around among great fallen slabs of rock, then up a narrower canyon where the sun did not shine. Now I was far from our place beside the stream, and I was alone.

What if there were men here? I could be attacked and killed, and then they would come quietly upon my people and kill all of them, for we were few, only sixteen men, twenty women, and the children. It was a small tribe, for we had lost many through war and hunger.

I paused. There in the sand was a spear-head.

I knelt to examine it. It was very small, very neatly done. The flakes of stone struck from it were done with great skill, nothing like our own clumsy spear-heads. But such a spear must have been used by very tiny men. . . . It was like nothing I had seen.

Straightening up, I looked all about me. I was in a shadowed place, a spirit-place. The canyon walls towered above me, and somewhere I could faintly hear the trickle of water.

I knew this place.

I knew this place well. And this chipped point of stone I held in my hand was not a spear-head. It was another sort of thing . . . something for which I had no name.

Yet now, suddenly, I knew where to go, and I ran on, swiftly, along the trail . . . and stopped.

Cut into the sandstone were steps leading steeply upward. Steps leading to what?

They were much worn, old; many rains and winds had beaten upon them. I started up.

Fear kept me from looking down. I climbed, across a shoulder of the rock and into a crevice, a split in the

rock where the steps were natural and easy and it was
wide enough for only one man at a time. I went swiftly up
to a wide ledge.

I stopped.

Before me was something I had never seen before.
Something . . . Yet, had I not seen this?

Stones fitted together to make a wall, an opening in
the wall for air. I walked slowly forward. Past the corner there was a door.

I stepped inside, my spear poised.

It was shadowed and still, but upon the floor lay the
skeleton of a man. The bony hand held a knife, a strong
thin blade of chipped stone.

I sat down and looked upon the man long dead. I took
the knife from the skeleton fingers. It was finely done,
much better than my own.

The room was bare. The floor was of neatly fitted
stones, upon one side a wooden seat. I looked at it,
studied it, then stood up.

The dead man had been killed, and he looked to have
fallen while running. Bending over him I saw something
else. On the floor beneath him, under his ribs, was another of those small spear-heads.

Looking at it, I scowled. There was something about
it that I should know, but did not know. Something I
should have . . . remembered?

There was another door. The spear in my hand, the
newfound knife held low in my other hand, I went through
that door. A long room . . . a shadowed room.

Empty.

Crossing it with running steps I went into the room
beyond. Smaller, almost square except for a sort of
closet in one corner, a closet or space but with no door.
The door might have been of wood, and burned. Peering
closer I could see the frame of the door was charred as
from fire. At the opening I stood peering into the alcove.

There was nothing there, yet there should have been.

From room to room I went. Some were in ruins, roofs or walls fallen in, a few more scattered bones, signs of fire. There had been a fierce fight here. At one place the center of the floor had ashes and the marks of burning as if something had been piled there and set afire.

For a moment I felt a chill of fear at the sight of that fire, but I did not know why it should so affect me.

I went out again into the air and looked around. The place where I stood should have been perfect for defense, and it needed only one or two men to protect it from invasion. Yet it had been attacked and its people destroyed. How, I could not guess.

It was late, and I knew I should go back.

But I was hesitant to leave. I looked all about me, disturbed by thoughts whose origin I could not guess. Somehow I believed I should have found something here, that I had been guided to this place by some strange influence, perhaps something from within myself.

In the dim light I went down the steps in the stone, then turned back toward our camp.

Emerging from the narrow canyon into the wider, I paused. The valley fell away before me with only the slightest of grades, and leaving out the trees the land was flat. I looked at it, and something nudged hard at my consciousness. . . . Why should it impress me so?

At the camp the fires were burning small, our place was hidden as well as might be, and our people were eating again, restoring their strength against the days to come.

The old man looked up at me, and in his eyes there was a question. But also upon me were the eyes of Pied Bull, the one who did not like me.

Did I like him? I thought of that and decided he did not matter to me. I had no feelings of liking or disliking, only of wariness. The man was too curious, too envious, and was dangerous because of his jealousy of me.

"You bring no game," Pied Bull said.

"I did not look for game," I said. "I looked for others, and there are no others. I think this is a good
place in which to stay."

He shrugged. "There is game. The women have found
roots. We can stay for a while."

Something stirred within me, and there lay before my
eyes the wide valley, the almost level fields with grade
enough for water to flow.

"We would do well," I said, "to move no more. This is
a good place to stay."

Pied Bull looked his disgust. "And when the game is
gone? And we have eaten the roots and fruit?"

"Where these roots grow, and these seeds, more will
grow. We will plant seeds and they will grow for us."

"Plant? What is plant?" The woman who spoke was Wolf
Boy's woman. She was quick and sure in her movements, one
of the best tanners of skins, one of the quickest to find
the food we gathered. Her name was Moon Daughter.

There was a knowledge within me I dared not tell, yet
there was a logic she would grasp.

"We have seen where seeds fell upon the ground, and
where seeds have spilled when we were eating, and later
when we came again the seeds had grown to plants.

"Why only gather what we find? Why not open the
ground and spill the seeds into it, then close the ground
over the seeds and when they grow, take what we need? We
can eat some, the rest we can store in dry caves. Then we
need move no more."

"It is foolish," Pied Bull said. "How do you know the
seeds will grow? And can you grow meat?"

"We can," I said quietly. "Do you remember the baby
deer Moon Daughter's child kept? Why can we not keep a
dozen such, or many more? Let the children guard them,
and when they grow we can eat them as we need, and need
no longer trust only to the hunt."

The old man who was my friend spoke quietly. "You speak wisely, my son. It is good, what you say. And it can be done."

"It is foolish," Pied Bull said irritably.

"No. It is good," Moon Daughter said.

Our chief, who was very old, sat quietly and listened. I had noticed this of him, that he let much talk go by before he spoke, and he listened well and then said what it seemed most of the people wished, or perhaps what he suspected they wished even when they had not spoken.

"We can stay here for a time. There is game. There is food. We have seen no signs of enemies. Our dry time has been bad, and we have suffered. Now we will rest, and we will grow strong again."

"And we will plant," I said. "All who wish to plant with me shall meet when the day comes at the meadow's edge, each with a sharp stick."

When they had scattered to their beds the old chief remained. He looked at me, his eyes old and wise and hard with thought. "Is it that you would take from me that which is mine? I am the chief."

"You are the chief. I speak only to help. To come here was hard. The way was long, and the land was dead and without water. Now we are here. Perhaps there is no one here. Perhaps no one has been here for a long time. Why should we move from a land of plenty?"

The old one, my friend, had come up to us. "Heed him," he advised. "Your troubles will be less."

The chief scowled, staring off down the canyon. "I am tired," he admitted. "We came far, and we are a small clan. Perhaps no one has ever crossed that waste before."

"Perhaps not," I suggested, but I was remembering the houses of stone. "Or if so, not for a long time."

"We will stay," the chief said, "while there is food. You may do what you will with your seeds."

CHAPTER 2

When morning came twenty-one people came to the
meadow, men, women and children. Each brought a sharp
stick.

The day before walking through the canyon I had come
upon a wide place where grew a sort of grass that had
many small seeds. As I walked through the grass the seeds
fell from the grass, striking the ground with a sound
like rain.

With Wolf Boy, Moon Daughter, and two of their young
ones we had returned and in the evening had filled bas-
kets with the seeds. Now we gave some to each and they
walked in a wide-spaced rank down the meadow, making a
hole with a sharp stick at each step. Four times each of
us walked the field's length dropping the seeds, and then
we returned to camp.

It was in my thinking to go back to the place I had
found, to the houses of stone, but I did not wish anyone
to know where I was going, nor to find them, not even my
old friend. It was something within me that warned me, so
I was wary, and when in the late afternoon I went out of
camp, I watched behind me with care.

So it was that I saw Pied Bull following me. I had
seated myself on the bank of the stream before he arrived
and when he came upon me I was staring into the water. He
came up to me and peered over my shoulder into the water.
"What do you look at?" he demanded.

"The water," I said.

"The water?" He was puzzled. "But it is only water.
What is there in it to see? Are there fish?"

"I do not know," I said solemnly. "I think the water
wishes to speak to me."

"What foolishness is this? You have lost your wits."

"Listen! Can you not hear it? It tells me things. Secret Things."

"You are foolish." He turned from me. "I do not know
how they can listen to you."

He strode away, leaving me alone, and when he had
been gone some time I got up and went on my way. When I
started into the canyon I could look back and see him
heading for our camp.

This time the climb was quicker. My toes were ready
for the narrow holds cut into the rock, and I went up
swiftly. Once on the ledge I paused, took my spear from
the strap over my shoulder with which I'd carried it, and
went into the building.

The bones lay where they had been, and I stepped past
them and went forward into the third room. Puzzled, I
stood before the alcove. There was something I must do
here, something I should remember.

Each time it had come to this, this moment when one
must not turn aside.

Each time?

Into the alcove I looked, and saw nothing. Only bare
walls, only the fitted stone, the silence of years. But
there was within my mind the haunting sense of recognition. But how? Why?

The old man said, "You knew," and I had answered, "I
remembered."

There was no time now--something warned me of this. I
might go away and never find the opportunity to return
here alone, and to sit down and think was not the thing,
not now.

There are memories within the muscles, memories of
actions performed long ago: the hurling of a spear, the
dodging of a blow; these things become instinctive. Stepping into the alcove, I raised my hands and touched the
wall before me. I found a crack opposite my chin, my fin-

gers dug, a brick came loose. Behind the brick an opening, and in the opening a gripping place.

The grip was also of stone, a dark stone, smooth and
polished. I put my hand in and I pulled.

For an instant, nothing happened. I braced my toe and
pulled the harder.

The wall swung toward me. . . .

I looked into a black, rectangular cavern. It was
deep and wide, and in the center, on a stone table, lay a
long box . . . a box as long as a tall man.

Inside the room were other things. On the wall, a
shield, beside it, crossed, a spear and a sword.

No man in my tribe had seen such a weapon, but it was
a sword. I knew it at once, knew its uses.

What was happening to me?

I stepped into the room. There were two smaller boxes
against the wall. There were other weapons . . . and the
long box?

I took hold and lifted the lid.

It raised easily under my hand, no squeak, no groan,
no grating of stone on stone.

From within came a faint scent as of something musky,
something faintly fragrant, and I looked upon the
skeleton-face of a man long dead.

He wore a breastplate of thin and shining stone, on
it a deer with one head and three bodies, a strange symbol.

The skull wore a heavy hat of the same thin stone and
there were fragments of a robe. A hide? No, some different material. It had fallen to bits. . . . It had been
purple.

There was a circle about the bony finger of the right
hand, a ring of strange design. And in the hand there was
a sort of blackened box as long as my forearm, the end
square, each side of the square as long as my thumb.

With careful fingers, I took the box from the
skeleton-hand, took it reverently, gently.

I had forgotten where I was, forgotten who or what I
was. What I was doing . . . it was something I had been
destined to do.

Now I knew that our tribe's trek north had not been
only to save them, to escape from enemies into a land
where there was water and a chance to live. I had needed
to come to this place. My feet had followed a trail
traced out by my mind, by some strange design woven into
the fabric of my genes.

What was it the Old One had said? <u>You are one of</u>
<u>Them</u>. <u>You are one of those who remember</u>.

The man who had been buried here in that long box
had once been <u>me</u>. It had been my hand that held that now
tarnished silver box, awaiting the time when I should
come again and take the gift I held for my sometime
self.

Gently, I removed the gold ring from the finger and
fitted it to my own, then carefully I closed the coffin
and, taking the silver box, I stepped back.

Tucking the silver box into my waist I took from the
wall first the sword, then the spear. I glanced at the
chests. . . . What awaited me there?

Well, they could wait.

Perhaps for another day, perhaps for another time, or
another life.

Out into the dusky twilight of the square room I
walked, and turning, I took the handle, closed the door,
then replaced the brick. Taking dust from the floor I
blew some from my palm into the thin cracks around the
brick.

Then I walked outside to the ledge and looked down
the canyon. I could see the narrow opening into the valley, the sky overhead with its few stars, and I stood
there breathing the cool air, knowing now that when I

went down those toehold steps again I should no longer be the man who climbed them, but something else.

Seating myself on a block of stone I placed the spear and the sword at hand.

It was a short sword, no longer than the length of my arm without the hand, as wide at the hilt as the length of my thumb, tapering only slightly to a short but sharp point. Each edge was a cutting edge, unbelievably sharp.

Taking the box in my hand I placed it across my knees and felt it carefully. It was so dark I could see only the glint of metal, but it was embossed with some strange design. Suddenly my thumb halted.

A small knob or button. Was it a catch? A means of opening the box? The box seemed to have no opening, yet from its weight it could not be solid. I pressed the

A handwritten version of the beginning of this draft.

COMMENTS: I have as many questions about this story as you do. Who are these people? On what continent do they live? Who is the man in the coffin and what civilization is he from? What matters really, however, is that Louis has given us one indication of how this concept of reincarnation and the discovery of knowledge handed down over generations might function in other variations of this story.

The versions you have read so far have been some of the later ones, possibly written in the mid-1970s. It all fits in very well with the alternative spirituality of the time, a time when Louis was experimenting with stories about mysticism and other universes in novels like *The Californios* and *Haunted Mesa*. However, the first time Louis sketched out the beginnings of his reincarnation concept was in the mid-1950s, in a proposal for a television series—an idea that was likely twenty or thirty years ahead of its time.

SAMSARA OR THE WHEEL OF LIFE

A Television Series by Louis L'Amour

Who can say what mysteries lie within the soul and mind of a man? Who can say that he alone has the answers to all questions? Since the beginning of time Man has longed for immortality in the Western world, and feared it in the Eastern. To every man and woman comes at some time the belief that this life is not enough; there is the desire to live on, to live in another world or in another life than this.

Beyond the grave lies hope, and many religions offer the promise of immortality; but only in the belief in re-

incarnation, or metempsychosis--the transmigration of
souls--is there something tangible, something real, something all men can accept and understand.

More people of the world believe in reincarnation
than disbelieve, and many millions look longingly and
hopefully in that direction.

This series will have romantic appeal for men and
women, who can escape the treadmill of everyday life by
imagining the people they once might have been; it has
enormous appeal and identification in that the hero, by
moving through his past lives, has access to and command
of all the knowledge and wealth of the universe.

He may know where lie the still unfound Maya libraries; or where the Pharaoh was buried and where he lies in
his golden sarcophagus, awaiting the lucky archaeologist.
He could know where Alexander's ships went, where Cleopatra buried her treasure. There is no secret he cannot
plumb, no life into which he cannot go.

Yet do we say we believe in reincarnation? Not necessarily. In the person of the scientist, the psychologist
DR. RICHARD MARKHAM, we introduce in each episode a different and varying word of caution in his conversations
with VAUBAN, our hero.

Perhaps the experiences come from stored-up knowledge
of history; perhaps from books of fiction; perhaps from
the very articles Vauban sells. We introduce much specu-
lation through the psychologist, and all of it will be
cogent, entertaining, and stirring to the imagination.

This is not fantasy; it is an adventurous step into
realms of spirit, of the unknown. Man may return to dust
after death, and that may be all, but millions believe
otherwise.

MICHAEL VAUBAN is an importer of art and antiques; he
is young, handsome, athletic, and he lives among the

vases, the carved stones, the jewels, the weapons of bygone years.

To his shop one day comes a woman to buy a rare vase;
she is waited upon by a clerk while Vauban writes busily
nearby. She likes the vase, and is assured that it is a
rare Etruscan piece. She, however, wants a pair. The
clerk assures her this is the only one, that there is no
other.

Vauban, still writing, comments aloud, "But of course
there's another! When Karchamal made that one, he made
another, identical to it."

The woman is surprised, the clerk astonished. Vauban
looks up, realizes he has spoken, and is confused.

After the customer has gone, the clerk comments, "I
had no idea there was another. How did you know?"

Vauban shrugs it off, but he is disturbed. He leaves
that night, and walking down the street, goes to the home
of Dr. Richard Markham. He explains, and he adds that this
has happened not once, but several times . . . and more
than once his hunch has proved to be correct. Can he be
clairvoyant? Markham discusses the idea, suggests he try
an experiment: Go home, relax, breathe properly. . . .

Vauban does so and emerges panting and gasping from
the sea. He is a galley slave who has escaped from a
wrecked galley. He has various adventures.

In successive trips into the past he is a Roman Le-
gionnaire; a priest of Isis in Ancient Egypt; a king of
the Hittites; a wandering mendicant in Mughal India; a
traveling minstrel in eleventh-century Europe; a prince
of India.

But there is danger. When in the trance states he is
in a state of suspended animation and if so found he may
very well be taken for dead.

This actually happens, and he comes to in a coffin
just before the funeral. This frightens him, and he knows
if he is to venture into the past again he must have a

room no one can enter but himself. It must be fireproof,
thief-proof, etc.

He goes into the past and watches the burial of a
Pharaoh; he is himself the priest; then he comes back in
his twentieth-century life and excavates the tomb. With
the wealth he gains from this sort of activity he builds
a secluded home.

There is a young woman with whom he has a strange relationship. He sees her on the street, they exchange
glances, but she evades him. She is dark, lovely, mysterious. He finds her in his dream-travel. He realizes that
certain people have an affinity for one another in the
reincarnation process.

Another time he wishes to see a girl whom he loved
and lost in another life. He finds where she is in this
life, but she is an ugly old crone who runs him off,
flinging things at him.

There is much humor, for he learns to distinguish who
people are in this life, recognizing them from the past.
A man comes to his shop to sell antiques whom he recalls
as a trickster in ancient Tyre. He refuses to buy. He
passes a pig in a marketplace that he knows is an acquaintance in another life, and he says, "Just as I
thought. I'd have known him anywhere!"

For this series there is no end. It is adult entertainment, but it has romance, it has many talking points,
in that each chapter will begin or end with a speculative
comment by Dr. Markham.

The hero can venture into any world, into any life,
can be anything, always returning to his own life. There
are many dangers. He always knows he will live again, but
he does not know when he will die in each life he returns
to. And in some of them he will die. . . . Here, for the
first time, we have a hero who can be killed and still
appear in the next chapter.

He can be anything, do anything, go anywhere.

REINCARNATION: the successive habitation of many different bodies by the same soul. The belief that the spirits or souls of men pass after death into other bodies is
a feature of many religions, especially in the East, and
is still held by the Buddhists and by many Hindus, and,
of course, by the modern Theosophists. It was taught in
Ancient Egypt, by the Orphic priests of early Greece and
by Pythagoras, was discussed by Plato, and was believed
in by some Christians.

My background to be the writer of this series, and I
would write all the episodes myself, is excellent. With
due apologies I might say that I have read several hundred books on psychology, metempsychosis, hypnotism, the
occult sciences, yoga, psychometry, multiple personali-
ties, clairvoyance, the subconscious, and the earliest
and latest ideas on the human mind.

I have an extensive knowledge of the arts, music, and
literature of ancient times; I have read widely in the
history and archaeology of all nations, am an amateur archaeologist myself, and have at hand both the knowledge
and the library for essential research.

My travels in many lands have fitted me with the
background to handle this series, and it is a theme that
intrigues me with its romance and unlimited scope. Before
us lies the entire field of world history; there is no
avenue we cannot explore. A Viking in early America? A
Phoenician sailing beyond the gates of Hercules? A cast-
away in the time of Rome?

Many of the early stories can be done with an eye on
the budget, but there are no limits to the possibilities.

Throughout the series there can be this one mysterious woman, one to whose life cycle Vauban is bound, who
continues to show up in the lives he leads. Sometimes he

is old, sometimes young; he is a cripple, a blind beggar,
a gladiator; he is Alexander the Great, he is anybody.

This is a series without a chance of being stereo-
typed. It cannot become monotonous. It appeals to the
spirit of romance, adventure, and speculation. It will
stir controversy. It will demand comment. And no man,
anywhere, can say it is impossible. We will, in the person of Dr. Markham, offer, as I have said, alternative
solutions. We make no claims; we offer stories and we
offer explanations. The viewer can choose the truth he
likes the most.

COMMENTS: *The Wheel of Life* is obviously a simpler approach than
the first two versions of this concept. It's a more straightforward,
"time travel through past lives" situation, where there is not so much
mystery, though perhaps a greater variety of adventure. It was also an
easier concept for a writer to pursue because the television series of
the 1950s were essentially episodic and open-ended, and thus it wasn't
so important to work out what the conclusion or meaning of the over-
arching story was going to be.

I have always wondered if Vauban's shop was based on one belonging to a very dear friend of ours, Harry Franklin. Harry had a
narrow storefront in Beverly Hills and inside it was a cabinet of wonders. He specialized in primitive and oceanic art and there were giant
carvings from New Guinea, masks and drums form Africa, and Roman
and ancient Chinese jewelry. As a little kid I found it to be both a fascinating and a kind of scary place—a shop very much like the Harry
Franklin Gallery also appeared in "The Hand of Kuan-yin," a story of
Dad's that was used as the pilot for *Hart of Honolulu*, a TV show
which, if the pilot had been picked up, might have become the first
detective series shot in Hawaii.

Over the years Louis made other attempts to get the novel version of *Samsara* started and to figure out how to write it. The most
powerful and personal version is the one that follows.

CHAPTER I

A man with gold rings in his ears . . . a vase of ancient glass . . . a fragment of carved stone . . . and a
girl.

Yes . . . a girl.

These things caused a door to open, a door I cannot
close, a door I am not sure I wish to close, yet a door
that has opened the way to a haunted past.

Alone I am, and alone I have ever been except for
those days, those moments even, when from out of the beyond
I have found again those whom I love, and who love me.

For the one thing I have discovered is that love need
not die, need not end . . . for even after millenniums I
have known it to endure.

Yet never have I been so alone as now when I possess
a knowledge I cannot share. Not, at least, in its entirety.

The man with the gold rings in his ears, the fragment
of stone . . . the girl . . . these were not a beginning
but rather a culmination of something that began . . .
how can I say where? Or when? Or how?

When I was not more than five years old a Gypsy said
things to me that I have not forgotten. That Gypsy set me
upon my path. My father was a veterinarian who also dealt
in farm machinery, and not far from the town in which I
lived were some farms owned by Gypsies. In the spring

they came to plant their crops, vast fields of wheat in
those days, and when the wheat was well above ground they
would depart, returning only for the harvest.

They built no house upon the land, preferring their
own caravans, but often they came to visit my father and
to trade horses with him, a business at which my father
and the Gypsies both were adept.

One year at harvest time they came to my father to
buy a complete threshing outfit; a steam tractor, separa-
tor, water-tank wagon, cook car, hayracks, and even
pitchforks.

Several days of discussion and bargaining preceded
the actual purchase, but the deal was finally consummated
in my father's office.

This was a small room in the corner of the great red
barn used by him as a veterinary hospital. It contained a
rolltop desk, a swivel chair, and an old leather settee
and had linoleum on the floor.

It was a day I shall never forget.

The Gypsies began to arrive at daybreak. The men wore
black suits and had bandanas tied over their heads under
their black hats, and some had gold rings in their ears.
The women wore brightly colored dresses and shawls, with
many necklaces of gold coins, and bracelets upon their
arms. By the time the last had arrived there were at
least thirty in our yard.

They knew my father and liked him, so there was much
talk and laugher as they relived old horse-trades in
which first one and then the other had been bested, before they settled down to business.

When the time came for payment they paid in cash on
the floor of my father's office. And they paid in gold.

The women lifted their outer skirts, revealing a series of petticoats containing hidden pockets around the
waist. From these they each took several gold coins until
my father was paid in full, a shining heap upon the lino-

leum floor. It amounted, I believe, to six or seven thousand dollars. I always intended to ask my father the
amount merely to satisfy my curiosity, but now it is too
late.

Too late?

Perhaps not . . . perhaps in some other time, further
along down the years.

Among the Gypsies who came that day was one who took
no part in the proceedings, for he was a stranger among
them, a man from another tribe, another land.

He was a tall old man, though very straight and
strong, with piercing black eyes, white hair, and a fine,
high-arched nose and high cheekbones. He sat alone on a
bench beneath the cottonwood tree at the end of our
porch, and the others treated him with great respect,
perhaps even fear.

He was sitting on the bench when I emerged from the
office, following some others. I felt his eyes upon me.
Others walked between us yet his eyes did not waver, so I
stopped at last and stared at him and he at me.

"So?" he said. "Here you are."

"Yes," I said.

"Do you know me, then?"

"I believe I do."

The sun was hot and I stood in the sun. The others
had drawn away, not seeming to be aware, not talking at
all, nor seeming to listen.

My father was in his office sacking up the gold, and
I could hear the chink of coins and a fly buzzing. A
horse stamped in the dust near the corner of the barn.

"It has been a long time. A very long time."

I said nothing, for I had few words, yet within me
there stirred a kind of awareness, a kind of knowledge,
and a listening.

"You will have much to learn, but it will come to you
quickly, to you above all."

The afternoon was still. Within the house dishes rattled and soon my mother would call me.

"You were born to him?" His eyes indicated the office where my father was.

"Yes."

"He is a good man, a strong man. This I have heard."

"Yes."

"You will be like him, I think. Like him, but different, for you will know. You, of us all, will surely know."

What he was saying to me was unlike anything that had been said to me before, yet the words seemed right and I found nothing strange in them.

"You will coor the drom," he said, "and if you need to know more, come to me in the springtime at the Sea Mary Church on the Gulf of Lyon, or at Burgos in the fall . . . and if you should meet a man with a golden dorje, tell him who you are."

My father came from his office then, and the Gypsies were drifting to their wagons. The tall man got to his feet and rested his hand on my shoulder. He looked at my father and said, "You have a fine son. Let him go his way."

When they were gone my adopted brother, who had stood listening, asked, "What does it mean? To coor the drom?"

"To go tramping," I said. "He meant that I should travel across the world."

Yet I could not have explained how I came to know Romany words.

Only a short time before I had become fascinated by maps, having them always before me. Already I could read the simplest books, and knew the continents and countries by their names and shapes.

"Pa," I asked later, "where is the Gulf of Lyon?"

"On the coast of France," he replied, and accustomed to my questions he did not ask why I wished to know.

That was the first indication, but nothing happened again for a long, long time.

And yet . . . ?

On a summer's day I had gone with my father into the country, and while he discussed business I walked up a low hill to where the sun lay warm upon the grass, and lay down near a big, old tree. After a while I dozed, yet what I then experienced was no dream, or if a dream it was unlike anything I would normally think of as such.

For I was not asleep. Distantly I heard the sound of a mowing machine, the murmur of my father's voice as he talked, and the lazy drone of a bumblebee. Occasionally wind stirred the grass, but when it ceased there was only the warmth of the sun on my back.

Beneath all of this I had been for some time aware of another sound, a faint but definite beat that grew in volume until suddenly I knew, I who at the time had seen nothing larger than a rowboat, that what I heard was the rhythmic beat of many oars moving in unison.

At the same time I gradually became aware of movement, of water rustling about a hull, and the realization that I myself was aboard that boat, moving with it, looking along the boat's length from some high point near the stern.

The sun was warm upon my back, for the sunshade above me possessed neither back nor sides. My finger stirred, and the hand I looked upon was my hand, yet much older, and upon the second finger was a ring bearing a strange device, a triangle with a peculiar design upon it. The ring, I knew, was important for what I was about to do.

"I will cross the bridge," I seemed to be saying mentally, "and enter the Red Pavilion."

The remark was puzzling, out of context, and did not belong to what I was then doing or thinking. Yet it was

the first of such random thoughts, all part of a recon-
struction that had begun to take place within the boy
that I was.

The boat glided to a stop, grated against a stone-
faced quay, and two slaves offered me their hands. I
stepped from the boat into the hot, bright sun, and
looked upon a city.

Turning, I glanced at the boat, seeming to really see
it for the first time. There were forty rowers, twenty to
a side, a high, curved prow, and a still higher decked
stern over which was stretched a fringed awning of green.
Under that awning was the single, fixed chair in which I
had been seated.

"We have been waiting, Master. We have waited a long
time."

Turning my back to the boat I found waiting for me a
covered chair with four stalwart bearers and two armed
guards. The man addressing me was a tall man with a fine,
high-arched nose and black piercing eyes.

"Mine was a far journey," I heard myself saying, in a
voice that was mine, yet not mine. "I had duties. I could
not come until now."

"A useless journey, I fear. They will not listen,
Master. They have been too long at peace, and they cannot
envision what will happen. The will to fight, if they
ever possessed it, is gone from them. They wish to treat
with the enemy, and believe he will come in peace."

"We cannot permit it. If this is lost, two thousand
years of knowledge goes with it."

Once more I looked at the river. The waters were
brown, moving with infinite power. Far off, where this
river began, its waters were clear and cold, flowing down
from mountains where glaciers were, down through dense
forests among green ferns and over moss-covered rocks. I
had come from there, and even beyond there. How long must
I remain in this hot and humid land?

Turning to the chair that awaited me I heard my father's voice calling, and the chair seemed to fade, and the hot, white glare of the sun, and I smelled the warm green grass below me, and the dark, rich earth. So I got to my feet and walked back down the slope to where my father waited beside the car, and I walked as in a dream, a strange question alive within me.

Who was I? What river was that? What was I? Above all, what had I been?

By that time I had been several years in school, my education no different from those about me. Ours was a pleasant, attractive, and busy town where two small rivers met in a valley. I played a little basketball, hiked along the rivers, boxed in the gymnasium, and spent long hours in the library. Of the dream, or whatever it had been, I said nothing at all, to anybody.

It remained within me, and with it a sense of waiting, of preparing for something that was to come. Preparing to begin something . . . or was it simply to begin again?

My mind was impatient with its progress, demanding more and ever more. When each day's school was complete, I hurried to the library, searching for I knew not what. Yet sometimes in my reading I would chance upon a name . . . or unbidden a name would come into my thoughts and I would search feverishly through books and maps to find it.

Thaneswar.

Why did such a name come to me suddenly, from out of nowhere?

There were other names, names found in no book, upon no map.

Sanathirtha . . . Jalandhar . . . Hari-Yupuya.

Suddenly I knew that last name. It was the city where I had left my boat to stand in the hot, white sun. Yet nowhere upon any map could I find such a city.

Of these things I said nothing, and after a time the memory of the boat and the landing grew dim, and I rarely gave thought to it.

Often, however, when reading old books I would find myself upon familiar ground as if some bygone knowledge had awakened within me. This struck me as absurd, yet it became increasingly necessary to guard my tongue to avoid seeming anything but normal.

Not that I came suddenly upon wisdom, for the foolishness every youngster must go through to grow up was still upon me. Often I succeeded in making an ass of myself, in saying or doing things that in a future time would make my ears grow red with embarrassment. Yet in those areas where I concentrated I found my thoughts leaping ahead, knowing what was to come, understanding arguments before they were offered.

Each year the Gypsies returned and several times they visited us and once I visited them with some youngsters of my own age.

The old man with the rings in his ears was not with them, nor could I learn anything about him. He had traveled with them a short time only. Vaguely they implied he had come from Hungary or Romania and was known to them through some obscure family connection.

There had been something familiar about him, something remembered or half-remembered.

More and more I spent time in the library, reading avidly from first one book, then another. Once, looking through an old book, rarely read by the look of the checkout slip stuck to the flyleaf, I came upon an etching of an ancient temple door. Under it was the caption: Unknown Ruined Temple.

Yet that temple was not unknown to me, for surely as I looked upon the picture I knew what lay within that door, knew I had been there, and upon occasion I had climbed those steps, stood within that door.

"Too much imagination," I told myself, and turned the page.

These things filled me with restlessness, and occasionally I wondered what would happen if I tried those same conditions again . . . lying on a hillside, the warm sun on my back . . . or possibly if I just relaxed and waited?

Yet even after the idea came to me I did nothing; it was not from lack of faith in the experiment, but simply the demands of day-to-day living. For the time had now come for me to go wide upon the world, to find my own destiny, in my own way.

CHAPTER II

There were bleak years before me, and hardships to endure. There were books to read, there was music to hear, and paths to explore. Often my feet were blistered with walking and my hands with work. Hunger made spare my flesh, and thirst parched my throat, yet I grew in strength, for strength does not grow out of softness but out of the use of strength.

My hands took easily to the ax and shovel. Never did I despise labor, nor the sweat of it. I hauled on the heavy lines on tramp freighters, swung a double-jack in the mines, or worked in lumber camps or on construction jobs.

Always I studied, finding my way slowly to knowledge, learning to strike quick and hard when the occasion demanded, and to move on before I became too deeply involved in situations not good for me, or ways foreign to those I preferred.

In San Pedro, while waiting for a ship to anywhere at

all, I lived the best I could, for hard times were upon
the land, and many were the men I met there. One of them
was Sleeth.

He came from where I knew not, and when he passed he
went to somewhere beyond my knowledge, yet for a few
weeks we spoke often.

When first I saw him he was coming into the library
of the Seaman's Church Institute, a dark, slender man
with good shoulders. He was of a medium height or somewhat less, wearing neat but shabby clothes, and he did
not look like a seaman, although the place was a club for
seamen.

What he read in that library I do not know, but after
a while we talked, of books and ships and far-off lands.
He was a romantic, as men who follow the ships are apt to
be, but what else he was or why he was there he did not
say.

Often I saw him about the hall, playing checkers or
chess, and at both he was a wizard. Nor was there any
limit to what he could do with figures. He was fantastic.

Several times I saw him watching me, and one day he
said, "When you get a ship, where would you like to go?"

"To the Far East."

"Why?"

I shrugged, I guess. "I don't know. It has always interested me."

"Yes, I suppose it would."

"Have you been there?"

"Many times. I am going back, someday."

"What's a dorje?"

He was tying little knots in a cast-off string,
quaint, intricate weavings that he created deftly with
amazingly quick movements of his fingers. It was a way he
had, playing with string. At my question his fingers
stopped.

"It's a Buddhist symbol," he said, "a thunderbolt

symbol. In fact, that's what 'Darjeeling' means . . .
dorje-ling. The place of the thunderbolt."

He stood up, putting his string in his pocket, then
drawing his palms along his thighs as though drying them.
"Where did you hear about a dorje?"

I laughed, to make nothing of it. "Oh, a man I met
when I was a kid . . . he was a Gypsy. He told me if I
ever met a man with a golden dorje I should tell him who
I was."

He did not look at me, merely said, "Stick around
here at night. When the shipping office is closed and a
ship comes in to refuel sometimes they'll take the first
seaman they can find."

"I don't have an AB ticket. Just a couple of dis-
charges as an ordinary seaman."

"I know a man who has one you can use. He took it as
security for a loan and never saw the man again." He
paused for a moment, looking out the window at the gently
falling rain. "I think I can get it for you."

"Thanks," I said.

He looked down at his hands. They were skilled, capable hands, hands of strength. The sort of hands one might
imagine a sculptor to have. "I wish we'd met further
along," he said suddenly. "There's so much you could tell
me, so much I want to know."

He looked at me suddenly. "I am caught in the middle,
you know, and I can't remember some of the things I must
remember. You could tell me how, you more than anyone.

"Look"--there was desperation in his tone--"do you
remember anything at all?"

His words made no sense, and yet, in a strange sort
of way I understood what he was getting at. "A little, I
think. I . . . I'm not sure."

"I have an awful feeling I'm needed," he muttered,
"but I don't know where, or how to find out. When I first
saw you . . . there in the library . . . I knew you, all

right. I just couldn't believe it. You of all people. And
then to discover that you haven't arrived . . . that you
can't help me."

I had no idea what to say, so I said nothing, yet I
was perfectly aware that something was happening to me,
that I was approaching a point of no return.

"The Gypsy . . . do you know where I could find him?"

"At Burgos, in the fall. Or at the Sea Mary Church on
the Gulf of Lyon. That's what he said." And then a
thought came to me. "His name was Adapa."

"I thought so. My God, Adapa! I've got to find him."
He put the accent on the first syllable, as I had, and
the sound of it gave me a curious sensation. "I hope
nothing's happened to him."

He looked at me sharply. "You're going out east,
then. Get word to me, will you? You'll know all about it
soon, and when you do, get word to me. Maybe by that time
I'll not need it, but do what you can."

He paused again. "Somebody has to get into Central
Asia. Somebody who knows where to go. We need a new location, something farther west. Or somebody has to write
something . . . you know . . . with the key words and a
guide for us. It's hell to have to blunder along.

"For so many years there were a half-dozen places a
man could go. You, for example, if you had access to the
records you could put yourself in tune within hours. You
could arrive."

The following morning I was drinking coffee at a restaurant counter, with only thirty-five cents left in my
pocket. Sleeth came in and sat down beside me, moving
quickly as he always did.

"There it is," he said, "the ticket. There's a life-
boat certificate, too. It might help.

"I know about a ship," he added. "It left Newport

News to go through Panama and was shorthanded. I am sure
they'll need some men, and they won't be too particular.
It's a hungry ship, but it's a living and it will take
you where you want to go. Most of the ships of that line
call at Japan first.

"I can't help you there; maybe your own sense will
guide you. But there's an old man in Shanghai, he's all
crippled up. Tortured, to make him talk. He never did,
and they left him for dead. He's in Shanghai most of the
time now, deals in arms for the warlords or anybody who's
buying. He will know you, and he will be able to help. If
you can get into western China . . . Well, leave it to
him. You could save us, put everything right."

"How will I find him?"

"He'll find you. His runners meet all the ships, anyway. He won't be able to come to you himself, as he should.
The man has difficulty moving, but he'll know. . . . I'll
send a cable.

"If you reach Rangoon, go to the Shwedagon Pagoda at
dawn or sunset. There are usually some people there to
hear the temple bells. . . . Don't miss it."

The restaurant was almost deserted, for the hour was
late. When the waitress refilled our cups, he said, "I've
never been able to settle down. Some of the others have,
but I've left too much behind. There are too many memories.

"When I was in Los Angeles I saw a girl. . . . I knew
her, but I did not. When she started to go into an apartment house she stopped suddenly and turned to face me.

"'You must go away,' she said. 'I waited, but you've
come too late. I am married now, and happily. There's
nothing to be done.' She went into the building and I
stood there, looking after her. She had known me, all
right, but all I remembered was that I'd known her before, and I didn't know where or when."

He turned suddenly and looked at me. "How old are you?"

"Seventeen," I admitted. "I've been passing as twenty-two."

He swallowed some coffee. "Seventeen . . . You're about due. You say you saw Adapa?"

"I was very young."

"But he knew you? Well, he would. He would know, or Nabu. The first time I arrived I was in Jenbeskala, and Nabu was there. In those days they spoke one language or a dialect of it from the Aral Sea to the Indian Ocean, we were all Munda-Dravids of one kind or another, and I'd come to the town just before the attack.

"We had no chance. They came riding in off the desert and into the town before we could close the gates. I was a warrior, but long since I'd learned there was no sense in dying for a lost cause, so I ran.

"I knew nothing about the town, you understand, and when I ran into this long stone-walled passage I thought I'd had it, yet something made me run on, even though there was nothing but a thirty-foot stone wall at the end. . . . Only there was.

"A section of the wall drew my attention, a large boulder, worked into the mortared stone, solid, and yet . . . I pressed myself into a man-sized divot in the rock. It was hardly big enough to conceal me but something, desperation or some form of knowledge, moved me. The rock moved behind me, rotated on a heavily greased column. I whirled as it moved to close. I was in a long room. There was a table at one end and a man was working there.

"'Sit down,' he said, 'I will be free shortly.' And there I stood with a bloody sword in my hand, gasping for breath with blood and sweat running off me, and he never turned a hair. That was my first meeting with Nabu."

Sleeth rambled on, talking of things of which I knew nothing, yet I did not wish him to stop and I found my mind waiting anxiously for each word, even while another part of me was filled with questions.

I had told him the old Gypsy's name was Adapa, but nobody had told me that, so how could I have known?

"What happened then? When you met Nabu?"

"He continued to write, then sat back in his chair. 'You came right to this place and it is a hidden place,' he said. 'How did you manage it?'

" 'They will find me,' I said. 'I am one of the last of the defenders. They were close behind.'

" 'They will not find you. In fact, they have already gone on.' He smiled at me. 'They think they just imagined that you dodged into that dead-end passage. They will be looking for loot now, not you.'

" 'Suppose they come here?'

" 'They cannot.' He gestured around. 'We are inside a rock. Unless they knew, as you did, they could never find the place.'

" 'I? I knew nothing.'

" 'In this life, no. But there have been other lives for you before this, and there will be others after. It is well you came when you did.' He looked at me. 'I am Nabu.'

"The Wise One." Sleeth looked at me as he said it. "I knew who he was but did not know how I knew. In the next few days he told me a lot, let me see what was happening and what I was a part of. Not over two hundred people know what we are . . . are what we are."

Outside in the street a taxi went by. The door opened and a man came in, shaking the water from his slicker before hanging it up. He was an old man, unshaven, and he looked tired. He sat at the counter a few stools away and ordered pie and coffee.

The cup holding my coffee was thick and heavy. It had

to be, in such a place as this. So it was with us. We had
to be durable.

"Would it be better if we never knew?" I asked the
question of Sleeth, and he shrugged. "For me it is simple. I must know. I am like Ivan Karamazov, who did not
want millions, but an answer to his questions."

"These men? Do they know each other?"

"Men and women. Yes, of course. One may be taller or
shorter, but the type remains the same, and the sex, of
course. Besides, there's something . . . a subtle thing,
but something we all recognize. You'll see it, eventually.

"There have always been places we could meet if there
was need, and our own libraries where we could bring ourselves up to date if the hiatus was too long. All that's
hard to reach now. Inaccessible because of politics or
war or natural barriers.

"I wasn't one of the first. In fact, I arrived late.
I wasn't like Adapa, Nabu, you, or some of the others."
He looked at me. "You were the first, I think. You and
Adapa."

"I don't know. All this, it's very strange. I am
talking without even . . . I mean, I really don't know
anything about this."

"No dreams? No day-dreams? No sudden recollections?"

"Well . . . maybe." I told him about my dream or day-
dream, of the boat coming to the landing, and the old man
waiting for me. "It was Adapa."

"Think of that!" He looked at me. "You did not make
it, you know. We'd all been waiting, hoping for your arrival before the invaders came. We hoped you could make
the rulers realize what was happening to them, and if
that failed, perhaps keep everything from being destroyed. We realize so little so late; we spend most of
our lives catching up . . . we can't move fast enough to
stay ahead of all the events around us."

"You said I did not make it?"

"You never got away from the riverfront. The street ran along one side of the state granary . . . a high brick wall. There was another on the other side, and they were waiting for you. If you'd been a young man--"

"What happened to Adapa?"

"Him, too. You see, the idea of a fifth column is not new. They had agents within the walls of Hari-Yupuya months before, and somehow they knew you were coming to stop the fighting, so you were killed."

"The city was destroyed?"

"Not only the city . . . everything. The people fled to the countryside or the jungle, and civilization dropped from them like a worn mantle. Fifty years later it was as though it had never been. Worse yet, one of our first libraries was lost. If there was ever a way to see how all this started we'll have to remember it, if we can. History, you know, it's chaos. So much is destroyed."

It was strange. I sat with a man I had seen first only a day or two before, and we talked of places of which I knew nothing and events I could not understand. And yet . . . and yet I did.

It was as if we talked of an old story we both knew, only somehow the feeling was sharper, more intense. There was a sense of loss, of loneliness, something that I could not account for.

We sat there together and drank another cup of coffee. "You're ready," Sleeth said quietly. "It isn't good to arrive when you're too young. A kid just can't cope, and he talks too much."

I stared into my empty cup. It was time to be moving on, yet I was reluctant to go, for there was so much to learn, and I had only the faintest grasp of what was happening.

The old Gypsy, and now this man.

"Adapa spread the word, that once you arrived again we could reorganize. We must have new centers, some farther west, in some safe place . . . if there is any place that is safe."

He got up suddenly and shook my hand. "I never expected this. Not to meet you, not like this, anyway. You get that ship now, and go to the old man in Shanghai. He'll put you on the right track, help you to reconstruct. . . . But it will come fast for you, and you'll remember more than any of us."

We started toward the door. In the street he turned suddenly. "Something I have always wondered . . . how it all began. I mean there at the very first. It must have taken some doing."

"I don't know."

"Well . . . well, anyway, the best of luck to you." He put his hands in his pockets and went away down the street. I looked after him, then turned toward the waterfront. A big Dollar Liner was coming up the channel from the sea. It had come from Asia, where I would soon be going.

COMMENTS: Though very much a mixture of fact and fiction, these two chapters contain a lot of legitimate details about Dad's life. There were Gypsies that came to Jamestown, North Dakota, in the years that he lived there. My grandfather, Dr. L. C. Lamoore, did, reportedly, sell them some farm equipment and my dad often told the story of the Gypsy women taking the gold coins out of their petticoats. Louis had an adopted brother, Jack, who was just about his age, although I don't believe that Jack was around when Louis was five. The description of the Jamestown property is pretty accurate also.

The same situation holds true for the chapter set in San Pedro.

Louis was "on the beach" (meaning out of work and waiting for a ship) there for many months. True or not, he has told other stories of Sleeth; you can read one of them, called "It's Your Move," in either *Yondering, The Revised Edition* or *The Collected Short Stories of Louis L'Amour, Volume 4*. And Dad did hang out at the Seamen's Church Institute and did ship out under similar and somewhat mysterious circumstances for the Far East.

This last draft also contains a wonderful metaphor for Louis's life: a child and a young man discovering the fertile imagination that will eventually allow him to blossom into a prolific fiction writer. Those "past lives" could be seen as the lives he would live in stories. When the writing is going well, a writer often feels like a channel or a medium for a flow of information that is coming, so it seems, from somewhere else. Another life? The spirit world? The collective unconscious? You are creating other lives and other times, and sometimes it feels like you are drawing on other realities to do so. I have had that experience occasionally, and my father had trained himself to live in it for hours a day.

Louis rarely mentions writers like Talbot Mundy or James Hilton as significant influences on his work, but in this book we see material that is a good deal more mysterious and spiritual than he is typically known for. In this particular case, it may be that Jack London's *Before Adam* had some influence. Though he probably first encountered it earlier in his life, I also remember Dad reading it to my sister and me at the breakfast table in the late 1960s or early 1970s.

It's also pretty obvious that Louis's experiences in, and study of, Asia had a profound effect on his creative life. Of course, his earliest successes both creatively and financially were in writing about merchant seamen and adventurers in Asia. Later, he occasionally even attempted stories like "May There Be a Road" and "Beyond the Great Snow Mountains" and *The Golden Tapestry* (included in this book) with Asian or Eurasian protagonists. In these versions of *Samsara*, we not only have a character marching eastward with Alexander the Great, but we have reincarnation, secret societies, and occult information hidden in "Central Asia." I'm thinking that Mundy and Hilton and maybe a few others I haven't yet discovered were more influential than I thought!

Now, just like our young/old protagonist, we are off to the Orient and a mysterious city that lies beyond the Jade Gate.

JOURNEY TO AKSU

The Beginning of an Adventure Novel

COMMENTS: *Journey to Aksu* is mostly set in western China in an area called Xinjiang or, in the westernized spelling of the time, Sinkiang. Sinkiang is to the north of Tibet at the base of the mountains that support the Tibetan plateau, wedged between modern China, Siberia, and Mongolia.

Though Louis worked on these drafts intermittently between the late 1940s and the mid-1960s, the story is set in the mid-1930s. It was a time when much of China was ruled by local warlords, only some of whom cooperated with Chiang Kai-shek's Kuomintang government. At the time, Sinkiang was, along with certain areas of central Africa and Antarctica, one of the most isolated areas on earth. Its isolation, however, did not keep it free from the sort of chaos found in the rest of China; political intrigue and warfare were common throughout the decade. The population of Sinkiang, especially in that time period, were mostly Turkic, rather than the Han people Westerners more typically think of as "Chinese."

There is a canyon in the Altyn Tagh, far west of
Sukhain-nor, from which, in a thousand years, no man has
ever returned alive.

This story is told in the marketplace of Suchow, east
of the Jade Gate, and it is whispered among the camel
drivers of Kashgar, far to the west, beyond the great
desert of the Taklamakan.

Yet it is but one of many such tales, for this is a
land that breeds legend and the story you hear tomorrow
in Tashkent or Hami may be the story that was told in the
same cities, and with the same inflections, at any time
since the first camels slogged westward, their goods
bound from far Cathay to Egypt, Rome, or Byzantium.

The massive, ice-sheeted range of the Altyn Tagh and
the mysterious Kuen Lun forms a vast rampart dividing the
province of Sinkiang from the fortress land of Bodh,
known to Westerners as Tibet. Yet that gigantic wall,
seemingly impassable, is penetrated here and there by
canyons and passes that allow access to the farthest
reaches of the mountains and the lands beyond. Some of
these passes lead from Sinkiang to Tibet . . . but who
can say, who dares to even guess, where others may lead?

To the north, along the Tien Shan mountains and the
far edge of the great basin, the camel and truck caravans
bound west from the Jade Gate now travel the route that
leads from Hami to Turfan and Aksu.

It was not always so. Two thousand years ago the silk
route lay to the south along the foothills of the Altyn
Tagh and the Kuen Lun. But with the passing of time the
bed of the Tarim River found a new course. The great lake
of Lop Nor vanished, creeks and springs dried up, and the
southern route was all but abandoned.

Still, in the wastes of the Taklamakan, one of the
earth's most formidable deserts, there remain ancient
walls and towers, the ghosts of forgotten cities. Some-

times seen, sometimes buried by drifting sands, their ancient walls are blackened by time, polished and hollowed
by abrasive winds. Others sink in salt-rimmed marshes,
lost in forests of dying reeds.

In the heat-waved distance mirages shimmer and mirror
fabulous towers and lush gardens where shadowy figures
move along cloistered halls and among sparkling foun-
tains . . . phantoms in the sky, images of another world.
And sometimes the men who look too long wander into the
sand and are seen no more, nor are heard from again.

Whispered in the bazaars and on the street corners of
towns bordering the great basin are stories of djinns and
hidden gold, of dragons and ghost caravans that move by
night, almost soundless and almost unseen.

Any man who has traveled these lonely wastes, who has
camped at night under the black loom of the Altyn Tagh,
with the vastness of the Taklamakan stretching away to
the north, will but agree that he has heard or seen the
shadows of these caravans.

At night when the camels are resting and the dung-
fires lend their thin smoke to the desert's emptiness,
there will sometimes come sounds from the distance. And
then suddenly, the talk will still, the camel drivers
will avert their eyes, the dogs will whine and bury their
heads in the blankets of their masters . . . and out beyond the firelight, out where it is dark and yet not
quite dark, there will be a ghostly movement, a soft
shuffling of feet, a jingle of accouterments, the mutter-
ing of camels and the far-off cough of a man: A caravan
is passing.

Nothing is said of the caravan, nor is anything said
when morning comes. . . . Only, there are no tracks. The
thick trail dust is unmarred, undisturbed. What manner of
men and camels are these, who leave no tracks behind? Who
pass, almost soundlessly, in the night?

The foothills and boulder-strewn slopes of the Kuen

Lun are said to be haunted by a species of devils who, as the water left the springs and the riverbeds grew dry, withdrew into the deeper fastness of the mountains, emerging only at times to prowl the desert. Sometimes if one looks quickly around, one may see the flicker of their shadows as they dodge back among the boulders. Sometimes, on the brightest day, one may see a shadow where nothing stands.

Far west of the Sukhain-nor there is a narrow canyon that opens upon a boulder-strewn slope, and this canyon is crossed by a stone wall that is very high and of a pale blue color. In the center of this wall there is a massive and very ancient wooden gate, but the trail that leads to this gate has been grass-grown these many years, for now that caravans no longer come and the rivers have died, the trail is no longer used, the gate no longer opened, not even for a walking man.

There is about this town, looked upon from the basin side, an appearance of death, yet the town is not dead, and not dying. For this town has lived and continues to live. Nurtured by what well of vitality no outsider can guess, it knows the hard-won secrets of survival. It lives, and yet now it fears. For armed men move along the southern road once more and the grapevine of the desert whispers a warning to the sentries in the mountains above the town . . . a warning of trouble, of men who come to capture or destroy or, simply . . . to change.

The man in the sheepskin short coat was cleaning a pistol, but beside him on a flat rock, and close to hand, lay another pistol, fully loaded. The man in the sheepskin short coat was not given to taking chances.

Along the banks of the tiny stream were scattered

sixty-four men who were bathing, washing clothes, or
cleaning their weapons. In the narrow-mouthed cove in the
mountain wall four mounted men watched over a herd of
horses.

At either end of the camp, well away from the stream
and the small noises made by the working and resting men,
were mounted sentries.

All the men were dressed alike in round sheepskin
hats and poshteens, the knee-long sheepskin coat common
to the area. All wore hand-stitched boots without heels.
From time to time the man cleaning the pistol turned his
head to look toward the sentries or at the blue wall that
blocked the canyon.

There was no outward indication that the gate had
been approached in many years, but the man cleaning the
pistol was not given to accepting the appearance of
things.

The waters of the stream were cold, clear, and fresh,
flowing down from melting snows in the glaciers far
above. All the way from Suchow there had been a scarcity
of water and now the soldiers basked in the warm sun and
drank deep and often of the stream.

There was about these men a tough competence, the appearance of battle-wise comrades who know their own
strength and have confidence in their weapons.

The man in the short coat had a face darkened by desert sun, honed by wind to a bleak hardness. The shirt
under the sheepskin was faded navy blue wool, the wide
belt of hand-tooled leather clasped with a silver buckle
kicked from the sand at the crossing of the Su-lo-ho.

A hired fighting man, a mercenary in the ever-
changing armies of China, he had almost a year ago been
given a mission that had more to do with lining the pockets of a general than with any military value. With
thirty-two men he had started west from Kansu, but long

ago that mission had been abandoned and now his little
army, its numbers increased, functioned as an independent
unit, existing by and for itself.

It has been said of China in the twenties and thir-
ties that anyone who could feed an army could have one,
and this was a force that lived well.

The beat-up, worn-out weapons which had been theirs
at the start had been discarded for modern, more efficient weapons from a cache along the way or captured during the fighting. Their firepower had been increased by
the addition of five light machine guns and two mortars.
They had learned that care of their weapons came first,
their horses second, and themselves third.

Only three of the number were Chinese. Six were Ladakhis from a country once part of Tibet. The Ladakhis were
wanderers, mountaineers, and fighting men. Twenty-two
were Torgut Mongols, scarcely changed from the time of
Genghis Khan, twelve were Kazaks, nine were Tocharis,
four were Lolos, fierce tribesmen from eastern Tibet,
never conquered by the Chinese, and four were Buddhist
monks. These monks were much more given to brawling and
fighting than to prayer and meditation. The remainder
were Tungans.

They were men from the bazaars of a dozen cities, men
who had been camel drivers, yak herdsmen, thieves, and
bandits. Of the original command only a few remained, and
those the toughest and best. During the months that had
passed they had won consistently in battle, had acquired
better equipment, horses, clothing, and food than they
had ever known, and they were a solid, closely knit
group.

They fought for money and the goods they needed, taking what they could from the warring factions of China's
far west. On occasion they had brokered peace, or at
least the temporary truce, based on their alliance with

one side or another. And they avoided direct conflict with the powers that could destroy them, the Kuomintang, the Chinese Communists, and the Soviets.

The man in the sheepskin coat closed the cylinder of the first pistol and tried the mechanism. It worked smoothly, so he reloaded the gun and placed it on the flat rock. He began to strip the second pistol. This one was an automatic, smaller, more compact. . . . This one was insurance.

The sentry nearest the wall spoke suddenly, sharply. The man with the pistol glanced up, waved a reply to the sentry's signal, and resumed his work.

He was seated upon a rock in a shaded place near the stream. It was cool, and the breeze from off the mountain was pleasant. His back was toward the empty space of the Taklamakan Desert, which lay, a low and shimmering brightness, beyond the trees.

When he lifted his eyes again there were three men entering the trees, and they rode horses that could only be from the Kara Shahr or Bar Kol oases, noted throughout western China for their fine animals.

What was the old saying about tribute to the emperors of China? Horses from the Kara Shahr, melons from Hami, grapes from Turfan, and girls from Kucha.

For the emperors, nothing less than the best of everything.

The riders stopped, uncomfortably aware of being sur- rounded by armed men and waiting for him to respond to them. Deliberately, he continued to work upon the pistol. Two of the men were Europeans, that in itself a surprise.

"All right, gentlemen. What the hell do you want?" As he spoke he looked up, sweeping them with a glance.

One of the men was tall, stooped, wearing glasses. "This is . . . well, it is unexpected. We had no idea . . . I mean, we did not expect a white man."

Or perhaps they had sent out the two Europeans precisely because he was a white man. He peered down the gun barrel, checking its cleanliness. "All right, what's on your mind?"

"As a matter of fact, we are preparing for an attack."

"So?"

"We . . . well, we hoped we might prevail upon you to ally yourself with us."

"How would that benefit me?"

The little man interrupted. "It is a matter of survival, my friend. Together we might cope with the situation. Alone you would be defeated."

"You assume too much. First, that I should remain here to receive an attack, and second that we should be defeated. The assumption is unwarranted and altogether stupid."

The little man stiffened. "Stupid? When you would be outnumbered ten to one?"

The man in the sheepskin short coat glanced over his shoulder and gestured, speaking sharply as he did so. A Torgut Mongol walked over and placed a Czech light machine gun on the rock.

"We have several of these and mortars. I know the force you expect to attack. They are a hungry rabble. My men are better trained, better equipped, more efficient in every respect.

"However, when we are rested we shall ride on. Marshal Chu will not arrive in time to disturb us, and I am sure he would like to avoid such a meeting."

The three exchanged glances. Obviously the meeting was not proceeding as they had intended, and the obvious unconcern of the commander of the small force worried them.

"Perhaps if you could come into the town," the tall

man suggested, "we could talk to greater advantage." Then
realizing his oversight, he added, "I am Phillip Laurent,
and this is Signor Villani . . . and Mr. K'o."

"I am Medrac," the man with the pistol replied.

"It is a French name, is it not?"

"I'm an American, not that it means anything out
here."

"Marshal Chu is going to attack us if we do not agree
to his demands. He wishes our young men for his army, and
our women. He has also made demands on our flocks, and
his force is noted for their looting."

"The precedent is timeless. It is the way of armies."

Villani nodded. "I agree. The Huns--"

"Signor Villani"--Laurent was impatient--"this is not
the time for a dissertation."

"You have come to request a favor." Medrac slipped
the clip into the automatic and stowed it away under his
coat. "So far you have said nothing to the point."

"Mr. Laurent or Mr. K'o," Villani said, "are more
competent to discuss that aspect than I." His manner became pompous. "I am accustomed to dealing with matters
after the fact. After all, I am an historian."

"Which probably means that you are an artist in ignoring all that does not conform to the truth as you wish
to see it. I have small use for historians."

"We are not here to discuss history," Laurent said
stiffly. "No doubt this officer--" He hesitated deli-
cately. "What is your rank, sir?"

"Rank is only important to martinets or officers'
wives." Paul Medrac got to his feet. "I take it you have
remained undisturbed for some time?"

"Since 1892," Villani replied proudly. "That was the
last time we were attacked. We have, I believe, developed
survival to a fine art here. In fact, we are dedicated to
it. As you can see, our town is remote, far from the
beaten track, and out of the mainstream of events. Conse-

quently we feel no need to share in wars, famines, epidemics . . . nor to pay duties or taxes. We particularly," he added, "dislike taxes."

"Who doesn't?"

"We have received a demand from Marshal Chu," Laurent persisted. "Three days ago an advance party appeared, and they informed us that Chu was advancing with a vast army--"

"Six hundred men."

"--and that we must provide them with quarters, food, recruits, and women. Otherwise they would capture, loot, and burn our city."

"We have never paid tribute," Villani said, "not even to the Mongol khans."

"We have strong walls," Laurent added, "and an ample food supply."

The walls did not interest Medrac, but the food supply did. Walls are of little use against a determined enemy and there is no more determined attacker than a lean and hungry soldier outside a fat and prosperous city.

He was far more interested in the people themselves than in the walls, for the strength of a city or a nation does not lie in its guns or walls, but in the hearts and backbones of its people.

"You will join us, then?"

"Nothing I have said implies any such decision. You ask me to risk my life and the lives of my men. . . . What do you have to offer?"

"But you're a white man!" Laurent protested. "There are white women here! I . . . we thought surely . . ."

"You were mistaken." Medrac picked up the other pistol from the flat rock and returned it to its holster. "I'm not of the opinion that a white woman suffers any more from rape than a Chinese or a Mongol. So if you have any idea of trading upon any inclination of European

chivalry, forget it. Such a sense in me is comfortably
dormant.

"Furthermore, let me tell you this: I have here one
of the toughest, best-trained outfits of fighting men in
Asia. We are few in numbers, but competent. I shall not
risk their lives without reason.

"However, I am willing to entertain an offer for our
services, but before you decide upon the size of the
offer, let me point out a simple fact. If we want your
town, we will take it."

Mr. K'o cleared his throat. "If price is a consideration, I believe we can talk to some purpose."

"Price is the consideration. And may I suggest you
begin with your best offer? We can grade it up from
there." Medrac glanced at K'o. "I am sure we will continue to understand each other."

Laurent started to interrupt, but Mr. K'o spoke
quickly. "You will accept an invitation to my house? I am
but a guest in the city, but my poor house is at your
disposal. Shall we say, for dinner?"

"You are a guest? How long have you been here?"

Mr. K'o smiled. "Twenty-seven years." His eyes twin-
kled. "At eight, then?"

"At eight."

Medrac watched them ride away, then turned to the
stocky Chinese with the scarred face. "Chen, I want five
men in that town within the hour. They will go quietly to
shop for fruit, and to inquire about horses.

"While doing this they will check the defenses of the
town and the morale of the people. Also, how many Europeans? Have they modern weapons? How long since a caravan
was here? They will be back no later than seven o'clock
with the information."

Chen departed and a tall young Mongol came swiftly
up. "Shan Bao, take four men and swing around behind the
town. Check the canyons leading into the mountains and

get a rough estimate of the flocks. I have an idea you'll find a number of connecting valleys and canyons, rich in grass and water. Don't take more than two hours. I want this information before I enter the town."

Seating himself again, Medrac drew from a musette bag a handful of maps. Each was a beautifully drawn map of some section of Sinkiang, and two of them were very good maps of the region where they now camped. A Chinese in Lanchow had provided these maps.

To the north and some distance away was the vast, salt-encrusted bed of old Lop Nor, the vanished lake. Rumor had it that the lake was filling with water again after many centuries. The Cherchen-darya River was to their west, and behind the nearby town loomed the massive rampart of the Altyn Tagh. Beyond that range lay Tibet, or to be more specific, that region of Tibet called the Chang Tang, and relatively unknown.

The town behind the pale blue wall was marked on no map at all, and from here the town might easily have been passed by as merely another of the ancient ruins everywhere along this route. Yet it presented a new factor, and a disturbing one, intriguing to the mind of any curious man. This town was a relic, something left over from the past, yet obviously not without some contact with the outside world, as illustrated by the presence here of Laurent and Villani.

Still, the town must have been known in the days of the caravans before the springs dried up and Lop Nor vanished. So how had it been forgotten? And there were white women here, too. But why not? There were white women in Tashkent, Samarkand, and probably in Aksu. So why not here?

Thoughtfully, Medrac considered the situation. The trek from lower Kansu to this point had been long and hard, and during the first part there had been almost continual fighting. Due to some luck they had been able

to resupply ammunition for their rifles, but their food
supply was running short. If they stopped here it would
give them a much-needed rest and a chance to renew their
supplies and repair equipment.

As for Marshal Chu, Medrac had learned of him long
ago. The old bandit leader was no bargain. They had so
far not crossed trails, but Chu was shrewd, cunning, and
capable as a military man. He had no political convictions, no leaning toward the Communists and less toward
Chiang Kai-shek. But Marshal Chu's weapons were worn and
old, his equipment was in bad shape, and his men were the
rag ends of a half-dozen bandit forces.

The Mohammedan outbreak had come on the heels of earlier fighting, putting too many strong forces in the
field with which he could not cope. Also, the Russians
were showing indications of moving into Sinkiang, which
they had been trying to do off and on for a couple of
hundred years--whenever, in fact, their country grew
strong. Russia had always, whether czarist or Soviet,
wanted this area, three times larger than greater Germany.

If Chu could take the town behind the blue wall he
might settle down in that relative obscurity and outlast
the current chaos. Chiang Kai-shek had failed to live up
to his promises with twenty years in which to do it, his
regime was coming apart at the seams, and now disturbing
reports of a full-scale Japanese invasion were filtering
in from Peking and Shanghai. The people of China were
looking for relief, and Marshal Chu wanted a storm cellar
to last out the trouble.

Shan Bao rode in at a spanking trot and dropped to
the ground, executing a smart salute. He was a lithe,
quick man with intelligent eyes, and he cared little for
anything but riding or fighting.

"You were right," he said, "there are many deep,

well-watered canyons. It is impossible to reach them by
circling, but we could see into some of them. They have
herds of sheep, goats, yaks, and camels, and there are a
number of great orchards and vineyards. This is a very
rich village, sir!"

"Anything more?"

"There are well-traveled trails leading into the
mountains, but the way to all the trails is through the
city."

"Any fortifications on the hills?"

"I believe so. There were rows of rocks that might bo
natural, but I believe are in part constructed, and there
are clumps of trees and brush that might offer a hiding
place for men or guns."

"Thanks. You'll be in command while I'm in the town.
I'll take Jepsun and six men with me."

He walked out to the edge of the trees, and looked
toward the town. Already the gate was only a darker
shadow against the wall. Medrac felt a growing excitement. A forgotten city on an abandoned caravan trail!

Down the long basin behind him the rays of the dying
sun touched the distant yardangs of the Taklamakan with a
fringe of crimson. Shadows crept out from the ancient
hills, and far off, the towering mass of a great, snow-
covered peak gleamed like a great white tower above the
basin. Far out over the wastes, a jackal called.

To the north and east there was a dark blotch on the
gray face of the desert. This was one of the great forests of reeds that covered what had been an ancient
lake--reeds that were sixteen to twenty feet high; once
lost in that forest no man could find his way out. It was
said that many of them grew from a deep slush, crusted
over enough to bear a man's weight in places, but if a
man fell through it was like quicksand, and there was no
escape.

The jackal called again. Medrac walked back and sat down. Jepsun would come soon with his horse, and they would ride to the strange gates . . . and beyond them.

COMMENTS: Although there is no hint that mercenary Paul Medrac is the youthful narrator of the last draft of the *Samsara* fragment, at one time, at least some of the pages you have just read were intended to be part of that story of reincarnation. The City of the Blue Wall was likely intended to be a repository of information that allowed the "arrived" reincarnated people to learn more about the process of reincarnation and their greater purpose.

In one out of the dozen drafts of *Journey to Aksu*, Louis's initial description of Sinkiang, the mysteries of the Taklamakan Desert, and the City of the Blue Wall were followed by these words:

For I, at last, had come to this place, a place I remembered, yet did not remember, brought here by a series of seemingly casual meetings, objects, ideas . . . even dreams.

And by several people . . . a Gypsy man in my own backyard, by Sleeth in San Pedro, a Buddhist monk on the Irrawaddy, and by Haig, that causal wanderer.

The night winds rustle the leaves. . . . The desert waits, softly, like a cat, crouching.

Then the manuscript goes into a flashback that is, for all intents and purposes, the version of the *Samsara* fragment that begins in young Louis Lamoore's home in Jamestown, North Dakota:

A man with gold rings in his ears . . . a vase of ancient glass . . . a fragment of carved stone . . . and a girl.

There is no indication of how we get from the boy who meets a mysterious Gypsy in his backyard, or from the uncertain young man trying to go to sea, to the cynical and worldly professional soldier, Medrac. Perhaps there were many other adventures between the time he shipped out and when he arrived in China, adventures that brought maturity and toughness. Certainly, the story mentions nearly a year spent in the west of China. . . . However, it is best to remember that these were *drafts*, written at different times and with different intents. It is fun to look at *Samsara* and *Journey to Aksu* as one consistent story, but that is not the only possibility.

It is much more likely that, over the years, Louis split this story into two separate tales, or was combining two tales to make just one. . . . I cannot tell.

What I do have is some other pieces of the narrative, so we can put together a bit more of what he intended. All in all, Dad left behind twenty-two separate fragments of *Journey to Aksu*. He attempted to begin it over and over. Sometimes these attempts were nearly identical and other times quite different. On many occasions, we have only a page or two from the midst of a more complete manuscript. The rest of the clues to what Louis was attempting are lost forever.

The following is from a flashback that deals with Medrac's first arrival in China:

To be frank, I was puzzled over my situation, but had accepted it with caution. From my arrival in Shanghai with forty cents in my pocket to my present predicament, events had moved without seeming purpose.

From that first evening when I came ashore from a sampan at Wayside Pier, my situation was clear. I needed money. Forty cents was not going to get me far.

My assets, except the obvious physical ones, were few. I was tall, dark, and broke. A satisfactory able-bodied seaman with the rudiments of navigation, a good hard-rock miner, a fair to middling lumberjack, and better than average at prizefighting, judo, and karate. None of these talents seemed calculated to help me find a place to sleep or anything to eat in a town where none of them were particularly in demand.

The theoretical skills that I possessed were hard to evaluate and had never been tested. From my grandfather, an officer in the Civil and Indian Wars, I had learned the basic fundamentals of military tactics, developed by much discussion of the methods used by Grant, Lee, Stonewall Jackson, Sherman, and Thomas, to name a few. Along with some mildly profane comments on Nathan Bedford Forrest and John Singleton Mosby, there had been out-and-out respect for the Sioux.

That initial curiosity had led me to a study of the tactical writing of Sun Tzu, Vegetius, Marshal Saxe, Napoleon, and a few dozen others. And along the way I had picked up the working fundamentals of various guns and weapons. In the China in which I had landed these were marketable talents.

My first move after landing was to find a seaman's hangout on the chance that I would come across someone I knew who would stake me to a few dollars until I could find a job or a ship. What I found was a girl.

Or she found me.

Contrary to the movies, merchant seamen do not go ashore in their working clothes; several of the men in the place were fairly well dressed, and most of them were neat, although occasionally one was rumpled and unshaved. These were usually the ones who had been ashore several days and were obviously influenced by the cup. My own suit was dark blue, tailored on London's Bond Street, my hair trimmed, my shoes

polished. Looking like someone to the manor born, I
had in my pockets just the price of a bottle of beer.

COMMENTS: Could the girl mentioned above be the one referred to in the opening lines of *Samsara*? Was she the emissary of the crippled arms dealer known to Sleeth? I have no idea. What I do know is that Medrac's background of learning military tactics from his grandfather is identical to my father's, and the story of jumping ship in Shanghai, which is also described in the *Jack Cross* fragment, is one he told too.

From Shanghai, the information we have picks up Medrac in Suchow (Suzhou) a city in the western Chinese province of Kansu (Gansu). This would have been weeks or months after his arrival in China, and certainly weeks or months before his arrival at the City of the Blue Wall. At some point during his stay in Shanghai, Medrac has been hired to perform a minor military mission by a corrupt Chinese general. He has traveled to the western edge of China proper, and with his small detachment of troops, is just about to head into Sinkiang. He must decide whether to follow the northern route or the more obscure southern Silk Route around the Taklamakan Desert to Aksu near the Soviet border:

"You go to Aksu?"

"Those are my orders."

"On the northern road there are Tungan soldiers, soldiers turned bandit since General Ma was defeated."

"Nonetheless . . ."

"Of course. It is your duty."

The words were gently spoken, but they posed a delicate question also, a question I had been asking myself.
How much duty did I owe?

The Ladakhi with the pockmarked face was, it appeared, a chance traveler, also going west. "A man must follow his destiny," he said. "If your journey is to Aksu, so be it."

He must have guessed my uneasiness, must have seen how alone I was. For that matter he was also alone, or appeared to be.

Throughout the day he had loitered about the camp, talking to me whenever the others could not listen, reaching out with tentative fingers toward my plans. Had we not been soldiers and well armed I should have suspected him of being a spy for thieves, but at the time I had thirty-two men equipped with modern rifles, five machine guns, and two mortars.

"Even to Aksu the southern way is best. You will find no Tungans there, and at a point due south of Aksu you may strike north across the Taklamakan and come easily to its gates. That is, if you still wish . . ."

The note was crumpled in my pocket and he had been close by when the ragged boy brought it to me. Had he seen it? The boy had been clever, so it was unlikely that the loiterer had seen anything. Yet the note was itself mysterious.

Using one hand only I had thumbed open the folded paper and glanced at it by firelight.

Come to the House of the Five Dragons.
The one who loaned you the Tao-Te-Ching sent
me. I have only three hours.

There was no signature, and I knew it could be a trap. Suspicion is a friend to the stranger, yet who could know about the loaning of the Tao-Te-Ching?

Only Haig had been present that afternoon in the apartment on Avenue Edward VII in Shanghai.

The wind was rising. Ragged clouds raced the moonlit

sky. A wall of wind struck the building in whose court-
yard we were camped. Ancient timbers creaked, dust
swirled.

Kicking dirt over the fire, I smothered the coals.
The man with the pockmarked, knife-scarred face had wandered off. When I stepped over the collapsed timbers of
the gate the wind tore at my throat, blowing the breath
back into my lungs.

The House of the Five Dragons had been pointed out to
me as one of the oldest in Suchow, dating back to the
time of the Old City.

The midnight streets were empty of all save the wind
that roared in from the western desert, bringing with it
a driving storm of fine gravel and sand.

Several times I hesitated at corners or in the shadow
of a wall to look behind me, but I seemed not to have
been followed. I had no idea why I should be followed,
but I was in a strange land, among strangers, and the
circumstances were unusual. Lately, I found myself growing suspicious. That was why we were still here when two
days ago we should have gone on, toward Aksu.

The vast old structure of the House of Five Dragons
was dark and silent but for the ocean of wind that beat
against its walls.

Undoubtedly I was a fool to have come here. Who, in
this place, would know Haig? Or know that I knew him? Yet
Haig was a peculiar man, with friends in all manner of
odd places, and he had, so I'd heard, a way of disappearing for months on end, going off somewhere inland. But
why should Haig send a message to me across more than a
thousand miles of China?

There was a huge wooden gate, and beside it, a door.
Lifting the latch--there was no question of knocking on
such a night--I stepped inside. Behind my belt my pistol
was a comforting thing, and I unbuttoned my coat with my
left hand.

The outer court was bare under the moon. An ancient cart leaned drunkenly against the far wall, poplars lashed about with slender limbs so the wind might know their agony, and down a long arcade there was a faint gleam of light. Like the house where we had camped, this was an abandoned place . . . or so it seemed. The wind thundered among the roofs. Opening the door, I stepped inside.

The room was large, drafty, and high of ceiling. At the far side was a k'ang . . . a raised portion of the floor heated by a stone fireplace and used as a bed. At a small table alongside the k'ang a solitary man sat smoking a cigarette. A lean, raw-boned man with a narrow, tough face and a lantern jaw, he wore a leather jacket unbuttoned down to the last two buttons, a gray wool shirt, and a scarf tied around his throat, cowboy style. His hair was rust-colored and there was a hint of freckling under the skin. "I'm Milligan," he said.

A battered coffeepot stood at the edge of a fire, and from the edge of the k'ang he took a spare cup and saucer and filled the cup with coffee, black and steaming.

"You got a friend, Medrac. A mighty good friend."

"How do you happen to be away up here?" I asked.

"I get around. Flew up to Kanchow for a fella. I got my own ship. Fly charters for whoever." He rubbed out his cigarette and started to shape another. "Haig asked me to tip this hand for you." He looked at me over the cigarette he was building, his eyes slate-gray. "You're in trouble, amigo, plenty of trouble."

"I've had a hunch."

"Why do you think you were picked for this job? Because you're a foreigner, you're the fall guy. If anything goes haywire, you get the ax . . . and I mean ax."

He lighted the fresh cigarette. "Haig steered me into half the money I've made in this godforsaken country."

The coffee was good. The last time I'd tasted coffee like that was in a cow-camp down in the Big Sandy, in Arizona.

"Did you ever think why the general picked you for this job? You ain't been in the country long and he's got you figured for a greenhorn. If anything goes wrong, if his buddies find those guns are going to the Communists, then this is your deal, not his. You get knocked off and you can't talk and nobody can prove anybody was in it but you. If you bring it off, then the general has sold a big load of contraband at four or five hundred percent profit."

"I was told to drive back six hundred horses."

"From Aksu? They've got horses there, all right, and those horses will be loaded with goods brought over from Alma-Ata, in Soviet Russia.

"As for horses, there's no need to go as far as Aksu if they want horses for the army, like they claim."

"Nothing was said about those horses carrying packs."

"Of course not. But you'll find they are. And the packs they carry will be machine guns, rifles, mortars, and ammo."

"The general is a Kuomintang man."

"Don't kid yourself, friend. He's like all the rest, feathering his own nest, playing both ends against the middle. I don't know about Chiang, but that crowd around him are a bunch of highbinders. They rob the country and they rob each other."

He gulped the hot coffee, then took up his cigarette.

"Look," he said after a pause, "you picked yourself a hot package. The way I see it you got two choices. First, you drop it right here and fly out with me, then grab yourself a ship out of Shanghai, work-away or anything you can get."

"And the other choice?"

"Go ahead with the deal. Accept the goods all innocent as you please, then meet me somewhere and we'll take
your cargo and fly it elsewhere. We sell the goods to the
highest bidder, split the take, and scram.

"Now you take Feng . . . the Christian General . . .
I know him and like him and he'd give his eyeteeth to lay
hands on that cargo. Say ten percent off the top for
squeeze and we split the rest any way you want it."

He squinted his eyes through the smoke. "You got any
idea what that cargo will be worth, delivered in the middle of China today? A quarter, maybe even a half-million
dollars. I know at least three places I could turn that
cargo over for gold money . . . cash on the barrelhead."

He paused again, finishing his coffee. "There's one
thing. Like I said, if anything goes wrong you get the ax,
and the man who'll use it on you is right along with you."

Well, I just looked at him.

"Fact," he said. "Haig told me that, too."

Mentally, I considered the men with me. There was no
reason to doubt it; certainly none of them owed any loyalty to me.

"Did he have any idea who it was?"

"No . . . and there might be more than one. I'd guess
there would be at least two." He grinned at me. "The general would be worried for fear one might sell out."

Of course, Milligan was right. The quickest, simplest, and smartest thing was to cut and run. Drop the
whole thing now, fly out to Shanghai, and grab the first
ship off the waterfront.

The trouble was I was tired of being broke. At fifteen I'd left home and since then had worked in construction camps, mines, and lumber mills, drifting from job to
job, going to sea occasionally and prizefighting when the
chance offered. It all added up to nothing except that in
the process I had gotten the edges of an education in libraries and from books carried along as I traveled.

Milligan picked up the cups and rinsed them out with
what remained of the coffee. "I got to take out." He
dumped the pot and the cups into a canvas sack.

"Thanks. I'll stay on."

"Your funeral." He glanced at me. "You got a rod?"

Pulling back my coat, I showed it to him.

"May be the only friend you got. Keep it handy." He
started buttoning his coat. "You bring that stuff here,
to this house. I'll find a buyer. We split and I'll fly
you the hell out of the country."

He picked up an old baseball cap and put it on. "You
get caught with this stuff and they'll shoot you. The
Chinese will believe anything of a white man; you're just
a renegade. That's why they picked you."

There were thirty-two men waiting for me on the edge
of town and any one of them might be the hatchet man. And
they spoke a language I did not know, except for the two
noncoms, who spoke English.

"You get back with those guns and stash them here.
There'll be a man around, a man you can trust."

Suddenly, he seemed to think of something. "Look,
you'll go from here to Anshi. Now in Anshi there's an old
house"--he drew a design on the wall with his finger--"it
stands about <u>there</u>. In that house there's a small cache
of guns and ammunition. Might be helpful, for your men or
bribes or some such.

"Joe Davenport was a buddy of mine. We did a piece in
the Marines together when I first came out. When he got
his discharge he went into the munitions business, smuggling and selling. This lot in Anshi he was supposed to
deliver to General Ma, but after he'd cached them some
trigger-happy son-of-a-bitch went and shot him. So far as
I know, those guns are still there."

"You've been here a long time."

He hunched his shoulders against the wind and grinned
at me with one side of his mouth. "I'm an old hand, son.

I came out in '21 with the Marines, and there was eight years of that; when I paid out of the service I stayed on, wanting to make a fast buck.

"Well, I learned to fly, bought myself an old crate, and went into business. This is my third ship."

"How about the fast dollars?"

"Oh, I had 'em! I had 'em three or four times, but have you ever been in Shanghai with twenty thousand dollars in your kick? It doesn't stay there long!"

He dropped his cigarette and thrust out his hand. "All right, boy . . . Luck. You'll need it."

He turned away from me and started off, walking into the wind, and for a moment or two I had to fight down an impulse to run after him. But I stood there until he disappeared in the night and then I turned and went back to camp.

My orders had been definite. Follow the route north of the Taklamakan to Aksu . . . but suppose I didn't? Suppose, without even suggesting it to any of the others, I cut off to the south?

It was a rare Han Chinese who liked the desert or the wild country, and from ancient times until now, these western deserts had been considered the end of the world. The route to Anshi and beyond would wind among the dunes somewhat, and there would be several changes of direction. Suppose I followed the advice of my pockmarked friend and went off to the south; how would that affect the plans of those with me, whose mission it was to eliminate me if anything went wrong?

Suppose I got them into wild country where nobody but me actually knew where we were?

By the time I had slid into my sleeping bag I had decided. At first light I would move them out to Anshi,

telling no one my plans. Barring the unforeseen, we could
then leave Anshi before daybreak, lose ourselves in the
desert, then strike south toward the oasis of Tun-huang
and the Caves of the Thousand Buddhas.

Lying on my back looking up at the stars and listening to the wind, I had another idea altogether.

What I needed was control, but not the sort of control I possessed now. The men I had were supposed to
drive and guard the returning horses. From the first it
had seemed like a lot of men but now it made sense. . . .
There was going to be a treasure trove of arms and ammunition too.

I had read Machiavelli and Kautilya. The answer was
plain enough. I needed more men . . . my men.

What did that suggest? First, that they not be
Han . . . or if Han, then local men holding no loyalty
to that far-off general.

Back in Shanghai I had heard an Englishman in the
Astor Bar say, "Anybody in China today who can feed an
army can have one."

Well, conditions were bad and that Englishman had
been right: The Chinese alternative to famine was solder-
ing or banditry, often nearly the same thing. Suchow itself was filled with drifters. The Mohammedan rebellion
had stopped the caravans, and the town was filled with
jobless, homeless men, many of them thieves or worse. I
had seen them standing or sitting around, men of a dozen
nationalities, for in the mountainous corridor through
Kansu to Sinkiang a Han Chinese was apt to be the exception. Here one found men of all sorts and no particular
loyalty.

The pockmarked Ladakhi . . .

Obviously, he had a reason for wishing me to take the
southern route, but that could be dealt with when the
time came. For now, he might prove useful.

Suddenly, I sat up in my sleeping bag and looked out through the gate to where several men huddled in a corner of a wall about fifty yards away. They were big, raw-boned men carrying old-fashioned rifles. Each had a saber slung across his back, the hilt showing above his left shoulder. The right shoulder was bare.

They talked to no one, and apparently had almost nothing to eat. I had watched them because of the way they had been looking at our horses, which I was sure they intended to steal.

Pulling on my boots and sheepskin coat, I picked up my rifle and walked over to where they lay. Two were asleep but as I approached, the three others sat up, as ready for trouble as ever men could be.

"Do you speak English?"

They merely stared at me.

"Do you want horses? Food to eat?"

They grasped the word "horses" quickly enough. One of them got up and tried me in what was probably a bastard Chinese, but I knew none of it.

Squatting on my heels I drew a rough map in the sand showing where we were. Touching the man nearest me with the drawing stick, then myself, and gesturing to show the country around, I made an X with the stick. "Suchow."

"Suchow!" he agreed, his voice harsh and strange.

"Anshi." I made another mark. "I give you new rifle!" I slapped the Mauser that lay across my knees. The men's eyes widened. "I shall go here." Drawing a line as I spoke, I indicated the Tun-huang oasis, the Kuen Lun Mountains, the crossing to Aksu.

"You"--I indicated them--"come with me. You ride"--I drew a horse--"and you eat." Gesturing to my mouth was enough for that. "Maybe we fight." I mimed shooting, slashing with a sword, and indicated a place for them on either side of me. When I stood up, I looked from one to the other. "You are not Chinese. What are you, then?"

One of the men, who wore a thin mustache, said, "Ngolok." Then taking up my stick he drew a region south of Tun-huang and considerably beyond it, drew the big bend of a river, then pointed to the space inside the bend and indicated that it was their country.

Turning, I walked back to camp, and they followed. I served up what was left of our supper and when I got back into my sleeping bag they grouped themselves around me.

Looking from one to the other I realized that for better or worse I had acquired the services of five fighting men. I knew nothing then of the Ngolok, the wildest, fiercest tribe in Asia, a nomadic people who have defied for centuries all efforts to penetrate their land. Nor had I any idea how rare it was to find any of them outside their own country.

Lying in my sleeping bag, I knew what it was I would do. I'd recruit, not an army, but a force at least comparable to the one I now had, a strong force of men whose loyalty lay only with me. Moreover, my recruiting must be done at once and before anyone could circumvent my efforts. By the time those whose mission it was to watch me realized what was happening, I wanted my force doubled.

At daylight I was on my feet and the Ngoloks with me.

We mounted horses and rode into the outskirts of Suchow, and with me was the pockmarked Ladakhi, who had appeared from out of nowhere once more.

If there was nothing else I knew, I knew fighting men, and it was fighting men I sought. The first was a Mongol with a gold ring in one ear, a stocky, powerful man with broad, high cheekbones.

"You!" I pointed a finger at him. "I want to talk to you."

He merely looked at me, then stared off down the street with an air of contempt that was beautiful to see.

"There is fighting to do, and traveling to a far land. If you are a coward, stay here."

My pockmarked friend, called Serat, translated for
me, and the Mongol got to his feet and spoke.

"He wants to know where you go."

"Tell him that if he comes with me he will eat each
day, ride a good horse, and fight, and that if he asks
any more questions I do not want him."

Serat translated and the Mongol looked at me, a hint
of a smile on his lips, then spoke and, turning, went behind the building. "He will get his horse," Serat said,
looking at me curiously. Then he asked, "Where do we go?"

"Where there is fighting," I said grimly. "If you
come with me, you shall go where I go."

"Where else?" He looked about him. "How many men do
you wish?"

"Thirty . . . if I can find others like these."

We found them. And we could have found a hundred . . .
perhaps two hundred more. In Suchow that day there must
have been a thousand aimless, footloose wanderers.

Brigands, some of them, and leaderless soldiers, too.
No doubt many were camel drivers and truck drivers rendered jobless by the unsettled conditions, but the men I
chose, I chose because they looked like fighters and because of their readiness to go. Any who quibbled or asked
questions I ignored, for I wanted only those willing to
commit themselves.

They were a hodgepodge of languages and nationalities, most of them in rags, all of them hungry, all of
them potentially dangerous, and scarcely one who did not
bear the scars of battle. Yet diverse in origin as they
might be, most of them spoke enough of the argot of the
caravans to make himself understood. I alone was defi-
cient in that respect. I, and those Chinese soldiers who
were in my command.

Of the original thirty-two, only five had actually
been Chinese from the coastal provinces, and of these two

spoke English enough to translate and to make themselves understood. Yet I now had Serat, if he proved loyal.

Serat was a doubtful quantity. Where he had come from and what he wanted were a mystery. Possibly only a job, a horse to ride, and food to eat, yet he was too glib, too ready with explanations, and a bit too concentrated on that southern route.

Certainly, it was not unexpected to find such a man in this part of China. The caravan route had made it a land of wanderers and the harsh conditions made it the home of nomads; in most places little had changed from the time of Genghis Khan or Marco Polo.

No stranger or more mysterious place lay on the face of the globe. Even Tibet was an open book by comparison. Up to a point the history of Sinkiang was a history of the Silk Road and life around the string of oases, but there had been a time, long before that, even long before the time of Christ, when vast, civilized cities had thrived there.

Who were the people who lived in those cities? What books did they write? What pictures did they paint? Who were their heroes? Their enemies? What was their history, their origin?

There was no use lying to myself. I was going south. It was good advice to avoid Ma's now leaderless soldiers along the northern route. But it was far less the whispered suggestions of Serat than my own desire to go south, into that never-never land west of Tun-huang.

Liu Hung, who was second in command, was pacing about and talking excitedly when I rode back into the court with Serat. The five Ngoloks were close behind.

"We leave in one hour," I said, and immediately moved to start organizing the camp for departure.

"We cannot, sir. No. It is too late in the day."

"It's not too late. I don't care if we only make thirty li. We're moving!"

He stopped, about to speak again, then he looked at the Ngoloks who stood around me.

"These men, what do they do?"

"They ride with us," I replied, "and there will be more."

"More?"

"The news is," I explained, "that the route is dangerous because of Ma Chung-yin's soldiers. The obvious solution is more men, a stronger party." It wouldn't do to suggest I was thinking of anything but the northern road. . . .

COMMENTS: So now we have one adventure leading to another. We learn the young mercenary, Medrac, hired to retrieve a herd of horses from the farthest frontier of China, has actually been tricked into running guns to the Communists by a corrupt Nationalist general. Medrac's friend in Shanghai, Haig, has sent the pilot Milligan to warn him, and Serat, the mysterious Ladakhi, is steering him toward the southern Silk Road and the City of the Blue Wall—a city that has staked its survival on secrecy, on no one ever leaving, or surviving an escape attempt. A city that certain drafts of Louis's *Samsara* fragment hint might be the repository of information archived by those who have "arrived"—those who can remember their previous lives, or incarnations.

Again, because of the way the bulk of the drafts of *Journey to Aksu* are written, I do not believe Louis seriously considered melding *Samsara* and *Journey to Aksu* into the same story for very long . . . but he did toy with the idea.

The most interesting part is that, just like the autobiographical aspects included in the last version of *Samsara*, this story is also strangely connected to Louis's life. Haig, Milligan, and the apartment on Avenue Edward VII are all part of the greater universe of "semi"-autobiographical L'Amour stories. Mercenary pilot "Tex" Milligan shows up in "A Friend of the General," with "the General" using Milligan as a method of escape:

> There was a charter plane at the field. You knew
> him, I think? Milligan? He would fly you anywhere for
> a price and land his plane on a pocket handkerchief
> if need be. Moreover, he could be trusted, and there
> were some in those days who could not. . . .

Haig, and his apartment in Shanghai, make an appearance elsewhere in this book, and in the short story "Shanghai, Not Without Gestures":

> It was not just a room but a small apartment,
> pleasant in a way. Drifting men have a way of fixing
> up almost any place they stop to make it comfort-
> able. . . . Yet the apartment was not mine. I'd been
> given the use of it by a Britisher who was up-country
> now. His name was Haig, and he came and went a good
> deal with no visible means of support, and I was told
> that he often stayed up-country months at a time. He
> had been an officer in one of the Scottish regiments,
> I believe. I had a suspicion he was still involved in
> some kind of duty, although he had many weird Asiatic
> connections.

Again, the apartment, though not the man, is mentioned in "The Man Who Stole Shakespeare":

> When I had been in Shanghai but a few days, I
> rented an apartment in a narrow street off Avenue Ed-
> ward VII where the rent was surprisingly low. The

```
door at the foot of the stairs opened on the street
beside a moneychanger's stall, an inconspicuous place
that one might pass a dozen times a day and never no-
tice.
```

And, most interestingly, Haig is also mentioned in *Education of a Wandering Man* . . . a book that is, supposedly, nonfiction! Louis describes "the old crowd," a type whose "ranks are thinning" but could be found "in every large seaport city." They were men who were smugglers, dealers in information, and those who wanted to "avoid the eyes of officials." He claimed a man named Oriental Slim, whom he met while "on the beach" in San Pedro, first put him in touch with this group:

```
    My first contact in Shanghai came in a sailors'
joint called, if I remember correctly, The Olympic,
having nothing to do with the games--although games
of other kinds were played there.
    It was a perhaps-accidental meeting with a Scots-
man, a former British-India Army officer named Haig.
He had left the service and become a Buddhist, but I
always suspected he was with British Intelligence.
```

I am not going to get into all the questions about Louis's actual experiences in Shanghai. Those questions are many and I wonder about them constantly (and uselessly). I will say that I have proof he was there, but at a time prior to when this story seems to be occurring . . . and at that time, he was there for only a few days. Did he return? It is still an open question.

Lastly, there is one final piece of the *Journey to Aksu* manuscript that has survived through the years, a denouement of sorts . . . not enough to satisfy but enough to suggest some sort of closure:

```
    . . . the city behind the blue wall remains in my
mind . . . no bit of it forgotten, and I find myself
wondering how they are faring there and if through
```

all that has happened since they have survived, they
who understood the art of survival better than anyone.

There is little about Sinkiang that is Chinese,
but even less than that of the city.

Perhaps the sharp reality of all my impressions
derives from the state of heightened sensibility in
which I undoubtedly was. Not so much from the task
for which I had been retained, but what I knew would
come after. Even at that moment I knew that once the
danger to the city itself was removed, then they
would find some means to remove me also, for fear
that I in turn should become a menace.

There were people there whom I called my friends,
and I flatter myself that they thought of me in the
same way, yet where the city and its survival were
concerned there was no friendship. The city itself
came first, and it always had, and that was the price
of its survival.

In the end it was a whim of mine that made the
difference, a whim and a sharp sense of the reality
of things even in that most unreal of all places.

It was odd that I, a newcomer to China, and in
many respects an innocent, should come upon the city
behind the blue wall. Haig, who knew more of China, I
think, than any other foreigner, knew of the city
only by rumor, and he did not quite believe in it.
The story, if one could dignify the vaguest of rumors
by such a name, was flimsy indeed. It had none of the
qualities of legend or mystery, nothing but a whisper
here and there among the marketplaces that such and
such a place had once existed.

Shanghai, the Shanghai of that era, is gone, erased by a world
war, a revolution, and what was supposed to be a Great Leap Forward.
Haig, Milligan, "the General," Oriental Slim, the apartment on the

alley off of Avenue Edward VII, the Olympic Cafe. I can't say it's all fiction, not by a long shot, for Dad left this tucked between the pages of a disintegrating scrapbook:

Flimsy evidence indeed, but more than a whisper that such a place existed.

ACKNOWLEDGMENTS

I would very much like to thank my mother who has been our cheerleader through every iteration of this project, Paul O'Dell (who worked on the earliest incarnation of this book and came up with the title for this entire program), Jeanne Brown, Angelique Pitney, Charles Van Eman, Sonndra May, Daphne Ashbrook, Jamie Wain, Jayne Rosen, Jessica Wolfson, Mara Purl, Cathy Sandrich Gelfond, Trish Mahoney, Jordan Ladd, and Paula Beyers for all their help and the sorting and transcribing of the original manuscripts.

On the publishing end of things kudos go to the great Stu Applebaum, Gina Wachtel, Ratna Kamath, Nina Shield, Elana Seplow-Jolley, David Moench, Kate Miciak, Joe Scalora, Cynthia Lasky and her crack team, Scott Shannon, Matt Schwartz, Paolo Pepe, Scott Biel, Heidi Lilly, Ted Allen, Larry Marks, Bill Takes, Libby McGuire, and Gina Centrello.

It took every name on this list and many more to make this book a reality.

ABOUT THE AUTHORS

Our foremost storyteller of the American West, Louis L'Amour has also thrilled readers with his work in the adventure, crime, and science fiction genres. He wrote ninety-one novels, a book of poetry, and over two hundred short stories. There are more than three hundred million copies of his books in print around the world.

Beau L'Amour is an author, art director, and editor. He has also worked in the film, television, magazine, and recording industries. Since 1988 he has been the manager of the estate of his father, Louis L'Amour.

louislamour.com
louislamourslosttreasures.com